KAREN T

A BOND OF
BLOOD
AND FIRE

THE GODDESS AND THE GUARDIANS
BOOK TWO

Cover art by Deranged Doctor Designs

Map by Gregory Shipp
https://www.facebook.com/gregoryshippmapmaking/

Map illustration by Kevin Heasman
https://www.facebook.com/dynamodoodles/

Edited by Monica Wanat

FOR SANDRA TOMLINSON
I HOPE ETERNITY IS AS BRIGHT AND
COLOURFUL AS YOU.
YOU WILL BE MISSED BUT ALWAYS LOVED
AND NEVER FORGOTTEN.

The Eight Kingdoms

THE ICE LANDS

HOURIA

THE ROUGH SEAS

GAR ANON

THE WET LANDS

RHODAINIA

STORMGUARD

THE BARREN LANDS

UNCHARTED WATERS

A Bond of Venom and Magic

PART ONE

TRUST AND TRAINING

KAREN TOMLINSON

CHAPTER ONE

Icy wind numbed Diamond's cheeks, whipping her silver hair into a frenzy. With a knotted belly, she realised they had nearly reached their destination.

Her eyes drifted to Commander Hugo Casimir's scarred profile. She breathed in through her nose and out through her mouth, just like her fae father had taught her, controlling the panic attack that threatened. Was it only yesterday Hugo had chosen servitude to the immortal Queen over their friendship? Diamond's eyes burned, unsure why he had thrown away their growing friendship. Her fingers flexed, a shudder rippling through her.

No matter how hard she clenched her fist, she still remembered the feel of hot blood running over her skin as she plunged the knife in the heart of her father's best friend—and betrayer. Learning to live with that act was her only choice. Edo was dead, and she had killed him— even if someone had controlled her actions through magic. She didn't want to think too deeply about whether or not she would have killed him if someone hadn't been controlling her with magic. Being kidnapped, rescued by Hugo, then recaptured by the Queen had left her mind in a whirl.

Now, to keep her friends alive she must become a weapon for the Queen. Today was the first day of her training, and Diamond had no idea what to expect.

The beat of Hugo's metallic wings filled her ears, and she determinedly blocked out any remaining thoughts of the day before.

Diamond watched the dusty surface of the training ground rush up to meet them. The flight above the clifftops, fissures and gardens of the palace grounds had taken only a few minutes. Hating heights, she was glad their time in the air had been short.

Diamond's breathing snagged, her whole body tensing as Hugo's feet hit the ground. Her worry proved unfounded when he landed with lethal precision.

His armoured sapphire and silver wings snapped into his back, almost disappearing. Diamond wanted to withdraw from the overpowering presence of Hugo's magic, magic that nipped at her skin, attempting to reach her own even though his face displayed only an unfeeling mask.

Ignoring Hugo, Diamond stared at the large warrior who awaited them. Hugo's grip was uncompromising, almost painful, as he eyed the other fae male. She had no chance of escaping.

The other fae wore a sleeveless leather jerkin, soft suede breeches and brown boots. Big arms crossed over his broad chest, displaying considerable muscle. He oozed impatience.

Around them the barracks continued its normal early morning routine. It was a huge area covered in ancient stone buildings and training grounds. Thousands of Prince Jack's Rhodainian soldiers and fae warriors were drilling or heading toward the mess hall for breakfast. Above flew Avalonian fae warriors wearing uniforms bearing the Queen's insignia; their golden-armoured wings glinted as they flew in formation, some diving and locking in battle above the grounds.

It was a noisy and busy place, but Diamond heard nothing of the other soldiers. She focused entirely on the warrior staring down at her; only the discomfort of Hugo's grip penetrated. It was hard not to feel weak and inadequate, but she vowed to hide these feelings. Diamond swallowed and lifted her chin. She had promised herself and her grandmother, the goddess Lunaria, that she would no longer be weak. It would be a hard promise to keep, but keep it she would.

Diamond had discovered many things about her heritage these last months. Her father had never been willing to talk of her mother. She had always believed he had been a woodcutter in the far northern town of Berriesford. But he hadn't. Her father had been one of the best general's in the Combined Army of Rhodainia but had left that life for the sake of her mother.

Since her father's murder by the Wraith Lord's hunters, Diamond had realized that what she had learned fighting in the backstreets of her hometown with her friend Tom was not enough to protect her. Hugo and Prince Jack's men had had to rescue her and her friends. Hugo had saved her life, then destroyed it by bringing her into the lair of the vicious fae queen. Diamond swallowed the bitterness she felt towards him. He really had no choice but to follow the Queen's orders.

Diamond's status as a half-blood fae meant very little in the Queen's lands of Avalonia, and she often needed to defend herself. Her father had taught her how to break a hold and slam her boot or fist into a male's vulnerable parts, but hadn't taught her how to fight against warriors like these.

The Queen's master-at-arms was supposed to help Hugo train her. Swallowing her nerves, Diamond studied the big male. This golden-winged warrior was almost as tall as Hugo. He was a lot older, probably in his forties, but fae males lived many years longer than human men. Clearly he was not a male to challenge. He exuded such an air of confidence and cool authority, Diamond's immediate instinct was to respect him.

Hugo nodded at the big warrior as he let go of Diamond, giving her a gentle shove away from him. She stumbled before managing to right herself.

"Tallo," Hugo greeted coldly.

Commander Tallo Nosco studied her with narrowed eyes as she scowled at Hugo and rubbed her arm.

"So, this is the general's daughter?" he inquired, circling and studying her.

At first Diamond was embarrassed by his scrutiny, crossing her arms over her chest, and hunching her shoulders to make herself smaller. Her skin prickled as Hugo's dark eyes watched her icily. No. They were not going to go away, either of them. Her breathing hitched and quickened.

Stepping off to one side, Hugo folded his arms over his chest, looking self-assured and completely detached. She wanted to storm over and slap him, demand to know why he was being so cold. Yesterday he had no choice but to do what the Queen demanded, but today should be different. They were no longer under the Queen's scrutiny. Diamond's violet eyes met his and narrowed. In response, those sapphire depths flickered, but his face remained harsh. Frustration turned to seething anger. With effort, she ignored Hugo. Her ire rose further as Tallo prowled closer, trying to intimidate her.

Grinding her teeth, she lifted her chin. Yesterday she had become a murderer. She could still feel hot blood against her skin. Someone had controlled her actions, making her kill without hesitation. General Edo, her childhood protector, had betrayed the people he loved because of misguided beliefs and a deep bitterness due to his enforced exile. Even after discovering he was responsible for her father's death, she had not wanted to be the one to kill him. Mainly because the hateful immortal Queen had given the order, but also because she had grown up with him in her life.

Diamond's chest tightened as she remembered those events, and the world spun. She was transported back into her strange dream from the night before. Images of an amazingly fast and vicious warrior goddess blasted through her brain; the way Lunaria moved, the way she fought, the way she saw her enemy, but most of all, Diamond could feel her burning fire of determination and self-belief. Lunaria had shared her absolute focus on surviving, on fighting for her people—on defeating her enemy.

Faster than she could comprehend, Diamond spun back from her dream to the cold damp of the training ground.

Tallo had ceased pacing, and Hugo stood tensely with his arms unfolded. Zoning out hadn't done her any favours. Diamond cocked her head to one side and stared warily at Tallo but did not drop her gaze.

Lunaria, the goddess of creation, was Diamond's ancestor. She had faith in Diamond's abilities. The least Diamond could do was try and succeed. No. She *would* succeed.

If she was going to live, if Jack and her other friends were going to live, she had to become a warrior. The first step was not believing herself weaker than everyone else. Lunaria would never have shown fear at this challenge, and she would never have been beaten by it— neither would Diamond.

Forcing herself to maintain eye contact, Diamond twisted on her heel and matched Tallo's stealthy steps. Her body felt fluid, her muscles tensing and relaxing with precision.

Hugo coughed in surprise, his eyes fixed in disbelief on her graceful movements.

Diamond immediately flicked him a steady look. During their dream world encounter, Lunaria may have given her a crash course in the fighting arts, but Diamond knew she could never beat these two hardened warriors. Even so, she hissed a challenge at Tallo like she had seen other fae do. After all, she was half fae and the daughter of one of the most renowned generals in the land; she would be damned if she was going to let these two males beat her to a pulp without at least trying to defend herself.

"Your weak female body will be bruised and likely broken, but I will not care," Hugo had once growled at her.

11

She finally concurred. They could not kill her; she belonged to the vile Queen just like they did, and they *all* needed her magic to defend them if they didn't want to end up becoming part of the Wraith Lord's army. For a moment Diamond wondered why the Wraith Lord would want to invade the lands of the Queen who worshipped the same dark lord he served. Not that it mattered, but still....

Sounds reached Diamond's ears, bringing her back to reality, heightening her awareness; officers shouting to their squadrons, the clink of metal as troops gathered in training formation across the barracks, banter from the mess hall. Her mind filtered out the noise until all she could hear was the sound of Tallo's controlled breathing and the creak of Hugo's leather armour as he crossed his arms again.

Tallo did not take his eyes off her, so she returned the favour.

"I thought you said she can't fight," he muttered to Hugo.

"She can't," Hugo responded flatly.

"Try me," Diamond said, her eyes flashing with challenge.

So Tallo did. He attacked with grace, speed and control. No weapons, just fists, feet and wings.

She managed to twist and avoid his first attacks, delving into her mind for the moves that might save her, but Tallo was far too experienced to be fooled. Even though Lunaria had given Diamond a crash course on how to fight, her body wasn't used to such activity. Her muscles were weak and slow. Tallo's fist hit her belly, and she sank to the ground coughing and gagging.

"Good, but not good enough," he said, squatting down by her. "At least you've got the balls to try. Now, get up," he ordered, his tone lazy and amused.

Holding in a groan, Diamond forced herself up on her feet, her legs shaking. Tears burned her eyes, and her stomach throbbed. Her eyes flicked to Hugo as her skin broke out in a cold sweat. His face remained blank: no regret, no compassion — even the touch of his magic was completely gone.

She concentrated on her breathing, forcing herself to ignore his oppressive presence. *I can do this!* she told herself over and over, as if the repetition would make those words true. Determined to not let Hugo see her cry, Diamond set her jaw and tilted her head defiantly.

Tallo attacked again, then again. Sometimes he would stop to show her how to block against a punch or a kick, other times he would show her how to attack.

After two unceasing hours of training, Diamond stumbled and made more mistakes. Knocked to the ground repeatedly by Tallo's hard fists and feet, her body throbbed. Welts that were turning into massive purple bruises peppered her forearms and shins.

"Enough," ordered Hugo from where he stood watching their progress.

Tallo straightened and stepped away from her. Suddenly his whole demeanour changed. He smiled, and slapped her shoulder. "Well, damn! You're not what I expected at all. You have done well for your first lesson," he praised her, turning to Hugo with a question on his face. This fae had no problem or prejudice against Diamond for being a half-blood *and* a magic wielder.

"One hour, then we will start again," answered Hugo.

Diamond bit her tongue. He really did not care how tired she was or how much pain she was in.

Tallo nodded and walked away with long, confident strides toward the large double-storied building off to the right. Eager soldiers headed that way, and a mouth-watering smell permeated the air, indicating it was the mess hall.

Breathing heavily, she put her hands on her hips and leaned forward, trying to calm her shaking limbs. Tipping her head back, Diamond was unaware of the way her shirt stuck to her damp skin and outlined the curves of her body. Her loose hair tickled her face. Irritated, she brushed it back, trying to swallow around her parched tongue.

She refused to give Hugo the chance to deny her a request to eat or drink. Standing quietly, she waited.

He glared at her for a moment. "Where did you learn to move like that?" he asked suspiciously.

Diamond was too tired to lie or come up with a clever comment. "I learnt it overnight. In my dreams," she panted, holding his gaze.

A muscle twitched in his jaw. His scar twisted grotesquely as he ground his teeth. His nostrils flared.

It was hard to hold back an exasperated sigh. That had sounded far too sarcastic.

"So you have been lying to me all this time? You are not as helpless as you made yourself out to be, but you are far more deceitful than I gave you credit for." His eyes were harder than ever, black through and through.

Diamond bit her tongue, knowing it was pointless trying to convince him that she told the truth. Instead, she forced a shrug. "Oh, I think you beat me on deceitfulness, *commander*," she bit out, forcing her voice to remain steady. After all, he was the one who had made a promise to save her from the Queen and smuggle her out of the city, only to break it. "Besides, everyone has secrets," she muttered.

For a moment something flickered in the darkness of Hugo's eyes, then he turned away. "Let's go. You have a long day ahead. You will need to eat to keep up with Tallo's training regime."

Diamond cringed when she realised her sweat had made her shirt almost see-through. She ignored the gaping stares of the young trainees and the intense gazes of the fae warriors as she marched behind Hugo into the mess hall. Human soldiers nudged and elbowed each other, whispering snide remarks. Even some of the female warriors appraised her far too closely, flaring their nostrils as they scented her.

Hissed comments about *the dirty magic wielder* and *half-blood* ignited her resentment, but it was the lustful growls and lewd remarks uttered by fae males that made her face burn. She shuddered as she felt their eyes devouring her body.

Hugo must have heard them too, but he did nothing. No snarled warnings, not like when they had been surrounded by other males while in the forest.

So be it. A fierce determination not to cower bloomed through Diamond's chest. Feigning belligerence, she squared her shoulders and stalked past them all, her head held high and a scowl on her face.

When they neared the entrance to the mess hall, she forgot to be bothered by the attention she was receiving. A groan escaped her as saliva gushed over her dry tongue. Insults be damned—she was starving. Shuffling down the serving hatches, she spooned eggs and bacon onto a plate and grabbed several mugs of cold water.

They sat at a long table near the master-at-arms, her hands shaking as she tried to eat. Tallo and a few other soldiers laughed more than once when food tipped off her fork. Diamond swore colourfully.

"It's probably for the best," Tallo chuckled. "In half an hour, you are going to be running around this training yard with the rest of this rabble. You need to be fit to be fast, and if you are going to wield a sword and other weapons, you need to be a lot stronger than you are now. So unless you want to vomit, I would suggest a bit of self-control." And he looked pointedly at the pile of food on Diamond's plate.

Sighing, Diamond reluctantly pushed her plate away. *What a dreadful waste!*

Hugo, who had finished eating, downed a pitcher of water and pushed his chair back. "When Tallo comes out, so do you. Do as he says. I will be watching you," he warned then left.

Tallo was true to his word. He gave her half an hour for her food to settle, then made her walk right through the ranks of soldiers in the training ground.

Tom's face dropped as Diamond stalked past his squadron of trainees. With her shoulders back and her head held high, she caught his eye and smiled tightly.

He paled and nearly fell over.

Diamond didn't blame him. She had changed dramatically since last seeing her childhood friend. All their lives they had been friends, but since their home and lives had been destroyed, they had moved on. Tom by choice, and Diamond because Hugo had effectively delivered her as a prisoner to the magic-hating Queen.

Tom had joined Prince Jack Oden as a trainee guard and was completely ignorant of what had happened to her in the palace. With a jolt she realised he wouldn't know she had killed General Edo. All Tom saw was a completely different person than the one he had grown up with. No longer was she the young girl who had dodged the groping hands of traders or run from bullies among the dirty streets of Berriesford; neither was she the frustrated teaching apprentice with unattainable dreams.

Tom was looking at her with wide eyes, taking in her bruised face and her sweaty, dirty clothes.

Diamond was to become a warrior and a magic-wielding weapon. For all her abhorrence of magic, the Queen wanted to use Diamond's to save the people of Valentia. Diamond swallowed hard. If she failed to impress the Queen in the coming weeks, Tom and Jack would be killed—by Hugo. *That will not happen*, she thought, clenching her teeth together. *I will succeed*. Diamond wondered why the powerful Queen

16

would not fight the Wraith Lord herself. *No matter*, she decided, brushing the thought away. The innocent people who had sought refuge behind the Rift Valley wall—whether Rhodainian or Avalonian—had already lost so much. None deserved death at the hands of the Wraith Lord, a lord who would consume their soul and condemn them to an eternity of darkness and pain.

Leaving Tom behind, she joined the squadron Tallo indicated and listened as he bellowed orders. Their assignment: to run around the edge markers of this training ground seven times.

By the goddess! That must be more than seven miles! Diamond had never needed to run so far in her life. She didn't even know if she could make it.

When it was her squadron's turn, everyone ignored her and took off. After two circuits, her lungs burned and she wanted to stop. Young trainees whizzed past her, and Diamond groaned in embarrassment. Her steps slowed in defeat until someone suddenly grabbed her arm and propelled her forward.

"Hey! You can't stop." The soldier grinned at her. "You're nowhere near done. If you stop now, the whole squadron will suffer extra training as punishment—and that will make you very, very unpopular."

Too breathless to talk, Diamond raised her eyebrows. *Really? Well, wasn't that just wonderful!* Diamond wanted to swear at Hugo and Tallo, but didn't have the energy. The soldier kept his hand under her arm.

"Come on. I'll run with you. Just don't stop. Okay? Regulate your breathing, keep your feet moving, and you'll be fine."

Nodding gratefully, Diamond concentrated on gulping air into her burning lungs. When the soldier let go, they jogged together in silence. It was nice to have a bit of support, even from a stranger.

"Come on," encouraged the soldier, "only a few more feet and you've made it."

Vaguely aware of Hugo watching her, Diamond fell over the finish line, landing in a heap on the dusty ground. Her lungs were on fire and she wanted to vomit. The soldier came over just as she made it onto her knees, gagging and retching. He patiently waited for her to finish, then held out a sweaty hand, which she took.

"Hi, the name's Reese, Reese Dunns," he said. Clear hazel eyes twinkled down at her as he grinned.

Grateful, she smiled back. "Hi Reese, I'm Diamond. Thanks for your help. I wouldn't have made it on my own. I'm so unfit it's embarrassing," she gasped, trying to push herself up but soon gave up. Her legs shook too much to stand.

Reese chuckled and lowered to his haunches. "Well, the Queen's fearless master-at-arms did beat the crap out of you before breakfast."

Diamond groaned. Great. They had all been watching her pathetic fighting skills. She uttered a stream of curses under her breath at Hugo.

"Don't worry, we were all rooting for you," Reese said, giving her a conspiratorial wink. "Maybe when you have learnt a few tricks of your own, you'll get to fight that miserable bastard who never takes his eyes off you. I expect you'll eventually learn how to land a few punches of your own. You might even land one right on his jaw. Now wouldn't that be satisfying?" he whispered, grinning wickedly and wiggling his eyebrows.

Diamond coughed and snorted a laugh. "Yes, it would," she agreed, smiling despite her heaving lungs.

Hugo sat on the ground, leaning against the inner barracks wall. Carefully and methodically, his big hands moved as he sharpened a sleek knife blade. He stilled; even from so far away, Diamond knew he had heard their conversation. Her stomach plummeted but Reese didn't seem to have noticed.

"I'll see you later." Reese winked and sauntered away.

CHAPTER TWO

Diamond's heart lifted a little. At least someone in this place wanted to be friendly with her. That feeling disappeared as Hugo strode over.

"Get up," he growled.

"Really? When do I get to rest?" she snapped, his coldness tipping her past the edge of caution.

"You don't. Over here now," he ordered, watching her struggle up before leading her to the edge of the training ground and away from the masses of sweating, swearing troops.

Nervously, Diamond wondered what she was in for next.

A mocking smile curled Hugo's lip as he cocked his head, regarding her sorry state. "This is where you begin to realise how hard your life is going to be until you become stronger. This is where you learn to respect me, Tallo and every other warrior here. Because we are going to help you become strong enough to fight for yourself as well as the people stuck in this valley at the Queen's mercy."

Diamond's eyes drifted over to where Reese watched them.

"What? Do you think your new friend will come and save you from this part of your training? No soldier is stupid enough to interfere. Besides, he's next on my list. He also needs a hard lesson in disrespecting a senior officer, which I am by the way. I am the one who is going to teach you how to kill with any blade placed in your hands, and I will be the one to show you how to wield your magic with enough skill to stay alive. As such, you will respect me."

His deep voice grated along Diamond's bones, and she flinched instinctively as he shifted his weight. Diamond remembered the brush of his fingers as he took her necklace, his betrayal in the throne room.

She squeezed her eyes shut against the horrifying memory of a dagger, the one Hugo had given her, sliding between General Edo's ribs and piercing his heart. Anger, grief and a terrible hopelessness at what she had been forced to do ripped at her insides. Her magic flared in response, heading straight to Hugo's as it always did.

With no effort, he stopped it and thrust it away from him.

"Not yet, Diamond. First you learn to respect me, then you learn to wield a blade. After that we will play with your magic."

Diamond felt his magical rejection deeply. But she would not let her hurt show. Ignoring the cold wind that whipped dust into her face, Diamond opened her eyes, set her jaw and adjusted her stance to face the elite guard.

"You have to earn respect. For me to respect someone, I need to trust them. I don't trust you anymore, Hugo. *You* destroyed that, not me."

Hugo's sapphire blue eyes darkened to obsidian, then he smiled coldly. "You don't need to trust me, only do as I say. If you want to pass the Queen's test, that is."

Diamond tried to block the kick he aimed at her belly, but as soon as he moved, she knew it was hopeless. Hugo shifted his weight sideways and propelled the roundhouse kick with such swiftness that his limbs blurred. At the last moment he pulled his kick, but his shin still connected with enough force that it drove the breath from her.

Diamond yelled. Her knees sagged to the ground and tears streamed down her face.

Hugo stared down at her, his face grim. "Next time don't be so insolent and foul-mouthed to me or about me. At least not where I can hear you."

Diamond glanced up and looked to Reese, who was watching them from across the dusty training yard.

"Oh, rest assured," he said, glancing at Reese too. "Your new friend is about to get the same reminder about respecting his senior officers." A slight snarl twisted the contours of his scarred mouth. "If, by some miracle, you *ever* manage to land a punch on my jaw, I'll take the whole squadron down to the East docks and buy them a drink. In fact, if you ever become that good, I'll buy them a whole evening of drinks, *little girl*," he sneered. "I'll leave it up to you to tell Reese that."

Diamond lifted her chin, determination shining in her eyes. "That's going to cost you a fortune one day, commander," she ground out.

Hugo brushed himself down. "I doubt it," he stated with a derisory twitch of his eyebrows. "Now, get up and re-join your squadron. You have weapons training today. And remember what I said—you will bleed these next weeks, but my only concern is that you become the weapon you are meant to be. Do not expect leniency from me."

Diamond didn't respond but watched him walk over to Reese. She stifled the sobs that threatened to burn a hole in her chest. It seemed impossible that she had ever been cradled in the warmth of his arms, that she had felt safe just because he was nearby. It didn't matter. She would stand or fall on her own. She didn't need his support or friendship.

By the time Diamond picked herself up out of the dirt, Reese was sporting a thick lip. Slightly stooped, she hobbled over to the squadron that was practising their archery skills. The mixed group of men and women, both fae and human, quietly made a space for her near Reese. It seemed he harboured no ill will for his thick lip as he gave her a sympathetic smile. She tried to return it.

"When I manage to land my fist in his face—and I will eventually—he's going to take this squadron to get drunk. So the more help I get from everyone, the quicker you all get your reward," she told him, a determined glint in her eye.

He nodded once, and she knew he would spread the word.

The rest of the day passed without incident. Diamond managed to trudge to the mess hall at lunchtime but barely said more than a few words to Tom before she devoured some food to regain her energy.

Explaining briefly what had happened with the Queen was a welcome respite from the incessant throbbing of her bruised body. Tom paled, looking sick as he realised the implications of the immortal monarch having Diamond as her weapon and the consequence if Diamond didn't achieve her given objective.

"What do you think she wants your necklace for?" he asked, his brow creased in a frown.

They were sitting alone on a bench at the edge of the mess hall. Tom was gaining weight fast. His shoulders and chest were broader, and he seemed older, more mature since joining the soldiers. He flicked back a brown curl from his eyes—a familiar gesture.

A weak smile tugged at her lips and she shrugged her aching shoulders. "Who knows? But I saw recognition and greed in her eyes when she saw it."

"Why? What does it do? It never looked anything special to me," he commented.

"I have no idea," Diamond sighed, rubbing her tired eyes. "Maybe it has something to do with the shield." She racked her brains, trying to figure out what was useful for an immortal fae Queen stuck in the prison of her own capital city. "Anyway, enough about that. How are things with Zane going?" she asked, wanting to banish her own problems for a short while.

Tom blushed, which instantly made her feel better.

CHAPTER THREE

Diamond made sure she was ready by dawn each morning, well before Hugo knocked on her door. During the day she worked hard, gritted her teeth and did her best not to yell when she was knocked down or battered.

By the end of day five she was utterly exhausted. Unused to such constant physical demands, her body protested with each tiny movement. Even walking required a mammoth effort.

Tallo spent all afternoon instructing her on how to pull back a bow string, then made her loose arrow after arrow. Her fingers and arms were bruised despite using gloves and arm guards. Her muscles trembled so much she feared she may fall over. A brisk wind dried her sweaty, dirt-caked shirt against her skin. She grabbed at the stiff material, pulling at it. Trudging through the outer gate, ignoring the guards completely, Diamond groaned and stared at the path she now had to walk before she could collapse into bed. It seemed like a hideous mountain looming before her, when in truth, it was only a gently sloping dirt track.

These last few nights, she, Kitty and Rose had all stayed up late to chat or visit to the library. She wondered if Kitty and Rose would mind if she didn't join them and just slept tonight. All she wanted to do right now was sleep.

It had been hard to see Rose after her part in Diamond's kidnapping, especially when it had resulted in Diamond's imprisonment and the death of others. Rose had admitted to knowing Diamond's kidnapper, a warrior with red wings and red magic. He had been powerful but not powerful enough to subdue Hugo. Incredibly,

Hugo had simply absorbed the red warrior's magic and continued to fight.

Diamond smiled a little. Rose had blushed prettily when she had admitted to knowing the red warrior. Diamond was pleased for her friend but hoped it would not be long before Rose could arrange for her to meet him. The rebel lord he served held information about Diamond's mother, which Diamond needed.

Hooves sounded on the gravel path. Curious, she looked over her shoulder. Her stomach clenched. Prince Jack Oden was swiftly riding up behind her. Diamond hadn't seen him since the throne room and wasn't sure how she felt about her friend since he had agreed with the Queen's plan to turn her into a weapon. Diamond took a deep breath and exhaled. She had found it in her heart to forgive Rose for her part in the kidnapping, even when it had led to bloodshed. She should at least give Jack a chance.

As usual, Jack was flanked by two guards. One she recognised as Roin, the burley captain of Jack's royal guard. The other was Zane, the arrogant fae warrior who had taken a huge liking to Tom.

The three of them easily passed Diamond, blocking her progress with their horses. Anger and guilt twisted Jack's handsome face as looked down at her. Even Roin, who was normally an affable man, looked shocked. Zane stretched his wings and folded them back in, a clear sign of fae disgruntlement. He raised his brows and pulled a face before gazing towards the barracks.

Tom.

For all his disapproval of her appearance, it seemed Zane was still more interested in Tom's welfare than anything else.

"Tom's fine, Zane. I think you'll find he has changed quite a bit in the past few weeks. He's stronger, faster and has a bit more meat on his bones now," she attempted to joke, reiterating Zane's words from when he had first met Tom. "And he might pretend otherwise, but I know he misses your company," she told him before meeting Jack's eyes.

Tight-lipped, Jack eyed her up and down. Diamond hadn't realised she looked so bad. Her head stung from a blow she had failed to block. Dried blood itched her cheek, and she had not bothered to wipe herself clean at all during today's training.

Perhaps I do look a bit rough, she conceded, feeling a little detached from herself. Exhausted, she turned away and walked up the path.

Jack swore and vaulted off his horse. "Hey!" he pulled her to a standstill.

Diamond paused and met his eyes. She swayed unsteadily on her feet. Cursing, she locked her legs whilst trying her hardest to regain her balance.

Without saying anything, Jack nodded at Roin, who jumped down off his horse and lifted her off her feet. Diamond began to protest but Jack cut her off.

"Be quiet," he growled as he swung back up on his horse.

Roin smiled sympathetically and passed her into Jack's arms. Gratefully, Diamond collapsed against his chest, closing her eyes as they made their way to the palace. Exhaustion made it difficult for her to concentrate while Jack muttered obscenities directed at the Queen and Hugo. Reining in, Jack lowered her to the ground then guided her to her room. He greeted Kitty briskly, ordering her to draw Diamond a bath.

The pretty, blonde maid took one look at Diamond, dipped a small curtsey and quickly began her assigned task. Jack helped Diamond sit on the bed, then his strong hands undressed her. She muttered a half-hearted protest as Kitty returned and helped him pull her shirt off. They both gasped at the sight of her bruised body.

"By the guardians, what in the name of Chaos is Hugo thinking? The way he was behaving before made me think he wants you as his mate. He should be coveting you, not beating you black and blue."

"I'm fine!" Diamond objected through gritted teeth. "And Hugo has never really wanted me. I think that was quite clear in the throne room. Besides, I'm training to be a warrior, not learning how to sew," she joked.

"Sure you are. Kitty? Find Rose. Please also bring some healing oil for the water. And would you ask if there's anything else Rose can bring for these bruises?" His voice was authoritative, but respectful.

"Yes, your highness." Kitty bobbed a curtsey and quickly disappeared from the room.

Diamond wriggled against Jack's grip as he tugged her boots off.

"Stop fighting me, you stubborn fool," he uttered, as she slapped his fingers away from the waistband of her leggings. "Regardless of what you think, I am going to undress you and help you into that bath." When she continued to struggle against him, he scolded, "Let's get one thing straight. You are my friend, and despite him being a stubborn bastard and an utter fool when it comes to you, Hugo is also my friend. You have both saved my life, and I owe you. So I am going to help you both to see the error of your ways. What I am not going to do is attempt to seduce you."

Diamond stared at him open-mouthed, shocked at his candid words. He smirked a little.

"Believe it or not, I *have* seen a naked woman before, but if you're that bothered, I'll leave your underwear on. Stop it!" he ordered harshly as she gripped his wrists. "You need to bathe, put salve on those bruises and rest." The determination in his eyes told her he meant every word.

It didn't matter; Diamond had no more fight left in her.

Kitty returned with Rose in tow. Rose glanced at her friend's battered body and immediately added spell-infused healing oils to the bath water. A minute passed before Rose declared that the water ready.

"Come on," ordered Jack.

He and Rose helped Diamond hobble to the bathing room. Jack steadied her as she limped down the steps into the sunken bath. She watched him leave; with a groan, she sank down into the softness of the steaming water.

Rose smiled sympathetically. "These oils might make your skin tingle a bit, but they will soothe the pain," she explained. "I'll bring you more tomorrow night. It looks like you're going to need them," she added before closing the door.

Alone, Diamond struggled out of her underwear and let the warmth seep into her aching muscles and bones, easing her pain. Tomorrow was going to be a living hell. Hugo would not be easy on her, despite her exhaustion. She sighed, deciding it would be best not to think of Hugo. She ducked her head under the surface and remained there for a short time, allowing the soothing softness and heat to engulf her.

Scrubbed clean and skin glowing, Diamond pulled a towel up off the floor to cover herself before calling for Jack. He came to help her out of the bath, telling her he had dismissed Kitty and Rose for the night. Nervously, she glanced sideways at him, hoping neither of her friends would jump to conclusions about her relationship with Jack. Not that Rose could—or would—judge her.

Diamond flushed as Jack glanced down at her wet body. She glared indignantly.

"Jack! Stop staring!" she berated him.

"Sorry," he grinned, not sounding sorry at all.

"You can wait for me in there. I'll be fine now," she informed him, flushing when he chuckled and flashed her a knowing look. They had become close after Diamond had saved Jack's life out in the forest but that did not mean she wanted him to see her naked. Discarding her wet towel, Diamond covered her bruises in the sweet-smelling salve Rose had given her.

Soothing warmth from a fire washed over her when she emerged from the bathing room. Tying the belt of her robe, Diamond almost giggled at the sight of the soon-to-be King of Rhodainia pouring out her tea. There was a tray of food on the dressing table, and the aroma of beef stew, bread and potatoes made her stomach grumble.

"Sit and eat," Jack ordered. He dried her hair, rubbing it gently with the towel as she ate. "Are you angry with me?" he asked, keeping his hands wrapped in the towel. "You know, for leaving you? For not getting you out of the palace before the Queen could truly sink her claws into you?"

"Yes," Diamond said, not wanting to lie. "You left me, Jack. After everything we went through together in the forest." She released a breath. "I was here on my own, in this *viper's nest* for over two weeks. Did it ever cross your mind to come and see me? To help me?" she asked, unable to keep the bitterness from her voice.

"I had to take General Edo to meet my commanders," he explained quietly, looking crestfallen.

Diamond hated to see him looking so upset. "It isn't your fault the general turned out to be so twisted, you know," she consoled.

"No, but I really didn't see his betrayal coming. I honestly thought Hugo would find a way to get you out before the Queen got to you," he said quietly. "The stupid ass cares so deeply for you, I really expected him to sweep you up, run — and screw the consequences."

"Well, you were wrong. He chose the Queen, not me. He is weak, a coward," she replied with bitterness.

"No, Diamond — he isn't," Jack disagreed. "He is far stronger than you think. Has it even crossed your mind that everything he did was to

28

keep you alive? He has ensured you are worth something to the Queen. Don't forget, Hugo spent many months fighting by my side. He has saved my life countless times and has fought hard for my people. When he first came to Stormguaard it took him a long time to trust us, me included. It wasn't until he saw my people using magic freely that he began to change. Once he realised he wasn't under the Queen's influence anymore, he became a different person. He lost that cold edge and befriended me and my men. He learnt about his gifts, and he was willing to use his magic to fight for us. As soon as we retreated here, she sent Lord Commander Ream for him. The next time I saw him, it was as if all the joy had been sucked from his soul."

Jack started working at the knots in her hair. Diamond patiently let him, only wincing occasionally.

"Hugo once told me his nightmares are haunted by the faces of all the magic wielders he captured for her over the years. Do you know what she makes him do to them?"

Diamond stared at him, a sick feeling growing in her stomach. "No," she whispered.

Jack snorted quietly. "Hugo has a special gift. He can absorb magic, like a sponge absorbs water. It's one of the reasons the Queen covets him. She too has that ability, but she cannot leave this city. Usually she sends her elite guards to hunt down magic wielders, but she only sends Hugo to hunt those who are powerful enough to threaten her: red-or green-winged fae who hide out in the forests far from here. He has to catch them by whatever means necessary and then absorb enough magic to make each victim compliant. He brings them to the palace; when they are weak and cannot fight her, she consumes their power until they die."

"Why does she do that? And why does Hugo help her?" Diamond whispered in horror.

"I have no idea why she does it. Hugo doesn't either." For a moment Jack looked sad. "He has never told me why he always returns to her. He says only that the elite guard have no choice but to return to her side. But I do know he has not hunted for her for at least two years, mainly because he has been with me. For some reason, whenever I leave this valley, she orders him to protect me—even Hugo doesn't know why. Neither of us complain. He can't wait to get away from her, and I like having my friend back."

It took Diamond time to process this new information. "Well, regardless of why he acted the way he did, it's too late now. I can't escape. The lives of my friends and the people in this city are my responsibility."

"No, they are not just your responsibility. Those people are both Rhodainian and Avalonian. They are counting on all of us, including me and the Queen, even if she is an evil witch," Jack responded, placing his hands on her shoulders as if to add weight to his words. "I am so sorry I left you, but I thought," his throat bobbed, "if the general had been so close to my father, if he had truly been my father's friend and primary general, that he would help me be a better ruler, that he would mentor me and teach me things I don't know. I've always felt as if I am expected to know how to do *everything*. People expect me to find solutions to problems, even without having experienced them before. Trajan was a great mentor and friend, but the Water Leopards need their ruler. Until Hugo came along, I never had anyone to throw around ideas with." He took a deep breath. "I just thought the general would be a person I could trust."

"Jack," Diamond stalled him, reaching up to touch his arm. "It's okay. I understand, really I do. I'm sorry about the general too. If it makes you feel any better, he fooled us all—my father most of all." Looking over her shoulder, she gave him a small smile. "We both trusted the wrong people. Let's make the best of this awful situation we're in and help each other. Deal?"

Jack nodded, leaning up against the wall as she finished eating.

"What do you think happened to that poor shapeshifter? You know, the boy?" asked Jack eventually.

Diamond stiffened and put her cutlery down. The young boy, Simeon, had only looked about twelve years old. Now he was the Queen's prisoner. It was his testimony that had condemned General Edo to death. At General Edo's bidding, the boy and his father had informed the Wraith Lord that her mother's necklace was in the north. Ragor's monstrous Seekers had wreaked death and destruction on her hometown of Berriesford looking for her crystal necklace, the necklace now resting in the Queen's vaults.

"I don't know what happened to Simeon. I think she took him back to the dungeons, but if I don't pass the Queen's test, she will kill him." Diamond gulped and put down her knife and fork.

Jack huffed lightly, "Well, that might be hard. According to my information, the boy escaped that very night. No one knows how."

Jack jumped as Diamond whirled around and stared at him.

"I'm sorry. I assumed you knew. The Queen has declared the boy a magic wielder. She is convinced he hid dark magic in his shapeshifting blood. The cell door was locked, and there were no signs of a fight. The boy just disappeared," he made a rippling gesture with the fingers of one hand. "She even questioned her elite guards, and you can imagine that she didn't do it gently."

Diamond felt a rush of relief. "Good for him," she whispered.

"He was clearly more resourceful than anyone gave him credit for," Jack responded, pushing her back around. He picked up the silver hairbrush and began gently teasing the knots from her hair.

31

"Or he's dead," Diamond stated. Tilting her head to look up into his chocolate eyes, she answered her own question, "No, she will not have killed him."

"Why not?" Jack asked.

"Because without him, she loses some her leverage with me."

"She has other leverage with you: Tom and me," he stated matter-of-factly.

"You know?" Diamond breathed, twisting around on the stool to face him once again.

"Of course I know. The Queen isn't the only one with spies." Jack chuckled. "But it isn't just Tom's or my safety that worries you, is it? Or even all those desperate people out there." The towel sailed through the air as he threw it aside. "It's Hugo. Your feelings for him have always been written on your face, and I know Hugo feels far more for you than a Queen's guard should. The Queen saw it too. It's why she took such pleasure in hurting you. You are her leverage with him, as much as he is with you. I know what she made him do in that throne room, and I get why you don't trust him anymore, but you must see he had no choice."

Diamond stared ahead, biting her bottom lip. "I do understand that. But I believe he will do anything for the Queen, and I can't trust him until he is strong enough to defy her."

Her heart ached for Hugo, especially after Jack's insights into his behaviour, but Diamond felt stuck in her whirlwind of feelings, which she had yet to sort through. She didn't want to see Hugo hurt, but he would be if she failed, just as Jack and Tom would be.

Jack grunted at her expression. "I thought so. You two are impossible. You will work yourself into the ground for his sake, despite your disappointment in him, and he will do anything to keep you from a greater harm." He huffed. "The Queen really is the mistress of manipulation, isn't she?"

"Jack, this isn't only about Hugo, or even you and Tom," Diamond said. "There are thousands of people in this valley who need my magic to help protect them. I might not be strong enough to do that yet, but I will sweat blood and take every bruise I have to until I can."

Jack grinned at the steely determination in her tone. "Now there's the real Diamond."

"I *have* to be good enough to pass the Queen's test, to keep you and Tom and Hugo safe. And I can only help the people of this valley if I pass," she replied.

"You do realise that insane female will kill who she wants, when she wants? It won't matter how many bruises you have or if you fit compliantly into her ultimate plans," Jack replied with raised eyebrows.

"Yes, but I won't give her the excuse by failing," she answered resolutely.

Stepping in front of her, Jack gave her a sceptical look before letting it drop. A mischievous glint crept in his eyes. "So become good enough. We'll need you at the wall soon enough. Have you finished eating?" he asked, changing the subject.

Diamond nodded, feeling so weary now, even the bed looked miles away.

"Come on. Bedtime," he said, pulling her up off the stool. He picked her up, cradling her against his chest.

Diamond gratefully relaxed against him, enjoying the comfort of his embrace. She winced as he lowered her onto the bed. Gently, he tucked her under the blankets.

"I've asked Kitty to wake you at five-thirty," he told her.

"Thank you," she murmured sleepily, staring up into his gorgeous brown eyes.

He contemplated her for a few seconds. "Diamond, do you really still have feelings for Hugo?" he asked, smiling at her droopy eyes.

33

"I don't know," she responded, not entirely truthfully. Of course she had feelings for him; she just didn't trust him anymore. Her cheeks flushed a little at her lie.

"That's what I thought," he retorted, smirking.

"Jack, it doesn't matter how I feel. Hugo doesn't feel a thing for me, not anymore," she declared, swallowing the ache in her throat.

"Of course he does. He simply needs to realise that unless he shows it, he will lose you."

"Really? And how do you propose to convince him of that?" she grumbled.

"No idea, but I have every faith in my friends. Although I might give him a little push if the opportunity presents itself."

"Fine," she grumbled, still not convinced Hugo was in the least bit bothered about her.

Jack kissed her eyelids, then pulled himself away.

"You should sleep. I will see you again tomorrow. I'll keep you company as much as I can over the next few weeks," he promised before he left.

Diamond was asleep before the door clicked shut.

CHAPTER FOUR

The fine drizzle plastered Diamond's hair to her face. In a fit of irritation, she pushed the loose strands out of her face, summoning all her self-control. *This could not be happening!*

Attion's hands were clenched behind his back. His shoulder-length brown hair was braided away from his face, his greenish-brown eyes regarding her steadily.

Diamond's chest tightened. Hugo could not be asking her to accept Attion, the guard who had groped her, as a training partner.

"Diamond!" Hugo warned. "Attion is here to train with you. He is experienced and good at what he does. He will help you learn. Also, Attion is required to report your progress back to the Queen on a weekly basis."

Her violet eyes flashed with anger as she whipped her head towards Hugo. "I will not train with him," she tried again, unable to keep the tremor of disgust from her voice.

Attion glanced at Hugo, but was otherwise stoic.

"Yes, you will. You both have to do this, so put your feelings aside and get on with it. Attion will respect you as a trainee warrior. If you feel like he doesn't, I suggest you become good enough to make him."

Diamond clamped her jaw shut, remembering her purpose: become good enough to protect her friends and the people of the valley. If that meant training with this abusive, cold guard, then that is what she would do.

Hugo worked Diamond into the ground. All day, every day, he pitched her against different training partners. Attion was always included and was never easy on her, but always remained respectful. Hugo knew Attion had not had many assignments away from the palace. He suspected the other guard enjoyed mixing with the Avalonian soldiers and warriors. Attion even seemed less cold towards Diamond.

Attion's life will change after the war is over. When Diamond and I kill the Queen, he will be free, Hugo thought. Pursing his lips, Hugo was painfully aware his plans of treason were still only seeds.

He hovered above the barracks, his sapphire wings armoured and glinting in the sun. The view of the steep city slopes was clear from the sky. Unable to stop himself, he glanced down to the area of the city where Diamond had been kidnapped. Whoever had taken her wielded magic. Red magic. A living adult fae with red wings and magic was unheard of in Valentia. If the Queen found out, she would hunt the culprit down. Thankfully she had accepted his explanation it had been human rebels who had initiated Diamond's kidnap. Hunting down the red warrior had become one of Hugo's main priorities. He needed the fae's help, and Diamond deserved to find out what her kidnappers knew about her mother.

Tallo looked up as Hugo lowered himself to the ground. Grinning, the master-at-arms gestured with his head to where Diamond and Attion were practising with short swords. Hugo knew Tallo was starting to lighten up her training to counter balance the onslaught of demands Hugo made of her, but never did she balk from her tasks. Whatever weapon Hugo thrust into her hands, she took it and listened to his words of tutelage. Not a single tear fell when her skin was marred by a knife or her face bruised by a sword hilt. Hugo saw her grit her teeth, lift her chin defiantly and try again and again, until her body shook with weariness. Her spirit and prowess as a fighter were growing more impressively than some of the guards Hugo had trained with since he had been a child.

Although he would not show it, his heart swelled with pride every time his beautiful silver-haired Nexus refused to give in. A Nexus was a rare magical bond that compelled a couple's magic to merge. Hugo had found only one dusty old book in the library that alluded to the bond, which indicated that two fae who bonded could become tremendously powerful if they had the chance to explore their pairing and each other's magic. They could sense each other, power each other—love each other.

Trying to distract her, Hugo pushed out a small amount of magic. As it touched her face, a zing of energy passed into him. He smiled. She didn't even stumble. No one else knew he had been doing this several times a day. When he'd started, it had distracted her but now she only grunted, did not fumble her block and sent a sharp stab of magic back at him. He felt it slap his face and his smile turned to a grin, which he swallowed quickly.

Tallo raised a brow, not missing a thing. "You really ought to take her to one of the training rooms and begin training her magic more thoroughly."

"I am training her magic, and her ability to control it. She just doesn't know it. If she did, she would panic and probably fry us all," Hugo replied dryly.

"Well, that's your department. I'll leave you to it. I'm going to swap out her partner," he informed Hugo before shouting for Reese.

Hugo began instructing the pair as soon as Reese arrived.

"No!" Hugo bit out harshly as Diamond dropped her guard too far to the left. Grabbing her arm, he moved it. "Here, your arm needs to be here. Don't drop your guard too far."

Her violet gaze met his. Thankfully he did not see so much anger or hurt in her eyes now. His belly tightened at her steady regard before she looked back at Reese. It seemed the soldier had become one of her regular training partners. Attion stood off to one side watching quietly. Occasionally he would catch Hugo's eye, asking for silent permission to walk over and correct moves or give alternative counter attacks. Hugo could tell Attion would never again disrespect Diamond. The fae guard wanted out of his life as the Queen's chattel as much as Hugo did.

Reese winked at Diamond as Hugo gripped her arm, moving the staff down slowly so she could follow the movements he made. Hugo smiled to himself. He'd seen the wink but chose not to punish Reese. Instead, he ignored his jealousy at their easy friendship.

"Again," Hugo ordered brusquely.

Reese feinted left and swirled his staff. Diamond caught the feint, blocking and countering with a viciousness that always surprised Hugo. Reese grinned and blocked, swirled on the ball of his foot and swept for her ankles. Diamond jumped his staff, twisted and slammed her fist into his kidneys.

Hugo stepped back next to Attion, giving them room. Diamond's body was toned and strong now; she also seemed to heal remarkably well. *Possibly because of her fae blood,* he mused. Regardless of the reason, he pushed her harder and harder each day, wanting to see how far her potential could go.

He didn't understand her abilities, not really. Diamond had never had any training; he couldn't comprehend how she could become so fast and so skilled in such a short space of time. He wondered if Arades Gillon had tutored his daughter before he died. Hugo remembered the fury in her face as she had killed the Seeker who had murdered her father.

Diamond had always denied knowing her father had been the primary general for Jack's father. It seemed Arades Gillon had hidden his past in order to try and protect his daughter. Hugo pressed his lips into a tight line. General Edo's betrayal nullified all those efforts.

Hugo wondered if Diamond still grieved for her father, if she had cried since that first night or if she still had nightmares. He gave a start. Reese had slipped through her guard again and jabbed her in her belly. She was leaning forward, spitting and gagging.

Attion strode over with a frown on his face. "Here," Attion motioned as she straightened. Diamond did not pull away as he gripped her wrist and showed her a flowing strong block. "Now dip and turn," he advised, and she tried again. Diamond nodded coolly and Attion returned to his spot, watching her movements closely.

A group of Jack's trainee royal guards practised nearby. Hugo saw Tom doing his best not to watch Diamond, but he couldn't seem to help it. Hugo grinned inwardly as Zane hit Tom hard on his shoulder with the flat side of a sword.

"Concentrate or suffer!" Zane advised, grinning widely as Tom swore at him. "And respect your senior officers, boy!" The big fae raised his sword and swung an attack.

"Stop calling me boy!" Tom growled, retaliating viciously.

Hugo turned away from the pair; he was pleased Zane hadn't given up on Tom. Clearly, he still coveted the younger man as a mate. Hugo silently wished them luck and turned back to Diamond.

He watched for any sign of weakness. There was none. He stood further back, scrutinising her, arms folded over his broad, leather encased chest. A thought occurred to him, and he narrowed his eyes suspiciously.

Maybe she doesn't have any human blood either, that would explain a lot. Hugo loosed a controlled long breath. Diamond's father had definitely been a fae warrior. But he didn't know about her mother; maybe she had been something else entirely.

His eyes followed Diamond closely as she executed an elegant spin. Using the moves Attion had taught her, she elbowed Reese in the back before throwing him with ease and skill over her shoulder.

"Enough," said Hugo firmly. "Reese, you may re-join the others."

Reese jumped up. "Yes, commander," he said, saluting before clasping forearms with Diamond. He jogged off to re-join the squad.

Hugo did not react. Despite his jealousy of Reese, he was pleased the men and women of this squadron had taken Diamond to their hearts. Human, fae or mixed blood, it did not matter to these Rhodainian soldiers. They would all fight for their prince and for each other, even die for each other if necessary. It lifted his heart to know Diamond had their support.

Seconds passed, then with a jolt, Hugo realised he was staring at her face, but he couldn't seem to tear his eyes away. He thought her so beautiful; from the moment he had laid eyes upon her, his magic had reached out for hers. Eyebrows as silver as her hair, long lashes outlining her large violet eyes. Her nose was small and slightly upturned at the tip; her lips full, possibly too big for her face—but they were so soft and...

Diamond coughed. A flush crept onto his face as she cocked a silver eyebrow at him. Hugo shrugged and gave her a sheepish smile. For a moment she looked stunned. Devilment took him. He slipped off his armour and tunic and dropped them at his feet then stepped over the pile, knowing his shirt clung to his body. Her wide eyes travelled over his flat belly, muscled chest and broad shoulders. He grinned as she flushed. Perhaps she wasn't so angry at him after all. Now all he had to do was encourage her to realise that—and trust him.

"Basic combination, attack and defence," he ordered, holding her gaze as he stepped closer than necessary. Slowly, he pulled the staff from her hands before giving her a sword.

Attion grunted and walked away to spar with the squadron.

Hugo and Diamond paid no attention, lost to everyone but themselves.

KAREN TOMLINSON

CHAPTER FIVE

The days blurred. Hugo moved into the barracks, using that as an excuse not to fly with her in his arms from her room in the palace to the training ground every morning. In truth, he found it hard to ignore the tension between them, not to mention the way their magic merged more each day. Holding her close every morning without showing her how he felt was becoming impossible.

The bitter cold made Hugo shiver as he waited outside the gates to the training ground with Attion. He wanted to push Diamond's magic further today, throw more at her and test her reaction. He needed to see how confidently she could stop him. Attion knew his plans; together they had formulated the report that would be delivered to the Queen tonight. Attion would detail Diamond's physical progress, but they had both agreed the Queen should not know Diamond could summon her magic within the confines of the city. It was safer for everyone if the Queen believed Diamond impotent under the influence of the ancient shield, like all other magic wielders.

Hugo's heart stumbled, his thoughts completely leaving his head. Jack's horse approached the barracks. Sitting behind Jack, with her arms wrapped tightly around his waist, sat Diamond. Hugo could not hide the sudden rage that rippled through him at the sight of her holding another man.

The prince reined in and steadily met Hugo's eyes before nodding a greeting. Diamond slid to the ground, cringing slightly, her cheeks flushing when she saw Hugo's anger. Jealousy and pain raged for supremacy, and he couldn't help the snarl that curled his lips. His reaction was immediate. His fists curled, and his whole body shook with rage. He clamped down on the urge to break Jack's jaw, closing his eyes and breathing deeply.

When the red cleared from his vision, Hugo snapped his eye open. Jack stood right in front of him. Hugo looked down at his friend, a snarl still on his lips.

Jack squared his shoulders and looked up, his brown eyes serious and steady. "What do you expect? She is a beautiful woman. If you want her for yourself, you need to fight for her, just like any other male would fight for the one they want. I know she still feels something for you, but she does not trust you. Gain her trust again, Hugo, before someone else steals her heart."

With that, the prince vaulted back on his horse and trotted away.

Hugo felt ready to explode with frustration after spending the day near Diamond, igniting then smothering her magic, followed by letting it flare and play. He wanted Diamond more than he had wanted anything else in his entire life. No matter how many times he reminded himself she was better off without him, he couldn't make himself leave her alone. He had taken Jack's words to heart. He wanted Diamond to trust him again. It would mean so much to share with her his plans to reach out to the rebels and the red-winged fae.

Hugo daringly let his touch linger as he brushed a drop of perspiration away from her temple with his thumb.

"That's enough for today," he said, his voice shaking a little. "You have tested me as deeply as I have you. We both need a break."

But despite his words, he couldn't stop himself stepping closer. His fingers slipped into her hair, cupping the back of her head. Tension and magic simmered between them. His head dipped slowly towards her. *Gods, I want to kiss her, so much!* Her eyes widened, and her soft lips parted, but it was the surprised gasp from that beautiful mouth that brought him back to his senses. With a soft, frustrated growl, Hugo reluctantly released her and stepped back. His eyes bored into her.

"You should leave," he ground out.

"Y-yes, I should," she stammered. "Goodbye." Red-cheeked and flustered, she hurried from the training room.

Hugo groaned loudly and swung a powerful punch at the nearest padded board, splintering it in two. He felt ready to burst with tension, and he needed to work it off. Hard. He went in search of Attion.

Bare-chested and sweating, the two fae warriors circled each other, honing in on the other's every move. Armoured wings glinted in the shafts of sunlight glaring through the training hall's high windows.

"If being near her does this to you, why don't you tell her of your feelings?" grated Attion, leaping sideways into the air and flipping elegantly. He landed and slammed a punch into Hugo's kidneys.

Anticipating Attion's attack, Hugo spun and lashed out with his armoured wings, then snapped a fist into Attion's jaw. The other warrior rolled with the blow, spitting blood from his mouth as he dipped and spun on his haunches. With his leg outstretched, he tried to take out Hugo's feet. The move was faultless—if doomed to fail.

Hugo leapt into the air and landed far enough away to call a halt to their match. These sparring sessions were building a fragile respect between the two warriors; however, Attion was right: their fights were more brutal when Hugo had been with Diamond.

"How can I?" Hugo growled, shaking his head. "How do I tell her and then keep her focused on saving this city? We both know that if the Queen learns of my interest, she will either kill Diamond or keep me from Diamond's side. Then how do I stop the Queen from harming her?" He raked a hand through his damp hair, ignoring the beads of sweat that ran down the muscles of his chest. "Gods dammit! My life is one long lie!"

"Commander! You are the one who told me we could escape our lives, lives wrought of destruction and death. *'Help me train her and keep her safe, and together Diamond and I will have the power to destroy our immortal Queen.'* That is what you said," Attion pointed out.

Hugo saw ice creep into the elite guard's eyes, the brown looking more green in the sunlight.

"Was that a lie, shadow demon? Is your Nexus bond with Diamond a lie? Is your claim that this half-blood is the most powerful magic wielder you have ever seen a lie?"

"No!" barked Hugo. "She *is* the most powerful magic wielder I have ever seen. When we merge, it feels so right, like we could do or be anything," he breathed, unaware his eyes had closed as he remembered the feel of their magic entwining in a dance that could bring joy—or utter destruction.

"Then the prince is right. Fight for her or you will lose her. Find a way to earn her forgiveness and respect, then seal your bond with blood. Not just for yourself, but for the innocent people of this kingdom."

Hugo huffed a laugh. "Since when did you become so bothered by the lives of the innocent, *spy?*"

"Since a half-blood and a shadow demon made me realise I could have more than death and killing in my life. Let's hope I wasn't mistaken." Attion cocked his head and contemplated Hugo. "Your magic is obviously worth more to the Queen than your death, or she would have taken your magic years ago and dumped your body in an alley. The Queen will keep you alive, even if you do declare yourself to the magic wielder."

Hugo snorted. "How the tables have turned. The guard who was ready to kill both of us a few weeks ago is now the only person who knows how tightly Diamond holds my heart."

Attion regarded him steadily, then did a most unexpected thing—he smiled. "Yes, I do, don't I, commander? Maybe I could use that to my advantage in some way."

Hugo smiled back. "Careful. Your sense of humour is showing. Don't go and destroy our reputation as cold-hearted killers."

"Hmm, you're right. I really shouldn't do that, because then you would have nothing to hide behind, and your female might realise you care."

"My female has a name, Attion. She fights with as much determination as you do, she is smart and tenacious and she never gives up. Those are admirable traits that deserve respect from any warrior, including you."

A thoughtful look on his face, Attion contemplated Hugo. "You can become shadow and death, but you are weak when it comes to that female. You made a deal with me for my life and now I will make one with you. Your heart and soul belong to her. Find a way to get her to trust you again; make her strong enough to defeat the Wraith Lord, and I will use her name with honour." Attion placed a fist on his chest, bowed slightly and left.

How swiftly time changes things, reflected Hugo, too shocked by Attion's words to react to that unexpected gesture of respect.

CHAPTER SIX

Although Hugo had taken charge of Diamond's training squadron, it was time to appoint a captain. Reese was the clear choice. He was not the biggest or strongest among the soldiers or warriors, but he was a decision maker. He supported his comrades but was willing and able to put down anyone with a smart mouth. More importantly, the others deferred to Reese to speak for them. In short, they trusted and respected him.

With that decision made, Hugo stalked toward Diamond. Despite Attion's regular jibing about pursuing Diamond, Hugo really didn't know how much he could push her.

Her back was turned to him, and she was laughing with some of the squadron. It was nice to see her relaxed and happy. Unable to prevent himself, he pushed his magic out to touch her. She turned to face him, her eyes locking onto his. Smiling, she cocked her head to one side. The others saluted and made their way back to Tallo.

"Are we sparring with weapons or magic today, commander?" she asked, violet sparkling in her eyes.

Hugo allowed his face to soften when he smiled back. "Why, both of course," he answered. "I need to see if I can distract you again."

Her cheeks flushed at his reference to the day before when he had deliberately nipped and stroked every available patch of her exposed skin with his magic. Eventually she had become so distracted, she had left herself open to an ankle sweep, thus finishing their session staring up at him from the ground.

Hugo's heart constricted when he saw hope softening her features. She allowed him to intertwine his magic with hers. He did not hide his pleasure at that contact. The feel of her magic caressing his face and sliding up his stomach simultaneously jolted him into inhaling sharply and blinking in surprise. That reflex cost him. The little minx launched an immediate attack, almost knocking him off his feet with a wave of power that rattled his ear drums.

Hugo was pleased her confidence in her magic grew more each day. He could sense her fear lessening, even if he still had to occasionally subdue its wildness.

Hugo's stomach tightened at the thought of his Nexus meeting the Wraith Lord in battle. Diamond was physically strong and could fight skilfully, but on the battlefield death was only one misjudged strike or stumble away.

When the sun's rays became tinged with orange, Hugo realised how much time had passed. Silver strands floated free of Diamond's braid and blew across her face. As she swore and thrust those strands back impatiently, her hands shook with fatigue. His eyes narrowed but he realized his muscles were shaking too.

"All right, that's enough for today," he instructed, lowering his Silverbore swords until the tips dug into the ground.

Under the impression their time together was over, Diamond's boots kicked up a plume of dust as she walked away.

"Diamond," he said softly.

"Yes, commander?" she asked, turning back immediately.

Part of him was nervous to see how she would react to his next words, but he had to get closer to her if he wanted her to trust him.

"There is a room opposite mine in the officers' quarters of the barracks. You may have three hours off tomorrow morning to move your belongings down here."

Confusion flittered across her face, and a small frown creased her brow. It was so comical, he had to smile.

"W-what?" she stammered. "Here? Near you?"

"Yes. It's too far for you to keep going back to the palace. Besides," he dared to reach out and tuck a strand of silver behind her ear. Wide, violet eyes watched him but she did not flinch away. "You need to rest when we are not training," he said, eyebrows raised meaningfully. "Jack is becoming a distraction."

His nostrils flared slightly as he felt an echo of embarrassment through the bonds he shared with her. She didn't know that he had bitten her, injected venom into her and swallowed her blood to save her life. Taking another's blood once formed the beginning of a mating bond between fae. He shifted uncomfortably. It meant he could sense some of her emotions, if he delved deep enough. Hugo very rarely allowed himself such glimpses of her heart. It felt wrong without her permission. He swallowed. Now was not the right time to tell her he could feel her emotions and control her mind. Any trust she had in him would be sorely tested by that news. It would have to wait.

Those violet eyes held his and her flush deepened at the mention of Jack. Jealousy bit into him but he curbed it. He did not own her or even deserve her. Yet.

"Yes, commander," she acquiesced with a nod.

Hugo sheathed his swords and clasped his hands behind his back, suppressing his desire to touch her again. "Good. Be ready to begin training by nine tomorrow," he said, nodding to a large stone building off to their left. "West quarters. I will make sure the door is unlocked. It's the first room on the left; mine is opposite."

Diamond saluted and walked away, but his heart lurched when she looked back over her shoulder and smiled.

CHAPTER SEVEN

Diamond called a cheery good evening to Kitty and smiled at the sweet, flowery scent that filled the room. Jack plonked himself in the armchair and grinned, amused by her distracted behaviour.

"Are you able to manage tonight, miss?" asked Kitty with a gentle smile.

Diamond, whose head was full of a certain warrior, gave a start. "Err, yes, Kitty. Sorry. We'll be fine," she reassured her friend, a little uncomfortable when Kitty glanced meaningfully at Jack, then quickly departed.

Diamond discarded her sweaty, dirt encrusted clothes. Jack watched appreciatively as she threw off her tunic and shirt, followed closely by her boots, socks and leggings. Diamond was beyond feeling embarrassed. She had grown confident in the way she looked over the past weeks; besides, Jack had already seen most of her body.

"By the goddess, Diamond! If you're going to strip, at least give me time to hide my eyes," he blustered.

Giggling as he covered his eyes with his hands, fingers apart, she stuck her tongue out at him right before she closed the door to the bathroom.

A satisfied groan escaped her as she slipped into the steaming water. Jack's cheeky sense of humour and support had helped keep her sane these past weeks. But there was something in his eyes tonight. Worry? Guilt? She wasn't sure. He had assured her he did not mind spending time with her, though she often felt guilty for keeping him from his responsibilities in the valley.

Diamond scrubbed herself clean with a bar of lemon-scented soap, wondering why Jack didn't spend time with someone special. It would not be hard for the charming and handsome prince to find a woman to warm his bed. Then she grimaced at her own thoughts. Fighting a war and maintaining authority over his deposed kingdom, not to mention keeping her company, probably didn't leave much opportunity for anything but the occasional dalliance.

Diamond's father had always been frank and open about sex, warning her she may be pursued by fae males to mate, especially as she was half fae herself. Her cheeks grew hot. Until Hugo, she had never wanted to share her body with anyone.

You need trust if you are going to give your body to another—fae or human, male or female, it doesn't matter. And that trust needs to be indestructible if you ever agree to bind yourself to anyone.

Diamond pulled herself from the water, dressed and left the bathing room. She was ready to tell Jack she was moving to the barracks. He would be happy Hugo wanted her closer, but Diamond's stomach tightened. She would miss Jack and Kitty and Rose terribly.

Seeing that dinner had arrived, she held her news as she tried to eat. It was hopeless.

"Hugo wants me to move into the barracks," she blurted out suddenly.

Jack pushed away his half-eaten food.

"That's great, Diamond. Besides, it's probably for the best," he replied in a resigned voice.

"Why?" she asked, worried about his lacklustre demeanour.

Jack leaned forward, taking her hands. "You should be with Hugo if things are improving. I also have to go back to the Rift Valley. The storms are making it too dangerous for me to continue traveling as often, and I need to keep control of what's happening out there." He rubbed his face with his hands, looking suddenly tired.

Diamond felt dreadful. He had been travelling back and forth to the valley to see her. Selfishly, it hadn't even occurred to her to tell him to stop.

"To be honest, I have been completely self-serving. These evenings with you and Kitty and Rose have been the most relaxing I've experienced in ages. But I have a kingdom in tatters and my responsibilities are in the valley with my army and my people." He sighed heavily. "There is unrest in the camps. Not only that, but we are running low on supplies, and I am powerless to stop the onslaught of the winter weather. Every day more people seek refuge behind the Rift Valley wall, and Master Commander Riddeon tells me Ragor will arrive with his host well before the Winter Solstice."

Diamond gasped, realising how much he had to deal with. "I'm so sorry, Jack. I didn't realise."

"There's no reason you should."

"Is there anything I can do to help?" she asked, sincerely.

"Yes," he responded, cupping her cheek. "Master your magic, and help me defeat the Wraith Lord. But most of all: forgive Hugo. The ice he wraps around his heart is only protection. Give him a chance to admit to himself—and to you—how he feels. He hasn't really had much practise at that sort of thing. Even with all his strength, he needs someone to fight *for* him too."

Before Diamond could respond, he pulled her into a tight embrace. "I'll see you soon," he whispered against her hair before he stood and bid her farewell.

Nightmares left Diamond shaking and drained. As she struggled to ready herself for the day, her heart was heavy with renewed grief for her father. Then how much she was going to miss Kitty and Rose hit her as she walked out of her room to where Rose waited for her in the corridor.

As they approached the door, Rose pulled on her hand, stopping their progress.

"I have to go this way," she said, indicating the stone flagged corridor that continued towards the healers' wing of the palace.

"Okay," Diamond answered, forcing a smile that did not reach her eyes.

"I have spoken with my friend," Rose whispered. "He has to go to the Rift Valley but he said to tell you he thinks your paths will cross there. If they don't, he will find you."

Diamond nodded, too tired and low to question her friend.

Rose kissed her cheek. "Good luck," she whispered.

Outside, the bitter wind whipped and tugged at Diamond's clothes. Welcoming its stinging touch, she trudged down the gravel path to the barracks.

The door to the west wing stood open. It took a moment for her eyes to adjust to the gloom. The corridor was clean but very basic with worn wooden floors, plain stone walls and the occasional oil lamp.

Trying the first door on the left, she found it unlocked. Her belongings had been piled in the centre. In the far corner, a single bed was pushed against the wall with a pile of woollen blankets stacked at the end of the bare mattress. A small window above the bed let in a small amount of daylight.

So this is it, she thought glumly.

The only other furniture was an old pine washstand, with a pot basin and jug, standing against the other wall. A small door led into a tiny bathing room; a short bath tub and a flushing water closet squeezed into the cramped space.

Diamond knelt next her trunk. Her fingers brushed the lid of a long white box. She carefully removed the item inside the box. Resting the delicate fabric on her lap, she smiled a little. This creation was the first beautiful dress she had ever owned, sent to her by her unknown benefactor. The stunning garment had floated around her like a star-spangled mist, and for the first time in her life, Diamond had felt beautiful. Reverently, Diamond leaned into the box and touched the precious hair comb, bejewelled with amethyst. Maybe one day she would wear it again.

Diamond gently replaced the dress in the box, not bothering to unpack any other clothes. An age-speckled mirror hung on the opposite wall. Critically, she frowned at her pale, tired reflection and stuck out her tongue. Her hair a mess, she took a moment to plait it before leaving her small room, sparing only a brief glance at the door opposite hers.

CHAPTER EIGHT

Arriving in the mess hall, Diamond deliberately sat alone. Thoughts of her father filled her head. She shoved her plate away as tears blurred her vision. A heavy energy pushed against her skin. Familiar magic tugged at her chest. A welcome discomfort.

With a resigned sigh and nervous flutter in her belly, she twisted to face Hugo. His hair was loose, the blue steaks catching the light as he inclined his head to the door. Heaving her tired body up, Diamond followed Hugo. She wasn't in the mood for practice today, but she knew there was no choice.

Wind lashed at them as they stood facing each other. Dust from the dry dirt under their feet blew into her already gritty eyes. Hugo's sapphire gaze narrowed as he took in her pale, tired face and red-rimmed eyes. It was as if he could read the raw emotions in her mind, see her grief over her father and her confusion over General Edo. Her defiance slipped. For the first time in weeks she dropped her gaze, opting to stare at his scarred boots instead.

Despite hearing his growl, she could not look up. Her stomach knotted at the sound. She had somehow let him down. When Hugo had told her this training might break her, she had promised herself it wouldn't. Her resolve to prove to him she could become a good warrior had held. But now all she felt was exhaustion. The terrible nightmares of blood and fear and fire had left a hollowness upon her heart, one that had been growing since her father had died.

Her fingers flexed, turning white as she fisted them. Staring at his boots, Diamond missed the narrow-eyed, concerned look Hugo gave her. A few uncomfortable minutes passed before Diamond's shoulders slumped under the weight of his gaze.

Turbulent energy whipped across the space between them, magic pushing against her as if trying to tunnel inside her skin. Her own magic responded immediately and defensively. Her magic snapped a shield into place, shimmering like a heat wave around them. Diamond gulped as their magic fought for supremacy. Only the shimmering air served as evidence of their silent battle.

Minutes passed. She trembled, her teeth clenched as a tremor tightened her spine. It was exhausting to fight him magically, more exhausting than physical sparring. Abruptly the onslaught vanished, causing her legs to wobble. It was a relief to give up.

"Join your squadron," Hugo ordered abruptly.

She recovered from her stumble. Dragging her feet, Diamond kept her gaze down on the ground and joined the others. All morning she did everything Tallo and the newly appointed Captain Reese asked of her, but she could not shake the grief that weighed down her soul. Even sparring with Attion changed nothing. She had no fire, no burning desire to prove herself to Hugo or anyone else.

Throughout the morning, Attion's eyes flicked uneasily from her to Hugo. Diamond never registered that his blows were tempered, almost gentle.

Listlessly, Diamond glanced at Hugo, her stomach clenching at the unfathomable look on his face. She could always pinpoint precisely where he stood, his magic a beacon.

Even Reese, who normally found something amusing to grin at, was subdued. From his position in the squadron, he kept glancing between her and Hugo. When Tallo ordered them to break for lunch, Diamond didn't even bother trying to eat.

Craving solitude and peace, she sat outside alone, staring at the iron grey clouds whizzing overhead. Soon that familiar play of energy assaulted her senses. She sighed in resignation. Part of her had been waiting for him, wanting him to come.

"What's wrong with you today?" Hugo asked, his voice not as harsh as she had expected.

She looked at his handsome and scarred face, then exhaled. *How do I tell this strong warrior about the grief and exhaustion dragging me down?* He had already said he wouldn't care if this training broke her. She remained quiet, hoping he wouldn't consider her silence as disrespecting him.

Or maybe that would be for the best, she reflected. Then he might beat her into unconsciousness, and she could sleep with no dreams and no nightmares to plague her. Her eyes closed, almost wishing for the brush of his icy cold anger.

"Get up," Hugo ordered.

"Why?" she asked, her voice flat and dull.

A snarl bared his teeth. "Because I said so," he growled, and stalked closer. The harshness of his voice made her wince. "Get. Up!" he ordered again, louder this time.

"No!" she barked, a spark of defiance igniting at his imperious tone. "I'm too tired to fight you. If you must punish me for insubordination, do it here."

Grabbing her by her tunic, he forced her abruptly to her feet. Dust blew into her sore eyes and mouth.

"So be it," he said, his voice hard enough to grate on her raw emotions. Letting go of her tunic, he stepped back. Diamond acknowledged there was no way out of this. He bent his thickly muscled legs and leapt. If she hadn't lunged sideways, he would have slammed into her and crushed her chest. Even as Diamond straightened, her emotions remained dulled. Her shoulders still slumped. She watched as Hugo stood tall and stretched out his glorious wings. Armour clattered across them, the stormy sky unable to dampen their beauty.

"Hugo, please," she pleaded, willing him to understand her emptiness.

A shadow crossed his rugged features, silver blazing in his eyes for a fraction of a second.

"I can't do this today," she whispered, sinking to her knees. From nowhere, hot tears pricked at her eyes.

Staring at her, Hugo stood impossibly still, as if hewn from stone. She looked up imploringly at him and watched his sapphire eyes turn to endless black orbs. Hastily, she dropped her gaze back down to the ground. The same thing had happened in the throne room. She recognised it as a sign he had shut down his heart.

Slowly, he approached. Despite her exhaustion, a shiver of apprehension ran down her spine. Hugo's steps were silent and deliberate; then she saw his worn, soft leather boots. Wings still outstretched, he squatted down and leaned forward. His voice was harsh in her ear, his breath hot on her wind chilled skin.

"Not today? Are you kidding me? Do you think your enemies will give a shit about how you're feeling when they come to kill you? Do you think they will care if you're tired or scared, or that your soul has been ripped in two?" Laughing harshly, he grabbed her head in one big hand, wrapping her hair around his fingers. A whimper escaped her as he pulled back firmly, forcing her to look at him. A mocking smile curled his lips. "Did you know I had started to believe in you? Believe that you could actually become a warrior and beat an immortal Wraith Lord? That one day you might even best the Queen? Was I wrong?"

Her shoulders tensed and the tears she had been holding back all morning tipped from her eyes.

Hugo raised his brows and snorted. "What's wrong? Do you think I don't know what's really bothering you? I can feel your fear and grief every time our magic touches. There is so much going on with your emotions, it makes me dizzy."

"You have no idea what's going on inside my head," Diamond sputtered.

He raised his brows. "No, not in your head. In here." And he touched a scarred forefinger just below the swell of her breast, against her heart. "Your deep confusion over your mother, your grief over the murder of your father. General Edo's death. Even Tom moving on. It's been building up inside you for weeks. And Jack leaving has clearly broken you." He cocked his head and waited, expecting her to refute his claims. "You aren't that fragile young woman who lost her father. Think about how much you have grown and the odds you have beaten to get this far. You need to believe that your father's death, and even General Edo's, is not your fault."

She blinked back tears and stared at his face.

His fingers loosened. "You must learn to control your grief and loss — we all have to. Everyone in your squadron has lost someone they love dearly, people they would gladly give their lives for — their souls for. They will need you to hold it together in a fight. Not just for your sake or for theirs, but for the people who can't fight for themselves."

Diamond still could not meet his eyes.

His wings shimmered as he tucked them tightly into his back. For a moment he simply contemplated her.

Silence stretched.

Swallowing hard, Diamond turned her attention from his wings to his face. Then wished she hadn't. Her stomach tightened. She must have imagined any compassion in his words.

Black, fathomless eyes glinted back at her, full of vicious amusement. Suddenly his fingers twisted in her hair, wrenching a pained gasp from her. "So you still believe you're that pathetic little girl? You really need to toughen up, *magic wielder*. After all, Jack didn't die. Or maybe that's what's bothering you, that he just upped and left. That he didn't care enough about you to stay." His voice was mocking and cold.

Diamond's face flamed as he ran his eyes over her body and raised one brow.

"Don't let it bother you too much. With a face and body like yours, it won't take you long to find another lover." A smirk curled his lips. "After all, it didn't take you long to seduce Jack, even after I told you to keep your legs shut. You'll only have to open them again and any of these hot-blooded fae will happily rut on you."

"Shut up!" Diamond hissed, her eyes flashing as she fought his grip. Anger and indignation flared hotly at his crass words. "Jack is not, and never has been, my lover!" She forced out, slapping and clawing at his hand. "Let me go!" she spat.

"Oh?" Hugo drawled, ignoring her demand. Gripping harder, he pulled her head back further. Something flashed in his eyes that she didn't understand. Triumph? Relief? She didn't have time to think about it before his eyes glittered darkly again and he nodded as if making a decision. His tone turned purring and insulting.

"That's it, isn't it?" he drawled. "The handsome prince got impatient. Maybe you simply aren't worth all the effort he put in. Picking you up every night. Dropping you off in the mornings. Gods, what did you do together all night if you aren't his lover by now? Is that it? Did you tease him? Get him so worked up he's had to go find someone else to—"

Diamond slammed her fist as hard as she could into his jaw. Satisfying pain exploded across her hand.

He jerked back, his mouth twisting into a wicked grin, blood bright against his teeth. "That's the Diamond I know. The one who shoved her thumbs into the eye sockets of a Wolfman, the one who turned an entire legion of Dust Devils to ash. It's about time she showed herself again. Bring her back to fight me with as much determination as you did those monsters. Work out your anger and your grief before it shreds your soul," he demanded, letting go of her hair before shoving her away from him.

Falling hard, Diamond tumbled across the ground, thudding as her back connected with the wall. Hot breath exploded from her lungs and she hissed with pain. But the impact shocked her out of her melancholy mood.

Blinding rage flashed through her blood. Her vision changed and she saw blinding rivers of colour encompassing them both.

How dare he treat me like this? All that compassion was simply for show, when he thinks me a whore who will open my legs for anyone. Well, I'll show him. Bastard!

She snarled, magic raging in her eyes.

Giving her a feral grin, Hugo spat a globule of blood on the ground, cricking his neck side to side.

"Well, well, *little* girl. Have I made you angry? Good. Come on then, defend your honour," he goaded, pacing impatiently while she scrambled up. "Let's go. Prove to me you aren't a pathetic little girl rolling in self-pity and grief. Show me the warrior you have become. Show me how hard you can fight. Destroy the grief and blame, here and now, before it can destroy you," he growled.

Fine! He wants a warrior, well, that's exactly what he's going to get.

Dodging sideways, she avoided the back-kick Hugo aimed at her chest, her elbow connecting with his back as he spun past. She danced away from him.

Lethal intent flashed in his glittering eyes as he faced her.

Realisation dawned. Hugo had manipulated her until she boiled with enough fury to blast the dark thoughts from her mind.

For the first time, he looked right in her eyes and gave her the slow, arrogant grin of a dominant fae male.

"There she is," he crowed. "So are you going to fight me, *little* girl? Or give up and spread your legs for a horny warrior instead?" he goaded.

Incensed, she loosed a wave of magic and their Nexus ignited. Power exploded, charging the air and her blood.

Hugo tipped back his head, the veins on his neck engorged. He roared into the sky. His body rigid, his eyes intense and full of silver fire when he looked back at her. A wicked grin distorted his face. Instead of shielding against her magic, Hugo sucked it inside himself.

Diamond gasped. It was exactly what he had done when the red warrior had attacked him. It did not matter.

He wants a warrior? Then a warrior is precisely what he will get.

CHAPTER NINE

Wind gusted around Hugo and Diamond. They ignored the cold fingers whipping at their hair and clothes, their eyes only on each other. Nothing and no one existed outside the bubble of emotions and magic that surrounded them.

Unaware the squadron had observed them fighting before being ordered away by Tallo, Diamond adjusted her balance as Hugo feinted with his right fist. Breathing had become hard, and blood stained her teeth. Diamond's anger was abating, leaving her body tired and her limbs heavy. Her magic reached out to Hugo, trying to pull some strength from him, but lithely he danced away. Shadow and mist disappeared instantly. A weighing look crossed his face.

"Ah, ah! That's cheating, even if you *are* tired," he smirked, but she could see how he was panting too. He launched a barrage of power at her. Matching his attacks while shielding pushed her to the limits of her energy. As her vision fogged, something wrapped around her ankles.

No.

He had distracted her and got beneath her shield! Before she could sever the shadowy ribbons, he yanked. With a squeal she fell backwards, so close to the wall her head connected with a sickening thump. She sprawled in a daze on the floor, her body becoming heavy, her arms and legs filled with a strange liquid warmth. It was as if she were listening through water.

He squatted down, his mouth stained with blood and said, "I think that's enough emotional release for today. It's time for us both to accept who we are and what we have done. We need to move on." His fingers were gentle as he brushed blood-matted hair off her cheek. "Maybe we can talk about what happened between us, too. If and when you are ready," he suggested softly.

Diamond could only look at him, still feeling dizzy—and now confused. Had she heard him correctly? He actually wanted to talk?

Hugo stood and stretched. Turning, he looked at the men and women of the squadron. They had stopped what they were doing and stood silently nearby, despite Tallo's order to train.

"Leave us," Hugo ordered, his voice no longer soft. "I will take care of her."

Diamond watched from the ground as dozens of booted feet moved reluctantly away. Hugo spoke quietly with Tallo, who tipped back his head and laughed loudly. Even Attion smiled at whatever Hugo said.

When Hugo returned, he didn't even give her chance to stand up before he swept her off the floor. Her head ached more than she thought possible and she winced, holding in her tears.

"Put me down, Hugo. I can walk," she declared.

"I know you can," he remarked, tightening his arms. His feet ground to a halt, and it became hard to ignore the weight of his gaze. "But I would like to carry you. If you'll let me?"

It was a question. He was asking for permission.

Diamond's throat dried out completely. Without looking at him she nodded.

Hugo resumed his progress, quickly covering the ground to the west quarters. With each movement of his body, his musky scent and warmth enveloped her.

Adjusting her weight, he bent to open the door to her room, crossed the floor, then lowered her carefully onto the small bed, supporting his weight with one knee.

For an unnerving moment Hugo silently studied her.

"I'll call a steward to fill your bath and order you food. You'll need to eat something after using all that magic, especially as you haven't eaten all day."

"I'm not hungry," she whispered.

"You'll need energy. We have to go out tonight," he informed her, looming over the bed like a great solid oak, unbending and large—she felt like the little girl he accused her of being.

"What? Out? Out where?" she croaked, gawking at him. She could hardly move let alone go out.

"The deal you made with Reese. Don't you remember? You landed a punch on the '*miserable bastard*'. So we are going to the old docks for me to buy everyone beer for the night," he said, looking amused.

Whooping and shouts of glee erupted from the yard. Tallo had obviously just told the rest of the squadron about their night pass. Feet thundered past her window towards the soldiers' quarters.

Hugo contemplated her intently. The weight of his regard had her wriggling.

"Why can't you go alone?" she asked when the noise had settled.

Hugo let his eyes roam over her bruised cheek and down her body as if assessing her injuries. Reclining, she closed her eyes, hoping that would settle the sudden tightening in her stomach.

"Because," he said, cocking his head to one side, arching one brow wryly, "this was your deal. You made it and you landed the punch, so you have no choice but to come with me for a night of drinking with your brothers-in-arms. Besides, you've wallowed in enough self-pity for one day. It really doesn't suit you," he said as he grabbed a pot of salve off the washstand and tossed it.

Diamond caught the pot in one hand.

"Fine," she said, rolling her eyes.

"Good. I'll be back in a couple of hours," he retorted, grinning as he closed the door.

CHAPTER TEN

When Hugo knocked on her door, Diamond was a mess of nerves. Trying to make sense of his earlier behaviour had thrown her into a whirlwind of confusion. He had been distant with her for weeks. And Attion's quiet but constant presence had served to remind Diamond of Hugo's true loyalties. Or were they his true loyalties? A sigh escaped her. She had been over these thoughts so many times in her head, she was dizzy.

She exhaled, trying not to think about how gently Hugo had lifted her off the ground or how carefully he had placed her on the bed. She swallowed and bit her top lip, twisting a lock of hair around her finger. He had even been concerned enough to send a phial of painkiller for her. That and the salve Rose had given her had dulled the edge off her aches.

Diamond jumped at a polite knock on the door. Swallowing hard, she waited a moment before opening it. Her mouth dropped open. Hugo had braided his hair back tightly, accentuating the hard angles of his shaven jaw. Unable to stop herself, her eyes travelled over his body. He was out of armour, and she could see a black shirt covering his broad chest under the edges of his cloak. His clean, spicy scent hit her, enticing her to inhale. Her cheeks flushed as he registered that tell-tale sign of fae interest.

His scar twitched as he smiled at her reaction. His eyes seemed even more blue than normal against the rich shade of his cloak. It was impossible for her to look away. Her mouth turned dry. *Gods, he really is handsome,* she thought, trying not to seem too overwhelmed by the fact she was going out and socialising with him.

He coughed and cleared his throat, "Good evening, Diamond. Shall we?" he asked, indicating the corridor with a sweep of his hand.

When they stepped outside the main door, she saw Attion waiting. Reality hit her like a slap in the face. Gritting her teeth, she passed by the other guard.

"Attion," she greeted in a cursory fashion. He nodded politely and waited for Hugo to pass before dropping in step behind them.

It was dry but cold outside. Shivering, she silently thanked her mysterious benefactor for purchasing the thick cape currently secured around her shoulders and the soft leather gloves she wore. One day she would find out who it was.

Hugo glanced back. Attion nodded and moved ahead to join Tallo. Diamond raised her brows in question. Hugo smiled a little and shrugged.

The squadron waited impatiently in the training ground. They cheered as she walked toward them. Embarrassed, she rolled her eyes, groaned and hid behind Hugo's back. Tallo grinned at her, while Reese gave her a flamboyant salute. Surprise flicked through her when she heard a soft chuckle from Hugo.

In a flurry of activity, the squadron set off, the voices of the eager soldiers loud in the night. It was going to be a long walk through the city to the docks, but none of them seemed to mind. It was an excuse to escape from the barracks for a while. The banter of the soldiers eddied around Diamond, and she wondered what her father would have made of her situation. Her eyes shifted sideways to Hugo's slightly swollen lip. Maybe Arades Gillon would be impressed. She smiled a little, hoping that was true.

When they left the palace grounds behind, Hugo looked down at her. The lamplight caught his eyes, making them glitter disturbingly from under his hood. He slowed to match his stride to hers until he walked by her side.

The weight of their past hung heavy in the air. It seemed neither were ready to talk about the day Diamond was kidnapped or what had transpired afterwards in the throne room. Perhaps neither wanted to destroy the fragile peace that had settled between them.

The squadron seemed eager to reach the docks and walked ahead at a faster pace, soon leaving her and Hugo behind. Diamond used the opportunity to study her surroundings. The last time she had been outside the palace gates was during her kidnapping. They had run for their lives that day. Hugo had rescued her, and then forsaken her for the Queen. Pushing those thoughts aside, Diamond made herself study the buildings. Their architecture changed as Hugo led her away from the palace. She stared at the beauty of the city. Representations of the guardians and fierce fae warriors covered the walls and columns of many buildings, reminding her of Lunaria.

Diamond glanced at Hugo, then quickly looked away when his gaze flicked her way. What would he say if he discovered she was a descendant of the Goddess of Creation? She swallowed that thought, still not entirely sure of his feelings towards her.

Further into the city, it felt strange to look into softly lit windows and see normalcy as people sat around dining tables or kissed their children goodnight. She felt so far removed from that life, as if her own father had been a glorious, comfortable dream that had wrapped her in love. But it was a dream that had dissipated in the harshness of her present life. She swallowed and kept her eyes averted from the tender, yet heart breaking scenes.

Soon the street lamps became less frequent and the shadows darkened. The rest of the squadron had long since disappeared. Alleyways and small backstreets led off the main cobbled thoroughfare. Hugo turned down one, and she found herself wishing to walk closer to him. Growing up in a trade town had not left Diamond innocent to the dangers of the darkness, but she had never wandered through such vast shadows as Valentia's before. Some backstreets appeared so dark it looked as if anyone who wandered into them would be devoured. She shuddered.

Hugo's voice rumbled out from under his hood. "Those streets lead down to the eastern docks and quays. It's a dangerous part of the city, run by a notorious crime lord. These docks haven't been used by big trading ships since the main harbour and west docks were built. Only local fishermen, smaller traders and captains trafficking illicit goods use them." Amusement coloured his next words, his eyes sparkling as he rubbed his jaw. "Although, if you fancy off-loading some of your anger on someone other than me, there are some vicious fighting dens down there. I expect their bloodthirsty audiences would lose quite a bit of money if you decided to walk in and challenge their fighters."

Diamond gaped. *Good goddess above! Hugo, with a sense of humour?* He was normally as serious as a cleric at a burning ceremony.

"Nah," she responded as nonchalantly as possible, her heart thumping as the mischief of a flower imp took her. She remembered their flirtatious conversation from weeks ago, the night he had told her she was beautiful. Maybe they could be like that again. After all, if she was going to lure him away from the beautiful Queen, she had to start somewhere. "You are the only challenge I need. Once I have triumphed over you, I will not need to best another warrior," she declare, holding his eyes and trying not to blush.

Hugo seemed momentarily stunned, then smiled widely and raised his brows,

"In that case, I might just let you win," he rumbled.

Diamond quickly turned away, trying to calm her suddenly erratic heart.

They walked on in silence, and Diamond became lost in thought. She had never really grieved for her father or allowed herself to think about what had happened with General Edo. Hugo had understood her low spirit far better than she had herself. He had purposefully given her a way to confront her grief. Ignoring it wasn't an option any longer, which he had made her realise. In his own way, Hugo had helped her deal with the emotions triggered by Jack leaving. A small cough was enough to clear her throat.

"Hugo?"

"Yes?"

"Thank you."

"What for?" he rumbled, looking puzzled.

"For making me confront my grief and guilt."

He snorted. "Oh, is that what I did?"

Out of the corner of her eye, she saw his mouth twitch into a smile.

"Yes, and you know it." She smiled. "I don't know why I felt so low today. I guess I let my feelings get the better of me."

He frowned down at her. "You'll miss Jack, but there is more going on in your head, and your heart, that you need to deal with. You saw your father killed—violently. You were forced to take the life of a man you had trusted since you were a small child. Your world has been turned upside down, mainly because of me. I know you think me weak for serving the Queen and even think me indifferent to your pain, but I am not. I have only seen you cry for your father once, and that was the day he died. You need to grieve for him, for General Edo and for the life you have lost."

"I didn't know you could be so insightful," she replied, not able to look at him.

"I know you didn't."

Her feet halted. It both disturbed her and lifted her heart to think Hugo knew her so well, that he could understand her like that. But she still felt she had let him down.

"Hugo, wait." Her hand reached out and tentatively touched his arm. She swallowed hard at the contact. "What I'm trying to say is that

I won't let you down again. I'm sorry if I did today. I know how much effort you and Tallo, and even Attion, have put into my training. It doesn't matter to me if it's only because of the Queen's orders. I want to succeed for all of you," she vowed.

Hugo pushed his cowl off his head, looking at her intently. "Thank you. I appreciate that, and I know the other's will too. But this isn't about me, and it definitely is not about the Queen and her damned orders. It's about you. You need to understand that if you let your emotions run wild, it could kill you; especially if you are fighting alone." His voice was firm but with no trace of anger. "If you lose control of your emotions, your magic will take over, just like it did before. That will make you vulnerable, and someone as ancient and powerful as Ragor will recognise that. He will use it to rip you apart, then he will steal your soul and throw you into Chaos to be tortured by Erebos." Hugo carefully tucked a strand of hair behind her ear. "And that would mean every soul in this valley would perish, because, powerful though the Queen is, I believe she would sacrifice every one of her people to Ragor before she will strike him down."

Icy fear slithered down Diamond's spine. "But why does she want me to fight him if she can ultimately beat him herself?"

Hugo shrugged, looking perplexed. "That's something I have been asking myself for weeks. It was only when I sent word that Jack was alive and needed sanctuary that she pulled her troops back from her borders. As they were gaining ground against Ragor's army, I don't understand her actions. Since then, whenever Jack has left the valley she has ordered me to protect him and make sure he returns. It's odd, but since she took your necklace she seems to have lost interest in the prince." He sighed and shook his head. "To be honest, her ultimate plan doesn't concern me right now. You do. And I cannot stand the thought that Ragor may send your soul to Chaos."

Diamond shuddered. Weeks ago, in that strange place between life and death, she had managed to escape the clutches of both Erebos and Sulphurious. It had been Hugo who had guided her soul back to her body. If he hadn't done, she would still be trapped in that place of never ending darkness and ice. Would he fight like that for her again? Her eyes dropped.

As if sensing she was about to withdraw, Hugo placed his other hand over hers. Warmth permeated through the leather of her gloves, the muscle of his arm solid under her fingers as he continued, his voice remorseful. "I have much to atone for in my life," he said, his fingers squeezing hers. "Too much to explain or apologise for right now. I have sworn to serve the Queen, and I will continue to do so to keep her attention from you, or at least until I know you are safe." He took a deep breath and expelled it slowly. "But she will have to lock me away in iron to keep me from your side when Ragor attacks. I will not leave you to fight him alone."

Words failed Diamond. After a moment of silence Hugo cleared his throat. Raising her eyes, she was surprised to see him looking uncomfortable, wary even.

"And I am sorry for using your friendship with Jack to insult you. It was a low blow, even if it did work to make you push past your sorrow. I couldn't bear seeing you so defeated. I really didn't mean the things I said," he finished earnestly.

Diamond gaped. *An apology?*

Her expression must have amused him because he gave her another gorgeous smile. "There, we have both apologised. Now, shall we try and enjoy ourselves?" he asked, readjusting her hand to the crook of his elbow. "We are out together with only the Queen's spies for company. So let me show you more of this overcrowded, stinking, yet gloriously beautiful city," he declared, pulling her closer before he continued walking.

After the tightness in her stomach settled, Diamond risked a sidelong glance at her escort, finding it hard not to stare. Changing her vision, she watched his energy as it flowed and swirled gently around him. An electric shock of current zipped through her as the silver serpents, his constant magical companions, drifted closer until they intertwined with her ribbons of light. One nipped playfully at her cheek. The contact tingled along her skin into her bones, heating more than her cheeks. Finding her courage, she caressed his cheek with the lightest magical touch.

His bicep tensed under her fingers, his eyes flicking to hers. Butterflies fluttered in her stomach. For a few minutes their energy danced then he began to slow it down until it wrapped gently around her arms, shoulders and waist. A wonderful calming warmth invaded her, as if he were a salve to her soul.

Hugo glanced down.

Ignoring her niggling doubts, Diamond held his eyes, smiled shyly and gripped him tighter.

CHAPTER ELEVEN

The wind blew viciously, tugging at her clothes and hair for the duration of the long walk down through the city. Pulling her cloak more tightly around her shoulders, Diamond shivered.

Hugo led her through the warren of streets. The people looked wretched and half-starved. Poorly clothed, they cowered in dark doorways and stinking alleys. City guards patrolled above in small squads. Their golden wings glinted in the moonlight as they dipped from the sky to move the homeless refugees back down towards the docks. The Queen did not seem to want these people straying to the higher, more affluent echelons of the city.

Hugo kept her arm tucked in his and pulled her closer.

As they neared the docks, inns and brothels became more frequent. The streets bustled with sailors and merchants, who wove through the crowds of begging refugees. The atmosphere felt heavy and volatile. Scuffles spontaneously broke out, to be quickly dealt with by the city guard.

Diamond held on tightly to Hugo, ready to fight if she had to. She did not like this part of the city. Instead, she concentrated on the brothels. In Berriesford, brothels had been confined to one area. Diamond had known that area was dangerous for a young half-blood girl, so she had done as her father asked and avoided them. Curiosity got the better of her now. Males and females of all shapes, sizes and state of undress hung around the doors and streets, lasciviously inspecting the passers-by. Diamond gaped, twisting her head back and forth.

Hugo snorted, and she found him smirking down at her.

Her cheeks flushed, her heart lurching at the glittering mirth in his eyes. Smiling sheepishly, she stuck her tongue out at him. He turned away laughing but that didn't stop her ogling the flesh for sale.

Fury seared her whole body when a slender fae whore pulled down her top, exposed her breasts and loudly offered her wears to Hugo. He grinned and refused, then winked. Diamond was incensed. He *never* grinned and winked. She stepped even closer to him. Her shoulder brushed up against his solid arm and she glowered at the female. When she turned her head back to look where she was going, she caught Hugo smirking down at her.

Annoyed, but unsure why, she tried to pull her arm away.

He simply tensed his considerable muscles, raising both brows. "Ah, ah. Temper temper, little girl," he chuckled.

Infuriatingly, she was unable to free herself without causing a scene. With no other choice, she stayed moulded to his side and kept walking.

The rumble of waves hitting the dock side became louder. It was a wonderful sound. Inhaling deeply, she closed her eyes and gripped Hugo's arm, remembering her father's voice as he laughed at her excitement upon seeing the sea for the first time. Her memories brought a smile to her lips.

The couple emerged onto the docks.

Stone quays stretched into the darkness, lined by the ghostly shadows of tall ships. *This must be near the Queen's harbour*, Diamond reflected. Her nostrils flared. Two hulking, shadowy galleons floated in the distance, confirming her suspicion. She frowned, wishing the resurrected guardian had turned them to ash along with all the other ships it had destroyed.

Fishing boats and trade vessels of all sizes loomed along the open dockside, their gangplanks guarded by armed men. Normally safe in the relative shelter of the quays, the boats were being tossed about like driftwood on the stormy winter tide.

Tu Lanah cast a silvery glow through the clouds. The ice moon became bigger and lower every night, almost touching the horizon now. The storms that raged daily would not abate until Winter Solstice passed and Tu Lanah rose back into the sky.

Guards in dark uniforms appeared like shadows, patrolling the skies and the ground near the moored ships. Diamond had seen fae like them before, the day she had been kidnapped.

"Don't worry, we aren't going that way," Hugo yelled over the mad chorus of clunking and twanging sails and ropes. He let go of her arm and pointed to a nearby inn. "Over here!" he shouted.

A strong gust of cold, briny wind caught Diamond's legs and propelled her straight into Hugo's hard body. He grabbed her arms quickly, holding her steady, his hood blowing away from his face. For a moment, his eyes held hers. Her breath caught in her throat as she felt his energy surge like the stormy winds around them, igniting that familiar heat inside her. But the moment was lost as he spun her swiftly around and propelled her past a huddled group of ragged vagrants. Diamond felt bad for them, stuck outside with no protection. Hugo pushed her quickly towards the door of the well-lit, but raucous inn. "Inside," he said gruffly, so gruffly she wondered if she'd imagined the fiery way he had just looked at her.

Diamond had not been in many inns and was unprepared for the heat and stench of stale beer and bodies. Lively music greeted her, and she couldn't stop her smile. It was bright and vibrant and happy. A duo playing fiddle and flute stood next to a far wall. Fae and human alike were talking loudly, trying to be heard. Tankards crashed together and barmaids rushed through the crowd, dodging unwanted attentions of their customers. Everyone seemed to be smiling, and the air was filled with good-natured banter.

Reese hurried over. "Commander." He saluted Hugo smartly, then winked jauntily at Diamond.

She grinned and flung her hood off her head. It was warm in the inn, thanks to the roaring fire in the hearth. Her face began to glow and tingle after the onslaught from the cold wind.

Reese raised his eyebrows, ran his eyes over her from top to toe, and grinned.

Diamond knew she looked different. She had made an effort with her appearance as she had wanted to look pretty for a change. Her violet shirt was cut low enough to show a hint of her reclaimed curves and the colour complimented her eyes. She wore a black, fitted tunic and grey leggings with black boots. The soft glow from the oil lamps reflected in the silver of her hair, her eyes glimmering like bright jewels as she undid the clasp on her cloak and let it drop from her shoulders. She blushed at Reese's open regard.

"Well, don't you look lovely?" Reese complimented, wiggling his eyebrows.

Hugo gripped her arm, pulling her towards him slightly. "Reese, send some men over to help carry the beer. Diamond, you can help too," he ordered, his voice growly and deep.

Her smile stayed in place as she rolled her eyes at Reese.

Choking on his laugh, Reese winked again and turned away to fetch reinforcements for the beer.

Hugo glared down at her, his mouth in a tight line.

"What?" she asked innocently, her smile slipping at the possessive light in his eyes.

"You know what," he growled at her and strode off to the bar.

Diamond frowned. She didn't know what, not really. All she'd done was look nice and smile at Reese.

"Hey!" She pulled hard at his arm. "Why are you angry now?" she asked in exasperation.

He turned, his gaze so intense she wanted to squirm. Bravely, she held his stare and raised her eyebrows, waiting for an answer. His eyes softened, his mouth curving into a sensual smile. "I'm not angry, Diamond. I'm jealous."

Her mouth dropped open, and she started as he leaned down next to her ear. Hot breath caressed her, sending a shiver through her whole body. "And he's wrong, you know. You don't look lovely; that's not a good enough description. Hmm, let's see, hair that looks like spun silver, eyes sparkling like amethysts and these soft, slightly swollen lips. Yes, beautiful or stunning are far more fitting descriptions for the way you look right now." He pulled back and allowed his eyes to travel slowly from the top of her head to the tip of her toes, and back up again, lingering on the open neck of her shirt.

Diamond's face flamed, her mouth dropping open. Deliberately, he met her gaze, his eyes dark and hungry. Completely thrown, she gazed at him. Gently, he put his fingers under her jaw and closed her mouth before turning away. He strode off to the bar, his cloak a flurry of blue as he flung it off.

Swallowing her shock, Diamond followed him.

KAREN TOMLINSON

CHAPTER TWELVE

The squadron occupied half of the inn, laughing and joking raucously. Diamond helped carry the tankards of ale and several pitchers of dark red wine, plonking them down in the middle of a worn-out, beer-stained table. There was a chorus of thanks before tankards were clunked loudly in Diamond's honour. Even Attion accepted a drink from Diamond. He nodded his thanks and gave her a small smile before settling back to watch everyone.

Utterly taken aback, Diamond tried not to react. *Thanks—and a smile? From Attion? Tonight is a night of surprises,* she thought in amazement.

It seemed the squadron found it hilarious that Hugo, a Queen's elite guard, had been punched in the mouth by a female trainee, even one with magic. To Diamond's surprise, he took their jibes good-naturedly.

Smiling indulgently, Hugo glanced sideways and muttered under his breath, "You do realise this is all your fault, don't you?"

She shrugged. "Sorry," she beamed, not sounding in the least bit apologetic. Steeling her nerves, she leaned in towards him. "It serves you right," she murmured in his ear.

"Yes, it does," he surprised her by agreeing. "It's taken me far too long to arrange a night out with you."

Before Diamond could answer, some of the other soldiers shuffled down their bench to make room and bade her to sit down. Diamond slipped in, pushing along a wall until she could settle herself into a snug corner.

Hugo immediately slipped in beside her, snarling at the others. They quickly backed off and gave him room, all of them recognising the challenge in his eyes.

Diamond's heartbeat ratcheted up a notch, her cheeks flushing with excitement and pleasure at that obvious sign of his interest. By the goddess, he was publicly staking a claim for her—with Attion only a few feet away. Nervously she glanced at Attion, but he coolly met her gaze and looked away, totally disinterested. His attention was focused entirely on the other patrons.

"Don't worry about Attion; he is on our side," Hugo rumbled in her ear.

His hot breath sent shivers down her spine.

Deliberately avoiding Hugo's challenging stare, Reese settled himself opposite and began regaling the table with ridiculous and fantastical stories about being a sea captain turned smuggler turned soldier. Next to him, Tallo took up a huge amount of space, nearly as much as Hugo.

Diamond tried to concentrate on their voices instead of the way her heart beat erratically every time Hugo's body brushed against hers. As the night went on, Hugo spent even more money, and the soldiers became even more drunk. Faces flushed, and Reese's stories became raucous and wild.

The fiddler and the flutist played jaunty folk songs and couples danced around the inn, laughing loudly. Diamond giggled as Reese stood, gallantly bowed and asked Diamond to dance. She felt Hugo bristle immediately but had already said yes before he could speak. It had been such a long time since she had let her hair down and danced.

Hugo reluctantly let her go, his eyes burning as she shimmied from the corner. Flashing Hugo a warning look, she took the hand Reese held out.

Hugo clenched his jaw and, with obvious effort, let her go.

Smiling, she let Reese pull her close—but not too close—and they danced energetically with the other couples, her hair streaming down her back.

The room passed in a whirl of colour and motion. Their laughter mixed with the music, but after three dances her sore muscles ached in protest. She excused herself from Reese, pushing her way through the crowd only to find her path blocked by a large fae warrior. Un-armoured golden wings framed his body, and his blonde hair glittered in the fire light. He was not as tall or broad as Hugo—or even Attion; but despite his lazy grin, there was something off about him. Diamond recoiled, her skin crawling. Recognition dawned. The warrior from the throne room.

Arrogance glinted in his eyes as he grinned down at her.

"Sorry," she stammered, trying to step around him, to get as far away from him as she could. He sidestepped and blocked her path. Quickly she shifted her weight to a defensive stance, her training kicking in.

"Oh, that's perfectly all right, Diamond. My fault entirely," he smirked, then executed a perfect small bow. "Allow me to introduce myself. My name is Fedron, and I have wanted to meet you for many weeks." He leaned forward conspiratorially to add, "Ever since I saw you half-dressed in the forest, magic wielder."

His eyes darkened, a predatory glint in them as his attention drifted to the open neck of her shirt. He inhaled. It was then she realised Fedron had lost his mind to his baser fae side. He was old enough to have passed his mating urge, but in some cases fae lost control of their feral instincts. They became obsessed with possessing others. Stretching out the forefinger of his right hand, Fedron hooked it into her blouse, pulling it aside to reveal the creamy skin of her breast and the large purple scar that marked it. His fingertip traced the raised skin.

Diamond froze completely, shocked that a complete stranger would dare touch her so intimately.

"Hmm, glad to see your wound has healed. Rose did a good job of healing your lovely skin." He tugged her shirt back in place, then traced his fingertips up the column of her throat.

Diamond's heart flipped and she jolted to life, slapping his hand away.

No. Surely not Rose's ex-lover? Diamond almost snorted. No wonder Rose's friends had not approved. This creep was arrogant—and dangerous. Seeing her incredulous expression, his whole demeanour changed into one of complete charm. Almost like a switch had been flicked. It was incredible.

"I can see that surprises you." A charming smile curled his lips.

Speechless at the change in him, Diamond just stared. He was definitely unbalanced, but she did not doubt that some women would find his charming mask hard to resist.

"Rose is a lovely woman but, alas, she will never be enough to hold on to someone like me. I have told her we cannot be together any longer. Perhaps, though, you would honour me with a dance and afford me some of the attention you have been bestowing upon others?" He hooked her shirt and pulled it aside, brushing her scar again. "After all, I did help rescue you from the forest, and I am *very* good at keeping secrets," he purred.

Diamond shuddered, yanking herself backwards out of his reach. Revulsion coursed through her at his touch. "I have no idea what you mean, and if you touch me again I will break your fingers," she hissed.

Again his mask changed, poise and politeness vanishing. His voice and eyes turned icy. "Oh, yes you do. Commander Casimir, the Queen's magic-wielding whore. I think I will tell her about the way he has been looking at you, about the way he is *claiming* you in front of all these people. Do you think she will believe he only wants to bed you, or will she finally believe he is a traitor? I wonder what she will do to break him?" he sneered.

At that veiled threat to Hugo, Diamond did not hesitate. Using all her strength, she punched the warrior straight in the face. Pain erupted through her bruised knuckles. He staggered back, taking some of the crowd with him. A look of absolute rage crossed his face. Before she could react, a large hand slipped around her waist, spinning her into a protective embrace.

Diamond tried to pull away, but Hugo tightened his grip.

"Stay there," he commanded, his voice like ice. His stare focused over her shoulder to Fedron, who had pulled himself upright.

Hugo's body stilled, controlled aggression pouring off him in waves. Diamond felt his muscles tense as the two fae warriors weighed each other up.

Fedron had almost lost himself to his wild fae side but she prayed he was not unhinged enough to attack Hugo. She leaned into Hugo's embrace and slipped her arms around his waist, longing for the other warrior to leave. Hugo would kill him right here, in this room full of people, and then the Queen would be informed. Her stomach plummeted knowing this situation could go so very wrong. She shouldn't have punched the warrior; she should have walked away. Hugo didn't need her to defend him.

A low warning rumble rippled from Hugo's chest, gently vibrating along her bones. His hand tightened, pulling her firmly against him as his other hand went to the hilt of a dagger on his hip. His head turned, tracking Fedron as he walked away. Diamond held her breath, aware that Attion had stepped up beside them. Both Queen's guards had armoured their wings, indicating they were ready to fight.

Despite Attion's presence, it did not occur to Diamond to pull away. Being in Hugo's arms felt right. Besides, Diamond could see Attion's attention was focused entirely on Fedron. Hugo's growl stopped, and he suddenly propelled her past Reese and the rest of the squadron. They too had gathered at Hugo's back in a show of support. Wings still armoured, he guided her to their table. The others gave them some space but lingered nearby. Diamond sank into a chair without protest and stared at the table top, visibly shaking.

"What did that warrior want?" Hugo asked quietly.

"I don't know," she stammered and looked up.

Hugo's face was dark, his eyes swimming with shadow and a deep possessive rage. "Did he hurt you?"

Diamond snorted a slightly hysterical laugh. "Err, no. *I* punched *him.*"

Hugo raised his eyebrows, his aggression remaining despite his grin. "I know. I saw you. What in the goddess did he say to make you do that?" he asked, tenderly brushing her hair back so he could see her face. Gentle ripples of energy stroked her skin, soothing her.

"He threatened you," she whispered truthfully. "He called you the Queen's whore and threatened to tell her…" Diamond's voice trailed off. Embarrassed, the words she wanted to say stuck in her throat. She stared at the buttons on his shirt instead, unable to speak.

"Tell her what?" he asked, his voice still gravelly despite the soothing touch of his magic.

Diamond took a deep steadying breath. This was not the time to be shy. Her eyes met his steadily. "Of the way you have claimed me in public, in front of all these people," she replied, trembling as she acknowledged what his behaviour toward her actually meant. "He said she would break you for it," she whispered, her voice catching.

Hugo's eyes widened. "You are afraid for me," he murmured, sounding awed. His eyes found Attion's.

Attion nodded, his face utterly cold, and then he left them.

Diamond watched him thread his way through the crowd to leave the inn. She didn't want to know where he was going.

Hugo's face loosened, softening. "It's been a long time since anyone has been afraid for me," he revealed gently.

Diamond took a breath. This dancing around their feelings was ridiculous. "Hugo, I don't know what's going on between us. I don't know if I can trust your behaviour towards me. You are fae, and Fedron is right—it's obvious that you have some intentions toward me, but I don't know what they are. I don't know what to think, not after what happened before. I trusted you, Hugo, and you chose the Queen."

An uncomfortable silence descended between them. His throat bobbed as he swallowed. Then he leaned towards her and gently took her hands. She stared at the way his rough, calloused fingers enveloped her own.

"Diamond, I cannot change who I am or what I've done, but I have never lied to you, and I am not lying now. I did what I needed to do to keep you safe. I wasn't prepared to deal with that situation in the throne room, and for that I am sorry. But please believe that you can trust me. I will always do whatever I can to keep you safe."

"Will you, Hugo?" Her lips pressed into a thin line, still unsure but wanting so much to believe him.

"Yes, I will. Look, I *am* interested in you. Deeply interested. But Fedron is right; the Queen knows I am in the urge and if she finds out I am pursuing you, especially after all her warnings, her wrath will not be pleasant—for either of us." The rough skin of his thumbs grazed the back of her hand before he let go. Gently he tilted her head up to look directly into her eyes.

Diamond's heart was racing madly, her mind finding it difficult to process his words.

"So I need to know: Do you want me to pursue you, or do you want me to leave you alone?" He seemed to hold his breath, waiting for her answer.

Diamond tried to swallow, but her mouth was too dry. Her feelings for this elite guard had never been in question, even when her anger at him burned brightly. It was trusting him to stay true to her, and only her, that made her hesitate.

Hugo's eyes narrowed astutely. Expelling a breath, he nodded. "I understand. You don't trust me. But perhaps you will give me a chance to gain your trust, then I will ask you that question again?"

Diamond nodded, relieved he wasn't going to push her for an answer. This was all happening so quickly. "I'd like that. But aren't you already in danger? Fedron will likely go straight to the Queen," she pointed out.

Looking at their joined hands, she missed the flicker of silver fire in Hugo's eyes. Against her skin, his magic writhed.

"No, he won't. Attion will prevent him," Hugo informed her coldly.

Diamond lifted her eyes, not really wanting to know how Attion was going to do that. Fedron, she decided, had cast enough of a shadow upon them.

"Fine. Then let's trust Attion to protect you. Now, let's forget about Fedron. This is our first evening out together, and if I remember rightly, we said we were going to try and enjoy ourselves," she reminded him, squeezing his hands.

Hugo gave her a tight smile.

"Hugo, I know you have never lied to me, and I really do want to trust you again, but what happened in that throne room cannot be changed. I have forgiven you. I know you had no choice but to follow orders." She paused, briefly closing her eyes. "I also know I didn't kill General Edo of my own free will. I was manipulated into doing it. It doesn't absolve me from his death and never will, but at least I can try and forgive myself."

"Would you have done it, if you had kept your own will? Would you have killed him to save the boy?" Hugo asked.

"I don't know," she whispered truthfully, then looked him straight in the eye. "Would you have whipped me if I hadn't?"

Hugo held her stare. His throat bobbed as he swallowed. "Yes," he replied hoarsely. "I am sorry, but yes, if it were the only way to save you from worse punishment at another's hand, I would do it."

Tears stung her eyes. She could feel the truth of his words, and the heavy regret he pushed through his magic to touch her.

"Well, let's hope it never comes to that and move on from that awful day, shall we?" After a moment of silence, she shifted uncomfortably then bravely met his gaze. "I do like you, Hugo," she told him, her cheeks flushing pink at her candour, "very much, but you are still a Queen's guard."

"For now," he interrupted. "But only as long as you need me to be, then who knows? Maybe I will find another calling." He shrugged, an amused smile curling his lips as she gaped.

Tallo declared they needed more wine and ale. He grabbed Hugo by the shoulder and yanked him backwards. Hugo allowed himself to be pulled up and to the bar where he dropped more coins into the waiting hands of the barmaid.

Diamond pushed the incident with Fedron aside and chose not to think about Attion—or what he was doing right now. Instead, she enjoyed the nerves bubbling in her belly every time she glanced at Hugo, both amazed and scared that he had declared his interest in her so openly.

Choosing to only sip her wine, she noticed Hugo did the same with his ale. Tallo gave her a beaming smile as he reached over and grabbed the pitcher of wine. She returned the smile, giggling at his gleeful expression as he swore colourfully at Reese, who slapped his hand away.

As the music and laughter became louder and raucous singing began, Hugo pushed himself up. "Stay there and don't go anywhere by yourself. I'll be back soon." He smiled down at her.

"Where are you going?" she asked, suddenly not wanting to be alone with all these drunken, loud people.

He raised his eyebrows, his eyes sparkling with mischief, "I'm going to relieve myself. Why? Do you want to come with me?"

"Oh, no, I don't," she said quickly, her face burning.

With a snort of laughter, Hugo walked away.

Diamond watched him push through the throng of people, brushing aside the barmaid as she grabbed him around his waist, her ample cleavage almost falling out of her bodice. Diamond's stomach lurched and she had to resist the urge to march over and slap the woman.

CHAPTER THIRTEEN

"D' you know?" Tallo slurred, smiling bleary-eyed at her. "I've known that male since 'e was a youngster. I 'elped," he hiccoughed and tried again. "I 'elped train 'im, and I 'aven't known anyone at all t' land a punch on 'im in a training fight. Not since 'e was 'bout thirteen." He tapped his nose, his finger slipping off as he toppled forward slightly. "I think 'e did it to distract you and make you ver' ver' mad," he finished, blinking furiously, like he was trying to clear his vision.

Diamond stared at Tallo, wanting very much to believe he was wrong, that it was the drink talking.

"What? No one has managed to hit him for that long?" she asked incredulously.

Tallo grinned stupidly. "I know 'e's one of the Queen's *special* guards. But I'd say 'e has a *very* soft spot for your pretty face and 'e let you 'it 'im so 'e could make you feel better." A low chuckle huffed from his huge lungs, "And take you out for the night." He looked inordinately pleased with himself after that last statement.

Diamond jerkily swallowed some wine, nearly gagging on the vinegary taste. It had not been difficult to figure out Hugo had riled her enough to lift her from a cloak of self-pity and grief. And he had already apologised for using Jack to do just that. But managed to hit him? Caught between a warm feeling in her chest and seething irritation, she crossed her arms. *I'm an idiot! Of course I'm not good enough to have landed that first punch — not when he expected it!*

Tallo wandered off, leaving her to sit and stew. No one else noticed her stand up and walk to the back of the bar. She would ask him. Her feet ground to a halt, her heart stopping in shock at the sight that greeted her. *So much for learning to trust him!* she seethed.

Hugo was holding either side of the woman's head. She had wrapped her arms around his waist and gazed invitingly up into his face. The sight sent Diamond into an instant rage. He wasn't even trying to get away! The barmaid's long fingers clutched at his back, running seductively over his wings as Hugo's eyes drifted down and lingered on the woman's bare cleavage. Diamond lost sight of his face as he leaned down to speak in her ear.

Trust indeed! she fumed, choking on her rage. *Let him have the barmaid then. But I'm not sitting here like a naive school girl waiting for him to finish with the big-breasted tart.*

Suddenly tired of the inn's raucous atmosphere, Diamond pushed her way through the crowd to the door. An icy blast of wind and the sight of the refugees huddled against the far wall of the quay almost sent her running back inside, but the image of Hugo being groped by the barmaid strengthened her resolve. She would make her own way back to the palace.

Frigid, salt-laced air stung Diamond's exposed skin as she stomped along. Away from the docks the street lamps had been extinguished. Around her the shadows rippled with menace, worsened by the frequent flashes of lightning. Thunder rolled across the sky.

Images of Hugo and the slutty barmaid drove her past the pleasure houses and through the dark streets, too incensed to pay attention to the huddled groups of refugees.

Her hands curled into fists, her fingernails biting into her skin. Not once in the months since she had met him had she considered Hugo could be with another woman. It hadn't even crossed Diamond's mind

94

that he may have physical needs that he would seek to fulfil. Queen's guards were prohibited from finding a life mate, but it had been made clear to Diamond that bedding whores—and barmaids— wasn't. Thoughts of becoming Hugo's mate had filled Diamond's mind more than once since she had met him. She ground her teeth with frustration.

Her eyes flickered shut as she imagined taking Hugo's blood. She was half fae, and it wasn't only Hugo who had desires, but having him was such a dangerous want, one that might break more than her heart if the Queen found out. *Especially if he wants to bed other women whilst pursuing me,* she thought, enraged. Magic blasted from her core and rocked the air around her. Her feet ground to a halt in shock. She was jealous—uncontrollably and insanely jealous.

Biting her lip as she walked, Diamond tried to bring her feelings under control. Concentrating on the shadows for anything suspicious seemed a lot more sensible than thinking about the way Hugo's hands had held her against him tonight or of the possessive way he had acted if another man wanted her attention. Hope and regret fluttered through her chest. She was running away again instead of fighting for him. *I'm a fool!*

Splats of icy rain landed on her head. She rolled her eyes. *Great, getting soaked will make things so much better.* It suddenly dawned on her how alone she was. The gloomy isolation of the enclosed street was unnerving. *This is ridiculous! What am I doing?* Her boot heel crunched on the ground as she turned to return to the inn. It was a shorter distance back to the inn than it was to the palace. At least she would be safe and dry back there. Besides, going back was the only way to persuade Hugo he didn't want that barmaid.

"Hello, pretty," came a reedy voice from a recessed doorway. A skinny man with broken teeth and a predator's smile stepped from the shadows.

95

Her heart sank in a flash of recognition. "Freddy," she breathed. Cold fingers of fear gripped her heart as she stared at the thief who had attacked her and Jack in the forest. Four more men crept out of the shadows, two staying in front and two circling behind her.

"Aw! That's nice, you remember me." Freddy smiled, his salacious gaze raking over her body. A blade glinted in his hand. "Now, where's that necklace?"

CHAPTER FOURTEEN

Hugo firmly pushed the barmaid up against the wall and pulled her groping hands off him. He didn't want to hurt the woman, but he had already tried walking away once.

"I told you, I'm spoken for," he growled resolutely. It was true. He had not taken any female to bed since he had returned from the forest. He couldn't stand the thought of touching another woman's skin, not now. Diamond was the only woman he wanted. Aching to be back by her side, he pushed his way through the crowded inn only to find her seat empty. Blood roared in his ears. He reached out with his magic, panicking when he couldn't sense her.

Spotting Tallo staggering around the floor, Hugo rushed over and grabbed the big male's tunic, hauling him up off his feet.

"Where's Diamond?" Hugo growled, his eyes flashing with fury and fear.

"Dunno. Wen' for some air maybe?" Tallo slurred, looking both confused and worried.

Hugo let his friend go. Throwing men from his path, he forced his way out of the inn, his heart thundering. *Where the hell does she think she's going? Why not wait for me? Gods, I've not been that long.* Then he remembered the barmaid and groaned. *Had she seen us? Surely she hadn't thought I would bed that trollop?* He swallowed his next thought and ran.

The dockside was empty other than the customs guards in the distance. Even the refugees had disappeared. Punching the wall of the inn did not assuage his rage or worry. They both had so many enemies. He inhaled, searching for her sweet scent. Nothing. He tried to calm himself. She was sensible enough to head back to the barracks, and she could fight to protect herself—if there weren't too many attackers. Images of the time she was kidnapped flashed through his mind. *Dammit!* He needed to find her.

Hugo sprinted down black alleyways, hoping Diamond would at least remember to take the same route. The wind whipped viciously at him; although he knew it was dangerous, he unfurled his wings, launching himself upwards. Pushing his magic to respond, metal armour clattered across the feathered membranes. He would see further and cover more ground from the sky.

Panic surged again. Fedron. That crazed male could have plucked her from the ground and taken her anywhere by now. *No. No. Attion will make sure Fedron doesn't bother her again.* Freedom was a powerful incentive, and Attion wanted it as much as Hugo did.

Rain lashed at his face. Never had Hugo wanted to know more about the venom link he had with Diamond's mind. If he understood it better, maybe he could reach out and find her. But when he tried, like he had done in the throne room, there was nothing. The muscles of his jaw bunched. It didn't matter; they were bound in other ways.

He pictured her face and filled his mind with her image. Their Nexus stirred. After so many months with Diamond, his magic was attuned to hers. Letting his magic claw through the night to find her was taxing. The shield constantly suppressed any magic it sensed. Panting, he forced his bond with Diamond into place. Calling on his darker gift he disappeared into a cloud of shimmering shadow.

Fear and pain, coupled with a fierce determination to survive, hit him like a blow to his head. Veering left, he beat his wings, fighting the wind to reach her. Rain pelted Hugo, freezing his body through his clothes. Seconds later a flurry of movement below caught his eye. He snapped his wings out to stop his momentum, his heart stumbling as he saw Diamond surrounded by five men. One of them grabbed her from behind, and the ringleader punched her straight in the face. Carried on the wind was the sound of another man goading his companions to attack.

Something inside Hugo exploded. Something far more powerful and animalistic than even his magic. The roaring inside his skull drove him to a red rage, the likes of which he had never experienced before.

A guardian of death, he dived.

By the time his feet slammed into the ground, Diamond had freed herself and knocked down the ringleader by slamming the heel of her hand into his nose. The attacker grabbed her arms from behind, but she kicked out forward, viciously catching another man in the belly. He doubled over and she kicked him in the jaw, sending him staggering backwards.

Hugo stormed forward, grabbed a handful of the man's tunic and slammed a fist into his face before throwing the attacker across the ground like a rag doll. The man smacked headfirst into the wall with a resounding crack before he lay still.

As Diamond's wide, violet eyes found Hugo's, a hand snaked around her neck, holding a blade to her skin.

"Oi, stay back or I'll slit her throat," the attacker warned, placing his hand on the top of Diamond's head and exposing her neck.

Hugo inhaled, disgust curling in his belly. The stench of fear belied the human's brave words. Hugo growled long and low, a sound that promised death. Murderous calm descended upon him at the sight of Diamond's ripped clothes and the metallic scent of her blood.

With lethal efficiency and aim, Hugo flicked his wrist and loosed a small blade. It buried into the man's forearm, and he lost his grip on Diamond. Before the man could react, Hugo spun behind them and buried another blade in the man's kidney, slicing swiftly upwards. An agonised scream ripped the night. A second later there was only gurgling as Hugo sliced the man's throat apart.

Diamond teetered on her feet, but she was free. Hugo gently leaned her against the wall and then turned his attention to the man who had been goading the others. He stalked his prey. Petrified, the man tried to run but tripped over the body of his friend. He began crawling.

"P-please. It didn't mean nothin'," he stammered.

"Not to you," growled Hugo. The scent of the man's fading lust sickened him. "But she means everything to me."

Hugo moved like lightening. The man did not have time to scream before his neck snapped. That was when Hugo recognised the ringleader Diamond had kicked to the ground.

Freddy pushed himself off the wet cobbles—and ran. A feral grin exposed Hugo's teeth. Freddy had escaped after attacking both Jack and Diamond in the forest. He would not be so lucky this time.

Gliding up into the air, Hugo landed in front of the skinny thief. Hate and fear flashed in Freddy's eyes as Hugo lunged forward and, without any hesitation or remorse, broke Freddy's arms. With all the force he could muster, Hugo smashed his fist into the thief's face. Bone and blood exploded.

"Gods, that felt good," Hugo muttered at the crumpled heap that had been Freddy. Hugo had waited a long time to do that. He turned back to Diamond where she sagged against the wall.

"Why the hell did you leave the tavern on your own?" he hissed at her, grabbing her shoulders and shaking her hard. He choked on his moan of relief when he realised she was more or less in one piece, even if her clothes weren't. Her head rolled around loosely, and he didn't realise how viciously he was shaking her until she begged him to stop.

"Please, stop. My head hurts," she whimpered, coughing blood down her chin and sagging against him.

He froze, ashamed of himself. They were not on the training ground, and he could see she had taken a vicious punch in the face. Unable to speak, he cradled her in his arms and launched himself into the wind.

Their combined weight was hard to control. They were buffeted up, down and sideways, rain saturating their clothes. Hugo gritted his teeth, keeping close to the shelter of the rooftops as best he could. He headed straight for the barracks.

Diamond gripped him tightly, her fingernails pushing through his shirt. His magic absorbed her distress, even as the smell of her blood stung his nostrils. Warm and sticky, it seeped from her onto his shoulder. His gut twisted. She was wounded. His large wings thudded against the air as he quickened his efforts to get back.

After horrible minutes of hard flying, the palace loomed ahead. He bellowed to the palace guards the call signal to let him pass, and landed solidly outside the west quarters. Without breaking his stride, he carried her through the entrance and into his room.

Hugo gently lowered her to his bed, trying not to look too horrified by the state of her face. It was a mess, even by his standards. Blood oozed from her nose into her mouth, staining her teeth red. Moving efficiently and quickly, he fetched a bowl of cold water and a soft cloth. His fingers yanked the bell pull, and he ordered a healer to attend them. Inwardly berating himself for missing her injury, Hugo pressed on her cut shoulder with one hand and began to clean her face with the other. A whimper escaped her as he gently wiped blood from her nose.

"Shh, it's all right, no one can hurt you now," he soothed.

Moments later came a soft knock upon the door. Relieved, Hugo opened it and stepped respectfully aside, beckoning a middle-aged man to enter the room. Sinking to the floor, Hugo watched, his eyes never leaving Diamond's face as the healer cut off her tunic and shirt and sewed up the slash wound on her upper arm with quiet efficiency.

Diamond hissed when the healing salve was applied, tears dripping down her cheeks. Wanting to comfort her, Hugo gritted his teeth. Using an immense amount of self-control, he managed to stay out of the way. But his magic sought to comfort her. It kept trying to escape his control and cross the distance between them. Echoing through their bond, her fear and disgust at being mauled by those men drove him into a seething rage.

To distract himself, he unsheathed his blood-caked daggers and laid them on the floor at his sides, then he pulled off his wet shirt, shifting his wings so they drooped down to the floor. Keeping his attention on Diamond, he leaned back against the cold wall.

After bathing her face, the healer decided her nose wasn't broken, then left. Diamond looked at Hugo, and his heart pounded with the need to both hold her and shake her. She dropped those amazing eyes from his wrathful gaze and squirmed. *She should feel guilty*, he decided, his anger mixing with relief that she was now safe.

"I'm sorry I didn't listen to you," she whispered, her face pale under her bruises.

He wondered briefly how someone could look so beautiful with such a bashed-up face. The snarl that escaped him was pure dominant fae, and even though he heard it and recognised it, Hugo could not feel sorry for it. That vocal rumble was meant to warn her how furious he was.

"I told you to wait for me. It was stupid to wander those dark streets alone," he admonished. She had been hurt, and he hadn't been there to protect her. Fear gripped his heart as he eyed the dressings over her knife wound. He had nearly lost her tonight. She eyed him warily as he pushed himself up. He stalked to the bed and sat on the edge, his weight making her roll towards him.

"Why did you leave on your own?" he asked, his voice still harsh. He was unable to stop himself from stroking her cheek gently with the back of his fingers.

She dropped her gaze and pushed her lips together, shrinking back against the pillow.

"Why?" he demanded again. He needed to know. "I told you to stay put. Those men were human, but Fedron—or any other fae—could easily have plucked you from the ground."

She tried to wriggle away from him. Deliberately, he put his hands either side of her head and gave her his most intense stare.

"Why?" he insisted, his voice gentle this time.

She stilled, her eyes moving back to his. Tears brewed in their violet depths. "Because you…I thought you…" she swallowed, a flush creeping up over her neck and cheeks.

He didn't have to pretend to be mad at her, his blood still thumped around his veins, his energy writhing protectively around her. "What? What did you think, Diamond?" he hissed. "Tell me what idiocy made you, a beautiful young woman, walk out into this overcrowded city, alone on a dark night? I know you can fight, but I thought you had more sense than that."

Giving a muffled cry, she tried to roll away from him. He leaned forward onto his elbows so he was only inches from her ravaged face, and raised his eyebrows expectantly. That only resulted in her squeezing her eyes tightly shut.

"Diamond, answer me," he whispered, his heart hammering harder now, not with anger but with understanding. He simply needed her to admit it.

"Because," she said, her voice shaking. "You were with that barmaid. And I did *not* want to wait until you had finished with her to decide to come back to me."

Hugo allowed a satisfied smile to curl his lips as she squirmed with embarrassment and fury.

"Hey, I wasn't going to do anything with that barmaid. I might have done once, but I have no desire to be with another woman. You keep me far too busy to even consider it—both in mind and body. So the next time you feel like running away from me—don't." His voice hardened, purely for effect.

She turned her head into his pillow. Her whole body trembled, maybe with shock, maybe guilt; he wasn't sure.

He grabbed her chin firmly and moved her head back to look at him. "Look at me. Freddy deserved what he got, as did his friends. Do not feel bad for them, if that's what's bothering you. Now, get into bed. You need to sleep," he ordered gently.

She nodded, trying to sit up. He stayed in her way, the naked muscles of his chest and shoulders contracting. Her cheeks flamed as she banged straight into him. Dumbstruck, she stared at his bare chest.

"Oh no, you are not leaving this room. You stay right here where I can keep an eye on you," he ordered.

Diamond fell back, looking utterly exhausted and completely dazed by his closeness. At any other time Hugo might have taken advantage of her reaction to his naked skin, but he was too worried about her right now. Grabbing one of his clean shirts, he wrapped it around her, helping her thread her arms through the soft material. Violet eyes watched him as he fastened each button. He hoped she didn't notice his hands shaking. He had wanted to be this close to her for months. Now her scent and body heat were doing crazy things to his equilibrium.

He tentatively felt for her magic, wondering why she hadn't used it to defend herself. She now had control over how much magic she could summon while under the shield. He frowned. Her magic was coiled so tightly inside her he could hardly feel its warmth. Understanding dawned. She was still scared of her power. To convince her she could master her magic, he need to take her to the cave. But that would have to wait.

When Diamond crawled under the covers, Hugo pulled them up over her shoulders. Wanting to stay near her, he sat down on the floor next to the bed and rested his head back on the wall. He had tried his best to control his feelings for Diamond, but he could no more change the way his heart and soul were intertwined with hers than he could stop breathing. Her magic was like a siren calling his own. His magic constantly searched for her even when she was not by his side. And her body. Hugo squeezed his eyes shut. He wanted to feel her skin, her warmth against his, to hear her moan at his touch, to whisper his name. He wanted that so much he ached. But even that physical yearning paled in comparison to his deeper desires. Inside him lived a being that he had been fighting to control since reaching maturity. The beast that he had yet to release from its cage was not a compliant part of his soul; it demanded the freedom to protect Diamond, and right now it was seething inside him, seriously discontent at his failure to keep her from harm.

Hugo knew he could do nothing to shield Diamond from what was to come, least of all from the certainty of the Queen's test. That was something she would have to succeed at with little or no interference from him. Survival beyond that test, however, would be down to both of them.

It was time to venture to the east docks. It had been too long since his last visit to Gorian. Set on a more positive course of action, Hugo leaned forward and watched Diamond. The gentle rise and fall of her chest reassured him she wasn't in pain. It was easy to hold her eyes when she sleepily opened them to check he was still there. He hesitated, then slowly stretched out his hand and took hold of hers, giving it a gentle squeeze. His heart clenched almost painfully when she curled her fingers around his, smiled and squeezed back.

"Go to sleep, Diamond. I'm not going to leave you," he said, his voice soft and reassuring.

The sound of her soft breaths became a regular pattern. For a while he was content to watch her sleep, then his eyelids became heavy. The murmur of protest she made when he moved to withdraw his hand made him smile. She half opened her eyes and watched as he cautiously climbed across her body to rest beside her, leaving a respectable distance between them.

Hugo listened to the wind as it howled outside, carrying the sound of the men returning in drunken, jolly groups. Gently he stroked Diamond's hair back from her face. He lifted a handful of silver strands to his lips, enjoying the silky feel of it against his skin. Both his body and his magic stirred, that growling voice inside him rumbling over and over, *Mine. Mine. Mine.*

Revealing to others that he wanted this woman had been foolhardy and would likely get them both killed. But that want was turning into a desperate soul-deep need that he could not control. Venom and magic bound them together, and yet he still wanted more. He wanted that blood bond too.

Sliding his body closer into her warmth, he sighed. Guilt was an old friend to Hugo; explaining their Nexus and the venom bond to Diamond was going to be inordinately hard. He wondered if she would believe controlling her mind and body was not the reason he had bitten her.

Discovering she still felt something for him—after everything he had done to her—was an astounding revelation. He swallowed, wondering how in the name of the goddess he was going to hide the depth of his feelings from the Queen's spies while building a relationship based on trust with Diamond. Courting was not something Hugo had ever tried before, and their circumstances were so mixed up that it could all go so very wrong. He shuffled closer and even the wild spirit inside him seemed to settle with contentment. Her body was softly moulded against his and, for a few hours at least, he could enjoy being close to her, with no prying eyes and no judgement.

CHAPTER FIFTEEN

Diamond heaved a breath and ran. The sound of metallic wings clashed above her as the squadron fought Jack's guards in the air and on the ground. A body dropped from the sky, almost landing on top of the fae warrior she had just knocked to the ground. The skinny, underfed new recruit hadn't stood a chance against Diamond. Now he coughed and spluttered behind her.

"Sorry!" she yelled over her shoulder. Thirty feet! That's all. I can do this.

Niall, one of the squadron fae, realised her intentions. Quickly he swooped and knocked Karl, one of Jack's warriors, sideways before he could grab Diamond off the ground. The two fae tussled, fighting hard with fists and wings. The more experienced Karl soon gained the upper hand, but Diamond had already passed him by.

"Stop her!" he bellowed.

Having all beaten their opponents, Tom, Zane and Somal blocked her target. Tom stood in the middle of the two fae, grinning widely. Zane and Somal flanked him, wings outstretched and armoured.

Zane gave her his best arrogant smirk. "Turn around, woman, or I'll set Tom on you."

Tom frowned at Zane. "Funny bastard, aren't you?" he responded, rolling his eyes before turning back to Diamond. She skidded to a halt. Her eyes rested on the red scrap of silk tied around the pole, the one that Tallo had set in the centre of the training ground. Jack's trainee guards had merged with their brothers-in-arms; this was an effective team building exercise for them. Tallo had given Jack's guard the job of protecting the pole and Reese's squadron the task of taking it.

Around them the noise grew louder. Fae who had been knocked out of the sky and humans who had been knocked to the ground all cheered, each egging on their respective teammates from the side-lines.

"Come on, Diamond, you can't take all three of us on," Tom declared, cocking his head and trying to sound reasonable, but it came out as smug. "Give in. We don't have to fight," he said. "You can't use magic under the shield, and you are outnumbered. Give it up."

Diamond looked left and right. Reese was fighting Vico to her left, grunting and sweating as he held his own against the more muscled fae. To her right, Paige, one of the only human women soldiers, fought Unis, the scariest female fae warrior Diamond had ever seen. And even though she knew Unis was kind-hearted, Diamond knew the female warrior would not allow Paige to win.

"Seriously, Tom?" Diamond crooned. "Do you really expect me to let my squadron down? To simply give up? Come now, surely you know me better than that?" While speaking, Diamond was concentrating on the warmth of her magic. It was harder to raise and command her magic without Hugo nearby, but it was also liberating to conjure it alone. Since the attack by Freddy, Hugo had been encouraging her to train her magic without his magic as a buffer, telling her she needed to become confident enough to control the amount she could summon under the shield. For days Diamond had been using magic to spar with the squadron, disarming them, shielding against them or forming weapons to fight against them. Hugo had secured their secrecy first, and all of them had agreed to keep their mouths shut.

"Now, Diamond!" Reese yelled as Vico twisted and knocked him down.

Without hesitation, Diamond threw her magic forward and knocked all three of her opponents on their backs. There was a chorus of shouts and loud grunts from the fallen men. Grinning, Diamond launched herself toward the pole.

Her fingers curled around the rag, ripping it from the pole. She swung the red material in the air as a cheer broke out from spectators on both sides.

Tallo grinned and took the rag from her. "Captain Dunns, your squad wins this one." He turned to Diamond, eyebrows raised. "Your control is getting better. If your magic becomes stronger outside the shield, we might stand a chance of stopping the Wraith Lord from breaking down our wall."

Diamond tried not to feel too uncomfortable as her squadron descended on her. After a few minutes of back slapping, Tallo ordered everyone to the mess hall to eat before the next session of training began. Both squadrons drifted away. After brushing themselves down, Tom and Zane walked over, bickering about whose fault it was they didn't see her magic coming. With new respect in their eyes, they congratulated her.

Tom gave her a tight hug. "That was incredible," he praised before the pair wandered towards the mess hall.

Diamond took a deep breath, happy to be left alone for a moment. She would never admit it to anyone, but using her magic on her friends still frightened her and left her feeling shaky. She looked around the almost empty yard and saw Attion holding out a hand to help up the young warrior she had knocked to the ground. The sight made her smile. Attion will have to be careful or he'll lose his reputation as a cold-hearted Queen's guard, she thought dryly. Diamond joined them.

"Hi," she greeted the boy with a friendly smile. Attion nodded to them both, then walked off to the mess hall. "So what's your name?" she asked.

"Mark," he answered, knocking the dust of his legs. "I've only been here a week. Don't really know anyone yet. Seems I don't know how to fight either," he said ruefully, looking at Attion's weapons and armoured wings in awe as the guard walked away.

"Well, Roin and Tallo obviously think you have potential or you wouldn't be training with the Prince Jack's guard, so don't worry about it," Diamond replied with a grin, noting Mark's golden-feathered wings, dark blonde hair and grey blue eyes. He was skinny for a fae but was still young. "How old are you?" she asked curiously.

"Nearly seventeen," he answered a little defensively.

Diamond raised her brows but stayed silent. Reality was cruel. If Ragor breaks through, it won't matter how old anyone is; they will all have to fight, she thought dismally.

"So, Mark, do you want to practise for a bit, whilst your lazy-arsed squad eats?" she grinned, hands on hips.

"Sure." He smiled eagerly. "Can you teach me to armour my wings?"

"Nope, but I know plenty of warriors who can," she pointed out. "Besides, you might as well make use of this next half hour, because we won't be able to reach the food with that lot in there."

"True," he laughed.

Diamond liked Mark, but he needed some mentorship. Perhaps Karl would take him in hand. Karl was a strong warrior but, unlike Zane, was not prone to arrogance or ridiculing others.

All her thoughts ceased as a shadow passed overhead and two heavily armed Queen's guards slammed down in front of her and Mark. Mark blanched. Their faces were hard and cold. No emotion. It reminded her of the first time she had seen Attion. Her pulse ratcheted up in anxiety.

In a natural, unassuming movement, Diamond stepped forward, positioning herself between Mark and the guards. Her stomach flipped with dread. The yard around them was almost deserted. Only two soldiers were chatting nearby. They eyed the guards suspiciously but, rather than coming to help, they walked toward the mess hall. Diamond silently cursed them.

One guard gave a contemptuous chuckle, bringing her attention back to him.

Diamond gasped. Even with a skewed jaw and bent nose, she recognised the guard who had attempted to arrest her in her room when she first arrived in the city. Ice coated her stomach; Hugo had broken this man's face because of her.

"Hello, magic-wielding bitch. Where's the Queen's dog?" he asked with a snarl.

"Not here," she replied. There was no point pretending she didn't know who he meant.

A dangerous light flickered in the guard's eyes and a malicious grin suddenly stretched his lips.

Diamond swallowed, her mouth dry.

"Who's this?" he asked slyly, nodding at Mark.

"Why?" asked Diamond, trying to keep her voice steady. Her magic churned in her belly, but she knew she couldn't release it on these guards. For as long as possible, Diamond needed to hide her ability to summon magic under the shield from the Queen. Her fingers curled around the hilt of her sword. It was a beautifully engraved, lightweight Silverbore blade that her benefactor had sent her two weeks ago. It fit herhand perfectly, warming to her touch as she drew it, ready to fight.

"Because I want a little revenge. This," he snarled, pointing to his jaw with a forefinger, "is your fault. But as I can't break your jaw, or the Queen's dog's, I'll break his instead," he threatened, menace in every line of his large body.

Mark began to shake but squared his shoulders and didn't back away.

"No, you won't," Diamond hissed, anger raging through her at his words. She might not be able to use magic, but she would not allow these vicious killers to hurt a young fae who had no hope of defending himself.

"You can't stop me," the guard growled, hate pouring from him. He looked with contempt at her sword.

"No, Thorn, she can't. Her skills aren't yet good enough," came Attion's voice from the direction of the mess hall. "But I expect all these soldiers and warriors together would be more than able to take you both down. Especially if you hurt her or the boy," he declared, his voice detached, his words more of an observation than a warning.

Behind Attion, the two squadrons of fae and humans banded together. Diamond did not drop her defensive stance or her blade, even as the guard turned to face the crowd.

"Attion. Mixing with Rhodainian filth, are you now? Even eating with them? Is that where your loyalties have shifted? To Prince Jack and the locusts who are devouring our land?"

"No, he isn't," Diamond answered immediately. "Attion is still a bastard, just like you. The only difference is I have to see his ugly face every day, thanks to the Queen," Diamond stated, putting enough disgust onto her face to make her statement believable.

Thorn's attention settled on her again. Soldiers and warriors surrounded them. Dismissing the group, Thorn's gaze flickered to Hugo, who leaned nonchalantly against the wall of the training yard behind Diamond, watching the proceedings. Diamond's stomach tightened painfully when she felt his presence. She wondered how long had he been there.

Thorn's eyes returned to Attion. "Oh yes, you are here to observe and report on Casimir's ability to bring this bitch to heel," he growled, no longer interested in Mark. "Well, I have a message for the commander," he stated, losing interest in his game now Hugo was present.

Holding in her rage, Diamond did not move out of Thorn's path as he strode directly toward her and Mark. Belligerently, she held his gaze as she gave a derisory snort, pushing Mark behind her and twisting to let Thorn pass. As Thorn and the other guard walked toward Hugo, the sound of swords being sheathed and breaths releasing filled the air.

"Well, you two sure know how to pick a fight," commented Paige dryly from next to Diamond. Mark chuckled, but it was a forced sound.

"I don't think we would have lasted more than a few seconds without my magic," Diamond breathed, relief and adrenaline making her shake now.

"Oh? We all think you would," replied Reese. The others nodded in agreement. "Either way, you were prepared to try for someone who is not a member of your own squadron and who could not hope to defend himself against their skills." There were murmurs of agreement, and Diamond felt herself blushing at the new respect she found in the eyes of her friends.

"Well, you two had better go and fetch food before it's all gone," advised Tallo with a cough, noting her discomfort. "Come on, back to your own squadrons. Reese? This lot is yours. I'm taking Jack's guard." With that, he bellowed his orders.

Diamond sought out Attion and gave him a smile of thanks, gratitude in her eyes. He nodded his understanding.

Her words of disdain had prevented Thorn from questioning Attion's loyalty, and his comment had not only concealed her ability to fight, but had ensured she wouldn't have to. Attion knew as well as she did that if it came to a choice between concealing her magic or saving others from death at the hands of those Queen's guards, she would have chosen to reveal her power.

CHAPTER SIXTEEN

After a day of training with Diamond, Hugo's body felt alive. Smiling, he remembered the flash of her eyes and the way her silver braid whipped around her head as she attacked time and again. Involuntarily, his fist clenched, still feeling the clash of her blade on his.

A strong gust of wind drove rain into his face, stinging his cheeks. Dressed in deliberately scruffy and dark clothes that hid his light armour, Hugo had been invisible as he walked out through one of the palace entrances. Now he hurried along the narrow streets, his head bent against the weather.

Leaving Diamond behind in the barracks had been inordinately hard. Since he had declared his interest in her over two weeks ago, they had spent most evenings together. He wasn't complaining. It was new and rather disconcerting to enjoy the near constant company of someone else. The only evenings he hadn't spent with her were when Rose and Kitty visited. He knew how much the other women meant to Diamond, so he left them to catch up. It was amusing to hear their high pitched giggles from across the hall.

Each day, after their training was finished, the couple ate with the other soldiers and warriors. There was a new respect in the eyes of many, especially when word circulated that Diamond had been willing to take on two elite warriors to protect a young fae she had just met.

Occasionally he and Diamond would sneak out after dark. Cloaking them in shadow to get past the gate guards was easy. He wanted to show her the city that was his home — not only the overcrowded seedy parts, but the beautiful areas too. When he wanted them to be recognised, he invited Attion to accompany them. Their friend became their silent shadow, one that kept his distance but who would give other informants no cause to report back to the Queen; if they did, Attion's words would be believed above all others. Hugo knew they were playing a dangerous game with the Queen and her spies, but it seemed she was happy to leave Hugo and Diamond alone.

When the couple wasn't out exploring the city, they sat in Diamond's room reading and talking about the other kingdoms beyond the Rough Seas. When they were too tired for that, he liked to listen to her stories of growing up in the north.

She talked freely of her father, her home and her life. Hugo decided he would have liked Arades Gillon. Diamond clearly adored him. Hugo couldn't help but wonder what sort of person he might have become if he had grown up with such a loving father. He shrugged. He had accepted what he had become. He had done terrible things, things that made him loath himself; but a small ember of hope glowed in his chest every time he looked at Diamond. For her, Hugo would change what and who he was.

Every moment with Diamond was a gift. Despite wanting to stay near her, Hugo needed to see the old man. Gorian was his only friend in this gods forsaken city, although Hugo didn't trust him with everything. As a teenage guard, the Queen had ordered Hugo to be part of a raid on the old docks. Her spies had passed along information that the old warehouses were being used by traitors to smuggle magic wielders out of the city. Instinct and curiosity had stayed Hugo's sword that day. Something in the older man's eyes had struck a chord in Hugo. In a warehouse full of chewed up old crates and blankets, he had immediately hidden the man.

Gorian's parents had come from the Fire Mountains and had travelled to Valentia before he was born. They had disappeared when Gorian was small and he had survived the streets of Valentia alone—or so Gorian had told him. Hugo didn't believe a word of it. The old man was holding back information. He was, however, a good friend, and Hugo needed a friend right now, someone he could trust to smuggle Diamond and him out of the city. Gorian was the one Hugo had been running to the day they had been stopped by General Edo.

Hugo ignored the drunkards that staggered by him. This low level of the city was rife with all manner of living filth. Thieves and cut-throats weaved between the homeless, desperate refugees, and no one flinched when a drunk was dragged off into a dark alley. Staying alert, Hugo increased his pace. He had sent word to Gorian he would arrive by midnight and didn't want to keep the old man waiting.

The freshness of the air when he neared Gorian's territory always surprised Hugo. It seemed to him this part of the city should stink like the sewer it was, but the ocean wind always seemed to blow the rot away. Hugo stopped briefly when he rounded the far corner of an alley. With narrowed eyes he called upon his magic and shimmered into the shadows to wait. He scanned the shadowy rooftops and doorways. Nothing. No ripples in the darkness to say the Queen was watching him. Satisfied, Hugo hurried on. The sooner he did what he needed to do, the sooner he could get back.

The dock was wild, open to the raging seas and winds. No ships graced the abandoned docks. A wave reared up, breaking against the quay and splattering Hugo with such force it sent him staggering. His wet clothes clung to his skin, no defence against the bitter wind that cut through the saturated material.

Dark, faceless figures watched from the shadows. Positioned strategically on rooftops and against the walls of buildings, he couldn't see all of Gorian's heavily armed guards, but he could feel them gauging him. Straightening his spine, Hugo adopted his natural prowling gait. They must have recognised his bulk as he passed unchallenged through their lines.

With blue lips and numb fingers, Hugo opened the door to the Eastlight, the large ancient inn that belonged to the old man. The stink of old ale and stench of sweaty bodies assaulted his nostrils in a nauseating wave. Hugo threaded his way through the throng of unsavoury characters. He flattened his wings and ensured his wet cloak hung down his back, covering them completely from any prying eyes.

The inn was busy and noisy. Anyone who lived on the wrong side of the Queen's law came here to carry out their business. Gorian insisted upon it, violently at times. No drug lord, thief or murderer dare operate in this part of the city without the old man's permission. Even the city watch avoided this place, especially at night. Gorian had his own small army, and his men watched the docks carefully. Any comings and goings they did not like were soon stopped, by whatever means necessary.

Gorian was waiting for him in a gloomy corner. Hugo smiled down at the old man, who nursed a tankard of ale between his hands.

"It's good to see you, old man," rumbled Hugo, sitting as far into the shadows as he could get. Out of habit, he leaned back against the wall and assessed the crowd, before regarding Gorian. Time had been kind to the old man; even so Hugo could see the lines etched on his face had deepened and his dark hair was now thinner, more grey than black.

Gorian returned his smile but his dark brown eyes were worried. "You too, son. This must be urgent if you're willing to risk coming here."

It was a statement, not a question. Hugo grimaced. Gorian always did get straight to the point. "It is," he replied. Gorian waited patiently while Hugo scanned the room again.

"Don't worry, my people are watching. If anyone from the palace has taken it upon themselves to follow you, they will not get far," he said in a slightly amused voice.

"Indeed," replied Hugo, raising an eyebrow, then he took a deep breath. "I need your help to leave the city," he stated quietly.

Gorian's sharp intake of breath was audible, even above the din of drunken voices. The older man shifted but held Hugo's steady gaze.

"Why? Is this because of Winter Solstice?" he asked, eyes narrowing.

Hugo remained silent.

"It doesn't matter. It's about time you came to your senses and ran. Glad to see you're going to do it before that viper sinks her teeth in to you or lets that twisted bastard Ream kill you."

Hugo leaned forward, the rest of what he said came in a harsh whisper. "Yes. It's partly because of Winter Solstice, but there's something else." He paused and took a breath.

Hugo quickly told Gorian of Diamond, her necklace and the Queen's demand for Diamond to fight for her. Hugo noticed the colour leeching from the older man's face.

After a long pause Gorian spoke. "There's something you're not telling me," he stated, cocking his head to one side. "You might be able to fool everyone else with your blank looks, but I know you. I know what you are." His eyes narrowed shrewdly. "You care deeply for this woman if you are willing to risk everything, including your life, for her. Why?" he asked curiously.

Hugo looked uncomfortable, embarrassed even.

A slow smile spread over Gorian's face as he registered Hugo's unfamiliar display of uncertainty and guilt. "You've bitten her," he breathed incredulously. "Does she know what that means?"

"No!" Hugo hissed. "I didn't do it to own her or control her. I did it to save her life," he said vehemently.

"Okay. I believe you. And I don't think for one minute you did it for less than noble reasons." Grinning, Gorian patted Hugo's shoulder. "It's all right, son. Your secret's safe with me."

Hugo sat back, his shoulders relaxing.

"So, considering the Queen can track you anywhere, where do you want to go?" Gorian asked.

"I don't know," Hugo admitted, leaning both elbows on the table. He and Diamond needed to leave before Winter Solstice, and he hoped Gorian would have some ideas. Hugo had never before crossed the ocean. The Queen had always kept him carrying out orders in Avalonia or Rhodainia. Other guards were sent to the far off continents to kill or spy, but she had never sent Hugo.

"I have a shipment of tea and silk and—err—other things, coming in from Gar Anon, two days before Winter Solstice; but it will take two days to unload. The captain's a sly bastard, out to make as much money as he can. But he owes me a favour. Likely he'll leave the morning of Winter Solstice on the tide. The city guard will not bother the ship as I have an agreement with their commander. He looks the other way, and I let him and his family live."

Hugo frowned but held his tongue. Gorian's business rules were his own.

"There might be other ships leaving earlier from the main docks, but they will be too difficult to get you aboard without papers."

And without being betrayed, thought Hugo cynically. "I'd rather take yours. The Queen will set her test soon. I know Diamond will pass it. She has to; there is no other alternative. But once she does, Diamond will be ordered to the wall. If we cannot get on an earlier ship, the battle with Ragor cannot be avoided." That thought grabbed Hugo's heart and squeezed. His voice was tight as he spoke, his nostrils flaring as he inhaled a calming breath. "If I can, I will get Diamond's necklace back, but nothing is as important as getting her on that ship."

Gorian frowned and took a big swig of his ale. "Is the necklace necessary at all? It might be nothing. Maybe the Queen is simply using it to influence her."

"No, the way that viper looked when she saw the crystal glow means it should not be in her hands. Besides, the dragon necklace is precious to Diamond; it belonged to her mother. I took it from Diamond and, if possible, I will return it. I owe her that much," he said heavily.

"A dragon necklace? That glows? Please, describe it — in detail — for me." Gorian asked slowly.

Hugo frowned, but complied. The older man chewed his lip as Hugo spoke.

"What's wrong?" asked Hugo suspiciously.

Minutes passed as excitement seeped into the older man's face and eyes. "I think I know why she wants it. If I'm right, if it's what I think it is, you have to get it back."

"Why? What is it?" Hugo demanded, a frisson of anxiety tightening his stomach.

Gorian took a deep breath. "A key. A guardian's key. For the gateway to Eternity."

"Eternity? The land of the gods and resting place of our souls?" Hugo asked incredulously.

"Yes," Gorian replied, his eyes bright and his face flushed. "There were only two keys." The older man reached out and gripped Hugo's upper arms. "I know this is a long story but you must hear it now. There will be no other opportunity. I must leave to visit old friends very soon. Will you listen?" he asked anxiously.

"Of course," Hugo agreed.

"You know the legends about how the guardians are the protectors of Eternity and of the gods. Thousands of years ago, Lunaria beseeched Krahto, the high ruler of the guardians to stop Erebos. Her brother had become a dark god who existed only to kill and take the souls of the living. Krahto could not harm or kill Erebos, so he cast an enchantment that imprisoned the dark god on this planet. Once in place, no other god could breech that enchantment. Lunaria was distraught, believing someone should fight for the souls of this planet. Krahto listened to her plea. But knowing the gods are immortal, his heart was heavy. The high ruler imparted knowledge no other god had. The only way to kill a god is to mix his blood directly with that of another from his bloodline. When he told Lunaria, she did not balk. She vowed to fight Erebos. Wanting to give the souls on this planet a chance, Krahto formed the crystal gateway, the only way to breech the enchantment he had set. Through this gateway he sent Lunaria under the care of two guardians, Zulad and Nareen. Each guardian possessed a key for the gateway. The keys themselves look like jewels."

Gorian paused and took a large gulp of his beer.

Hugo did the same, not wanting to rush his friend.

"The guardians eventually had two sons. One son, Vaalor, swore to fight alongside the goddess and his parents; the other son, Sulphurious, was cruel and bloodthirsty. Forsaking the goddess, he sought to serve the dark god. Erebos did not turn Sulphurious away. They worked together; Erebos taking the souls of his victims and Sulphurious consuming their flesh."

"So Erebos resurrected Sulphurious? Not Ragor?" Hugo asked, lips pressed into a tight line. A shiver of dread ran down Hugo's spine.

"I would imagine so," Gorian agreed.

"So what does this tale have to do with the Queen?" Hugo asked, trying not to sound impatient.

Gorian turned the tankard of ale between his fingers. "Lunaria and King Arjuno had a child. Did you know that?

Hugo shook his head. "There are stories, but it's hard to know what to believe."

"Hmm, that's true. Well, the night King Arjuno of Avalonia died, many events were set in motion. That was the night Lunaria gave birth to her child, and Griana, general of the king's fae army, betrayed the king and became imprisoned in this city."

"What? The Queen used to be a *general*? And she was a traitor to her own king?"

"Indeed she was, son. That evil female was never meant to rule this land."

"Then how did she become a queen? How was she trapped here?"

"I only know the stories passed down to me. Prince Lexon, the king's younger brother, took an oath to the goddess to protect her child, and all her descendants. Lunaria gifted him with powerful magic, and when the Queen returned from the battlefield and tried to kill the baby, Prince Lexon cursed her. He bound her to the city she coveted and cursed her to be barren as punishment for the harm she wanted to inflict upon a helpless child."

"But what happened to Lunaria? To her guardians? Could they not save the king? Or even kill Griana?" Hugo asked, leaning forward on his forearms.

"Again, I am only repeating what was taught to me," Gorian said.

Hugo wondered by whom, but remained quiet. Gorian's secrets were his own.

"To lure Vaalor away from the goddess, Sulphurious attacked his parents before the battle. Sulphurious knew his brother would feel their pain as they died, and he ripped their keys from their foreheads."

Hugo felt a sudden sense of foreboding and the beast in his soul stirred uneasily. "Gorian, what do the keys look like?"

Gorian took a deep breath, and held his eyes. "They are the size of a small jewel. One a polished ruby. The other a rough diamond."

CHAPTER SEVENTEEN

The barmaid threw more logs on the fire. It sparked, bellowing acrid smoke back into the room. Both Gorian and Hugo coughed.

"Come, let's get some air," Gorian suggested, waving his hand in front of his face.

Hugo stalked after the old man, moving around the back of the bar and through the small kitchen to the rear door. They descended the wooden steps that led down to the side of the inn. Hugo's mind whirled with questions.

Clutching their hoods up against the wind and rain, they descended into the storm and stood huddled against the wall for a little shelter.

"So Diamond's necklace is the key to Eternity?" Hugo growled.

"It doesn't matter if it is," Gorian answered, waving his hand dismissively. "Trying to get it back will get you both killed," he shouted against the onslaught of the wind.

Hugo's face darkened under his cowl as a wall of shadow descended like a shroud around them, protecting them from the storm.

"Only me. And only if the Queen catches me," Hugo replied. "Diamond doesn't know I want to get it back."

"Just leave it, son. I have friends who can help retrieve it. Besides, the Queen needs a guardian for it to be of any use, and she doesn't have one."

"No, but Ragor does."

"No, he doesn't. Think about it. Sulphurious is not helping Ragor. The Wraith Lord would have used him to burn Avalonia to the ground and his Dust Devils would have consumed the ash to travel faster. No, Sulphurious is not Ragor's."

Hugo rubbed his temples as a headache started.

"It seems your priority is keeping your young lady alive and then getting the hell away from this city," Gorian pointed out. "You will need to run fast once you leave. And you know eventually you will have to fight for your freedom. The Queen will send Ream to track you wherever you go."

"Not if I destroy the blood tether she holds," Hugo growled.

Gorian cocked his head and raised his brows. "Shit! How many obstacles do you want to put in your way? I hope the woman's worth it."

Hugo gently knocked the back of his head against the wall, squeezing his eyes shut before looking at Gorian again. "Yes, she is. But gods damn it! I've done so much to hurt her. I don't know if she will ever trust me." He rubbed a hand over his face.

Gorian smiled sympathetically. "Hugo, why don't you tell her what you're planning? How you feel? If you don't know if she trusts you, how the hell are you going to convince her to run away with you? Damn it, son! You're sacrificing everything for her. The Queen might want your body to try and break that damned curse Prince Lexon bestowed on her, but if you run and then get caught, she is as likely to kill you as bed you. Diamond should know that," he said.

Staring at the shadows for a moment, Gorian seemed to make a decision. He turned and bestowed an intent look on Hugo. "I have not been totally honest with you about my origins. I was not born here. I am from the Fire Mountains. I was born and raised there. If you make it to Gar Anon on that ship, head for the Fire Mountains. There are people in Salvir who will help both of you. Seek an audience with Queen Ilya. Tell her I sent you. Tell her of Diamond's magic, of your Nexus, of that necklace."

126

A sudden shout of warning came from the front of the inn, carried in by a gust of freezing wind along with the clash of metal on metal. Hugo cursed and pulled his blades.

Splashing through the deep puddles, Hugo and Gorian ran swiftly around the side of the building. Both skidded to a halt at the same time. Hugo could only gape at the sight that met them and, for a split second, his arms hung slack at his sides. His hood blew back and freezing rain pelted into his eyes. He rapidly blinked the water away.

Two dark shadows viciously attacked the slim figure. Diamond was holding a blade in each hand, grunting with effort as she blocked the strikes from the much bigger and stronger men. Her hood blew back, her silver hair glowing in the flashes of white lightening.

What the hell? How did she have any idea where to find me? Hugo tried unsuccessfully to make sense of her presence. In that second, she moved so quickly he struggled to see her through the rain. There was a sickening crunch as she slammed the hilt of her sword into one man's nose. The guard crumpled to his knees, holding his face. Hugo roared at her to stop. But she did not hear him and slammed a kick into the side of the guard's face.

Diamond skipped aside as the man fell. The second guard bellowed with ill-contained fury. Throwing his considerable bulk behind his sword, he attacked. Highly skilled, his sword blurred through the air and slashed at her ribs.

"*No!*" Hugo roared into the wind.

But Diamond met the attack with devious intent. Blades singing, she used the man's rage against him; blocking another attack, she spun on her haunches and knocked his legs out from under him.

Gorian's man fell, splashing water up into the air.

Diamond's boot slammed down into his groin, eliciting a scream of agony even as her blade lifted high. The man lay on his back in the water moaning, helpless against her wrath.

Catapulted into action, Hugo moved before Diamond could finish her killing strike. Launching himself forward, he straddled the fallen man's outstretched legs and faced his beautiful, fierce Nexus. "*Diamond! Stop!*" he thundered, meeting her blade with his own whilst slamming a wave of energy forward to shock her. Her sword stilled but her eyes remained bright and unfocused.

"Diamond," he repeated, his voice gentling. "It's me. It's all right, they're friends. They will not attack again," he soothed, lowering his blade.

That look in her eyes was painfully familiar. Warriors, particularly inexperienced ones, could become completely focused on their victim, sometimes at the expense of their own lives; they lost awareness of the situation around them. Diamond was now so skilled at fighting, he sometimes forgot her inexperience with actual battle.

The man on the ground shuffled away from them.

Gorian helped him up. "I'll deal with you later," he promised. "See to your wounds, then get back to your post."

The guards waiting in the shadows melted away into the darkness. Oblivious, Diamond blinked, staring wide-eyed at Hugo. Holding her gaze, he carefully stepped closer and guided her weapons back into their scabbards. Rain pelted down upon them, but neither moved. Her unbound hair blew around wildly, whipping against her shoulders and face. She pushed it behind her ears, hissing with irritation as it blew straight out again. Hugo couldn't stop himself reaching out, gathering it in one hand and sweeping it over her shoulder to hold it there. "What are you doing here, Diamond?" he asked harshly.

No answer. She stared at his face, his hair, his eyes. He couldn't look away. Suddenly, she threw her arms around him and hung on tightly. Stunned by her frantic embrace, he slowly wrapped her in his arms, then carefully folded his wings around her.

"I thought they had hurt you. They wouldn't tell me where you were!" she cried, her voice muffled by his chest.

Her softness and warmth seeped into him, and he forgot they weren't alone. He forgot the rain that drove down upon them, and the waves that boomed against the docks. He forgot everything as their magic twisted in a desperate attempt to merge into one—until Gorian coughed uncomfortably.

"So? This is she?" he asked, stepping forward with a speculative smile.Diamond bristled immediately, as if she too had forgotten everything else in that one moment.

Hugo felt her begin to withdraw. He pulled his wings back but quickly grabbed her around the waist, pulling her hard up against his side. "Yes," he answered, his eyes shining at Gorian's lopsided grin. "Gorian, meet Diamond. Diamond, meet Gorian," he chuckled throatily. The after effects of their magic making his body burn.

The look upon Diamond's face was a picture. Utter shock, followed by a tight smile and a nod of her head. The old man returned the greeting, but Hugo didn't miss the flash of surprise in his eyes before it was replaced with frank curiosity.

The rain beat down mercilessly upon their stagnant figures as they studied each other. Gorian nodded. "Come on, you two. Inside," he ordered.

Hugo squeezed Diamond's waist reassuringly, glad she did not argue. They all shivered with cold. The wind and rain raged, whipping at their legs as they walked. Gorian led them up the rickety wooden steps and in through the side door. They followed him through the busy kitchen, up the main staircase and into a small bedroom.

Hugo gripped Diamond's wrist as though she might try and run away.

Located at the back of the inn, the room was cold and drafty. There was a bed, a washstand, one high-backed wooden chair and a small bedside table. Gorian lit the oil lamp.

The room was sparse, but at least it was dry.

Hugo still grasped Diamond's wrist despite her tugging at him. He set his jaw in irritation, growling a warning. Her snarl back was pure defiance.

Tension and the heavy weight of magic fizzled through the air.

Gorian, clearly recognising it, flicked his attention from one to the other. "Stay here until you are dry. Perhaps it would be best to stay until morning. It's dangerous out there tonight. And Hugo? This might be a good time to speak frankly to her," he advised, raising his eyebrows meaningfully. "I will bid you a goodnight. I, too, need to get dry."

Hugo grunted his thanks as Gorian left and the door clicked shut.

Warily Diamond and Hugo stared at each other, the sound of their breathing barely audible above the raucous noise of the inn below.

Hugo let go of Diamond's gloved hand and stared down at her. "Right. Start talking," he said, his voice ominously low as he fought the urge to crush her into his chest.

CHAPTER EIGHTEEN

Diamond's wet clothes stuck to her skin, making her itch mercilessly.

"What d' you mean?" she asked sulkily, although she knew exactly what Hugo meant. She had disregarded his advice to stay away from the disused docks. That was twice she had wandered around the city at night on her own. It was his fault. She had awoken just as her door clicked shut behind him. It had been impossible to settle again, especially when the storm raging outside had done nothing to calm her nerves.

Diamond had hastily dressed. She'd had no idea where Hugo had gone, but she wanted to know why he had snuck off under the cover of darkness. She worried it was something dangerous. Her anxiety, tinted with mistrust, won. Stepping out into the storm, it had not been a surprise when a trace of his magic lingered in the air. Nervously, she had followed it.

He was staring down at her, waiting for an answer.

"I, err, wanted to see where you'd gone. Make sure you were safe," she sputtered, chewing her bottom lip. His eyes widened in disbelief. Diamond fidgeted, rubbing madly at her itchy arms.

"You wanted to make sure—gods damn it, Diamond! I'm a Queen's guard! Of course I'm safe. You mean you nearly got yourself killed—again—because you wanted to make sure I was *safe*!" he blustered incredulously.

Sighing dramatically, Diamond turned her back on him, throwing her wet cloak over the back of the wooden chair, then she collapsed on the side of the bed to hide her embarrassment. "No, I didn't nearly get myself killed *again*. I'd already beaten both of them when you stepped in," she bit out, crossing her arms indignantly over her chest. It was impossible to stop shivering.

Hugo smiled widely.

Diamond's mouth dropped open.

"Yes, you had," he agreed softly. His silver-specked midnight eyes shone. His voice was not harsh like she had expected, but rumbling and soft. His gorgeous, toe-curling smile transformed his severe face like it had done every evening for the past two weeks. Her mouth dried out as she ran her eyes over his tall, muscled frame. He was right: her worry seemed ridiculous now that he was standing in front of her, looking so damned healthy. His lips stretched wider, his scar twisting upwards. He watched her studying him. Heat flamed across her cheeks, and she dropped her gaze.

"I wanted to know why you left me," she whispered, suddenly feeling foolish.

Hugo sighed and flung his cloak on top of hers. "I didn't leave you. I came to visit a friend," he said.

Mortified, she rolled her eyes, then cringed. "Oh no, I'm so sorry. I didn't think. I shouldn't have followed you. Sorry," she babbled, wishing the floor would swallow her whole.

Hugo flung back his head and laughed. Her pulse jumped, and a shiver of pleasure skittered up her spine at the richness of that sound.

"Will you stop that," he chuckled, sitting next to her and nudging her with his shoulder.

"Stop what?" Gods, she felt so stupid right now, but it was almost worth it to see him smile.

Hugo caught her face with his strong fingers. Turning her to look at him, he held her eyes with his. "Assuming that I'm sneaking away from you to jump into bed with some other woman," he drawled with a crooked smile. "There are no other women," he whispered, close enough now that his breath warmed her lips.

Diamond couldn't breathe — or move. Her heart banged so hard against her ribs that it was painful. A flush crept over Hugo's cheeks, and his throat bobbed. Heady and overwhelming, magic scorched the tiny amount of space left between them.

"Sorry," Diamond mumbled breathily as he slowly let go of her face. His fingers shaking a little, he brushed a drop of water off her temple. Diamond frowned. "So what friend were you visiting?" she asked. "No offence, but I didn't think you had any friends; well, you know, proper friends," she said, biting her lip.

"Thanks!" he replied sarcastically, although he was smiling again. "Tallo is my friend. So is Jack."

They were both shivering now. Standing up he paced over to the door and turned the key in the lock. Diamond's eyes grew wider as the lock clicked. Pulling off his worn outer clothing, Hugo unfastened his light leather armour and dropped his sword scabbards and weapons on the chair. The linen shirt he wore underneath was sodden and sticking to his skin. Powerful muscles rippled across his chest and shoulders as he undid the small buttons that secured it around his wings. Wriggling a little, he pulled it off.

Unable to tear her eyes off his beautiful, sculpted body, Diamond watched him turn away and hang his shirt on the back of the door to dry. The view of his wide back and heavily muscled shoulders left her flushed, but it was his wings that stunned her. She had never been brave enough to study them this closely before; besides, when not armoured, they were usually tucked in tight to his back.

Lamplight bathed the thousands of tiny feathers, giving them a beautiful midnight blue sheen. *Like liquid silk,* she thought, unable to tear her eyes away. Except they weren't simply blue. Diamond tried not to gasp at the greens, reds and purple hues that shimmered among the sapphire. The beautiful silver whorls that had glowed so brightly the day of the guardian's attack on Valentia now created a soft radiance that illuminated the stunning colours.

Unconsciously, she curled her nails into the bed clothes. Her fingers twitched with an overwhelming urge to touch him, all of him. She wanted to run her fingers over the entirety of his wings just to see if they were as silky and smooth as they looked.

Hugo folded them until they were astoundingly flat, almost as if he could pull them inside his skin to make them smaller. That shifting movement revealed a pattern at the joint of each wing that looked like scales. As beautiful as his wings, the silver and sapphire scales followed the ridge of muscle down either side of his spine and disappeared to a point under his waistband.

Her mouth tightened into a thin line as she noted the many scars that crisscrossed his back and shoulders. Her heart lurched, sickened by the pain he must have suffered throughout his life. She wondered how many battles, how many enemies—whether real or invented—had he fought for the vile Queen.

Hugo twisted that gorgeous body around, presenting his naked chest to her hungry eyes.

Breath hitched in her throat. *Oh! By the goddess, where do I look now?*

Suddenly the floor boards became very interesting.

"I came to see Gorian," Hugo said. Three strides ate up the room, and Hugo flung his leg over the wooden chair, straddling it. He propped his forearms on the high back. When Diamond looked up again, he smiled at her. She felt his magic reaching out, brushing her cold face. Her heart beat faster, and her magic stirred.

"Gorian is the only person in this city that I trust," he told her quietly.

Diamond stilled and cocked her head to one side, ready to listen. It was unsettling to see Hugo as someone with friends and secrets, not just the Queen's servant. He paused, pursed his lips and made an unsure a face. She gave him a small smile. "Go on," she encouraged. Against her will her body started to shiver again. The room was warmer than outside, but her clothes were saturated and sucked heat from her.

Hugo stood up. "Come on. You need to get those wet clothes off," he said.

"What? No. I'll keep them on, thanks."

"Oh, for pity's sakes, Diamond, you're shivering and wet through! I'm not suggesting you undress in front of me. I'll wait outside. Get undressed and wrap yourself in a blanket before you get hypothermia," he told her, a concerned frown creasing his brow.

When the door clicked shut behind him, she pushed herself off the bed. He was right: she was frozen. With numb and clumsy fingers, she fumbled with her boots, pulling them off with difficulty. Peeling off her wet clothes, she hung them over the washstand to dry. Even her pretty underwear came off. It was all soaking.

Wrapped in one of the roughly woven blankets, she let him back in. Quickly, she scurried across the floor in her bare feet to sit on the bed again.

There was no hearth for a fire and a fierce draft blew through the gaps in the old window frame. Her fingers were white and her toes numb.

Hugo unlaced his leggings.

Diamond nearly choked with embarrassment.

A soft chuckle escaped him at her expression. "Diamond, stop looking at me like I'm going to eat you alive. Close your eyes if my nakedness bothers you that much," he drawled.

She hastily squeezed her eyes shut just as he pulled off his remaining wet clothes. She refused to open them again until she felt him grab a blanket and he said, "There. You can relax now." Grinning widely, he finished wrapping the blanket tightly around his waist. Goose bumps covered his mottled skin.

"You're cold," she stated, biting her lip.

"So are you," he replied, walking confidently around to the other side of the wooden double bed. "Get in," he said, lifting the sheet and blankets.

Diamond blushed furiously and shook her head. A huge gust of wind howled around the inn, rattling the old walls, as well as the windows.

"Diamond, get in. We are both cold. Please, trust me. I only want to keep us warm."

The softness of his voice washed over her, melting her insides along with her embarrassed protest. "I do trust you," she whispered, giving a watery smile. She realised that it was true.

"Well then?" He smiled, raising his eyebrows expectantly.

The old bed creaked as they climbed in. As her feet hit the icy depths, she shuddered. The bedding was freezing and slightly damp against her exposed skin. Even bringing her knees up to her chest did no good. Her feet felt like blocks of ice. The wool blanket was rough, but she would not take it off to feel the sheet next to her skin, not with them both being naked.

It wasn't the most comfortable bed in the world. The mattress was lumpy and hard, but at that moment it felt wonderful. Diamond was exhausted, her muscles aching from fighting and shivering.

Hugo lay on his side facing her. Bending his elbow, he rested his head on his hand. Diamond blushed again, cursing her fair complexion and hoping the light was dull enough to hide it.

"Relax," he said, his voice an amused whisper.

They remained quiet for a few minutes, just studying each other. Diamond wanted to dive under the covers but instead made herself return his scrutiny. His dark hair was still pulled back tightly, exposing his chiselled features. His lips curled in a gentle, indulgent smile that sent a wave of heat through her insides. And she would never tire of looking at his beautiful eyes.

"Why did you come here so late at night?" Diamond asked curiously, trying to fill the silence and distract herself from her bizarre situation. The sight of his naked chest just inches from her made her stomach do somersaults. Shocked, she realised how much she wanted to touch him. Curling her fingers into fists, she bit her bottom lip but held his eyes.

Hugo brushed an errant strand of hair from her mouth. Helpless to stop it, a shiver of pleasure tingled wildly down her neck and through her body. That smile spread into his eyes at her reaction.

"I have a lot to tell you, Diamond," he said, his voice husky, if a little shaky. "But before I do, promise you'll hear me out before you respond."

CHAPTER NINETEEN

Hugo sounded unsure, completely unlike himself.

Anxiety tightened Diamond's stomach. "I promise," she nodded.

He took a breath. "It's hard to know where to start," he said, silencing her with a look as she opened her mouth to speak. "Shh, you promised. Please believe me when I say I had no idea what was going to happen that day in the throne room. I am sorry for—well, becoming so distant from you." He swallowed and his voice lowered. "It must have been so hard for you to learn General Edo was the one who betrayed you and your father."

Diamond squeezed her eyes shut against the awful memory of that dagger plunging into General Edo's flesh. An old feeling of panic tightened her throat, but she took a breath and pushed it away.

"I had no idea the Queen was going to take your mother's necklace that day either, and for my part, I am sorry. I am sorry I ever brought you to this city." Sadness and bitter regret crossed his face as he hesitated. "The Queen is such a heartless soul. She has ordered me to torture and kill people with far less magic in their whole bodies than you have in your little finger. Her plans for you will be cruel, and I fear somehow she is going to use me to hurt you." He swallowed, looking at her warily, like she might flee.

Diamond looked right back, her gaze not wavering. She knew what Hugo was, what he was capable of. The regret in his voice and the sadness in his eyes were enough for her to believe he was sickened by the acts he had been made to do in his life.

"I know what you are, I've always known," Diamond said. She did not understand what all this meant, why Hugo was here with her, telling her these things. It didn't matter, a quiet joy was growing in her heart that he was. Bravely, she wrapped her fingers around his and held on to his calloused hand. "I'm willing to trust you, even though common sense tells me I shouldn't. It's true you brought me to this city, I have even hated you for it, at times. But I don't anymore." She contemplated their joined fingers. If only the fragile relationship that had been building between them could be held together so easily. "If you hadn't, we wouldn't be together now." Her voice shook a bit, and she looked up through her lashes at him. "I have been trying to figure out why the Queen allowed you to train me. From the way she touched you in the throne room, I wouldn't have thought she'd want you near any other woman."

Diamond's face flushed as that last comment came out. To cover her discomfort, she quickly continued. "She must know how much time we spend together. After all, Attion reports back to her."

"Not on everything, he doesn't," Hugo answered.

Diamond raised her brows. "Really? Why not?"

Hugo smiled. "Once he was blinded by loyalty and fear, but Attion's perspective is different now," Hugo told her. "I don't want to discuss Attion, I want to talk about how we are going to get you away from the Queen."

Diamond sighed, her shoulders slumping even as she hid her surprise at Hugo's words. "It's not possible. Look what happened the last time we tried to leave. I can't help but think she is simply playing with me—with us. I don't understand why she needs me as a weapon. Not when she has an army under her command. And not whilst she has you. You have magic, Hugo. Why can't you be a weapon for her?"

"My magic is different to yours. I can hone weapons from it. I can use it to cloak myself in darkness. I can absorb the magic of others. That's how I manage to bring them back to the city. I can make them weak enough not to fight—for a time. But I cannot cause destruction on such a massive scale as you seem to be able to do with yours," he told her.

"But if you train *me*—a magic wielder—to kill, surely she believes I will become a threat to her." Diamond's voice dried up as she tried to word her next question. "Do you think that's why she wants us together; so you can kill me when she is ready for me to die?" Her eyes dropped from his face, praying to Lunaria for the right answer. Whatever else Hugo was, he wasn't a liar.

He squeezed her hand. "Look at me. I am likely damned for all the things I have done in my wretched life, and I am truly sorry you have to ask that question of me." His voice was heavy with regret. He swallowed hard. "But I promise, I would rather die than follow that order."

Diamond's shoulders drooped with relief, a breath escaped her lips. Slowly, giving her time to pull away, Hugo lifted their entwined hands and tenderly brushed his lips against the soft skin on the inside of her wrist. For the briefest moment, Diamond felt her pulse beat against the warm caress of his lips. Warm magic slid across her chilled skin. In response, hers slowly bloomed. A flush crept across his cheeks and silence settled between them. Both of them seemed unsure of what to say next.

Hugo coughed to clear his throat. "As soon as the battle with Ragor is finished, you need to get away from here. If we win, the Queen will want her prize: you. If we still live but we lose, she will want her revenge. On both of us. I have found passage on a ship. It leaves this dock the morning of Winter Solstice. It will sail with the early morning tide. Gorian will arrange it for us."

"What? But where is it going? I don't know anything about living anywhere else." Panic slammed into her at the thought of ending up alone in a kingdom she knew nothing about.

Hugo smiled and put his fingers over her lips, staunching her words. It was hard to fight the urge to kiss them.

"I said us. I'm coming with you."

"Coming with me?" she stammered. "But the Queen won't let you go. She'll hunt you down."

"Yes, she will," Hugo agreed quietly. "And eventually whoever she sends will find me."

"Surely if we run far enough and fast enough, she won't find us," Diamond countered.

Hugo's sapphire eyes darkened. "She will. The Queen can track all her guards. Wherever they go, she can find them. When we are young, she takes our blood. Do you know of the Acolytes?"

Diamond nodded. "Yes. Rose told me of them, and of the Prevost, their leader who answers only to the Queen. Rose knew an Acolyte who gave her a potion to heal my broken bones. It was disgusting!" She grimaced. The memory of tincture of petrified fire toad was not pleasant.

Hugo chuckled at the look on her face. "The Prevost of the Acolytes casts a spell on a phial of our blood, which the Queen keeps. A drop of our blood dabbed on a map, any map, will lead to us. It's why none of us can ever leave."

"So she will hunt you down and force you back—or kill you?" Diamond breathed.

"Yes," he agreed. "Unless I can destroy the phials," he looked at her intently.

Diamond gaped at him, unable to process his words.

"But even if I can't, then we leave—together. Running will mean always being on our guard. But I can deal with that if you can. Besides, you know nothing about living in another kingdom," he gave a half-smile, lifting her hand to kiss her fingers, then shrugged. "And neither do I, but I would like to learn—with you."

Diamond wasn't sure she heard him right. She blinked. "With me?" she asked hoarsely.

"Yes. I have never wanted to be a Queen's guard. This life was not my choice, but I have never let myself hope for anything more, until now," he breathed. Sitting up, he freed his other hand to brush his fingers down her cheek, "You make me believe I can become something other than the puppet of and murderer for an ancient, crazed queen." His fingers cupped her cheek, shaking slightly. "Do you like the way our magic dances?" he asked, although from the sparkle in his eyes she guessed he already knew the answer.

Diamond nodded and dropped her eyes to his bare chest, her long silver lashes brushing her cheek.

He gently tilted her chin up. "I have never felt anything like it before," he told her.

Diamond huffed slightly. The Queen had caressed him with her vile magical touch.

Hugo's eyes narrowed. "No, not even hers," he said in understanding. His magic pushed against her skin as if he were trying to reach inside her soul and reassure her. "Yours is beautiful, the perfect match to mine." His throat bobbed, and she couldn't tear her eyes away from him. "We have such a rare and special connection," he continued. "It's called a Nexus bond. It is a powerful, goddess-given gift. Our magic simply fits; it belongs together. A perfect match. I don't know how a Nexus bond works, not really, but maybe when this war with Ragor is over we can find out—together?"

Diamond's heart tightened in her chest. Being with him was what she had yearned for, but he had let her down. She breathed out slowly and steadily through her nostrils. No, she trusted Hugo now. He was right: their magic did belong together. She felt stronger, more powerful with him nearby.

Diamond took a leap of faith, believing in her heart and her magic. She nodded. "I'd like that," she answered, her cheeks slightly flushed.

Hugo leaned back, settling himself on his elbow once more. His face remained serious, though his eyes absorbed every detail of her high colour and bright eyes. "We must escape the Queen right after the battle. We cannot be anywhere near the palace on Winter Solstice."

"Why? What has she got planned for you?" Diamond asked, dread curling in her belly.

A shadow crossed his face, clouding his eyes. "I forget sometimes how little you know of this place and of the Queen's rituals." The intense sapphire blue in his eyes turned almost black and his magic withdrew. Diamond shivered at the loss.

"On Winter Solstice, all the Queen's guards gather in her throne room. None are permitted to be absent. That vile female then picks one, or more of us to, err ..." he coughed uncomfortably, searching her face as if unsure of whether to continue or not.

It dawned on Diamond; he had stopped because he thought her too naive to hear his next words. She squeezed his fingers, reassuringly. "It's all right, Hugo. My father was fae, remember? I am not as ignorant as you seem to think. What does she do to them?" She raised her eyebrows expectantly.

"Use them for sex," he said bluntly.

"Oh," was all she could reply, instant jealousy searing through her magic, battering them both.

"Whoa!" Hugo grimaced, leaning back from the onslaught before a satisfied smile stretched his lips. His thumb stroked over her wrist, sending little electric shocks up her arm. "What was that?" he asked, a little too smugly.

Diamond scowled. "What?" she muttered, dragging her magic away from his.

"Diamond, you can't hide your feelings from me. Your magic and mine; remember?" He grinned, entwining his fingers with hers and bringing them up for them both to see. "Are you jealous?" he asked, his voice full of a heat that made her insides melt.

"No," she denied, mortified when her face burned.

He chuckled but let it go. "Let me explain, before you blast me off this bed. The Queen chooses one of her guard she thinks is not utterly loyal. She craves complete control over us; our emotions, our memories, even our bodies. And she possesses an ancient fae method of achieving that. She can cloud a mind with thoughts and desire and make any of us do anything she wishes. Sometimes those she has bitten remember what they have done; other times, they don't," he finished, disgust heavy in his voice.

Diamond swallowed the bile that rose in her throat. She remembered her lack of control in the throne room. But she hadn't been bitten by the Queen.

"You mean she rapes her men, not just physically, but mentally too? Only on Winter Solstice or whenever she wants?" Diamond asked, horrified for them.

"Always one or more on Winter Solstice, but if any of her guard show signs of wanting to mate, she will bite them immediately. The venom in that bite is what gives her control over her victims," he explained, blowing air out through pursed lips. "I have managed to make her think I am still hers to command, until now."

"You mean she could bite you and control you—forever?" Diamond whispered, her face almost as white as the sheets.

"Yes," he answered, grinding his teeth until his jaw muscles bunched and his scar twisted.

"But how does she bite? Can she shape change into some sort of beast?"

"No, at least I don't think so," he replied with a snort. "Some fae are born with a second set of teeth. It's a rare trait, left from our wild beginnings in the forest. But I have seen the Queen use those teeth many times. When they are embedded in her victim's skin, she releases her venom."

Diamond narrowed her eyes when she felt a shudder ripple through him. "Why do such a thing? She is beautiful, powerful and rich. Surely she does not want for male attention?"

"Oh, a number of reasons I think. Power is like a drug. The more you have, the more you want. When she bites her men and has absolute power over them, they can never leave or betray her." Hugo cocked his head, not dropping his eyes from hers. "I have heard stories, ones that have never been proven of course, but Gorian..." He paused, a thoughtful look on his face. "Never mind, but perhaps they are more true than I ever thought. The Queen is said to be cursed. She is barren, except for one single Winter Solstice in all time, when she can conceive. Raping her men is not simply about lust or power. If those stories are true, it is about her desperate need to have a child."

"Are you telling me that she has not forced you to, err, lay with her yet?" Diamond asked through gritted teeth. Jealousy seeped into her magic again but she tightened it around her chest, not allowing it the freedom to touch him. It nearly suffocated her.

Hugo's nostrils flared and he rumbled a low growl. "No, she has not."

CHAPTER TWENTY

An irrational amount of relief stole Diamond's sense at his words. "Well, why can't we run then?" she blurted. "Before Ragor gets here. We could just leave."

Reluctantly, Hugo pulled back. "We can't. You know that. If we could, I would have smuggled you out of here weeks ago. Besides, there is no way out until Gorian's ship arrives. And there's something else." The wariness in his eyes made her stiffen. "Gorian thinks your necklace is a key to a celestial gateway."

Diamond went utterly still. "A gateway? To where?" she whispered.

"Eternity," he replied. "The first guardians had jewels set in their foreheads. The jewels are the keys. They will allow only the guardians who possess one to pass from our world into theirs."

Diamond blanched. "I've seen the guardians in my dreams. It was the night of the throne room. Lunaria pulled me into another realm. She gave me armour to wear; it was like a living thing." She swallowed and closed her eyes. "I remember the heads of guardians appearing and disappearing on it. All had a jewel in the centre of their foreheads."

"So it's true," Hugo breathed.

Silence fell. Both of them were lost deep in thought.

Hugo spoke first, his voice determined. "We leave the necklace. I don't know why the Queen wants a key to Eternity, but she doesn't have a guardian. And it seems one is useless without the other. Besides, it's more important that you survive Ragor and get away from her. I don't know how she is going to test you, but I do know that it will push you both physically and mentally."

"What do you mean?" Diamond gulped.

Hugo studied their entwined fingers.

"Do you know what the test will be?" she pressed, dread tingling the nape of her neck.

Hugo hesitated, his eyes shuttered. "No, but *when* you pass it, you will be taken outside the shield and pushed to call your magic." He pressed his lips together. "Soon you will join Jack on the wall."

Diamond dropped her eyes, shuffling away from Hugo's heat. In truth, she had not thought of her friend much since he had left. Guiltily she wondered if that made her a bad person. "But she will send you there with me, won't she?" she asked, her stomach clenching at the doubt in his eyes.

"Whether she does or not makes no difference. You have to go. There are thousands of people in the Rift Valley who will die if Jack and Commander Riddeon lose control of the wall. You are powerful enough to save so many lives. Not like me, all I have ever done is destroy people." Self-loathing coated his words.

"That's not true. You saved me, more than once."

"Did I?" he asked, a note of bitterness seeping into his voice as he ran his index finger along the skin of her collar bone down to the hollow between her breasts where her necklace usually sat.

Diamond held her breath.

"I'm sorry for being so messed up, for being so many things I shouldn't be."

He paused and shifted his weight towards her, his face and eyes softening so much she couldn't speak, let alone move away from him.

Hugo gently kissed the back of her hand, then let it go and brushed some loose silken threads behind her ear. Her eyes fluttered closed involuntarily. A shiver of pleasure travelled through her and she arched her neck to the side. Trying to hide her response to his touch was impossible. Magic trembled around them, pushing against their skin.

"All the training, the way I've pushed you and your magic, it isn't for the Queen. You have to be able to survive on your own—through this coming battle, and after. And if she finds out about our plan—and stops me—you have to run. Promise me you will run. Don't stay here for anyone; not Jack or Tom. And definitely not for me. "

His gaze was so intense it frightened her.

"I promise," she whispered.

"Thank you," he replied, relieved.

"But the Queen won't find out about our escape. How can she if only we and Gorian know?"

Hugo sighed, his face grim. "Because this city is like a den of snakes; anyone could betray us. Gorian's guards, the ship's captain, the thieves and murders that saw me enter the inn earlier. She has spies everywhere."

Adjusting his weight, Hugo cradled her face in one large hand. Diamond rested her cheek against his palm, trying to understand why this complicated male was willing to put himself at such risk for her.

"I know everything I've said is a lot to think about. I understand. Let's get some sleep. Maybe we can talk more tomorrow," he said, sounding weary.

Giving him a tired smile, she nodded, then snuggled under the thin blankets. Her eyelids closed, but she was painfully aware of Hugo's strong energy and the length of his hard warrior's body, inches from her own. Tentatively, she reached out with her magic and wrapped it around his waist and arms, like she so desperately wanted to do with her body.

A low rumbling groan vibrated through his chest.

As their magic entwined, a sensation of deep belonging spread from her core, seeping through her bones. But that belonging soon became something much more. Gritting her teeth, she tried to remain still. Then he shifted his weight closer.

"Diamond? Can I hold you?" he asked, his voice no more than a low growl.

Anticipation fizzled through her. She nodded, her mouth too dry to speak. Warm, hard muscle wrapped around her, then a gentle rustle filled the air as he shifted her weight and lifted her into his body. Beautiful silken wings encircled them.

"Just to keep you warm," he whispered, his voice strained. "Trust me."

"I do trust you," she murmured, feeling safer, yet more on edge than she ever had in her life.

Their magic melted together, pulsing in time with the beat of their hearts. There was no shame when Hugo pulled her in closer, only warmth and delicious, simmering desire. She propped her head on his shoulder and, with her heart thumping madly, dared to rest her cold hand on the curve of his waist. His skin was impossibly hot under her fingers. The urge to explore him further nearly broke her self-control. Engulfed by his warmth, Diamond was painfully aware of the roughly hewn blankets separating their naked bodies. Her breath caught in her throat at a light brush of his lips against her forehead. If she leaned her head back he would be able to kiss her lips.

Before she could drum up enough confidence, he ran his hands through her hair. Murmuring contentedly, she savoured the closeness and warmth of his body as it seeped into hers. The touch of his hands in her hair excited her, but lulled her too. Under her cheek, she felt the muscles of his chest shift as his fingers moved. Her warm breath fanned his skin. Like his wings, the silver serpents of his energy curved around her. They gently explored her chilled skin and awakened nerve endings she didn't know existed. New sensations were drowning her.

"Diamond," he whispered before burying his face in her hair. "This is madness," he mumbled.

The truth of those words struck a chord in her heart but she didn't care. It didn't feel like madness being next to him or feeling his hands in her hair. It wasn't enough. She wanted more. She wanted to feel the rough skin of his fingers exploring her, the warmth of his lips on hers and the glorious length of his body pressing against her, skin against skin. Instinctively, she moved her hips into him, stunned when he groaned her name.

The noise of the inn faded. All Diamond could hear was the sound of her heart beating wildly and her panting breath. A gentle growl filled the air, and Hugo's arms tightened before he whispered into the shell of her ear, "Sleep now." Something flared in her mind and in an instant, deep sleep claimed her.

CHAPTER TWENTY-ONE

It was long before dawn when Hugo dressed in his damp clothes. Shivering, he was sorely tempted to slip back into the glorious warmth beside Diamond. The lamp flickered dully, casting a soft amber glow across the softness of her curves. Pulling on his shirt, he sat on the small wooden chair, smiling indulgently. He had almost lost his thread of self-control when she had pushed against him last night. A ferocious need for her had consumed him.

In desperation, he had searched out her mind. It had been surprisingly easy to find the channel created by their venom bond. With a little push, her mind had bloomed open. Her need and desire, mixed with excited trepidation, had swirled into him.

Hugo rubbed his hands over his face and groaned. Invading her thoughts and manipulating her mind had been beyond deceitful. Nothing he did when it came to Diamond ever seemed right. But neither was making love to her when she had so many obstacles to overcome—all of which demanded her utmost attention. He knew taking a lover for the first time would distract Diamond, even put her at risk. Besides, he didn't want to be only a lover, he wanted far more than that from her. He wanted to be hers completely—body, soul and magic—and for that to happen she had to know—and accept—everything about him.

Latching onto her will before he had lost his nerve, he had commanded her to sleep. Just like that, she had dropped into a deep, peaceful slumber, her body yielding against his. This had been the most difficult and wonderful night of his life. It had been sweet agony to hold Diamond so close but not explore her. Eventually his ardour had settled and, surrounded by her sweet scent, he had slept. For the first time in years, the faces of the dead had not haunted him.

A mass of silken hair tumbled over Diamond's face and shoulders, fanning out across the pillow they had shared. His gut twisted. *This,* he thought with a jolt, *is how she will look every morning, if I ever get the chance to make her mine.*

Hugo resisted the urge go to her side and run his fingers through her hair again, to brush it back so he could see her face. The blanket had slipped enough to reveal the upper swell of her breasts and the bite mark he had given her. A frown shadowed his features. As soon as they were away from the Queen he would tell her. Maybe when she knew why he had bitten her, she would forgive him. The alternative didn't bare thinking about.

Stirring and mumbling incoherently, Diamond rolled towards the empty side of the bed as if looking for him. His chest tightened when she pushed her face into the indent on the soft feather pillow, right where his head had been. Hugo suddenly wished he hadn't forced himself to get up. The thought of waiting for her to awaken, to watch her face as she saw him next to her, was enticing. Gripping the chair back with his hands, he tried to resist, then pushed himself up.

Diamond stretched and moved as if feeling his gaze. Quickly he threw on his damp tunic and fastened on his blades. How would she react to him this morning? Would it be better for him to be gone when she awoke?

The inn was quiet, but he knew Gorian would be in the kitchen making breakfast. Glancing out of the small dirty window, Hugo gave a satisfied grunt. The glass was thick with dust and salt from the sea, but he could see through it well enough to tell the sky had cleared. The sides of the dilapidated warehouses were illuminated by Tu Lanah's silvery glow. Men busied themselves, carrying boxes from a sturdy boat that banged against the quay. Every now and then a *boom* echoed as a large wave broke against the unyielding wall of the quay. Stealthily, Hugo walked over to the bed and perched on the edge.

"Diamond?" he whispered, delighting at the goose bumps that appeared on her skin when his breath fanned her ear. Daring her wrath, he couldn't resist brushing his lips in a feather light kiss under her earlobe. She gave a secret smile and stretched her neck back invitingly. It was such an unconsciously sensual move that his body stirred in response. He swallowed hard. Gods, it was difficult not doing it again and again.

"Diamond?" he repeated, his voice huskier than before. His mouth burned to trace kisses along her exposed skin.

Murmuring, her eyes fluttered open. Confusion fogged their depths for a moment, then her brows furrowed into a frown. "Hugo?" she whispered. A shy smile bloomed across her stunning face before it flushed bright red.

A grin stretched Hugo's features when she pulled the blankets right up to her neck. She looked adorable with her messed up hair and bashful expression.

"Morning. It's time to get up. I'm going down to find Gorian. We'll be in the kitchen. Eating," he informed her, still grinning.

"Don't grin like that," she muttered uncomfortably.

"I'm not," he said, trying to purse his lips together. It didn't work. He couldn't stop smiling at the memory of her sleeping wrapped in his arms. Inhaling, his grin spread. Her sweet scent was mingled with his now. "Did you sleep well?" he asked in a drawling voice.

Nodding, she dropped her eyes.

"So did I," he said, brushing a finger lightly down her hot cheek.

A hesitant smile curved her lips as his gaze lingered on her mouth.

"I'm ravenous," he told her, deliberately infusing his voice with double meaning, "so you had better hurry up and get dressed." He slowly ran his eyes down the full length of her body and back up again.

Her flush deepened.

Satisfied by her reaction, he winked, then almost laughed out loud when Diamond's mouth dropped open.

"Also, if we get back to the barracks too late, it will start tongues wagging. And you'll never hear the end of it from the squadron, especially the love-struck Reese, if we don't get back before they know we've been out together all night. You'll break his heart," he warned.

Diamond huffed at him. "Reese is not in love with me," she uttered defensively.

A sputter of laughter exploded from him at her indignation. "Yes, he is," Hugo grinned and attempted a mock frown.

Smiling now, she placed her hands flat on his chest and shoved him off the bed.

Hugo let himself be moved.

"Oh, stop it. No, he's not. He's a very nice man who is my friend. Just like Jack is."

"Really?" Hugo said, raising his brows quizzically. "You sure?"

Diamond rolled her eyes. "Go downstairs, you fool, then I'll get up."

Chuckling, he caught her face in his hands. Holding her eyes, he slowly leaned forward and touched his lips to hers in the lightest, most gentle kiss. The taste of her almost drove him to his knees. It was so damned hard to pull away. Leaving her stunned, Hugo rallied his self-control and sauntered to the door.

Wide, violet eyes watched him as he grasped the handle, winked and stepped into the hall. He caught her stunned expression before he closed the door. It was understandable really; he was acting completely out of character and he had never kissed her before. He blew out a deep breath as his stomach flipped. He would find the right time to tell her about the bite—he would. Taking a few large strides, his feet hit the first stair and he descended into the stale aroma of the rickety old inn.

CHAPTER TWENTY-TWO

The soft murmur of voices rose from the kitchen. Hugo cocked his head, his keen fae hearing missing nothing. Two males. The sound of pots and pans being thumped down and the sizzle of bacon. His stomach rumbled at the aroma. It had been a long time since he last ate.

Gorian was an early riser; he had to be if catching the early tides meant the difference between keeping his illegal activities low key and forcing the city guard to act against him. Hugo did not judge Gorian. The older man had helped keep Hugo sane over the years, but Hugo wasn't stupid; he knew Gorian was not a noble man. Most of his profits came from whorehouses, underground magic rooms and fighting pits. Hugo guessed he had made a lot of money in the past few years due to so many desperate people flooding into the city. Sometimes it sickened Hugo to think about it, but life was cheap in this war.

Reluctantly, his thoughts turned to the impending battle with the Wraith Lord. Hugo had fought many battles alongside Jack and his army in the Grasslands of Rhodainia. He had fought against the Wraith Lord's vile creatures, that army of animated dead that could turn into swirling columns of dust. But it was not himself he worried for.

Diamond would face them. An ache bloomed in his chest. He knew she could die. No matter how hard he had trained her or how good she became, she was not a warrior. Hugo didn't know if Ragor would simply attack the wall or if he had spies and traitors skulking among the filth-ridden backstreets of this city.

He tried not to think about how the Wraith Lord had been freed from his warded prison. Every sickening detail of day the Queen had set Ragor free was etched into Hugo's brain. The Wraith Lord had been freed for a purpose; Hugo had never discovered what. The Queen had used Hugo's shadow magic to move her spirit from Valentia. Using him that way had nearly killed both of them, but she had needed to be there to use the blood of king Oden, and cast the spell that had set Ragor free. Once his part in that nightmarish day was over, Hugo had been sent away.

After hearing Gorian's story, Hugo wondered if setting Ragor free was something to do with the keys to Eternity. Arades Gillon had commanded King Oden's armies. Hugo wondered if the Queen had been searching for the necklace even back then. Had she killed the king to make her quest for the key easier? It was highly likely. Though, it was unlikely she had expected Ragor to turn on her. It shouldn't have come as much of a surprise, Hugo supposed. If legend were to be believed, the Wraith Lord's only allegiance was to The Lord of Chaos. *And*, Hugo reflected dryly, *the Queen did help put Ragor in his prison in the first place.*

Warriors from all Eight Kingdoms had kept the borders between Rhodainia and the Barren Lands secure. It had been that great combined army, forged by the immortal rulers of the Eight Kingdoms, that Jack's family had commanded. The Combined Army had contained Ragor's demonic creatures in the Barren Waste Lands for a thousand years—until the rulers from across the oceans began to forget, and the Oden dynasty's strength had fallen. Hugo swallowed the rush of bile that hit his throat, his footsteps faltering. *Until their king had fallen.*

Taking a deep breath, Hugo pushed away his guilt. He stepped into the kitchen.

Gorian nodded and bid him a cheery, "Good morning."

Another man stood by the back door, facing the yard. He was a hulking brute with wide shoulders and a thick neck. As the guard turned to glance at Hugo, it took all of Hugo's self-control not to snort with laughter. Dark eyes glinted from the guard's messed up face. Maintaining a blank face, Hugo swallowed his pride in Diamond's fighting skill. This man was obviously one of Gorian's best guards. It was in the way he stood, in his scrutiny of every detail of Hugo's weapons but, most of all, it was in his eyes.

"This is Max," explained Gorian with a warning look in Hugo's direction. *Do not goad him*, that look said.

Hugo nodded, keeping his face blank. He sat down where Gorian indicated. *Well, it should be interesting when Diamond comes downstairs,* Hugo smiled to himself.

"So? Where's the young lady?" Gorian asked with a smirk. "Tired, is she?"

Hugo treated him to a warning scowl. "Gorian."

Gorian smiled and slapped Hugo on the shoulder good-naturedly. "Relax, son. I'll be on my best behaviour. Did you talk to her about your plans?"

"Yes, I did."

"And?"

"And there are still things left unsaid, and things she will need time to think about."

"Time to think about? By the goddess, Hugo, you don't have time to think about it. And neither does she. Doesn't she want to live?" Gorian exclaimed incredulously.

"Yes, she does," said a musical voice from the doorway.

Even Max gave a start.

Hugo frowned. *How did she get down here without me hearing her footsteps?*

Diamond greeted Gorian, then treated Hugo to a stunning smile. Irritatingly, a swift flush heated his neck. Caught off guard, he could only stare stupidly at her.

Noticing Max standing by the door, Diamond's smile faltered. Instead of sitting down as Hugo expected her to, she walked straight up to Max and held out her hand, an apologetic look on her face.

"I'm very sorry about your nose," she said earnestly, flicking her wrist in Hugo's direction. "I was worried about him. He forgot to tell me what he was up to. It was nothing personal."

Max stared down at her, his mouth a bit slack, but he took her slim hand in his big paw. Apparently no one had ever before apologised for hitting him. Hugo watched like a hawk, ready to launch himself at Max if he even twitched in the wrong direction.

" 'S alright," Max said, his voice rough and deep. Intelligent, alert eyes weighed up Hugo's body language. "Never met a woman who can fight like you. Besides, can't fault you for caring about your friends," he said with a lopsided smile.

Diamond grinned back, relieved. "Thanks," she said, her shoulders relaxing. Max returned to his vigil at the door. The chair creaked as Diamond sat down opposite Hugo at the table.

Hugo silently raised his eyebrows.

"Something wrong?" she asked sweetly.

Hugo shook his head innocently. In truth, apologising had been the last thing he had expected her to do. "Nope," he denied, biting into his bacon.

Gorian placed a plate in front of her. "Eat up. Then you had better get going before it gets light. Diamond?"

"Yes?" she mumbled, stuffing a fork full of food into her mouth.

"Hugo told you about the ship?" His eyes flicked to Max, "And your necklace?"

Diamond nodded gravely. "Yes."

"Good. Don't try and retrieve it. Leave it where it is. Both of you." He looked meaningfully at Hugo. "I am leaving to visit friends. I will tell them of it, and I guarantee they will want to see it returned to its rightful owner."

Hugo felt a spike of suspicion at Gorian's words. He was a crime lord after all. But Gorian's face and eyes were utterly sincere.

"The ship will leave at four-thirty am for the spice continent of Gar Anon. There will be a row boat waiting on the quay near the main warehouse. Be here by three-thirty at the latest to board it. They will not wait longer than that," he said solemnly. "I will arrange your passage. The captain is a greedy and untrustworthy bastard, but, well, let's just say he owes me a favour. Do not turn your back on him or he will likely stab you in it and take everything you own."

Diamond finished her food, while thinking that comment over. Hugo stood and reached into his pocket pulling out a bag of coins. "Here, this should cover our expenses. And keep the captain's mouth shut, for now," he said, his fingers releasing the bag. It dropped with a solid thud into Gorian's hand. Diamond's eyes widened but she didn't say anything.

"What's this captain's name? Just in case," asked Hugo, his face blank but his voice oozing threat.

Gorian smiled tightly, nodding in understanding. "Captain Sabiliar. Don't return here unless you have to. It's too risky," he said, his smile full of regret as he looked at the younger man. "Take care, son. I'm glad our paths crossed all those years ago. You're the closest thing to family I have known in a long time." Then Gorian cocked his head to one side. "When you get to Gar Anon, make sure you head to the Fire Mountains. There will be answers in Salvir for both of you. The fire people are in your blood, Hugo; it's where your family is from. I will be leaving to meet with my friends soon, but we will meet again one day," he said with certainty.

Hugo was at a loss for words. Before he could recover and ask Gorian what he meant, the old man walked over to Diamond, his eyes flashing a warning as he took her hands in his.

"Hugo is like a son to me. He is risking a lot for you—and will always risk a lot for you. Being a guardian of those he loves is who he is underneath the mask he wears. If you let him, he will care for you until his dying day. Don't throw that back in his face," he warned, while his eyes promised to hunt her down if she did. Gorian let her go, then embraced Hugo before departing with Max.

Hugo and Diamond stared at each other, the air crackling with tension and unspoken words.

"We should go," said Hugo quietly. Still wondering at Gorian's words, he led the way out of the back door and down the steps to the docks. *A guardian? An interesting choice of words for someone like me*, he thought, curling his lip in derision.

Frigid air gusted around them, leaving the dawn sky free of clouds. Beautiful stars peppered the sky, twinkling brightly beside the ice moon that illuminated the dilapidated buildings of the dockside.

"Come," Hugo rumbled, holding out his arms as he unfurled his wings. Armour shimmered across them, their markings intensifying in the silvery moonlight. Without hesitation, Diamond gave him a little smile, reached up and wrapped her arms tightly around his neck. He embraced her slim body, picking her up and lifting them smoothly off the ground. It was hard to ignore the warmth of her breath against his skin and the way she unreservedly leaned her body into his, holding him tightly. His concentration flickered as her warm thighs wrapped around his waist, gripping him tightly.

Focus! He scolded himself as heat spread through his veins, then pooled in his lower belly. They passed over glimmering rooftops, avoiding the watch towers and city guards. Warrior fae challenged

Hugo as he reached the palace walls but there was no trouble when they recognised him as a Queen's guard.

Landing softly in the deserted barracks, Hugo smiled. Diamond now looked flustered as he slid her slowly down his body until her feet could touch the floor. Taking her hand, he led her inside. It was harder than it should have been to let her go. They agreed she should meet the squadron as usual and continue her training. Hugo watched Diamond reluctantly enter her room, not turning away until her door clicked shut.

KAREN TOMLINSON

CHAPTER TWENTY-THREE

Rain fell in loud torrents on the roof of the training hall. Tallo had relented and let the squadron train indoors instead of out in the brutal weather.

Diamond nearly missed blocking Paige as she glanced at the door, looking for Hugo. *Concentrate!* she berated herself. Diamond hadn't seen Hugo since returning from Gorian's inn nearly a week ago. He had all but disappeared, leaving her training to Tallo and Attion. The latter was a hard taskmaster but was never disrespectful. Coldly courteous was a good description, Diamond supposed. All Attion could—or would—tell her was that the Queen had recalled Hugo for other duties. Anxiety had squeezed Diamond's heart at the brief flicker of worry she had seen in Attion's eyes.

Diamond told herself not to fret. But not feeling Hugo's magic, not knowing what was happening to him after everything they had discussed, was hell. Every evening she went to his room hoping he would be there. Every evening, as her worry worsened, she curled up on his bed, praying to Lunaria he was safe.

Tallo frowned and called a halt as Paige struck a sideways blow and whacked Diamond on her arm. Diamond yelped. It had not escaped Tallo's notice how distracted and tired Diamond had become.

"Concentrate, Diamond!" he admonished, treating her to a spectacular frown. "Captain Reese! Niall! You're up next. Diamond, Paige, get a drink! And Diamond? Get your head back in the game before you get hurt."

Chastised, Diamond turned away. Reese winked as she walked off the floor to the water table. She forced a smile at him. The two men chose their weapons and began to spar. Tallo grunted his approval.

Diamond downed a pitcher of water and wiped the drips off her chin before turning around.

Her blood froze instantly.

Lord Commander Ream, the cruel and scarred leader of the Queen's elite guard, studied her from the doorway, Attion by his side. Ice slithered down her spine. Both males approached. Reese and Niall stilled. The whole squadron, even Tallo, watched the two Queen's guards closely. Out of the corner of her eye she saw Reese, then Niall, swing their swords ready to strike, but not at each other. Fearing for their safety, she almost imperceptibly shook her head at Reese. If Attion noticed, he did not show it.

Rooted to her spot, the blood drained from her face, leaving her pale and lightheaded. Sweat beaded on her brow. Swiping it away, Diamond forced herself to meet the Lord Commander's cold scrutiny. Lifting her chin, she waited.

"The Queen wishes to see you now." Attion's voice was as cold as it had ever been, but she did not miss the minute nod of his head or the warning in his eyes.

Prepare yourself, that nod said.

"Of course," Diamond replied, her heartbeat picking up. "Do I have time to freshen up?" she asked, keeping her voice steady and neutral.

"No," responded Commander Ream icily. He stood to one side, indicating Diamond should proceed ahead of them. As they left the training hall, Attion came to her side.

"This way," he said, motioning for her to turn left down a corridor that led to another large training hall.

"Nosco!" Commander Ream barked over his shoulder. "You too. The rest of you stay here." There was stark warning in his voice.

Captain Reese and his soldiers watched with barely concealed animosity as the small party left the hall.

Fear turned Diamond's legs to jelly. *Is this my test? Or has the Queen tolerated as much as she was willing between her favoured guard and the half-blood magic wielder?* Bile rushed Diamond's mouth. She swallowed it painfully. Being this close to Commander Ream terrified Diamond, reminding her of the temple and the throne room. *No. No panic attacks. I can survive this. The Queen will not kill me unless I am of no use. She wants a weapon, not a corpse.*

By sheer effort of will, Diamond put one foot in front of the other, trying not to succumb to the desire to lean on the wall or to turn tail and run.

Attion led her through a heavy oak door and into a large training room. A lump formed in Diamond's throat. She would not cower from the immortal tyrant who sat awaiting her arrival. Unceremoniously, Lord Commander Ream placed a hand on Diamond's shoulder and shoved her forward.

The Queen sat on a plain wooden chair at the far end of the room; beautiful, regal, immaculately dressed—and coiled like a snake ready to strike. A thick black cape hugged the monarch's shoulders, gold buttons pulling it tight across her shapely breasts. The fall of her long golden hair was twisted over one shoulder, shining like spun gold against the sable material that hung down to her feet. One foot— encased in a warm, fur-lined, deerskin boot—tapped impatiently. Diamond hid a small smile of satisfaction at the Queen's outward sign of irritation.

A line of elite guards stood either side of the Queen, all staring blankly forward. Attion walked forward and stood at the far end of the line. Her stomach lurched as his eyes flickered toward her. He lifted his chin and squared his shoulders. At his silent order, she mirrored him. Satisfied, he focused forward.

Right, no cowering. Emotionless and utterly still, the twelve other guards resembled marble statues. Diamond's feet ground to a halt.

"No!" she gasped in shock.

Two young women cowered on their knees in front of the Queen.

Kitty stared forward blankly, her face grey with fright. The wet patch that stained the maid's dress broke Diamond's heart. Something had petrified Kitty enough to soil herself.

Diamond's eyes shot to Rose. A large bruise marred her cheek and blood trickled from her nose. Visibly trembling, Rose met Diamond's gaze. It was all Diamond could do not to run to her friend.

The Queen smiled spitefully and glanced at Kitty before sliding her eyes to Rose.

Diamond deliberately looked away from the only two women who had ever befriended her, trying to take control of the fear that twisted her insides. *Breathe,* she told herself.

Then she noticed the male lounging lazily against the wall behind the Queen's right shoulder. Diamond was unable to tear her eyes away from his face. It was unlike any she had ever seen, distinctive and absurdly perfect in its own way. Amused and arrogant, his deep blue eyes studied her right back. Skin as blue as a summer sky glowed and shimmered in the shafts of sunlight that illuminated him. Along his cheekbones and across the bridge of his nose, there was a ridge of cerulean and silver scales that disappeared under his silky blue hair. He was easily as tall as Hugo. Although not as heavily muscled, this male's body exuded strength and power. His athletic form was clad in material so silky that it looked like he were swathed in liquid sapphire.

His lips twitched into a wide smile at her scrutiny, and she scowled back in instant dislike. Removing his hands from his pockets, he crossed his arms over his chest in one flowing motion, arching a blue brow at her. Diamond looked away. This perfectly astonishing male, who was neither human nor fae, was the least of her worries.

Ream shadowed her as she approached the line of elite guard. The Queen wasted no time on a greeting, no smile at all upon her face. There were no council members for her to pretend for now.

Diamond dipped her head, the only sign of subservience she could force. Resentment and fear tore at her heart. Hugo was not among the elite guard. Diamond firmly pushed thoughts of him away. They would crush her if she let them.

CHAPTER TWENTY-FOUR

A sly smile curled the Queen's lips. "Well, well, half-blood. I have it on good authority that you are excelling in your lessons to become a warrior. It seems your tutors feel you are ready to move on to honing that hideous but useful magic of yours."

Diamond stayed quiet, her heart thumping in her chest. Kitty began to shake. Rose bravely reached for the other woman's hand and grasped it. The Queen flicked her gaze at them, then seemed to dismiss them from her mind.

"Along with the rest of mine and Prince Oden's army, your squadron will leave for the wall tomorrow. However, before I agree to let you leave with them, you need to prove your abilities." The Queen flicked her attention to Rose, who stared at the floor, before moving her green eyes to contemplate Tallo, who stood with a guard at his back near the edge of the room.

Sweat broke out on Diamond's brow. Tension simmered in the air. Even some of the elite guard swallowed hard.

The Queen's eyes suddenly turned dark and stormy.

Trance-like in his movements, the guard behind Tallo pushed the compliant master-at-arms to his knees. Slowly he unsheathed a dagger from his waist and buried the tip in Tallo's neck right under his right ear.

Tallo's eyes widened, but he did not utter a sound of pain, nor did he fight. The look on his face told Diamond he knew it was pointless to resist.

Diamond's head whipped back to the Queen. Cold fingers of terror danced along her spine, her breath escaping in small panicked huffs as another guard stepped forward from the line. His face and eyes were dead.

Cruelly, he yanked Kitty's head back. Kitty mewled like a frightened animal. Before Diamond could utter a word of protest, the guard dragged his blade over the soft skin of Kitty's neck. Blood spilled down her chest. Within seconds the light had faded from her friend's cornflower blue eyes, and she crumpled in a heap.

"*No!*" Diamond cried, launching herself forward, but cruel arms caught her and held her fast.

The Queen narrowed her eyes and laughed coldly. "Just so we are clear. I don't make idle threats. I have another guard close by your friend—Tom, isn't it? I think you have met Thorn before? And of course the prince has a shadow. Not a guard, of course; that would be too obvious. But someone who is more than capable of destroying him if I so wish it. So, if you don't want to lose any more friends, you had better hope you are good enough to be of use to me."

Vomit rushed Diamond's mouth. Sweat slicked her palms. Her eyes stayed fixed on the blood that dripped from the guard's dagger as he stepped behind Rose. Rose squealed and began to sob.

"Quiet! Or I'll have my Lord Commander silence you again," the Queen barked harshly.

Rose took big gasping breaths, trying to master her terror. Diamond felt her admiration for her friend soar.

The Queen stood and prowled over to Rose until she was standing behind the blank-faced guard. He pulled Rose to her feet, then moved to one side. Stepping close enough for her body to brush up against the young healer, the Queen played with Rose's rich brown hair, gently running her fingers through it as if she were caressing a lover.

Diamond clenched her jaw. Rose whimpered and trembled—her legs shaking.

"Shhh," the Queen whispered into the shell of Rose's ear. Her right hand slid slowly over Rose's shoulder and her left hand travelled up into the trembling woman's hair.

Diamond froze with horror, unsure what to do to help her friend. Holding Diamond's eyes, the Queen smiled. Sharp green teeth snapped down behind a row of perfect white ones.

"No!" Diamond gasped. Again, those iron-hard arms grabbed her from behind, instantly clamping her in place.

"Still yourself," Ream hissed in her ear. Repulsed by his closeness, Diamond froze. "Keep your eyes on her. If you look away, I will crush the life from you," he threatened, wrapping a hand around her throat.

Wide-eyed, Rose looked at Diamond, but before either could utter another sound, the Queen sank her teeth into the soft skin on Rose's neck. The young healer went suddenly ridged, her eyes rolling back. A sucking sound came from the Queen's mouth.

Disgust shivered through Diamond, saliva and bile burning her throat. After a few seconds, Rose's body became limp. The Queen held her up as if she were no heavier than a baby. The column of the Queen's throat bobbed as she feasted.

Diamond could not tear her eyes away from the sickening scene. Horrible seconds passed until the Queen dropped Rose's limp body to the ground. Ruby red blood ran down the Queen's chin as Rose convulsed in the large, congealing pool of Kitty's blood. The Queen delicately wiped her chin with her fingers, sucked the blood from them and returned calmly to her seat.

"Well, it's been far too long since I've tasted a woman. Maybe I'll do it more often. Her blood was far sweeter than any of my guards'," she smiled demonically, blood staining her single set of white teeth.

Rose stopped twitching and lay inert next to Kitty's bone white corpse.

Revolted by his proximity, Diamond struggled against Ream's grip. Tears blurred her vision. He gave a satisfied chuckle and gripped her tighter, mockingly nipping the exposed skin of her neck before letting go and moving behind his Queen.

Silent seconds ticked by.

The Queen studied her nails.

She's waiting for something, Diamond realised.

Less than a minute passed before Rose awoke in a daze. Pushing herself into a sitting position, the healer stared around in horror. She did not seem to remember what had just happened. Covered in Kitty's blood, her fingers fluttered to the bleeding wound on her neck. She winced.

"Oh good, you're awake," purred the Queen.

Rose's green eyes darkened as she stood. Unlike the guard who had murdered Kitty, Rose's eyes remained clear, but her poor face contorted into a mask of utter confusion and fear. Diamond swallowed in recognition. This is what had happened inside her head the day she had killed General Edo. Awareness of what was happening, but no control to stop it.

Tallo tracked Rose's progress towards him.

Horrified, Rose pulled another dagger from his guard's waist. Tears ran down her pale cheeks as she was forced to push the point of the blade into the other side of Tallo's neck. The big warrior grimaced but held completely still.

Diamond met the Queen's arctic gaze.

"Prove yourself now and Tallo will live. Fail to impress me and I ensure your friend slits his throat—right before I order one of my guard to slit hers. Or maybe not. Perhaps I'll give her to my esteemed commander for his entertainment, then kill her. Oh," she said, addressing Ream almost as an afterthought. "You did remember to let

Commander Casimir know his student is being tested today, didn't you? I should hate for him to miss the fun."

"Yes, my Queen. I sent a messenger," he replied, bowing his head.

"Not to worry. It *is* a long way from my chambers to the barracks. I expect we will see him very soon."

Triumph resounded in her voice, stealing Diamond's breath. *Her chambers?*Rose was forced to twist her blade. A rivulet of blood ran down Tallo's neck, dripping onto his shirt front.

No, Diamond would not allow herself to think about Hugo. Concentrating on this test was the only way for her friends to survive.

"Prove to me my master-at-arms is worthy of his position, that he has completed the task I gave him to train you." Elegant shoulders shrugged. "Then he can live. Fail, and this traitorous whore, whose friends seek to usurp me, will kill him. If you prove your worth, you will be taken outside the shield where you will learn to summon and control your magic. Make no mistake though, if you still live when this battle with Ragor is done, you *will* return here, to me. You will not try to escape, or I *will* kill anyone and everyone who has ever spoken kindly to you."

"I understand," answered Diamond, rage growing in her belly. Wrathful magic burned a path along her bones. She subdued it, not allowing it to flare. This test had to be completed without magic or the Queen would know the shield did not smother Diamond the way it did other magic wielders.

"Do you?" the Queen asked softly, her eyes drifting now to Attion. Diamond's mouth dried out as her sharp, green teeth glinted menacingly. Then they were gone.

Wrong. This was all so wrong, and Diamond was helpless to stop it. She had never thought she would care what happened to Attion, but she found she did. The threat of those teeth made her blood run cold.

"And just so we are clear, Commander Casimir is mine. His infatuation with you has been amusing and no doubt will be useful, but do not think for one moment I will allow it to last. Oh, and in case you are curious, he's been serving me—*every* night this last week, as he is sworn to do."

Those words, accompanied by her satisfied smirk almost shattered Diamond's world. *Serving her?*

The Queen gave a reptilian smile at the devastation on Diamond's face. "I *know* where your magic comes from," she told Diamond coldly. "You look so much like that whore of a goddess. She stole what was rightfully mine: my throne, my marriage, my child," she spat those words with such venom even Attion's eyes flickered to her. "I knew you were her descendant the moment I laid eyes upon you. I don't know where you came from—neither do I care—but you will use that female's legacy to save all the souls in this valley. Unless you want them to rot in Chaos because of your failure. If Ragor triumphs and I am forced to fight him myself, there will be no valley and no city left. Our warring magic will suck the life from everything. Do you hear me? There will be no survivors save the victor of our fight. So if you want your friends and all these wretched mortals to live, you must stop Ragor from arriving in this city."

The Queen stood. She skirted the congealed blood and came to stand in front of Diamond. Soft lips brushed Diamond's ear. Warm, sweet breath fanned her skin when the Queen spoke. Her voice was so quiet only Diamond could possibly hear her.

"Understand this, *magic wielder*, the blood in your veins is diluted by hundreds of years of breeding with mortal filth. I will *never* allow someone like you to place a claim to my throne. If you try, you will die. But if you love Commander Casimir, then you will do *everything* I ask of you. If you do not, I will use and destroy him. I will get him to commit such atrocities against his friends, against the people of this city and against you that he will wish for death."

It was all Diamond could do to hold back her tears of distress.

Smirking, the Queen returned to her seat.

"I have been contemplating what to do with your disgusting hide when I am done with your magic. I cannot abide to keep you in my city. Lord Firan?" she said imperiously.

Diamond's knees nearly buckled. *Lord Firan? Immortal Lord of the Wetlands?* His reputation as a cruel and arrogant ruler matched the Queen's. No outsiders were ever allowed into his kingdom. Those that tried to enter were never seen again. The blue-skinned male stepped forward, ensuring the Queen did not have to twist to see him.

"Lord Firan, in return for your loyalty, this female will become yours. I cannot tolerate her blood in my kingdom but she will meet your needs," the Queen drawled.

Lord Firan lazily ran his glowing gaze over Diamond. Her stomach tightened with anxiety as the perfect curve of his blue lips twitched into a sensuous smile.

"Indeed she will," he agreed. "My bloodline needs new magic to rejuvenate it. I am more than happy with the terms of our treaty, your grace. As long as you leave some magic in her blood for me to play with."

The Queen nodded once in agreement before both immortals assessed Diamond as if she were a pleasing purchase. Tension simmered in the air. Before she could even snarl, urgent footsteps thumped down the corridor. The heavy oak door slammed open behind Diamond, crashing into the wall.

The Queen's smile quickly left her face. "Commander Casimir, I wondered when you would deign to join us, or even *if* you would." She shrugged gracefully, giving a feline smile. "Now I know."

Diamond whipped her head around, her stomach flipping as the other guards tensed.

Hugo was panting heavily, a light sheen of sweat covering his skin. His magnificent wings were armoured and thrown wide, their silver markings vivid against the shining sapphire blue. The growl that rippled from his throat was more savage than any she had ever heard. He clutched his Silverbore swords, the muscles of his neck and throat bulging and rigid with tension.

Diamond gulped. He seemed taller and more menacing than ever. It was then she noticed his eyes. A strange, feral light glowed from them. Fire, but much more, as if another being glared through them.

Those eyes quickly scanned the room.

"No," she whispered.

In that split second, Diamond realised he was assessing where—and who—to attack. Before he had time to act, a wave of powerful magic slammed across the room, knocking his massive bulk straight into the wall. Plaster dust exploded into the air.

With a wave of her hand, the Queen's magic cleared the dust to show Hugo pinned to the wall, a foot off the floor, unable to move. His swords, still clasped in his big fists, were forced flat against the wall.

"Commander! You may wish to consider your actions from this point on *very, very* carefully. Remember your oath to serve *me*. Remember how your past indiscretions ended." There was such quiet lethal warning in the Queen's voice.

Tense silence hung in the room. Only the sound of Hugo's heavy breathing and frustrated growl filled it.

Slowly Hugo met the Queen's gaze, and his eyes returned to normal.

Smirking, she lowered his bulk to the ground. He inhaled, exhaled, then he pushed himself away from the wall.

Terror and elation filled Diamond's heart in equal measure. *He came for me!* That snarl at the Queen had been for her. His armoured wings and swords proved his intent to fight for her. But at what cost? Fear rippled down Diamond's spine. Such an outward sign of dissent, of aggression against one's monarch must be considered treason.

Hugo's swords were ripped from his grip by a flick of the Queen's wrists.

"You do not need those, commander," she informed him coldly. "Calm yourself."

Hugo ground his teeth, his chest heaving as he fought to control his rage. He slowly folded his wings down into his back.

"There, that's better. Now, come to me," the Queen ordered.

Diamond blinked at that command. Hugo's jaw muscles tensed, and his eyes were full of pain as they met hers. Then, like an obedient dog, Hugo stalked to the Queen's side. Diamond swallowed her nausea, pain jolting through her heart. In return, sorrow seeped through his magic, which flickered like the touch of a butterfly's wings against hers before it was gone.

Ream remained close behind his queen, his eyes not leaving Hugo for a second.

The immortal monarch twisted gracefully. Her venomous green eyes lingered on Diamond before she raked them wantonly up and down Hugo's body. Her tongue flicked around those ruby red lips as if wanting to taste him.

Hugo ignored his monarch's attention, fixing his gaze on the far wall.

The blue-skinned stranger, however, observed the Queen and Hugo steadily. The lord carefully took in every detail of the unfolding events before he turned his deep blue eyes back to Diamond. There was something strangely familiar about that gaze.

Diamond swallowed, holding that ocean-blue stare. She would not give into the fear poisoning her heart and mind. She could survive this. For Hugo, for everyone else, she *had* to.

CHAPTER TWENTY-FIVE

At a nod from the Queen, the elite guard formed a circle around Diamond. She blanched, her legs shaking. Her head twisted to behold the circle of fearsome warriors. They all wore light, leather breast plates over linen shirts, knee-high leather boots with re-enforced shin guards and close-fitting leggings. Diamond gulped. She had no weapons, only her hands and feet.

There was no warning before a boot landed in her back, but she had been waiting, her senses alert. Throwing out her front leg was instinctive. She bent her knee to stop her forward momentum and kept her body upright, even as her spine screamed in pain. Directly in front of her, a guard shifted his weight sideways, aiming a kick at her ribs. Diamond swiftly dropped onto her side, and his boot passed harmlessly above her. Bending her upper knee, she kicked him with all her strength between his legs. A high pitched yelp of pain filled the air as her boot connected with his groin. The guard sank to his knees at her side.

Thanking the goddess for the weakness of males, Diamond grunted with effort, swung her leg in an arc over the back of his neck and swiftly slammed his face down into the floor as hard as she could, leaving him unconscious.

Without a doubt, Diamond knew she fought for the life of her friends. If she showed any fear or hesitation, the Queen would see it as failure. Wrapping her heart in ice and blocking out Kitty's corpse, Diamond moved swiftly and efficiently. All those long, painful days of training, of drilling now took over. The elite guards did not hesitate to attack, intent on breaking her into little pieces. Randomly, they struck, one opponent at a time. Diamond fought and fought, constantly holding back her magic as her fists struck leather and flesh.

Will there be no end to this?

Her muscles and bones throbbed with agony, tiredness slamming into her in great waves. It became harder and harder to ignore it. They were deliberately wearing her down, destroying her piece by piece. A mistake now would cost her dearly. Moving swiftly, her bruised arms blocked a barrage of vicious punches from a sinewy guard. Her lungs burned and she blinked away stars from her vision.

Sensing her fatigue, the Queen laughingly instructed two guards to attack simultaneously.

Diamond did not have time to think, only react as Attion complied. Rapid and powerful, he moved against her right as she threw her last opponent over her shoulder. Spinning on the balls of her feet she blocked and struck against Attion and the other guard until her forearms screamed and her knuckles—already split and bruised—splattered blood across the floor. Dragging in ragged breaths, her chest burned. The air seemed too hot, too thin to appease her body's demands.

Fatigue slammed into her. Trembling violently, her weak legs sent her off-balance as she spun to defend an attack from behind. Mis-timing her block, Attion's large fist collided with her bruised cheek and nose.

A sickening snap—and her nose broke. Pain raged through her face. Diamond screamed. Her legs immediately buckled, and she fell face-first into the hard floor. Her forehead struck the flagstones, rattling her brain and stealing her sight.

Before she could even attempt to struggle up, Attion dropped to his knees and grabbed her. With no remorse, he wrapped his fist in her hair and yanked her head back until she had to struggle onto her knees or lose a chunk of hair. Choking and coughing on the blood that filled her airway, Diamond stared into his eyes. His hand rose to strike at her throat. Realisation made her heart miss a beat. Unless the Queen said otherwise, he would kill her.

I will not yield! She snarled and fought, frantically sucking blood into her mouth. Gambling that somewhere under his mask was the male who had trained her, who had patiently corrected her time and again, who *could* respect another, she forcefully spat in his face. As she hoped, big clots landed in his eyes and shot into his mouth.

Attion recoiled and approval flashed in his eyes before he loosened his grip.

Grabbing that small advantage, Diamond spun herself about in his grasp, ignoring the pain as a patch of her hair ripped out. Mustering her remaining strength, she drove her elbow up into his jaw. A loud crack, and his teeth smashed together. Attion toppled backwards into a heap, landing with a disgusting squelch in Kitty's congealed blood.

"Enough!" yelled the Queen.

Diamond was still on her knees breathing hard. Blood ran down her chin, dripping onto her shirt. Blowing the bright red drops from her damaged nose, Diamond pushed herself shakily to her feet. Her glare at the Queen was demonic and full of hate. Rage buzzed through Diamond's veins, dulling the pain in her face as she watched the Queen reach out her long slim fingers and wrap them around Hugo's hand, possession oozing from her.

Hugo flinched at her touch, but his eyes remained forward, his hand limp in hers. His face blanched of colour but no matter how much Diamond willed it, he would not look at her. Her heart lurched painfully at the sight of his hand clutched in the Queen's. It seemed such an obscene, intimate gesture above Kitty's glassy-eyed corpse.

Grief and guilt and raging, jealous anger at Hugo's impotence threatened to tear Diamond apart. But she fought. Fought with everything she had for control of her emotions and panic. Blood dripped from her nose, pain sparking stars across her vision as she gingerly wiped her nostrils.

It did not matter that Diamond was managing to control her emotions. The tempestuous force of her magic escaped her control, swirling around her in an invisible storm.

Hugo's eyes widened in alarm as his own reeled forward.

None could see the wave of shadow and serpents that merged desperately into the ribbons of Diamond's light. Mere seconds passed as anguish seeped from Hugo's raw magic into her, belying the blankness on his face. She could feel him pushing through her skin into her blood, his magic licking along her bones. Dark magic pushed hers to react, almost as though he had lost the ability to control it. She smothered her gasp, feeling his need to protect, to rage against the threat surrounding her.

Almost using up her remaining energy, Diamond forced Hugo from her body, pushing him away and suppressing her power with sheer effort of will.

Directing a snarl at him, she hoped he would understand. He needed to take control of himself, and quickly. It was stupid to think the Queen would allow Diamond to live if she sensed her magic was not subdued by the shield and the Queen's influence.

With no warning, a wave of exhaustion hit Diamond and the room spun. She took a shaky step forward to regain her balance. Of course the Queen chose to misread her action.

"Really? You think to attack me?" Her laugh was pure venom. "Oh, I don't think so. Hugo." An order. "Let's see how well student and teacher are matched, shall we?"

Out of the corner of her eye, Diamond saw Lord Firan straighten up and uncross his arms. A strange reaction from someone supposedly neutral to the events unfolding in front of him.

Attion, who had regained consciousness, grunted as he quickly pushed himself across the floor. Spitting blood from his mouth, he shook his head as if trying to regain his equilibrium. But for the first time, Diamond saw a flash of revulsion in the elite guard's eyes as he looked at the Queen.

Hugo stepped past Attion, his eyes wholly black, his face dark and unforgiving.

Diamond's throat hurt. *It's only a mask,* she told herself, but gulped as fear shuddered through her whole body. It was clear Diamond could never triumph against Hugo, not broken and bleeding as she was. It seemed the Queen was amusing herself at their expense, and even Lord Firan had realised it.

"Hugo?" Diamond wheezed through ravaged lips. "Please. Don't do this," she ended on a desperate whisper.

But no matter what emotion Diamond had sensed a moment ago, one look at Hugo's unbearably blank face told her he would not hold back. Without hesitation, he launched himself through the air, kicking out sideways at her stomach.

With no hope of stopping him, Diamond spun agilely out of his reach. On any other day she could swiftly outmanoeuvre his bulk, but she was so tired. Her arms and legs quivered with pain and exhaustion. It was impossible to hold back a sob of despair at the lack of emotion in his face and even harder to take control of her panic.

One long stride and Hugo spun on his leading foot, swinging his shoulder into a vicious back fist that would have taken her out and broken all the bones in her face if it had connected. She stumbled out of his reach, knowing neither of them had a choice but to fight. That knowledge did not stop her anger at the Queen, at Hugo and at the whole gods damned situation.

Diamond blinked, forcing her magical sight in to play. Breath-taking colours and energy swirled around the living souls in the room, filling it with a kaleidoscope of light. Diamond paid no heed to such beauty. She hardened her heart and her resolve. Her life would be worth nothing if her friends died.

I will not give the Queen reason to brand me weak or a coward! Suppressing her fear, Diamond bunched her fists and cricked her neck. She would fight with every last bit of her strength to keep them alive.

With sudden clarity, Diamond saw the midnight shroud of Hugo's energy. Silver serpents snapped wildly through the sapphire-stained shadow. They pulsed right before Hugo attacked again. Like lightening, Diamond dipped under his punch, twisted fluidly and landed her fist with as much force as she could muster into his ribs. Her knuckles screamed as yet more skin ripped off against the tough leather. Swiftly, she shifted her stance and slammed a foot down onto the back of his knee, screaming with effort.

A grunt and a flicker of surprise registered in Hugo's eyes as she passed from his line of sight. Not having the luxury of satisfaction, Diamond pivoted on her standing foot and aimed a kick at his back. Her instep smashed hard into his kidneys before she snapped her leg back, then shifted to swing her leg upwards and slam her heel into his jaw. Hugo grunted and there was a sharp intake of breath from the Queen.

Lord Firan smiled broadly.

Too experienced to falter, Hugo whirled to face her.

His face blurred and the room tilted. *No.* She couldn't faint, not now. No one else was going to die today because of her. Anger and grief raged in her heart as her eyes found Kitty's drained corpse.

Attion stared wide-eyed from Diamond to Hugo to the Queen, using the pause to drag himself to his feet and out of harm's way.

A slight snarl curled Hugo's lips, his obsidian eyes narrowed as he noticed Diamond sway unsteadily on her feet.

Her body was almost done. Spitting a globule of blood and saliva at his feet, Diamond raised her chin defiantly even as her heart fractured. This was not the fae who had sought her company night after night, who had proudly escorted her around his city or who had held her in his arms so gently and vowed to save her life. This unfeeling warrior was not that friend. Logic told her Hugo was doing this because he had no choice, but Diamond did not want to listen to logic. All she understood was, just as before, his promises had become hopeless dreams. Once again, Hugo had become the Queen's cold-hearted killer.

Violet eyes met endless shadow and—time stopped. His eyelashes flickered, then Hugo launched into a barrage of punches at a frightening speed. Now she knew how much he had been holding back all these weeks. Hugo was not fatigued and far outmatched Diamond in both strength and experience. Quelling her despair, she fought as hard as she could, managing to evade his fists for mere seconds only. He swung a vicious hook punch. Diamond jumped back. Her foot slipped in Kitty's blood. Unbalanced, she flailed her arms.

Hugo swiftly kicked her off her feet.

Air left Diamond's body in a rush. Retching, she plummeted onto her back, her head slamming into the stone floor. Blinding light shot through her skull, stars exploding across her vision as she lay choking on her own blood.

Before she could comprehend what had happened, Hugo's bulk landed on her. Somehow he did not crush her. His powerful thighs squeezed just enough to pin her battered body down.

Goddess help me! I can't breathe! He's going to suffocate me!

Remorse flashed in Hugo's eyes at the same time merciful shadow swamped Diamond's thoughts. Cool and dark, it stole her conscious mind, willing her away from the pain in her body. She gladly let herself fall into the blackness, right before his punch landed on her jaw.

187

CHAPTER TWENTY-SIX

The Queen narrowed her attention on Hugo. He could feel the heavy weight of it bowing his shoulders. Leaving Diamond inert and bleeding beside him, he changed position, bending onto one knee. This act was one of necessity, not respect. He could do nothing else. He was utterly drained.

What have I done?

Pain and remorse ripped at his heart. He clamped his teeth together so hard they hurt, bitter in the knowledge his reaction to this test had been what the Queen wanted to see. She had used his desperation to help Diamond against both of them. This despicable female had ordered him to guard her chambers this week in order to keep him and Diamond apart. The Queen had learned of the time Hugo had spent by Diamond's side, but no punishment had been given, which had only served to increase Hugo's anxiety. His only orders had been to conduct Diamond's training via Tallo and Attion, and not return to the barracks. Hugo had, of course, requested daily reports about Diamond's progress. Tallo and Attion had wanted to ask what was going on. Neither did, and Hugo had ignored both their silent questions and the pity in their eyes.

It had not come as a surprise to learn the Queen had summoned Diamond this morning. And no matter how stupid he knew it to be, he could not stop his desperate need to protect her. The knowledge that Diamond was alone and facing the Queen had stolen his common sense. As soon as he had entered the training room, a savage urge to rip the Queen limb from limb had taken hold of Hugo. He would have destroyed everyone in that room if that wave of magic hadn't knocked him off his feet. The force of it had shocked him from his protective rage.

Beside him, Diamond gurgled and moaned.

Once again he had failed her. Once again he had capitulated to the Queen to save Diamond from further pain. Head down, Hugo stared at the blood-covered floor, thankful beyond reason for the venom bond that had allowed him to sweep Diamond into unconsciousness before his fist had landed on her jaw.

A wicked smile crossed the Queen's perfect features as the noise of Diamond's bubbling breaths filled the room. Hugo's heart beat a rapid rhythm against his ribs. She was choking, drowning in her own blood.

He needed to help her.

To stop himself from reaching out, he gripped his own thighs until his nails broke the skin under his leggings.

The Queen approached and placed a slim finger under his chin, raising his face. She looked into his eyes and smiled. Hugo knew he had condemned himself to her bite. It was only a question of when. Tenderly, she stroked a finger down the line of his scar. His teeth clenched at the contact, a wave of disgust rippling through him. His stomach tightened, but he hid his fear at that contact.

"You have done well. Her body certainly *has* become a weapon. Maybe in more ways than one," she mused in a purr of satisfaction. Icy green eyes glittered as she glanced at Tallo.

The master-at-arms sagged with relief as the two daggers were pulled from his skin. Blood ran freely down his neck, adding to the metallic stench already filling Hugo's nose. It was hard to prevent his sigh of relief at seeing his friend free.

"I'm so pleased my master-at-arms will not die today. Although maybe that whore of a healer needs to. Her lover informed me she is working with the rebels. A pity he has disappeared. I should like to have spoken with him further about that group of betraying filth."

Contemplating Rose, the Queen addressed the quaking healer. "Oh, don't worry, child. We will soon see how much—or how little—you know. Lord Commander Ream is going to have a little fun with you when we get back to the palace."

Rose cried out in terror as Ream grabbed her arm.

Hugo kept his eyes on the cold green depths of the Queen's, not daring to look at Rose even as his gut twisted in alarm.

"Hugo, you will take my new weapon to the wall. I have released my hold on her magic. She will be able to summon more than just a spark now, and the further from the city she gets, the less influence the shield will have. Make her use her legacy. I *want* it to grow. She needs to stop the Wraith Lord, especially now that I have the necklace. Oh, and whilst you are away from my chambers, do not think to visit hers." She laughed coldly. "Remember what happened to your last whore, Hugo. Spare her that fate. You are there to stop her losing control, that's all." Sharp fingernails curled around his jaw and dug into the sensitive scar tissue on his face. Hugo forced himself not to wince.

"She may have charmed you and awakened forbidden feelings, but make no mistake: you are mine. That half-blood filth belongs to Lord Firan now. The souls and ships he has pledged for the price of her body are far more important to Valentia than she will be after this battle is over. But don't worry, if she lives through it, I will not take all her magic. I have agreed to leave Lord Firan enough to make use of." She sucked in her bottom lip, as if savouring Hugo's pain. "Did it make you angry seeing these men beat her bloody? Think how you will feel this time around if you give me cause to let Ream have her. Something tells me Lord Firan will still take the leftovers." She chuckled. Soft. Venomous. Satisfied. "You see, heirs with magical blood in their veins are so important to him, just as mine will be to me when you break my curse on Winter Solstice."

Hugo could not think straight. The urge to rip her throat out nearly undid him.

No. She can still kill everyone in this room.

"I expect, commander, the next few weeks will be most unpleasant for you. After all, you are fae. You should have protected the female who has stolen your heart. I think she will hate you very much now. You, who was too late to stop me from selling her like the whore she is. You, who stood by and watched these males attack her. And you, who beat her when she was already broken and bleeding," she tsked. "You really are a bastard, aren't you?"

Hugo's gorge rose, burning his insides.

Curling her lips at the turmoil in his eyes, she ran her fingers over his cheek. "Oh, Hugo, my poor, young love. You simply needed to remember that you are mine. Don't forget again. The Lord Commander is itching to play games with you both. Go back to being that cold, powerful guard who I find so fascinating." Inclining her head toward Diamond, the Queen's bejewelled crown glinted. "It won't matter to her anymore. You played such a brutal part in destroying her, I think she will seek comfort from someone else now, don't you? I doubt Prince Oden will turn her down; after all, he *has* been there to comfort her before."

Hugo swallowed as the Queen leaned in and brushed her mouth lightly against his.

"And Hugo? Do not try and escape your fate. Your blood and your body are mine."

Hugo loosed a big breath as the Queen and her guards left, though his reprieve was short-lived. The Lord of the Wetlands squatted on his haunches in front of Hugo.

Eyes as deep blue as Hugo's own glinted as the immortal lord glanced down at Diamond's ruined face. "Now that will never do," the lord said softly and reached out an elegant blue finger.

Hugo held his temper in check as Lord Firan touched Diamond's broken nose. It immediately cracked back into place. Hugo felt queasy with relief as Diamond moaned. At least she was conscious enough to feel pain.

"There, that's better. I don't want my prize marred forever," he said, wicked amusement shining in his eyes. Without hesitation, he laid those elegant blue hands on Diamond's head, running his palms down the length of her body to her toes. A haze of magic emanated from him, flowing over her. The purple bruising peppering Diamond's body lessened, and with shock, Hugo saw her damaged skin begin to knit together.

Despite the relief and gratitude he felt at seeing her wounds heal, Hugo tensed. He balled his fists, a feral instinct making him want to break this lord's immortal neck for assuming he could touch Diamond like that. She was not and never would be Firan's prize.

Smiling arrogantly, right into Hugo's furious eyes, Lord Firan lifted Diamond's broken, bleeding hand. His tongue flicked over her knuckles licking her blood. Shuddering with pleasure, he swallowed. "Hmm, pure as the driven snow." His smile spread into a wide grin, showing small perfect teeth. "I wonder if she will remain so after being at the handsome prince's beck and call." He dropped his voice almost conspiratorially. "If I were you, commander, I would keep her away from the amorous prince or make her yours completely. After all, we both know you can." The lord reached out a finger touching Hugo's lips even as he bared his teeth. "If you understand me?" he grinned.

Hugo wanted to wipe that satisfied and knowing smirk right off this male's face. With that same finger Lord Firan scooped up more of Diamond's blood from the side of her ravaged mouth and sucked it. Holding Hugo's eyes, he swallowed.

Hugo clamped down on his absolute white-hot rage. How did this arrogant prick know about Hugo's ability to bite? Hugo's whole body became fluid, ready to move, to kill. Challenge roared to life in his eyes, turning silver flecks to bright burning flame. He would not hide his magic, his power for destruction from this bastard.

With narrowed eyes, Lord Firan cocked his head and waited, seeming more curious than concerned about what Hugo would do next.

Hugo battled with his rage and instincts to kill this lord who dared touch Diamond. *It will not help her or me to kill Firan — yet.*

Hugo dropped his eyes to the floor. He could wait.

The Lord of The Wetlands gave a satisfied chuckle and put a hand on Hugo's shoulder, patting him. His voice dripped with amusement as he stood tall. "Your self-control is admirable, commander. I know you want to kill me. But do not fret, my young friend, your secret is safe with me. Rest assured, when Miss Gillon returns here and becomes mine, I will take extra special care of her."

He grinned as he walked away.

CHAPTER TWENTY-SEVEN

Hugo allowed himself to collapse, falling from his knees to sit next to Diamond. Shaking from head to toe, he took a ragged breath to calm his tumbling emotions. He made himself look at her. She was ravaged, swollen almost beyond recognition.

Bile rose in his throat as he relived what had just happened. She had fought so hard and so skilfully. He was so incredibly proud of her— and so utterly appalled at himself. Hugo's shoulders sagged, the face of another pretty young woman merging into Diamond's as he closed his eyes.

This beautiful, brave woman, who held his heart in her hands, would never trust him again. She would believe he had abandoned her for the Queen. He wouldn't blame her in the least. Every little bit of mistrust and resentment would be deserved. Despair threatened to overwhelm Hugo and, for the first time in his life, he felt helpless tears burn his eyes.

A horrible gurgling sound bubbled with each heaving breath Diamond took.

"I am so sorry," he whispered in her ear, his gut twisting as he rolled her sideways, letting the blood run from her mouth. It pooled under her cheek as she coughed and gagged, but at least the horrible noises eased.

"I had to do what she said or everything would be lost. Your friends, this city. She would have destroyed you. I couldn't let that happen..." His voice broke. Sickened, he tried not think about Rose.

Urgent footsteps entered the room.

Reese blanched as he beheld Kitty's corpse. He sprinted across the blood-covered floor, the rest of the squadron close behind. Swearing at the top of his voice, he looked as though he wanted to slit Hugo's throat. "Stay away from her, captain," Hugo growled. Though Hugo didn't blame him.

To his credit Reese ignored Hugo and dropped to his knees next to Diamond. The rest of the squadron fanned out around them, standing close enough that cold, hard steel glinted in Hugo's peripheral vision. Apparently their respect for him had just disintegrated. A growl rippled from his throat. He didn't have time for this. They needed to go so he could take care of her. He had to try and put this right. "Reese. Stand back," he ordered quietly.

"Or what? You don't get to decide what happens to her right now. *Look* at her!" Reese spat, meeting his eyes. "Why? Why do this to her when everyone here knows she means more to you than the Queen ever will?"

"Because the Queen knows it too! Because if I hadn't, the Queen would have destroyed her in far worse ways than I ever could, you ignorant fool!" bellowed Hugo, gesturing at Kitty.

Tallo did not interfere, but he could not look at Hugo.

Hugo understood their reaction. His stomach roiled in self-disgust. Forgiveness would never be deserved. Blood rushed through his ears as his inadequacy and failure hit him. Diamond had called him pathetic all those weeks ago. How very right she was.

Diamond stirred at his raised voice. They all froze as she whimpered his name. Immediately, and with infinite gentleness, he lifted her head into his lap and stroked her blood-matted hair out of her battered face.

"Please. Hugo. Just. Leave. Me. Alone," she rasped, tears running down her cheeks and mixing with her blood. Speaking brought on a bout of coughing.

He watched helplessly as she curled into a foetal position. He was the cause of her agony; he had done this. An invisible hand gripped his heart and squeezed. Pain and despair like he had never imagined stole his breath. She didn't want him near her. She would not forgive him. His hand stilled upon her head. When he didn't move she repeated her words, louder this time.

"She wants you to go," said Tallo softly, placing a hand gently on Hugo's shoulder. The older man's eyes were full of pity and understanding. Hugo did not notice. He only felt his composure begin to crumble. He wanted to scream and shout and beg her forgiveness, but he was aware the whole squadron was watching him. They were ready to rip him apart if he didn't leave, and he had no stomach for hurting any of them right now.

Summoning all his willpower, Hugo shut down his heart, wrapping it in a cage of shadow that turned his eyes obsidian. Wiping all expression from his face, he placed Diamond's head gently on the floor and stood. It was the hardest thing he had ever done to walk away from her.

CHAPTER TWENTY-EIGHT

The next morning came far too soon for Diamond. She stayed still, listening to the sound of rain and wind lashing the loose window frames. Icy gusts howled, working their way in through cracks in the old stone walls, seeping between the fibres of her thin blankets. Diamond shivered, her muscles screaming in protest.

Agony flashed behind her eyes as she turned on her side. She gasped. Such wretchedness only served to remind Diamond that yesterday had been real, that Kitty's death was her fault and that Rose's nightmare was only beginning. Diamond sobbed into her pillow. Tallo had gravely informed Diamond that Rose had been taken to the palace. Her impotence was a crushing, guilt-ridden weight on her heart. Diamond could do nothing to help her friend. Is this how Hugo felt when he had no choice but to comply with the Queen's wishes?

It took enormous effort to push herself upright and even more to fight the wave of nausea set off by her pounding head. Taking deep calming breaths, she waited for the room to stop spinning, then gingerly moved her legs off the bed until she could sit on the edge.

The squadron was to leave with the rest of the army today, and she was to go with them. With a heavy heart Diamond surveyed her body. Her nightie was small enough that it did not hide the swellings and purple bruises that deformed her arms and legs. Surprisingly, her skin was not as damaged as she had expected.

Tallo and Reese had helped her back to her room yesterday, both of them saying very little; but they had tried their very best to be gentle as they laid her on her bed and called the healer. After reassuring them she would be fine, they reluctantly left her to the healer's ministrations.

Bathed in spell-infused tonics, then covered in salve, she had allowed the healer to bandage her hands and check her for internal bleeding before crawling into bed to rest.

She preferred to concentrate on the pain throbbing through her body rather than acknowledging the agony in her heart. Burning tears slipped from her eyes. She knew how Hugo felt; she now had a taste of the powerlessness he struggled with. But he had taken part in beating her unconscious.

Another wave of nausea made the room spin wildly. Diamond breathed through it as she tried to sort through the sickening jumble of emotions that vied for supremacy. Cold and shaking, she put her hands over her face. What should she believe? That he truly felt something for her, that he would fight for her; or that he was willing to drop to his knees like a coward every time the Queen ordered it?

As if he knew she was thinking about him, the door opened. Hugo loomed in the hallway, a huge silhouette against the yellow glow of the lamps. Diamond lowered her hands from her tear-stained face, unable to speak.

Stepping inside, Hugo closed the door, leaning his back against it. His onyx hair hung loose around his shoulders, the deep blue streaks shimmering brightly. Haunted sapphire eyes moved from her toes, up over her bare legs and arms. His muscles clenched as he ground his jaw and raised his eyes to her face. Then his whole body slumped, making him look defeated in a way she had never seen before.Diamond hid her shock, biting down on the tears that threatened to overwhelm her at the sight of him. "I didn't invite you in," she forced out coldly. "You can close the door on your way out."

"Diamond, please," he said softly, reaching out to her. Almost immediately he dropped his hand, recognising the disappointment and pain she allowed into her eyes.

"Please what, Hugo? Swoon into your arms? Show you forgiveness for letting the Queen sell me like a piece of meat, or for standing by whilst I was beaten black and blue? Oh no, let me think. Of course! You want forgiveness for serving the Queen who slit my friend's throat in front of me, who bit Rose and drank her blood!" Her voice shook with suppressed rage.

"Diamond, please. I tried. She would have killed everyone you love. Please. Forgive me." He sounded wretched, pleading.

"No!" she yelled, her ire only fuelled by his desperate face. "She killed my friend! And you! Where were you? In her chambers, *serving* her? You were too late to stop any of it! Was that your plan, Hugo? Be so late you would not have to fight for me or for my friends?" *Unfair,* screamed her rational mind, but she was too angry with herself and with him to thrust those thoughts away. "No, I will not forgive you. What happens the next time you are ordered by that evil witch to do her bidding? Will you slit my throat as easily as that guard slit Kitty's? Will you watch me bleed at your feet?" she raged bitterly, not caring who could hear.

"No!" he spat. "By the goddess, Diamond, I had seconds to make a choice, and I made it. I don't give a shit what anyone else thinks, but please, try and understand why I went to her when all I wanted to do was rip her apart. Her magic stopped me in my tracks! If I had fought for you, she would have broken you and me into pieces, bone by bone, and killed everyone you care about. There would have been no help from the guards. You saw what she has done to them, and those she hasn't bitten crave the chance to exact revenge on me for receiving the Queen's favour, for still being alive when they *know* I have magic!"

He took a tentative step towards her, expelling a steadying breath.

Their gaze met and locked, and that magical bond twanged in her core as if a chord had been pulled tight. Belligerently, she fought it and stared him down. She heard what he said, even understood it, but the mountain of rage and disappointment in her heart seemed insurmountable.

"What happened to Rose?" she hissed, almost not wanting to know.

He paled even further. "Ream has her in the dungeons," he answered quietly.

Diamond swallowed her nausea, trying not to think about the tortures her friend could be suffering even now.

"Diamond, please. I had to back down. At least this way you have time to learn about your magic, to strengthen it. You can fight for your friends and the people of this valley. At least now you stand a chance of getting away."

"Shut up!" she hissed. Hurt spilled from her heart into her violet eyes. Ignoring her pain, she pushed herself off the bed, limping forward. Her glare flayed his soul. It was agony to breathe let alone talk. "Don't justify Kitty's death or Rose's torture with my life! I would rather die than subject my friend to the suffering that will be hers. If by some miracle I live through this battle with Ragor, I will become Lord Firan's property—or had you forgotten that? But what of you? You will not die, at least not until *your* Queen gets what she lusts after, and that isn't too far away, is it?"

She cocked her head to one side. Curling her top lip contemptuously Diamond looked him up and down, just like the Queen had done. Fresh resentment, coupled with raging jealousy, burned her heart.

It did not matter what Hugo had done, she wanted to touch him again, to feel his hot skin under her fingers, to feel his arms hold her and his whispers tell her she would be safe. Instead, she swallowed those damning thoughts and bunched her fists, taunting him, "Or maybe, for all your protestations, that's what you really want? Hmmm? Is this all some elaborate game? Am I your amusement, a bit of cheap entertainment until Winter Solstice arrives? Until you get to—" she never completed her sentence.

Skin flushed with anger, eyes swirling with dangerous silver fire, Hugo stepped right up to her, baring his teeth savagely. "Stop it! Don't you dare demean what I feel for you! I came here hoping you'd understand, even forgive me for what I had to do. Gods! I was so proud of you, fighting so hard, for so long. Hurting you so badly was the hardest thing I have ever done in my life—and believe me when I say I have committed many vile acts at the behest of that immortal bitch." The fire died from his eyes only to be replaced with sorrow. Hugo looked at his Nexus, his venom bound soulmate, and dropped to his knees in front of her. "Diamond, I am begging for your forgiveness, for your understanding, but I would do it all again if it stopped her from killing you and everyone you care about," his voice wavered as he looked up at her.

Shock at seeing him on his knees left her speechless.

"Diamond, please..." he implored as her silence continued.

Unable to stop herself, her hand snapped out to strike him hard across his cheek. Her bandages muffled the power of her blow and did nothing to ease the pain and confusion in her heart. An expression of raging hurt and despair swamped his face and, for the first time since she had known him, Hugo dropped his eyes. Frustrated and angry, she pulled off her bandages.

The Queen's guard knelt in a state of misery as though waiting for her punishment.

With a sharp *crack*, her hand connected with his scarred cheek.

Hugo took her blow, not even trying to defend himself. An air of utter defeat and dejected acceptance settled upon his broad shoulders. It smothered his energy until she could barely feel it. Her palm stung as she stared at this proud fae warrior, who had both saved her life and destroyed it. But causing such suffering in someone she cared about so much, no matter what he had done, shamed her. Deep down Diamond knew he had saved her from a fate far worse than one beating.

Agonising silence stretched between them. Hugo continued to stare at the floor, his shoulders slumped. Pain etched the golden contours of his face and he shut his eyes. Regret squeezed her chest tight, making it difficult to breathe.

"Get out," she whispered, tears burning her eyes. Turning away from him, she found herself suddenly exhausted. "I need to be alone for a while."

Hugo lifted his head and stared at her, his throat bobbing as he swallowed.

"Was I not clear, commander? Leave," she sobbed, tears running down her face now.

Hugo pushed himself up, his eyes shining darkly.

"Don't let her win, Diamond. Even if you can't forgive me, the ship will still be waiting on Winter Solstice. Please—be on it."

With that he turned and left.

CHAPTER TWENTY-NINE

Dressing in her armour was a painful and slow process. The tough leather hurt her swollen limbs. Persevering, Diamond struggled to fasten the laces and ties with her stiff, swollen hands. She buckled her Silverbore sword around her waist, slipped two throwing knives into her vambraces and fixed her sleek Silverbore daggers to her hips and thighs. By the time it was done, she was exhausted.

Sitting on the bed, she listened to the rain pounding against the window, and grimaced. It was going to be a miserable journey. Downing a phial of painkiller, she grabbed her thick, waxed cape and drew it on. Gingerly, she lifted the sack containing her meagre belongings, flicked her cowl up and joined the squadron in the winter storm.

After this battle, if she still lived, Diamond *would* be on that ship to Gar Anon. It was time to discover who she really was, who her mother had been. Busy thinking of the Queen's words about her blood and heritage, Diamond did not register her booted feet sloshing through the surface water or the mud that splattered the back of her legs, nor did she register the hidden scrutiny of the warrior who sat proudly upon his stallion, distancing himself from the scurrying men and women of the squadron.

Diamond hurried towards the stables.

And what of Hugo? He knows nothing about who he is. Guilt burned inside her. At least Diamond had known her father, had been loved by him. Hugo had never experienced anything other than coldness and abuse. She swallowed her sorrow for him. These thoughts were too much to consider right now.

Tallo led forward Luna, a gentle mare Diamond had ridden before. He did not speak, but nodded grimly and continued his task of organising the masses of troops leaving for the wall. Diamond blinked as he walked away. Her heart lifted to see him alive. Struggling onto her mare's back, she caught sight of Hugo. His horse rose above any other, sleekly muscled and shining wetly in the moonlight. From under the cowl of his hood, sapphire eyes caught her gaze, and her stomach tightened painfully.

She wanted desperately to forgive him, but she couldn't. Not yet. Lifting her face to the icy rain, she let it hit her bruised face. For a moment the pain served as a distraction from the confusion in her heart. She understood, even empathised with, Hugo's situation, but she was still angry with him.

Diamond tugged on Luna's reins, urging her forward at a steady plod. The crack of whips and the protesting growls of Ometons filled her ears, as the great northern snow beasts pulled on the chains and winches that opened the reinforced palace gates. The column of warriors, horses and supply carts wound its way down through the cobbled streets of the city.

Hugo briskly walked his horse up beside her. The magnificent animal whinnied at Luna, who turned her silver head and huffed back.

Diamond's skin prickled beneath her armour as tendrils of Hugo's magic reach out, and whether she wanted it to or not, his very presence made her feel more alive. Anger, disappointment and something far deeper sparked in her bruised heart. No smile reached her lips, though Diamond steadily met his gaze. The warmth of understanding filtered through their magic.

Unbidden, her eyes strayed to the distant ocean where tall, white crested waves broke fiercely on the grey expanse of water. Before Diamond could discover who she was, Ragor needed to be destroyed; to do that, she would have to allow Hugo close enough to help her gain control of her true magic. What she had been playing with in her training was only a fraction of her power. Her heart stumbled at that knowledge.

Diamond switched her vision. She watched as the silver serpents of Hugo's energy tentatively reached out for the pale violet ribbons of her own. Without glancing at him, she allowed them to touch, just a little. Sensing her acquiescence, the serpents entwined around her magic until warmth snaked around her wrists, her waist and her shoulders, stroking her, beseeching her for forgiveness. The feeling was so right, so familiar, she couldn't pull away.

Hugo snapped his spine straight and turned his sapphire gaze on her. Warmth and strength seeped through her ravaged body as his magic attempted to sooth her—until it felt as though Hugo could push those silver serpents through her flesh and bones and wrap them around her bruised heart. Without warning, the serpents snapped taught and tugged at her chest. A small gasp escaped her. Hugo tightened their bond, and she was pulled closer to his side.

Neither of them smiled as their eyes met. Simultaneously, they glanced back at the palace. In their own ways they both feared the future. One day they would have to return here, whether that would be to death or something far worse she did not want to contemplate right now.

Karen Tomlinson

PART TWO

THE WALL

CHAPTER THIRTY

The highway wound deeper into the valley, through rolling farmland and into the gloom of the forest. The army column made its way along the mud-blighted road, passing what had once been quaint villages that were now swollen with ragged refugees and temporary shelters.

A thumping reached Diamond's ears. Hammers and axes. It was clear more shelters were needed for these wretched people. It seemed they had been provided with a few tools to make that happen. Diamond was relieved at least some would have shelter. The rain had stopped now but the storms would get worse until Tu Lanah touched the horizon and the Winter Solstice passed.

At first Diamond kept her gaze down, not wanting to see the poor conditions or the tired, dull eyes that watched the army pass by. *But this is who I am fighting for,* she realised. Lifting her eyes, she forced herself to absorb every detail of their squalid living conditions, every family huddled in the mud, every shivering soul, every hopeless cry. She inhaled the putrid smell of sewage and unwashed bodies. It was hard not to cover her nose and mouth with her hand. The conditions were appalling.

Diamond vowed she would fight with every scrap of her soul so these people might know a home and a future that was safe. No matter how hard this got or how scared she was, she must never lose sight of that goal.

After what seemed like hours, Tallo called a halt. He was at the front of their section but his deep voice carried to the rear. It was abhorrent to Diamond that the tough but kind-hearted Tallo could have been killed yesterday.

Hugo brought Midnight Fire to a stop nearby. Her emotions still rode high. Unsure how to handle them, Diamond refused to look at him.

A frigid wind had cleared the storm clouds from the sky. Dry it might be, but the temperatures had plummeted. Diamond shivered, making her sore body ache even more. Reining in Luna, she scowled at the ground, not at all sure she could dismount.

Reese, who watched her from a few feet away, narrowed his eyes and approached her with a determined air. Hugo's nostrils flared as he scented Reese stepping nearer. Before the soldier could get within touching distance, Midnight Fire blocked his way.

"Do you want to dismount?" asked Hugo gruffly, before half-turning his head and glaring down at Reese.

Reese defiantly held Hugo's gaze, but catching the shake of Diamond's head and her apologetic gaze, the squad captain clenched his jaw and turned away.

Diamond's ire rose. Only the concern in Hugo's eyes convinced her to bite down on her reaction to tell him to go and lose himself far away from her. *The Queen cannot win,* she told herself twice before she finally looked at him.

"Not really, but unfortunately I need to," she informed him stiffly.

With a smooth controlled movement, Hugo dismounted and looped Midnight Fire's reins over his arm. Three powerful strides and he stood by Luna's side. Shoulders stiff, jaw clenched, he waited. With his height, he wasn't much lower than Diamond was, even from the back of her horse.

Diamond regarded him steadily. She was well aware the squadron was watching them. It would be so easy to rebuke him. To humiliate him. Instead, she haltingly lifted her right leg over her saddle, a hiss of pain escaping her. Teetering precariously on the curve of the saddle, she allowed Hugo to put his hands on either side of her bruised hips.

Wincing, she gritted her teeth as he lowered her carefully to the ground.

Diamond knew Hugo would feel the weight of the squadron's mistrust. Her time with him had proven he was not as unfeeling as he would have others believe. Still, he ignored them, his attention solely on her.

"Thanks," Diamond said, giving him a small smile before limping off into the trees without another word. When she came back, Hugo handed her bread and cheese.

"Drink this when you've eaten," he said, passing her a phial of blue liquid. "It will help with the pain."

For a moment Diamond could only look at the phial. Stupid tears burned her eyes. She blinked them back. "Thank you," she whispered, unable to meet his eyes this time.

A river of mud had been left by the stream of horses, men and carts. It sucked at her boots as she hobbled to a fallen tree trunk away from everyone else. Tucking her cape underneath her, Diamond sat down. Bolts of pain shot through her swollen jaw and face as she chewed on a piece of slightly stale bread. She sighed and gave up after a few bites. Her appetite had disappeared. Gulping the icy water made her teeth ache, but she used it to down the painkiller. Its bitter aftertaste stung her throat and lingered on her tongue.

The fact that Hugo had actually been thoughtful enough to bring her painkillers—after what she had done this morning—made her shrink into herself.

The bottle was smooth and cold as she rolled the empty phial between her fingers. With her energy levels at rock bottom, she plummeted to new depths of misery.

Hugo sat with his back to her. Unmoving, he seemed to be staring into the gloom of the forest, lost in thought. Tears stung her eyes. This is what the Queen had wanted—to drive them apart. To hurt and weaken them both. Hugo was more alone now than he had ever been. These soldiers and warriors no longer respected him because he had done the only thing he could to give Diamond a chance, capitulate. If he hadn't done, the fate of everyone in this valley would be so much worse.

Diamond sat up straight and contemplated Hugo's broad back. The Queen would not win.

CHAPTER THIRTY-ONE

Diamond shivered through the afternoon. Despite the painkiller, her body jarred with each of Luna's steps. The drug had only made Diamond drowsy. Every now and then she felt magic, magic as dark as the shadows of the forest, wrap around her shoulders and pull her back into balance on her saddle.

Midnight Fire continued to walk as close as Luna would allow. Occasionally the two horses huffed and whinnied at each other. Diamond was dozing, so tired she even welcomed Hugo's large hand holding her upright, when she heard voices raised in challenge.

Blinking her heavy eyes, Diamond peered through the thinning treeline. In the darkness, yellow torches flickered brightly, illuminating a large structure. Jack's compound. They must be in the heart of the valley.

Diamond made out a large area of cleared ground that seemed to surround a huge fortification. A wide ditch, its scarp steep and muddy, encircled the structure for as far as Diamond could see. Solid wood gates were already thrown wide.

The squadron filed into a large yard surrounded by wooden pens and stables. The horses tossed their heads and snorted at the prospect of food and rest. The compound was crowded and noisy—and quite overwhelming. With hands and feet like blocks of ice, it was far too painful for Diamond to move. She swore under her breath. Her body had seized up. Beyond her seat in the saddle, Diamond spied a large wooden building. It looked solid and safe. She groaned; what she wouldn't give for a nice warm bed, right now.

Flags billowed above the building, emblazoned with the dragon of Jack's house, and there were many well-armoured guards around the doorways, walls and guard platforms on the roofs. Diamond expelled a sigh. Jack was her friend, and he had told her he had spies in the palace. Word would have reached him of her test. Fervently, she hoped she wouldn't see Jack tonight. Facing his questions and inevitable wrath over her ravaged appearance would be far too draining.

Tallo reined the squadron in across the muddy central yard, after being directed to the only space left by a very harassed-looking captain.

Diamond used the opportunity to switch her vision. Energy from the forest pulsed forward, as if drawn to her. It was easy to relax and welcome that spark of growth and life as it washed over her. Warmth invaded her mind and the smell of sap and damp earth tickled her nostrils. Closing her eyes, Diamond gave herself a moment to relish the feeling, wishing she had opened herself up to it earlier. A tiny nudge on her cheek from Hugo's energy brought her back to the here and now.

Masses of energy flowed around her, swirling around the warriors and the horses. Her heart tightened, and she fleetingly wondered if Tom or Zane were nearby.

Diamond let her vision return to normal. It did not matter; they would have their own duties now.

"Dismount!" Tallo bellowed, jerking her out of her reverie.

Before Diamond could even think about getting herself down, Hugo was standing by her, his large hands gripping her hips again. She flinched, and he hesitated.

"You don't have to be near me every time I turn around," she snapped. "I *am* capable of doing some things for myself."

"I know that, but it doesn't mean I can't help you," he replied patiently, holding her eyes.

Firmly but with care, Hugo lifted her down. Her numb feet hit the ground, and she obstinately pushed him away. Her knees collapsed; to her shame, only his quick reactions saved her from landing in the thick mud. Muttering and cursing her stubbornness, he swung her up in his arms, paying no heed to her protests as he strode off towards the wooden building next to the prince's.

"Hugo!" bellowed a voice from behind them.

Hugo froze. He instantly threw his wings wide, armoured and glowing. Slowly he turned around, his feet squelching in the mud. Diamond felt his whole body tense, his muscles pushing uncomfortably against her bruises. She changed her vision. The silver threads of his energy were thrown out in a similarly defensively way to his wings.

Jack covered the ground in long strides until he stood an arm's breadth in front of Hugo, oblivious to the energy that tried to attack him. Diamond felt it in her chest when Hugo gripped that energy with his iron will and yanked it back. The serpents reluctantly recoiled until they wrapped around her, holding her protectively.

Diamond hastily let her vision return to normal. It wasn't necessary for Jack to see evidence of her magic.

"Give her to me," Jack ordered, his voice hard.

She felt Hugo pull her in to his chest and knew he would not follow Jack's order.

"Hugo, you will release her or, may the goddess help me, I will give the order to strike you down where you stand. Queen's guard or not. Friend or not. You do not deserve her," said Jack, his voice icy.

Diamond wanted the ground to swallow her.

Familiar faces stood tense and ready behind Hugo, their swords drawn. Her heart flipped. Enough. There would be no more blood spilled on her account. This was unnecessary. Ridiculous even. Hugo did not deserve this treatment. And Jack had no right to decide who was worthy of her attention.

A movement in her peripheral vision cemented her concern. Gunnald stood in the shadows, his bow ready. Its strange magical markings glowed, mirroring the tattoos visible on his neck and arms. The human's incredible vision was centred directly on Hugo.

"Hugo. Put me down. Please," she breathed, squeezing his tense arm between her fingers.

A feral snarl curled Hugo's lips as he took note of his position, but he glanced down at the sound of her voice. His eyes turned to glittering obsidian, a shadow darkening his face. She briefly pushed her magic against him, wanting to comfort him, to erase the darkness that took his heart away from her when he knew death or pain was closing in.

"I am not worth dying over," she whispered, knowing only his fae ears would hear her. Hugo's eyes lightened a fraction. But even as he nodded, she felt his utter disbelief in that statement filter through his magic. She gulped down her tears. He really had come to fight for her yesterday. He had stopped, not for his own safety, but for hers. Guilt for how she had treated him burned her heart.

"It's okay. Put me down," she told him. "I'll go with him."

Ignoring Jack's outstretched arms, Hugo reluctantly lowered her feet to the ground, not letting go until she had gained her balance.

Diamond found she could not watch as Hugo turn his back on them and walked away.

CHAPTER THIRTY-TWO

Jack was silent as he walked her to his quarters. He gently guided her to his soft bed and pushed her down.

"Jack, I can't stay here!" she protested, staring up at him.

"Yes, you can and you will. Now stop arguing," he ordered sternly.

"Don't tell me what to do, Jack. I'm not one of your men," she bit out.

Looking slightly chastised, the prince dropped to his knees by the bed. "I'm sorry," he said, taking her hand, full of concern. Deep brown eyes studied her swollen features. "Word reached me about what happened right before you arrived. What the hell was Hugo thinking?" he ran his hands through his curly brown hair. "I thought he cared about you, everyone did." He ran a gentle fingertip over her swollen lips.

"I'll be fine," she bristled, pulling away. "It was a test. One I had to pass. Besides, you're Hugo's friend. You know what his life is like. You know he had no choice." Defensiveness made her voice harsh.

"Yes, he did. He could have fought for you."

"What? Like you did in that throne room? Be honest, Jack. You were thinking about more than only me that day. You agreed to let me become the Queen's slave because—just like her—you know how powerful the magic inside me is. You need a weapon to keep your people safe. You bargained more for that weapon than for me, and then you walked away. So don't you dare judge Hugo for the mess that is his life. He has never known anything different. Besides, he tried to help me, he tried to fight. But I am glad he stopped. He would have died along with you and Tom and every other person I care about."

Diamond stopped her barrage of words, almost as surprised as Jack at her defence of Hugo and her condemnation of the prince.

They studied each other silently, then Jack cocked his head, nodded and gave her a lopsided smile. "Point taken, and I apologise wholeheartedly for this shitty situation you are in. You're right. I am as much to blame for all this as Hugo. I could have gotten you out of the city months ago, but I am selfish. I was—no—am thinking of my people. We do need a weapon. One with enough power to defeat an immortal lord. And you are it." He reached his hand out and brushed some hair behind her ear, smiling ruefully. "I am sorry. Am I forgiven?"

Diamond sighed. "Jack, there is nothing to forgive. You have a responsibility to your people. They should come first."

"Glad you feel that way," he said, then he grinned. "By the goddess, it's good to see you. I missed you. Even Zane and Roin have been grumbling about not having a reason to leave this compound. Zane's been moping around here like a lovesick puppy, missing Tom. Thank the goddess Tom's back with us—permanently. I'm hoping those two hurry up and sort out their relationship. Zane's moods have been giving me a headache! A bit like two of my other friends. So, have you and Hugo talked things out since the beating? He didn't look too happy to give you to me, did he?" he winked and grinned ruefully.

Diamond groaned, fell backwards, and threw her arms over her face. "No. He wasn't."

"Well, I'm not going to apologise. I was pissed at him," Jack grinned.

"Really? I would never have guessed," she replied sarcastically.

"Don't worry, I will eventually, but not tonight. He can sweat it, wondering what we're up to. And you haven't answered my question. Have you even tried to sort things out after yesterday?"

Diamond groaned. "No. I'm not sure how to."

"Why?" Jack asked.

"Well, for one, because you just dragged me off to your bedroom," she pointed out bluntly.

"And?" he encouraged, chuckling.

"Because I was angry, and I wouldn't forgive him." She paused, throwing her arms down by her sides. "And I hit him."

Jack snorted. "Well, he's used to being hit. Besides, sounds like he deserved it."

"No, you don't understand. I slapped him, and he didn't even try to stop me. He simply let me. He was on his knees, he practically begged me to forgive him, and I didn't. I am a horrible person," she choked out.

Jack smiled sympathetically. "Hey, it's all right. Hugo will forgive you. I know he will. It will do the stubborn fool good to realise that he will lose you if he doesn't make a choice between you and the Queen. So tonight you are going to stay here, and we'll see what that does to stir up those possessive fae instincts. You can share my bed," he stated, chuckling as she glared at him. "Err, okay. I'll sleep in the chair if you're still declining to be my lover," he teased, wiggling his eyebrows suggestively.

"Jack, you're an idiot. No, I don't want to be your lover. I couldn't cope!"

"No, I guess I am far too much too handle for a half-blood magic-wielding maiden from the north."

Giggling, Diamond chucked a pillow at him. "Far too much," she agreed.

"Well, maiden, I'm glad you're here, even if you *are* a bit bashed up, wiping mud all over my bed and refusing to be my amusement," he teased.

She laughed as he pulled off her boots. It was easy to relax back and snuggle into the soft velvet and woollen throws on the bed. Jack put the muddy footwear outside the door. Diamond sighed, letting the luxurious textiles on the bed caress her skin. "How on earth did you get all this luxury out here?" she asked, looking around Jack's room appreciatively. A fire burned in a stone hearth, making the room gloriously warm after the numbing cold of her journey. Rugs covered the wooden floor, and she noticed two armchairs near the hearth.

"Comes with being heir to the throne, even if it is of a kingdom lost to monsters and shadow," he laughed bitterly. "Stuff appears from people who want to be on your good side. What can I say? It beats the open forest. Now, you need a nice warm bath and food. Which would you like first?"

"Oooh, a bath," she said with a sigh. "There's absolutely no contest."

"So be it, my lady," he said, bowing low.

Jack walked from the room, and Diamond heard him ordering people about. It was lovely to hear his voice again. She turned her face into his soft pillow and, wonderful though it was, no matter how much she wanted to stay in this comfort, she knew she could not. The gossip around the camp would be unbearable. Her eyes followed Jack as he walked back toward her. Carefully, he pulled her to her feet, just as a small bird-like woman appeared behind him. The woman, who looked to be in her fifties, indicated a door off to the left.

"This is Mary. She will help you bathe. Then you can come back in here and we'll eat together," Jack informed Diamond with a cheeky smile, knowing she would wonder what the maid would think.

Diamond raised her brows but smiled gratefully as he kissed her hand and strode out.

Languishing in the bath was pure heaven. After washing her bruised body and rubbing herself dry with a rough towel, she allowed Mary to help her dress in a simple but well-cut peach satin gown.

What an odd garment to find out here, Diamond mused, chuckling as she wondered who it belonged to. Jack's reputation as a kind but fickle lover had not passed Diamond by. A smile pulled the corners of her mouth up. She could see why, but she loved Jack as her friend, nothing more. They were both happy with that.

Jack was sitting in one of the armchairs when she walked back into the bedchamber. He smiled appreciatively at her.

Glancing down, Diamond realised she hadn't worn a dress for months. Leggings, breeches and tunics had become her norm. She needed functional clothes that she could fight in. Still, it was nice to feel pretty. Sitting in the chair opposite Jack, she curled her feet underneath her, staring at the flames.

"So? What's really going on between you and Hugo? And that wicked fae who calls herself a queen?" Jack asked quietly. He seemed to have been mulling things over whilst she had been languishing in the warm water.

Diamond sighed deeply and rubbed her eyes. "I have a lot to tell you," she stated. Jack only interrupted a couple of times as she told him about the weeks since he had left. He frowned at the story of the guardians and the keys. His gaze drifted to where his sword stood propped up on the wall, but he said nothing until she told him of the test.

"She sold me to Lord Firan for the price of an armada," she told Jack, her voice fading when she heard someone turn the door handle.

"Lord of the Wetlands?" Jack queried, frowning. "He's in Valentia? I'll get my spies to find out what agreements have been signed. Look, don't worry about that for now. We have a Wraith Lord to fight, and while we plan to do that, we are going to convince Hugo he *can* get you out of this place, *and* that he deserves to be with you. Even if the Queen can track him, you can at least try and run," he took her hand and gave it a squeeze, loneliness evident in his eyes. "Diamond, I would give anything to find someone who is as perfect for me as you are for him, and he is for you. Fight for it while you can."

It was a relief when Mary rattled through the door with a tray and set it on the small table between them. That conversation was a little too deep to be having with Jack.

At that moment her belly growled loudly. Jack laughed as she grasped her stomach and apologised.

A bowl of steaming beef stew and a glass of red wine later, Diamond's eyelids drooped. Heat from the fire, not to mention the alcohol, flushed her cheeks and, although Jack smiled as he put his glass down, there was concern in his voice. "Come on, your body has a lot of healing to do. Half fae or not, you need to rest."

Diamond meekly let him lead her to his bed. Her head cleared a bit when he sat her down on the edge.

"Jack! I can't sleep in your bed. What will people think?"

He brushed off her protests, lifting her feet up. "It doesn't matter. You need to sleep properly—in a decent bed. Just this once, stop worrying about what anyone else thinks, hmm?"

The sheets were smooth against her feet, but she was glad Jack did not suggest she get undressed, that would have been too much. Warily, she watched Jack take his shirt and boots off. She suddenly felt very uncomfortable. He looked fitter and more muscled than he had a few weeks ago. Thankfully he had recovered from being so ill. The scars from the knife wounds to his back had faded to a light purple. Diamond squeezed her eyes shut. Without a doubt her friend was gorgeous, but it wasn't him she wanted in her bed.

"Diamond, relax. Go to sleep," Jack said soothingly. "I'm going to sleep in the chair." He brushed his fingers gently down her cheek and kissed her lightly. "Believe me when I say this will do Hugo some good," he told her before settling himself down under some blankets in the armchair. "Goodnight, Diamond," his voice drifted over her.

"Night," she echoed, snuggling into the warmth of the bed.

CHAPTER THIRTY-THREE

Howling winds woke Diamond. Jack was nowhere to be seen. She released a moan and smacked the bed with the flat of her hands. Hugo would be insufferably moody today. She cursed Jack for leaving her to deal with him on her own.

After she had eaten the breakfast Mary served, she strapped her armour securely on her body. Stretching her stiff limbs, Diamond cricked her neck. *Right*, she decided with resolve, *this is best done now*. Avoidance was not going to make things better.

Stepping out of Jack's quarters, she flung her cloak around her shoulders and set off in search of Hugo. Soldiers were busy all around the compound, carrying out their orders with purpose. The bulk of the column had already headed out to the wall.

Forcing her feet to move, she walked to the building that Hugo had been heading towards when Jack had stopped him. After asking another soldier where to find him, she knocked on Hugo's door. No answer. Maybe he had gone out with the squadron somewhere.

Back outside, she headed to the stables. Midnight Fire would still be stabled if Hugo was around. Hugo wouldn't fly anywhere today, not unless he had to. It was too windy.

The stallion stood patiently in the stall next to Luna. Both horses snorted a greeting and pushed their heads out to reach her. Smiling, she leaned on the wooden bar of the stable door and indulgently fussed them both. *The darkness and the light*, she thought ruefully. Her face was leaning against the stallion's neck when she felt a presence behind her. He tugged almost painfully on their bond.

"Good morning, Hugo," Diamond responded, trying to stop her voice from shaking.

"Morning," he answered, his voice flat and unemotional.

Nerves made her belly flip. She was dreading this. Still, she may as well get it over with. Kissing the neck of the stallion, Diamond turned around.

With his arms crossed over his leather-encased chest, the Queen's guard stared at her coldly. But Diamond had spent months studying Hugo and his expressions. She probably knew him better than he knew himself. Even though he was holding his emotions away from her, his rage was evident. His mouth and jaw were tight, twisting his scarred lips.

Bravely, she walked right up to him and found herself staring up into glittering black eyes. No sapphire blue or silver. Nervous though she was, she found her own anger responding to those endless eyes of shadow. He had shut down his heart, hidden it from her again.

"Go on then," she challenged, resentful of his withdrawal. Violet sparked brightly in her eyes.

"What?" he growled through clenched teeth.

"Get it over with. Call me Jack's whore. Go on. Just like you have before. Call me names if it makes you feel better, but don't you dare give me the silent treatment."

Nothing. Not a sign of the warrior who had wanted to fight to keep her in his arms last night. Her stomach sank. *Is that all it took? Surely he doesn't think so low of me as to believe I would actually sleep with Jack to get my own back?* Indignation seared her heart. "Is that all it takes for you?" she snarled. "Just one night to give up on me? After everything you have done to me these past months? You insufferable bastard! How dare you judge me!" Her eyes dropped to his fingers.

Hugo's knuckles had turned white where he gripped his own bicep. Unfolding his arms he clenched his fists by his sides.

Tears burned her eyes and, though she tried to stop, her words kept tumbling out. "And I didn't ask to stay with him. Jack has always been kind to me, and I was so tired. And I didn't want you both to fight. G-Gunnald. He had his bow on you. He would have killed you if Jack ordered it." Diamond knew she was rambling, but her words stumbled at the thought of an arrow piercing Hugo's skin.

Hugo stared at her. Unwavering. His body completely still.

Dropping her eyes, she kicked hard at the ground, a tear running down her cheek. *Why doesn't he believe me?* "Oh you know what, Hugo?" she hissed. "I knew you wouldn't believe me. That you wouldn't *want* to believe me. I'm not sure you believed that Jack was only ever a friend. Why should I care what you or anyone else thinks? I can share *my* body with whoever *I* want," she said cuttingly. "Tell you what, *commander*, you fly back to that cold-hearted bitch queen, and when you're gone, I'll go back to Jack's bed, and we'll busy ourselves giving the rest of this camp something interesting to gossip about. After the way he touched me last night, I doubt he'll say no." The words were out before she could stop them. Damn her mouth. *Why did I say that?*

Hugo paled before his face flushed and his eyes shone dangerous and dark against his golden skin. Metal clattered across his wings. The growl he emitted was so animalistic and savage, Diamond warily backed up against the stalls. Around them soldiers began to stand and watch. Hugo's blue-armoured wings were a novelty for most soldiers.

Those armoured wings now glowed brightly, almost as brightly as they had when Sulphurious had attacked Valentia. Shadows swirled around Hugo's face before he took a deep breath and sucked it inside himself.

The horses snorted and shuffled around in their stalls. Midnight Fire stuck his head out to see what all the fuss was about. He nudged Diamond's shoulder with his big head as if to say, *Take that back.*

227

Absentmindedly, Diamond stroked the stallion, her face flushed with shame. Tears tipped out of her eyes. She had to get away from this hard-hearted warrior. He threw her emotions and control completely off kilter. Quickly dropping her head, she stormed past him.

"Diamond!" he uttered sharply, grabbing at her upper arm so hard she couldn't go another step.

"Ow!" she exclaimed. "Let go of me!"

"No," he said firmly, but his fingers loosened as his eyelids closed.

Diamond glared up at him, about to yank her arm away, but when he opened his eyes she stilled, caught in the thrall of sapphire and silver.

His fingers released her, and his expression softened. "I do believe you," he whispered. "But regardless of what I—or anyone else—thinks, if you really want to be Jack's lover, that is what you should do. I will not stand in your way." His jaw clenched and it was clear he forced those words out.

Without thinking, Diamond reached up and placed her gloved hand on his cheek. "I don't want to be with Jack. I want to be with—"

Someone coughed, cutting off her last word. Her hand dropped like a heavy weight to her side.

A man in a sergeant's uniform stood behind Hugo. His face was carefully blank, but his eyes appraised Diamond as he informed them Jack wished to see them in the council room. "It's in the same building as his chambers. I am to escort you there. If you can't remember the way, that is," he smirked.

Bristling, Diamond decided she would like the opportunity to wipe that smile off the sergeant's face. *But I suppose the whole camp knows I spent the night in Jack's bed,* she reflected. *I only have myself to blame.*

"Thank you, sergeant. I can remember the way. You may leave us," Diamond informed him, trying to keep the irritation out of her voice.

228

The sergeant raised his brows. "But the prince has ordered me to fetch you."

"Well, the prince can wait," Diamond bit out, instantly annoyed with Jack. He need not start ordering her about.

The sergeant made to step forward.

"Listen to her," growled Hugo, standing at her back.

The sergeant jumped, having forgotten Hugo's presence. He swallowed as the weight of Hugo's icy cold eyes rested on him. Threat radiated from the huge Queen's guard, and his wings shifted dangerously, the rivulets of silver sparking. The sergeant sputtered and coughed, staring up at Hugo's scarred features.

Diamond could smell his fear. He flashed her a look, one that indicated he didn't like being thwarted.

"Leave," Hugo snarled, his voice lowered and rumbling with threat. He was in no mood for any challenge resulting from last night's demonstration of Jack's authority.

Meeting the man's resentful gaze, Diamond raised her brows. "You may tell your prince I will be there shortly."

The sergeant managed a reluctant salute, then stomped away, his face flushed and angry.

Diamond smothered her laugh. "Well, he deserves a smack in the face," she commented as she watched him go. When she turned to Hugo, he was smiling at her. Her whole body heated.

A few seconds passed before he spoke. "Diamond, he was only trying to follow his orders, but it will not hurt to show the males here that you are not weak. You are a beautiful young woman in a predominantly male soldiers' camp. You will come across many like him and some who are a hell of a lot worse. And you are going to attract attention, especially wearing that," Hugo pointed out, openly appraising the curves of her body, which were enhanced by her fitted armour.

Diamond did not bristle at his regard, instead she tried to hide her delight at the flush that appeared on his neck. Her lips twitched in a smile. Deliberately, she kept her eyes on his face as he stepped close, tapping her swords with one hand and the knives strapped to her thighs with the other.

"Keep these close to you. It may not only be the enemy you need to use them on. And a smack in the face might not be enough." There was a stark warning in his voice.

Standing so close, his warmth seeped into her. Diamond inhaled. *Gods, why does he have to smell so good?* His scent did weird things to her mind. No longer able to hold his eyes, it was her turn to flush. A tiny smile curled his lips. She coughed and gulped. "We better go," she managed to croak.

Hugo ran one finger down her hot cheek and nodded.

CHAPTER THIRTY-FOUR

The council room was large and dim, smelling of wood smoke, stale bodies and metal. Diamond wrinkled her nose in distaste. The only light came from lanterns dotted around the walls and the large open fire. A roughly hewn oak table dominated the space, so large that it had likely been erected in the room. Crudely made stools and benches provided seating, but most of the occupants stood.

So this is where Jack holds his court and councils. She glanced round. *No wonder he wants to escape whenever he can,* she thought wryly. *I would too.* Heavily armed soldiers and warriors occupied the room, their blades glinting ominously in the lamp light. In times of war they were not asked to set down their arms when in council, but Jack's personal guard surrounded them on all sides, some with bows at the ready.

Zane gave her a wink. Roin nodded. She smiled at them both, her eyes searching for Tom. Disappointment and worry dragged at her belly. He wasn't there. *Surely the Queen wouldn't have harmed him, would she?*

Hugo brushed his fingers against hers as if he understood where her thoughts lay. She summoned a watery smile for him.

The stools and benches were occupied by men clad in garishly coloured robes, which contrasted starkly with the drab browns, blacks and greens of the soldiers' uniforms.

Jack's council, Diamond surmised. She smiled; they did look like the self-serving hypocrites Jack had called them months ago.

The prince stood behind the huge desk. He scowled a little at Hugo but inclined his head in greeting. He gave Diamond a warm smile, his eyes holding hers for far longer than necessary before his gaze flicked over her armour clad body. A wide grin stretched his mouth. Attempting to stop her embarrassed flush at his regard was useless. Acutely aware of Hugo, she glared at Jack. Later she was going to slap Jack for winding Hugo up.

Hugo gently but firmly took hold of her arm. With a low growl, he led her to a space at one side of the room; near enough to hear what was being said, but far enough away to not draw the attention of those at the table. He pulled her close enough she could feel the heat from his body. That sensation, coupled with his musky scent, made her head swim. Taking a steadying breath, she fought the urge to lean up against him.

"It's not possible that the Wraith Lord has come so close already," said a grisly-looking man at the table. His voice matched his appearance, rough and challenging. His shock of curling hair was streaked with grey, matching the bushy beard that blurred the lines of his face. His small, dark eyes were very alert.

"Lord Stockbrook, I assure you Ragor will be here within the next two weeks with his main host. Their attacks on the wall test our strengths and weaknesses. I also know that these strikes will get more frequent and more severe. Ragor did exactly the same thing to Stormguaard before he attacked with his full force," responded Jack, his voice even and authoritative.

"Aye, and look how that ended, your highness. Now we have no homes and cower behind a woman's skirts," retorted Lord Stockbrook bitterly. "What makes you think you can beat the Wraith Lord this time, prince, when you lost your father's lands in such a spectacular fashion against him before?"

There was a tumult of voices around the table. Jack's supporters heckled Lord Stockbrook, whose chin rose in challenge. Tension crackled in the air. Jack stared down the grizzled lord. It was Lord Stockbrook who lowered his eyes first. It probably had something to do with Roin and Zane, who stood on either side of their prince. Zane's large hand came to rest on his sword, his eyes promising violence. One word or motion from Jack and Lord Stockbrook would be dead.

"Enough!" Jack thundered, slapping his palms down on the table and making it rattle. "Lord Stockbrook, I understand you lost more than your home when Ragor sacked the grasslands. I am truly sorry for your loss. However, there are a number of reasons why we may emerge triumphant from this battle." Jack's eyes searched for and found Diamond's.

Her heart sped up. *He's relying on me*, she realised with a slightly sick feeling.

"Here we have more men and more seasoned warriors. Rhodainian or Avalonian, they are not battle weary as we were when Ragor took Stormguaard. Magic shields this city, and the Rift Valley is on our side. There is also no dust for the Dust Devils to use against us, like there was when they sacked our lands and killed our people; quite the opposite, in fact. Gentlemen, if we work together with Master Commander Riddeon and fight as brothers with the Queen's warriors, we have a better chance of triumph." He nodded at the fae commanders, who stood quietly to one side, watching carefully. "But in order to triumph, I cannot have anyone at this table who wishes to undermine my authority. This is *my* army. Queen's warriors or not, you are all my men, under my command until Ragor is defeated. All the Queen's commanders know this."

Diamond's chest tightened with recognition as she looked to Master Commander Riddeon. Her heart stopped, then started again. She remembered how he had watched with narrowed, golden eyes as Diamond's necklace had been taken. He had reacted strangely when it had been placed on the table in front of him. Her teeth clenched. He had known what it was, that much was clear now.

Jack continued to speak. "Therefore, Lord Stockbrook, I will suffer no insubordination from you—or anyone else. Discussions and questions about our campaign, yes; challenge to my authority, no. You will follow my orders and fight for me—as you are sworn to do—or I will execute you for treason. I do not have time for debates or trials, and I will not tolerate dissension." He fixed Lord Stockbrook with a stony glare, then allowed his eyes to travel over each one of the warriors and lords at the table.

The silence stretched. Many shuffled uncomfortably.

"Is that understood?" His countenance remained hard as he cast his eyes around the entire room.

A chorus of agreement rippled around the crowd.

Lord Stockbrook's gaze turned speculative and slightly more respectful.

In turn, Jack stared the older man down until Lord Stockbrook dropped his head in a bow of acquiescence.

Diamond gaped, then glanced up at Hugo's face. Jack did not sound like the young prince they both knew, but a grown man who could command armies, a man who would soon be a king.

Hugo's mouth twitched in a smile. He was proud of his friend.

Jack continued, not allowing the change in atmosphere to affect his voice at all. "Commander Riddeon will outline the strategy we have been working on and answer any of your questions. Let's begin. Commander?" Jack sat down and indicated to Master Commander Riddeon to take over.

Hugo listened intently to the meticulously laid plans Master Commander Riddeon laid out. His body remained completely still, other than his eyes, which moved around the room, constantly judging the men who spoke, listening to the questions they asked and the comments that were made.

Diamond tried not to fidget. The heavy weight of someone's gaze fell on her.

Commander Riddeon stood to one side as Jack took the floor again. He watched the room in the same manner Hugo did. In appearance he looked to be in his early thirties. He was a handsome male, who was tall and broad with shoulder-length brown hair.

Diamond's chest tightened. This fae was as ancient as the Queen. Immortal. Powerful. And he had served her all these years. *Why had he shown me any sympathy in the throne room?* The golden-eyed commander nodded his head in a greeting. Utterly confused, Diamond nodded back.

Commander Riddeon had such an air of reserved power and stillness that he seemed able to melt into the background. He held her gaze, a smile toying at the corners of his mouth at her obvious confusion and discomfiture, then his attention moved elsewhere. Leisurely, he observed each of the men in the room, his golden gaze coming back to rest on the warrior at her side; that is, until he sensed Diamond watching him. His attention moved on when Hugo tracked Diamond's gaze.

Various voices washed over her and she soon wondered where she and Hugo would fit into this huge battle plan. It was a mammoth undertaking, coordinating so many men. Diamond looked at Jack with concern. He might sound like a king, even behave like one, but his face looked pinched and tired. For a moment he caught her eye, giving her a small smile.

She wondered who else would go to the wall with Jack. As part of the royal guard, maybe Tom would go. Zane stood vigilantly at Jack's back. He caught her eye but did not smile. Zane was an arrogant fae male, but she knew he had fallen for Tom in a big way. Jack had said Zane was miserable without Tom. Diamond wondered if their relationship had progressed or if they were both held back by their responsibilities to Jack. She sighed; it was strange to have recently experienced so much without sharing it with Tom.

Eventually the atmosphere started to tell on her. Her magic reacted to the buzzing energy in the room. Unbidden, her stiff and bruised body began to use that energy, absorbing it to heal. Even so, her tired muscles still protested at standing still for so long. She shifted her weight from foot to foot whilst trying not to grimace.

Hugo looked sideways at her, then slipped his fingers around hers, giving her hand a gentle squeeze. Utterly surprised by the supportive gesture, her eyes flew to his. Silver glinted as he held her gaze. Cool air caressed her fingers when he let go. For a moment it was hard to hide her disappointment, then his gorgeous mouth tilted into the ghost of a smile. Compelling her to hold his gaze, his hot hand slid around her waist, pulling her against him. Raising one eyebrow in a most un-Hugo like way, he turned his attention back to the room, angling his body so no one else could see where his hand had ended up.

Her heart banged against her chest; she was sure Hugo could hear it. A few moments later a gasp escaped her. Hugo kept his eyes on the meeting, his face remaining expressionless as his hot hand moved up under her armour. Hard, calloused fingers smoothly traced the curve of her waist, making her stomach clench. Her chest tightened until she could barely breathe. Her face heated and she desperately wanted to turn into his chest and wrap her arms around his waist. Thankfully, before she could give in to that urge, Jack called a halt to the meeting.

The lords, warriors and council advisors drifted out of the room. Hugo allowed his hand to fall from her skin. She stifled her groan.

Hugo studied the men striding purposefully from the room, including Commander Riddeon, who once again allowed his golden eyes to rest speculatively on the couple before he bowed his head and walked out.

When the room was clear, Zane relaxed. Grinning widely, he walked over to Diamond and Hugo. It took Diamond another moment to piece herself together. Now would not be a good time to look at Hugo, she decided.

"Hello, Diamond, commander. It's good to see you both." Zane smiled. His eyes narrowed, then he glanced at Hugo. Sympathy flashed across Zane's face. It was clear he empathised with how hard the Queen's test must have been on both of them, but he said nothing about her swollen, bruised face.

Hugo stiffened but did not snarl. There was no condemnation in Zane's acknowledgment of her injuries, only understanding. Sensing Hugo's moods had become second nature now, and his energy bristled defensively as Jack approached.

"Hugo," Jack greeted his friend stiffly.

Diamond hoped this would not end badly. She gently brushed Hugo's fingers with her own. A plea for peace.

Hugo did not look at her. Instead, magic brushed her skin in the lightest caress. "Jack," he responded, no aggressive inflection in his tone.

Jack regarded his friend steadily. "I apologise for last night. I did not fully understand what had happened." He paused and looked from Diamond to Hugo.

"Now I do. Diamond told me in no uncertain terms she has forgiven you, so I should too. She also gave me a roasting over what I did to you last night." Then he grinned as Hugo turned his head and stared in surprise at Diamond. She flushed. Jack chuckled at the warning glare she shot him. It was good to know he was back to teasing both of them again.

Zane and Roin grinned at her pink cheeks too.

"So it seems you've learned to fight better than your skinny friend, if you can beat all those elite guards. Tom's still as weak and clumsy as a new-born foal," Roin stated, glancing at Zane with a taunting grin. "He can't even fight off one warrior, let alone a dozen big males."

"What? He's not weak! Tom's a good fighter now, he always beats everyone in his squadron…" Zane immediately jumped in defensively. Then he saw Roin's face. "Prick!" he muttered.

Grinning, Roin smacked Zane on the back. Diamond couldn't help but smile too.

"So is Tom okay? Where is he?" she asked.

"I've sent him to the wall to ensure the fourth tower is ready for me," Jack answered. "I will run our campaign from there. Commander Riddeon will oversee the wall from tower one to three, me—three to five, and Lord Stockbrook gets five to seven."

Diamond had heard this in the long talks, so nodded but did not ask any further questions.

Roin and Zane stood back as Jack gestured to the table. The three friends took a seat.

Jack got straight to the point. "I'm deploying two battalions to hold each section between the towers. They will join the men already there. Tallo will command my section, along with Captain Dunns. I will need Tallo to help me whilst I am planning and co-ordinating." Jack placed the flat of his hands on the table, took a deep breath and lifted his head to look directly at Hugo.

"Hugo, I need you to assume a command role. You will be responsible for destroying the giants. There are five clutches in Ragor's ranks, and one clutch is pushing their way up the coast. They'll reach the wall before Ragor's main host. You've seen what they can do. They are the advanced attack force, exactly as Ragor used at Stormguaard. If we leave them unchallenged, they could weaken the wall using nothing but their fists."

Diamond's breath stuck in her throat. Giants were creatures from the Barren Wastes. With fists as hard as rock, they could destroy virtually anything.

"So far giants have arrived at the wall only in pairs, and we have been able to destroy them before they could do much damage. This time, thankfully, we have explosive devices that will blow a nice hole in their skulls. Getting rid of even one clutch before it reaches us could make the difference between the wall standing or falling. You saw them tear through the walls and armoured gates within hours at Stormguaard. We can't let that happen here."

"But these walls are ancient. Solid marble and protected by the Queen's magic," Diamond uttered, truly horrified at the thought giants could destroy their defences so quickly.

Jack's tone of voice was tight, the only indication of his anxiety. "The shield will fail if the wall is destroyed, and the Queen's magic protects *nothing*," he informed them, leaning forward until he was close to them both.

"How do you know that?" Hugo asked quietly.

A grim smile stretched Jack's lips. "Commander Riddeon. Don't forget he is as old as the Queen. He was around when the magic that created the shield was wielded."

"What did he say?" Diamond asked, anxiety tightening her gut.

Jack lowered his voice, holding her eyes. "The shield was never formed to stop dragon fire. It was cast by a member of the royal family that the Queen usurped; it was cast to imprison *her*. It seems they cursed her to never leave this city, once she took it."

CHAPTER THIRTY-FIVE

Hugo stared at Jack, his face blank and unreadable. Now was not the time to go into that story further. He made no comment or question about Jack's revelation.

"So what do you want us to do?" asked Diamond.

"Hugo will lead the attack on the clutch," Jack said, letting the matter of the shield go. His chair grated on the floor as he stood. "The Queen has sent orders for you. Here," he said, thrusting an envelope bearing the Queen's seal at Hugo. As a Queen's guard, Hugo was not subject to Jack's orders, not as the rest of her men were. Queen's elite guards would take orders from only the Queen or their lord commander.

Hugo's large hands broke open the wax seal and read the contents. His face gave nothing away as he crumpled it in his fist and met Jack's gaze. He nodded once.

"I am under your command, prince," he informed them with a slight smile.

He didn't seem resentful of his orders at all, then Diamond remembered this had been the way for them for years.

"Good, just like old times then," Jack replied, smiling back at his friend. "You will take a squad of the best fae warriors Commander Riddeon has and lead an attack on the giants. Kill the clutch before they get anywhere near the wall."

"How many warriors does that give me?" asked Hugo, planning already.

"Twenty," replied Jack. "Tallo will show you the explosives. There is a plentiful supply."

241

Diamond stood quietly and listened to their planning. She wondered if she could summon enough magic to help, if she would lose control and burn everyone near her to ash. For the first time in ages she felt a bloom of panic. The reality of using her magic outside the shield was truly terrifying. She feared losing control near Hugo or the other warriors. She could kill them. Her breathing hitched. Closing her eyes she felt a sheen of sweat tickle her brow.

A tug on her chest.

Diamond looked to the source of that tug.

Hugo returned her gaze, his sapphire eyes steady, his magical caress calming. Silver sparked in his eyes. He took a deep breath and expelled it slowly. A reminder to breathe. In. Out. Slowly. She swallowed and nodded, understanding.

"You won't hurt them or me," he said, his confidence in her reassuring. Leaving her to calm herself, his attention returned to Jack. "Where is the clutch now?"

Jack pointed to a detailed map spread out on the other end of the large table.

"This is Master Dervin," Jack said, indicating a tall, slightly stooped man standing by the map.

Diamond frowned. He had been so unassuming, she had missed his presence in the room. Or he had entered while everyone was paying attention to Jack. Intelligent grey blue eyes twinkled out from a lined face. Diamond smiled at the man.

"He is my master cartographer. This is the route the giants are taking." Jack traced a finger along the map. "If you have any questions about the terrain out there, Master Dervin will be happy to answer them. He is very adept at covering large amounts of terrain quickly and reproducing it in exacting detail on maps."

Master Dervin nodded, an acknowledgement of Jack's praise.

Hand drawn with delicate and colourful illustrations, the beautiful map immediately drew the eye. Intricate gold writing identified where important landmarks and villages could be found. Colours melded together, making structures and land masses so real and vibrant they seemed to stand off the thick vellum. Diamond gasped at the beauty of it.

It occurred to Diamond that although the Queen had managed to all but erase magic from her lands, Jack's father had done no such thing. He had protected and ruled his gifted citizens with laws, not killed them. Master Dervin was gifted, to produce such a magnificent piece of art. She eyed the man curiously. Maybe Master Dervin was far more than a cartographer.

Cover a lot of ground? Probably a shapeshifter then.

His twinkling eyes crinkled at the edges when Diamond came to that conclusion, as if he perceived when she figured it out.

"Our scouts expect the giants to have reached this area in four days. Another report confirming their position is due when I reach the wall this evening," Jack said. "We have been watching them for the last week, and they have not deviated. This clutch has been travelling the coastline, using the beaches and shallow water when the forest is too thick to walk inland." Jack's jaw muscles tightened as he gritted his teeth. "They are destroying the small coastal villages as they pass through them. Our scouts say most towns and villages near the wall have been abandoned for a while, but we still find stragglers. If we don't stop this clutch, they will wreak havoc on the wall within the next few days."

Diamond glanced at Hugo, but there was no way to know what he was thinking.

"Tallo is waiting in the armoury for you both. As he had a hand in developing them, he is the best one show you the explosives. Zane, please show the commander where to go."

243

Zane stepped up. "Follow me."

Hugo nodded farewell to Jack and followed Zane outside.

When Diamond started to follow, Jack's hot hand grabbed her wrist and held her back. "Wait," he ordered and closed the door as Hugo left. "Diamond, I wish I didn't have to put you in such danger. But your magic may make all the difference to this war, especially if you can wipe out those giants."

"Jack, disregarding the Queen, I *want* to try and help you and the people in this valley. They don't deserve death at Ragor's hand, nobody does."

He sighed, suddenly looking like the weight of the world was on his shoulders. "No, they don't. I've seen—and so has Hugo—how quickly those giants can destroy a city. How much pain and death the Dust Devils can wreak in mere minutes if we fail." Pale-faced, he gulped.

"Jack, we won't fail. You won't. And I won't. Your people deserve their homes back, and so do you. You are to be a king. I will do everything in my power to make sure you are crowned in your own kingdom, where magic is welcomed and protected; not like here, where such gifts are shunned and feared."

"I still don't want to put my friends in such danger," Jack told her.

"Jack, you have to do what's best for your people. They are relying on you for their lives, and the lives of their loved ones. They will need you to lead them home to their own lands. Your responsibility is to them, not us."

Jack laughed but there was little humour in it. "Is it? I'm hardly a reliable monarch. I didn't keep them safe before. The best I could do was scatter them, send them across the seas to the other kingdoms. Those that made it here did so without me. I was fighting to survive with Hugo in the forest. What makes you think they need me?"

"Jack, stop. You have been leading your people since you were a child. Everyone makes mistakes, even princes. It's clear your soldiers trust you or they would not have stayed here with you. They would have run far from this place or escaped with others across the seas." She smiled. "But you are not a child anymore, Jack. Even Lord Stockbrook saw that today. You have the respect of powerful men and warriors. You are leading the army of two kingdoms, and you have the ear of an immortal commander. *You*, Jack, have organised this valley and negotiated a place of refuge for your people. You have to stay in control and lead them because, from where I'm standing, no one else can."

Jack stared at her open-mouthed.

It had been quite a speech, Diamond decided, giving his cheek a pat.

"Gods, I wish you loved me and not Hugo," he grinned. "That idiot better make his move soon or I might just change my mind about being your friend."

"No, you won't," she quipped. "You might be able to rule a kingdom, Prince Oden, but you could never handle me and my magic."

Jack snorted. "You are absolutely right, my beautiful half-blood friend. I couldn't. So run along and find out if I've managed to make your soulmate jealous enough to admit his feelings."

Diamond rolled her eyes. "You are a bad man, Jack," she said. Smiling she kissed his cheek, then opened the door to step into the dim corridor beyond, closing it gently behind her.

CHAPTER THIRTY-SIX

Hugo was disappearing around the side of a large building at the back of the compound. Squelching and slipping through the mud, Diamond half-walked, half-ran to catch up. Tallo was greeting Hugo and Zane when she ran up behind them, breathing heavily.

"Sorry," she apologised, panting.

Zane and Tallo grinned. Hugo, on the other hand, eyed her sullenly, his nostrils flaring as he inhaled. His eyes shot accusingly to hers. Diamond almost groaned out loud. Jack's scent must be all over her after kissing his cheek.

"In here," said Tallo.

Hugo turned away from her.

They silently followed Tallo past several well-armed guards and into the large warehouse. It was dry inside and smelled of pine and metal and something else—maybe chemicals. Diamond gaped. Weapons were everywhere, all stacked neatly side by side. Old and worn weapons were piled up against the walls. Nothing would be wasted. If they were beyond repair, they would be smelted down in the nearby furnace and re-forged.

Tallo took them over to a large, reinforced trunk and opened it carefully. Diamond peered in at the small explosive devices. They looked remarkably innocent. Just small Silverbore spheres. Tallo lifted one and held it out to Hugo. Eyeing it suspiciously, Hugo took it. His big hand dwarfed the deadly item.

"I know it looks small and harmless, but it isn't. They're deadly little suckers when you use them right. All you need to do is take this cap off and press here. Then run—or fly—like hell. You have five seconds from pressing that button before—*boom!*" His hands flew out in demonstration.

"Five seconds?" breathed Diamond, peering at the metal sphere as if it might go off all on its own.

"Shit," muttered Hugo under his breath. His wary gaze did not move from the sphere, and he nearly dropped it when a massive roar shook the very ground they stood on.

"Sulphurious," Diamond breathed, recognising the owner immediately.

Tallo grimaced. "Yes, that's your old friend. Since he burned the Queen's armada, he has begun turning up at random, as if he's testing the integrity of the shields. It seems he has a thing for the prince too."

"Yeah, if Prince Oden goes anywhere from this compound, the black dragon will show up near him. Weird that he is so interested in a human prince," reflected Zane.

Hugo and Diamond shared a look, both frowning. Another loud bellow rattled their ear drums, and they flinched. Some of the young soldiers looked petrified. A moment later the dragon's wings thudded off into the distance.

They all looked at each other.

"Like I said—weird," uttered Zane.

Hugo had moved closer to Diamond, his body now a barrier between her and the wide open entrance to the armoury. She flushed, realising he had done it to better protect her.

"Where were we? Damn dragon, too distracting by far. Yeah, I had some friends develop these little beauties. They did a good job," Tallo said, scratching his upper lip with his thumb.

Hugo looked down at the silver sphere nestled in his hand. "Are these things safe to carry?" he asked dubiously.

"Sure, so long as you don't rattle 'em around enough to press that button." Tallo grinned.

"That's nice to know," replied Hugo dryly, raising his eyebrows and rolling his eyes at Diamond.

Diamond perched on a wooden post with Midnight Fire and Luna, waiting for Hugo. When they left the warehouse, Diamond's stomach had rumbled loudly enough to make him laugh, so he had gone in search of food. At least his mood seemed to have brightened again.

After he returned, they munched through their simple lunch. Diamond tried not to grimace her way through it. Her jaw and face still hurt when she chewed. Hugo kept eyeing her with concern. It was clear he had noticed her discomfort, but she was grateful he didn't bring it up.

After they had finished, he threw himself into his saddle. Feeling his eyes track her progress, Diamond also mounted her horse, choosing to fix her attention on Luna instead of him. Her cheeks heated when she remembered the feel of his hand on her skin.

As they urged the horses toward the gates, a group of warrior fae marched up to them. Clad in light but tough Silverbore and leather armour, the whole squad saluted smartly.

"Commander Casimir? We are ready to go. Shall we meet you at the first tower later this evening?" asked the one at the front of the group. There was something familiar about him. Diamond squinted, unable to figure out what.

Hugo shook his head brusquely. "No, Elexon, we will not arrive until very late. I have somewhere else to go on our way to the wall. Guard the explosives Tallo has given us, and I will expect you at the tower at first light."

The warrior tapped his left shoulder with his right fist. He nodded respectfully to Hugo, then—to Diamond's surprise—at her too.

Following the warrior's example, the other nineteen tall, heavily muscled fae spread their impressive golden wings and raised themselves elegantly into the air. Diamond watched them head out toward the wall. She had seen fae in the skies around the city, but these warriors looked breath-taking in their beauty, flying as a fluid single unit, even when fighting the high winds.

"Should they fly in this wind?" she asked with concern.

Hugo smiled indulgently at her worried face, then leaned over and gave her braid a little tug. She gaped, completely thrown. This sudden playful side to Hugo was as disconcerting as the smile he was giving her. She gulped a mouthful of air. That smile flipped her belly and made him look unfairly handsome, even with his twisted scar. It pained her to realise how much she had missed his gentle teasing this last week.

Still smiling, Hugo coughed and cleared his throat. Diamond dragged her attention from his mouth.

"They'll be fine. Don't worry, they're used to it. They'll get safely to the tower and be ready to discuss our plans first thing in the morning. Which is more than can be said for us if we don't get a move on, especially as we have somewhere else to visit first. So, come on. Let's go," he said briskly.

The large forest tracks were churned into a muddy soup by horses and men. The going was tough. Carefully, they guided their horses past the slower columns of foot soldiers, only urging to a faster pace when there was rare, but welcome, space.

The Rift Valley wall soon disappeared out of view, obscured by the tall trees and rocky glens. Hugo led Diamond down ever smaller tracks, some no more than animal paths. The reds, golds and greens of the winter forest surrounded them, a veritable canvas of vibrant colour, all breathtakingly beautiful.

Diamond inhaled deeply and closed her eyes. She loved that earthy aroma of wet soil and pine trees. A small smile tugged at the corners of her mouth, a sense of peace and gentleness settling on her. This forest was content. She could feel it. It reminded her of Berriesford, her childhood home. Her thoughts drifted to her father. Sharing her memories of her childhood with Hugo had been both painful and wonderful. Unsurprisingly, it had helped Diamond come to terms with her grief. It was nice to think of her father without bursting into floods of tears. Hearing his deep voice in her head and picturing his face, she drifted into her past with a sad kind of joy.

CHAPTER THIRTY-SEVEN

Hugo watched Diamond's face. Her content little smile as she closed her eyes made his heart ache. He had tried to give her the time she needed to sort out her anger and disappointment in him, but it was becoming harder with every moment that passed. Jealousy had slammed into him when Jack's scent had lingered on her. Hugo knew he had no claim on her, but he could not stand the thought of her touching someone else. It was difficult to control his soul-deep need to express to her how much she meant to him. Fisting his reins, he shifted in his saddle, his wings shivering under his cloak. Midnight Fire snorted his objection. Hugo immediately reached down and patted the beast's muscled neck to apologise.

A soft humming washed over Hugo. When he turned, Diamond's eyes were opaque, a smile curling her generous lips. The gentle tune stopped when she felt his gaze.

"I've never heard you sing before," he commented. One day he would ask her what she saw when her eyes took on that milky appearance. "Your voice is beautiful. It fits the gentleness of this forest. Will you continue humming for me?" he asked.

Her eyes shifted back to their normal vivid violet, colour staining her cheeks. Hugo loved that he could make her blush so easily. He guided Midnight to Luna's side. Cheeks still flaming, Diamond resumed her humming. Her gaze avoided his. After a moment, she closed her eyes, trusting him to lead Luna on a true and safe path.

They headed deeper into the forest, the symphony of the wind in the trees their only company. Hugo kept his senses open but felt no other presence nearby. He needed to assess Diamond's magical control. A low growl, too soft for Diamond's ears to pick up, rumbled out of him. How fate must be laughing. It seemed the only place he never wanted to visit again was the only place where it would be safe to do that very thing.

Hugo knew every bit of the forest here and, with very little effort, threw up a wide cloud of shadow that rippled through the trees, shrouding them from any prying eyes. Valentia's shield did not affect him as much out here, and he believed that applied to the woman at his side, too. He slowed their pace and guided Luna between two moss covered boulders.

Diamond glanced around, noting the shadow but remained silent, trusting him with whatever he was doing.

Soon they dismounted and gazed up a small cliff face. The glen was cold and damp, spray from the thundering waterfall saturating the air and their clothes. Diamond shivered by his side.

Hugo smiled. "Come here," he said, opening his arms. His heart thumped as she flushed at his deliberately quiet tone. *Oh gods, self-control,* he told himself sternly. They both had other things to deal with. Their feelings for each other needed to wait. Even so, his breath hitched as she stepped close. Hesitantly, her arms wound around his neck.

In turn, he wrapped his arms around her lithe body and lifted her, determined to ignore the way her warmth seeped into him. Throwing out his un-armoured wings, he raised them in to the air. Spray covered his feathers until every beat resulted in a blast of shimmering droplets that exploded in rainbow cloud of colour around them. Flying with his wings un-armoured was one pleasure Hugo never tired of—one he did not indulge in often.

Grinning widely, he took them higher than the waterfall then glanced down.

"No," Diamond gasped at the devilment in his eye.

Hugo swiftly twirled them around, spiralling higher into the air. Then dived. Diamond squealed, forced to fling her legs around his waist and grip him tightly. A loud unadulterated laugh bubbled from his chest. Diamond's hair floated around him, lifted by the rush of air and water. Inhaling the scent of summer and flowers was another pleasure he would never tire of.

Another scream came from Diamond as he headed for a rocky outcrop. It was cruel, he knew, to make her think they were about to crash. Grinning widely, he threw his wings wide and halted them in mid-air. A hidden cave mouth appeared below. With perfect balance, Hugo landed on a lip of slippery rock.

Gasping, his Nexus stared at him, totally stunned.

"You laughed," she whispered breathlessly from the circle of his arms.

He cocked his head. "Yes, I did," he agreed softly, realising it was the first time he had laughed with such glee since being a boy. Not sure what to say, he shrugged and lowered her gently to the ground.

"This way," he said and avoided her gaze as he stalked off in front. He pushed past a protrusion of grey rock that acted like a curtain. Inside, the air became drier, but still he shivered. Diamond's magic wasn't the only reason he had brought her here. He heard a gasp as she slid past the natural screen.

"What is this place?" she whispered in amazement, gaping at the natural beauty of the cave.

Hugo took a breath.

Trust.

"This is where I used to run when I was a young teenager. With my friend. His name was Tawne. When our lives got too much, I would call upon the shadows and we would escape Valentia. Even if it was only for a few hours, this is where we would come."

"It's incredible," she whispered, then turned to him.

Hugo braced himself.

"Tell me about Tawne?" It was a hopeful question, not a demand.

Hugo swallowed. If he wanted to build a relationship with Diamond, he had to share things about himself—things that were both painful and filled him with shame.

Silently he prowled down the natural steps and further into the cave. Luminescent crystals lit his way, casting a constant but gentle purple glow. They hung from the cave roof like natural chandeliers and adorned the cave walls like glittering sconces. He stopped next to a pile of old bones and ash that was almost hidden in the shadows at the back of the cave. He toed it with his boot.

"Hugo?"

A soft enquiry.

Diamond had followed him across the cave, so close that her body heat warmed him. Her magic made his body tingle as it sought to soothe him. He wanted so much to hold her close, to kiss her—to be the one to make love to her for the first time. His face heated, and he expelled a shaky breath. He knew Diamond had feelings for him, but he would not take advantage of her. They could not truly be together until she knew everything about him. And that included the bite he had given her. The first step was to trust her with his past.

Hugo gave her a grim smile. "Tawne was a trainee guard too. We were both taken from our families as babies. I have no idea where I'm from, and neither did Tawne. When the Queen says a baby has been gifted, it usually means it has been taken from its home or left at the palace gates by some sycophantic parent. I learnt this when I was a teenager when I took part in ripping poor helpless children from their mothers..." his voice shook. It took a moment to control the self-loathing that surged through him. The Queen had ordered him, but even as it had sickened him, he had locked down his heart and done it.

"Hugo?"

The concern in her voice as she uttered his name made his chest tighten. "When we were about eleven, Tawne found this cave by accident. He had been climbing the waterfall. Tawne was a shifter, a wolf with pale blue eyes. He was so large, his head nearly reached my chest." Hugo stepped sideways and sank onto a smooth rock, pulling her down next to him. "We used to come here to get away from the horror of our lives, even if it was only for a few hours. The Queen already had our blood so we could not leave the valley, but we could sneak out of the city. When we were fourteen, I fancied myself in love with one of the young healers who cared for the Queen's guards. Her name was Amy. I trusted Tawne and told him how I felt. It seemed he had a crush on Amy too. As teenage boys tend to do, we challenged each other. Our fight was brutal. Tawne could not control his wolf and often turned when he became angry. He ripped a chunk from my back but thankfully the fight was cut short by one of our captains — Tallo. We were bleeding badly, but Tawne had changed back by the time we were taken before Commander Ream. Neither of us would admit what caused the rift between us. Even though the Queen sent us to the healing quarters, neither of us admitted anything to Amy. From then on it became an exciting competition to pursue her, to see who could win her affections. We made every excuse in the book to see her, or at least I did. During training I would get injured on purpose so I had reason to visit the healers. I even threw myself off my horse once and broke my arm." He glanced at Diamond's face. She didn't speak, only looked at him with her brows raised. "Amy eventually worked out what was happening. I suppose she thought it was flattering." He coughed as Diamond smiled. Quickly, before he could change his mind he continued. It was uncomfortable sharing his life, his failures like this. "She chose me and became my first lover. It caused a huge rift between me and Tawne. As you would expect, the Queen soon found out how accident prone I had become, and it didn't take her long to figure out why—or who I was doing my damnedest to see. At least that's what I thought. It seems Tawne was more bitter than I expected. When she questioned him, he betrayed me and Amy." Hugo's voice stumbled a bit then.

"Go on," Diamond encouraged quietly.

"Amy was dragged to the throne room. In front of me and the other trainee guards, she was beaten without mercy—by Ream. A lesson to us all about what would happen if a guard chose another female over the Queen. Afterward, the Queen used magic to break Amy's body. One bone at a time. She tortured her for hours, then gave me a choice: knock her into unconsciousness or let her suffer her pain. I couldn't do it, may the goddess forgive me. I let poor Amy suffer because I was weak and couldn't smash my fist in her jaw." He blanched. "The Queen laughed in my face."

Hugo stared at the floor, bile burning his throat. Revealing his biggest failure as a male, as a potential mate and protector, made him quiver inside. Diamond may loath him after this. Without meeting her eyes he continued. "Commander Ream drove iron bolts through my wings so I could not armour them. Then he beat me until I was too weak to fight. They..." he took a deep breath and tried again. "They made me watch as Commander Ream and some of the other guards raped Amy. She pleaded for me to help her, but I could do nothing. If I had knocked her out, they may have spared her from such treatment." His voice was but a whisper, full of self-disgust and pain. "Amy was barely conscious when the Queen threw us in the dungeons together. She wanted me to see the damage, the suffering I had caused. Between them, her and Commander Ream, they had broken Amy." For a moment Hugo could not speak. He took a long deep breath and loosed it slowly. "All the time we were locked in that cell, Amy begged me to help her, to kill her. It was too late; I could do nothing. The Queen had me trussed in iron so that I could not move. I was useless. All of it, all of Amy's suffering was my fault." He raked his fingers across his tightly braided hair, catching and loosening a few dark silky strands.

"What happened after?" urged Diamond, her throat bobbing. Her small fingers enfolded his, her magic reaching out to soothe him.

"That night, Tawne attacked the guards and ripped a bloody trail to the dungeons. He freed us. I picked up Amy and ran. Tawne refused to follow us, he knew they would be able to track him, so he led them away. I don't know even now how we managed to escape, the goddess or some benevolent deity must have helped us that day. I was young and not strong enough to fly with us both, not with damaged wings. I had grown up hiding my gift, but the darkness and shadows were always my friends. I used them to screen us from the palace guards, to form a shield that kept Amy's pain from their ears. Shadows can become an illusion, so I used them to blend into my surroundings, just like I do now. When we were out of the city, I brought Amy here. I waited a few days for Tawne, but he never came. Amy got sicker and sicker." He gulped at the awful, dark memories. "She lost her will to live. Every time I went to touch her, she cowered from me and cried and cried. I couldn't do *anything* for her. I was utterly helpless. I made the decision to leave her, to hunt for herbs that would ease her pain. I never made it back. The Queen knew I hadn't left the valley. Some elite guards found me at a nearby farm, stealing food. You don't need to know what happened next, but it was months before I made it back here. I did not see Amy again. Tawne had been captured and was tortured alongside me. Neither of us gave up the location of this cave. When the Queen was done with us, she gave Tawne to Commander Ream. I can still remember the defiance on his face as they dragged him away. He and Amy paid dearly for being my friends." His fingers drifted to his scar. "Before the nightmare ended, the Queen gave me this." He heard Diamond swallow. "To remind me every day what would happen if I ever allowed myself to care for someone again."

His eyes drifted down. Diamond's fingers were gripping his so hard as to cause him pain.

"I'm so sorry, Hugo. I-I don't know what to say." Her warmth seeped into his damp clothes as she shuffled closer.

The sympathy in her eyes was like a weight bearing down on his soul. He didn't want her pity, he only wanted her to understand. Shaking himself, he squared his shoulders. "I just wanted you to know, to understand…" his voice trailed off as she leaned in and brushed her lips against his cheek.

"Thank you for trusting me enough to share your past," she whispered. "I can't begin to understand what horrors you have been through."

He inhaled, then wished he hadn't as her scent filled his senses. His voice was impressively steady and strong as he addressed her, not even a hint of the emotions raging through him at that moment. "I still have more to tell you. But not yet," he said.

"When you are ready," was all she said.

Hugo felt his heart swell. There was no judgment in her eyes, only understanding. Bringing her hand to his lips, he swiftly kissed it. "This is also the ideal place to re-acquaint yourself with your magic," he said briskly, completely changing the subject.

"W-what?" she stuttered.

Pushing away the ghosts of his past, the grin he gave her was genuine. "Up. Now. These crystals will absorb any magic you throw out, and I'll help you with the rest. No excuses," he added, holding up a hand as she opened her mouth to speak.

CHAPTER THIRTY-EIGHT

Diamond allowed Hugo to pull her to her feet. The revelation of Amy and what she had suffered clattered through her brain. Though it made her sick to her stomach to think of Hugo being forced to stand by helplessly and watch, to carry such harrowing memories. Her heart was heavy with sorrow for him. Capitulating to the Queen was not cowardice, it was the only way he knew how to keep those he cared for safe. And Tawne. She didn't know him, and never would know him, but she still hoped his nightmare in Commander Ream's company had been short.

Diamond squeezed Hugo's hand and held on when he went to drop it. They stared at each other. In that moment, Diamond vowed to destroy the Queen; for Hugo, for Amy, for Tawne, for Attion, for Rose, and for everyone else whose lives had been destroyed by her evil.

Hugo cleared his throat as her magic tugged at their bond, fuelled by her vengeful thoughts. His voice sounded rough when he spoke.

"There it is," he said, cocking his head. "That beautiful magic. Now, don't hold back. Don't restrain it. We are nearer the wall, and the effect of the shield will have lessened. It's time to see how all our magical fights have helped with your control." He gave her a wolfish grin and tugged hard on her chest.

"Hey! Stop that," she gasped.

"The Queen believes you have no ability inside the shield. All she wants from you is to blast Ragor and his army into oblivion. She does not care if it kills you and all the men on the wall when you do it. But sheer power may not be enough to best an immortal like him. You have to be able to wield your magic with control, without the influence of the shield. So today is where we find out if your training has given you that control." He chuckled at the anxiety on her face. "Honestly, it's safe here, these crystals absorb energy. It's why they glow."

"You're serious," she whispered.

His face hardened to granite and his persona changed to that of lethal Queen's guard. "Summon your magic," he ordered. "You need to feel its strength and control it. You need to *own* it and be its master — *before* you meet Ragor."

Diamond knew better than to argue with him. Besides, he was right. Shying from her magic was not an option. Closing her eyes, she grasped the ember of power he had tugged to life. It flooded through her body, sending crackling heat and light surging through her blood and licking along her bones. The sensation was overwhelming. Panic gripped her, sweat beading her brow, when she realised she had summoned it with little effort. Her breathing quickened.

"I can't!" she cried out, fear of losing control, of burning Hugo just like last time, stole her reason. Her chest tightened until she couldn't breathe. The cave. The walls. They were closing in. Blackness sparked at the edge of her vision.

"Diamond?"

She focused on him, on that rough, bass voice.

"You can do this. Believe in yourself. You will not harm me."

Diamond stared into his eyes. Sapphire and silver flames encircled with shadow. But deep inside his gaze held something else. Belief? Her heart tightened as her body relaxed. He believed in her, now she had to believe in herself. He had been pushing her hard to control her magic. If she could master it in training, she could do it now.

Nodding to indicate she understood, Diamond controlled her breathing, exhaling as she allowed her body to relax further.

"I want to try something," he said, in a husky tone.

Strong fingers turned her around. Diamond felt him step close behind her, his body heat seeping into her as he gripped her shoulders. Her eyes fluttered closed as his breath fanned the shell of her ear.

"Think, Diamond. Remember how you felt when we fought side by side in the forest. Remember your anger, your fear. You fought for yourself, for Jack, for me. You believed in your magic. You gave it freedom, and it protected us all from Sulphurious. It razed demons to dust. It might be the only thing that can save you—and me," he hissed. "Don't fear what is part of your soul. Become master to your magic, and it will respond," his voice was a low rumble, his proximity making her shiver as he gave a tug on their bond. "If you can't command it, we will all die next time."

Magic ripped up from her core. Diamond cried out, her hands shooting back to grip at Hugo's legs. She needed to hold him, any part of him, to keep her grounded. She breathed him in, filling her senses.

"You used your magic to save me. Your magic knew it was my match, even then." He hesitated, then took a deep breath, gripping her harder and pulling her back against him. "Diamond, we are meant to be together, and no matter what happens or who tries to tear us apart, our Nexus, our magical bond, will always be there. Only death can break it," he whispered, sending shivers rippling from the top of her head down through her body.

"Let me in," he whispered in her ear, his lips lightly grazing the skin under her earlobe.

Diamond felt all her barriers melt away. Under the pressure of his hands, her skin tingled until warmth spread through her. Heat and magic crackled in the air, sending silver sparks flying into the shadow that surrounded them. Joyously, their power entwined before Hugo pushed his magic gently through her skin. It seeped inside her, wrapping itself around her bones. Such a glorious feeling of belonging swamped her, more intimate than anything she had ever experienced.

Diamond gasped, revelling in it. Her breaths quickened to short gasps, even as a delicious ache pooled in her core. A groan escaped her lips.

Hugo growled, lightly grazing his teeth on her neck. His breathing became harsh as his fingers gripped her hips hard enough to be painful.

Diamond didn't care. Tilting her head back, she arched her neck, inviting the attention of his mouth. Another moan escaped her as his tongue flicked out, exploring, tasting. Fighting the urge to turn around, her fingers dug hard into his thighs. She wanted him so badly. Now. Here in this cave.

"Hugo, please," she moaned, not caring that she was begging. Fae. She was half-fae, and right now her need for him was soul deep and burning.

"No," he hissed. Swearing under his breath, he stepped back until cool air caressed the back of her neck. "Focus," he panted, his voice hoarse. The scent of his desire made her head swim.

He wants me as much as I want him. That thought alone nearly stole any reason she had left.

"Remember how you called your magic to save me. That focus and determination. I need you to do that right now. Remember, Diamond, and let my magic guide yours."

Diamond gasped as she felt him open his soul to her. His memories filled her. The forest, the Queen—the throne room. Fear and anger, and utter desperation slammed into her, awakening memories of her own that she wanted to forget: General Edo's blood dripping down her arm and between her fingers, her father's ravaged body as he pleaded with her to run. Diamond quickly forced those memories away, gladly falling back into Hugo's.

He was in the forest, surrounded by monsters, fighting so hard to keep them alive. To keep *her* alive. All the rage and fear she felt from Hugo's mind was amplified in her own. She embraced their bond.

And magic seared her soul.

Power sizzled along her veins, burning through her every cell. Gritting her teeth, she tried to stop her reaction. But her magic was free, searching out its mate. Diamond felt the moment it dived into Hugo's soul, binding itself to the very core of his power. A cry escaped her.

"Let it *live*," he breathed, stepping closer again, seemingly unable to keep any distance between them. His hands found their place on her hips. "Let your magic become. Give it the freedom to grow." His words were so steady, so full of conviction. The insistent command in his voice destroyed her will to contain her power. Her eyelids snapped open and she gave her magic freedom.

Glorious light and heat poured from her skin, searing away every dark shadow in the cave. Hugo did not let go like she expected, but pulled her back against him, wrapping his arms around her abdomen. Her energy seemed to flow into him, keeping her grounded and in control.

"You can control it if you want to," he told her. "You know how to, just the way you have mastered every other weapon," he encouraged.

Overhead, the purple crystals pulsed as they absorbed more and more of her power. They glowed like nothing Diamond had ever seen. Cocking her head to one side and making an arc with her hand, she wondered what would happen to the cave jewels if she continued. A kaleidoscope of sparks fell as her magic hit them, again and again. *Will they explode if I overload them?* It was a detached, distant thought. Hugo must have wondered the same thing. "Now stop," he ordered, calmly and quietly.

Diamond closed her eyes, tightening her hold on the heat that raged so deep inside her, heat so powerful that she had no idea where it came from. She couldn't grasp it, couldn't find the source. It existed with no beginning and no end. Pain tugged at her insides, a fiery taste, like burning embers, beginning to fill her mouth and nose. Terror gripped her.

"I. Can't. Stop," she ground out.

Hugo tightened his hold on her, and she felt him tug their bond. "Put your hands over mine," he growled.

Diamond did, and the most extraordinary sensation took her. A surge of shadow invaded her. It swirled and tugged insistently at her chest, and although she could feel her magic hiss and spit in defiance, the shadow did not listen. It consumed her unruly power until nothing more than a gentle trickle flowed from Diamond.

Hugo's body radiated heat.

Diamond glanced over her shoulder at him, swearing he seemed taller, as if his body had become swollen with the merging of their Nexus.

"Now master your magic. Trust me to keep you safe whilst you train it. I won't allow it to get out of control or harm either of us. *Force* it to do your bidding, just like you have your body and mind. Think of your magic as a living being, one that desires boundaries. I know it's wild but it needs you to live. If you die, it dies. It's yours to control, like my shadow is mine," he told her.

He was right. Honing the power that flowed through her veins was like learning to control her thrusts with a weapon or a strike with her fists. She *had* to take control. This magic could be the salvation of so many souls. It would only rage and destroy if she allowed it.

"Loosen your hold on me a little," she rasped.

The pressure of Hugo's hands relented a little. Sensing a release on its enforced containment, her magic surged. Angered by her attempts to subdue it, her power exploded out through her skin, her eyes, her mouth. A swirling storm of bright white and violet threads, shot through with sapphire and silver ribbons, swirled around them both. The cave glowed. Gritting her teeth, Diamond pushed and fought.

I will not yield.

She fought until a crack appeared in her magic—the first sign she was winning. She re-doubled her efforts to grab it and mould it to her will. Concentrating on nothing but the heat and defiance of her power, she pulled it back towards her, then thrust it away, again and again.

Joy flowed through her as her power began to respond. Diamond's neck stretched back in ecstasy. She rested her head back against Hugo, her hair glowing as it fell in a silver cascade down his body and across his arms. Huge hands pushed gently against her abdomen, moving her until her body was forged to his. Diamond smiled, covering his hands with her own, holding them against her. She did not want this feeling to stop. It wasn't just the power Diamond craved but this feeling of belonging, of their Nexus. Such a glorious gift. Inside their bodies and out, their magic danced, the feeling nothing short of perfect. A small groan escaped her, and she pressed back against the solid mass of muscle behind her. He responded by gripping her harder, his voice gravelly and shaking as he spoke.

"Now, Diamond, you have to stop it now. It's beginning to control you again," he breathed, his chest rising and falling in heavy pants. His hands tightened into fists against her abdomen.

"But I don't want this to stop," she whispered. "I want to stay here with you, like this." *Well, maybe not entirely like this.* The longing in her voice surprised her and she blinked, gripping him tighter.

"That's why you have to do this. Your magic is stealing your self-control. You have to force it to obey you. I cannot absorb any more magic, and I cannot dominate it any longer—it's too strong. *You* are too strong," he told her, clenching his jaw.

In her heart Diamond knew he was right. Hugo had been consuming her power to give her time to learn control, but it had become too overwhelming for both of them. She could feel her magic's arrogance, its knowledge that it could wrest control of her once again.

Diamond gritted her teeth and battled her power. It didn't want to leave Hugo's. It hungered for contact with its other half. And like any other living being, it fought for what it wanted. Stamping down on the raging heat and the fiery emotions in her heart, Diamond pulled—and pulled her power away from its Nexus. Hugo kept a grip on her, murmuring encouragement as his magic withdrew.

Diamond screamed as her magic challenged her one last time. Heat and light poured from her in a storm that burned the air in the cave, but she felt it, the moment her magic broke and bowed to her wishes. Eyes squeezed shut, she commanded it to still. It finally capitulated, curling despondently inside her. Diamond soothed it like a child, even as her chest heaved and sweat trickled down her spine.

Her face glistened with sweat. Unable to stop shaking, Diamond gave in and leaned hard against the solid strength Hugo offered. For a moment neither of them spoke. Diamond kept her eyes closed, trying to recover her equilibrium—then a slow grin spread over her face. The power she held was mighty, but not enough to overwhelm its master: her. For that is what she was now, its master; not the other way around. The fear and anxiety she had harboured for months, ever since she had seen the burns on Hugo's face and hands, slowly melted away. Her limbs settled, and her heartrate slowed towards normal.

Hugo stared at her intently, the silver of his eyes reflecting the glowing purple light that thrummed through the cave crystals. His body radiated a ridiculous amount of heat. She wondered if that was how he reacted to their Nexus.

"You knew," she accused him gently as he held her eyes.

He gave her a slow smile and released a heavy sigh. "No, not really; only suspected. You have mastered your body and your emotions—except with me sometimes." He grinned wickedly and those powerful shoulders lifted in a shrug. "Now *you* know you can control your magic. It will take a little time to learn what you can do with it. First though, you need to discover how to control it every time you summon it. When you have done that, it will become your most trusted ally. It will fight for you whenever you wish it and never leave you." His voice faded and he seemed to remember he was still holding her. His arms dropped abruptly to his sides, and he stepped away.

The heat Diamond had been enjoying vanished with him.

"Again," he demanded, back in his commander persona.

And so it went. They practised for hours, until Diamond could summon and cease her energy flow independently of Hugo's help. He made her continue until her whole body shook with fatigue, only letting her stop when she proved she could summon and control but a tiny tendril of magic, not a storm.

She manipulated one tendril toward him, smiling widely as she entwined the gentle ribbon of light with a silver serpent, letting them dance. Joy seeped into her. Their magic was happy. *Is this how he stopped my magic burning us alive last time?* she wondered dreamily. *Did he use our Nexus to smother it?* But the sight in front of her distracted her from that question.

"I wish you could see your energy. It's truly beautiful," Diamond whispered, lifting her gaze to his face. In that moment she saw his face soften. He opened his mouth as if to speak, then snapped it shut. She didn't miss the strange glint in his eyes before he looked away. Diamond frowned. *Had that been guilt?*

Confusion and unease rippled through her as Hugo abruptly pulled his energy back and turned away.

"It's getting late. We should go," was his only reply.

CHAPTER THIRTY-NINE

Hugo rode in silence, lost in thought. Diamond's heart lurched for the hundredth time since they had left the cave. Feeling their magic merge had been such an intimate and beautiful feeling. She swallowed; it had felt so right, like she belonged with him. Her body had *ached* for his, and if he hadn't been more in control—she swallowed hard, deciding now was not the time to push him into talking about their feelings for each other.

Fingers of icy cold grasped her toes, the chill wind finding any gaps in her cape and her armour, just to spite her. Diamond shivered, the day taking its toll. "Is it far now?" she asked as the first drops of rain splattered on her head.

"No, we'll reach the base of the cliff in about half an hour, but the trek up to the wall will take longer," Hugo answered, giving her an encouraging smile. "Let's pull your hood up, keep the rain and wind off your head," he said softly, reining in Midnight Fire until they were side by side, then he leaned over and did it for her. "There," he said.

Diamond gave him a small smile of thanks, her breath hitching at the flash of affection in his eyes before he led them forward. They broke through the treeline. She gasped.

The Rift Valley cliff loomed above them.

"How are we going to get up there?" she breathed.

Hugo chuckled softly. "Don't worry, we don't have to climb. At least I don't."

"Ehh?" she exclaimed. Her heart sank as she wondered if *she* was going to have to climb. She was far too tired. And there were their horses.

"Hey, relax. I'm kidding." He laughed at her dismay. "There's a track cut into the cliff-side. Of course you don't have to climb. There's a town up there. Don't forget there are a lot of people in this army to feed and shelter. Jack has already arranged for us to have a room in the tower, though. It seems he wants you to be comfortable." He paused as if thinking. "I guess it doesn't hurt to be close friends with the gallant crown prince, especially if you want favours, like a luxurious bedroom to share," he finished, glancing sideways at her with a mischievous glint in his eye.

Diamond glared at him defensively, then flushed. She was unsure if he was referring to sharing Jack's room or something else entirely. *Does he mean we are going to share?* She gulped, then noticed the obvious amusement in his eyes before she dropped her eyes as she urged Luna ahead.

Behind her Hugo gave a satisfied smile.

Soon they switched positions. Hugo weaved between camping soldiers and supply carts, leading her toward the track. It seemed these men had sensibly decided to wait until morning to ascend the tall cliff face. Camp fires burned and horses whinnied. Diamond could even smell food cooking, which was torturous. Her stomach grumbled a protest, so empty now it ached.

Gritting her teeth, Diamond tried not to appear as scared as she actually felt when they urged their horses, side by side, up the slippery track toward the cliff top. A vicious wind blew their cloaks, which were no protection from the driving rain. Soon they were both wet through to the skin.

Hugo set his features in a determined mask and grabbed Diamond's reins. Holding them tightly, he pulled Luna along when she faltered on the wet shale and rock. Diamond's heart was in her mouth even though Hugo positioned himself on the drop side of the track. Midnight Fire calmed the mare, urging her onwards with his muscular body and familiarity with the track, a steady and calming influence. By the time the ground levelled out, Diamond shook from the effort of staying on the mare's sloping back, her thighs and arms aching mercilessly from gripping her saddle so hard.

Hugo led the exhausted mare to the door of the turret. Clutching her saturated cloak tightly around her chest, Diamond hunched her shoulders against the freezing rain that struck painfully at the exposed skin of her face. Hugo slid down from his horse. Even his movements seemed laborious and slower than normal. With a few short words, he handed the reins to a waiting stable boy, who nodded as he hunched his shoulders against the storm.

Luna whinnied pitifully, dropping her head.

Damn! The ground was a long way off. Diamond suspected her legs would collapse under her when she dismounted. Gritting her teeth, she swung down, unfastened her pack and shakily made her way up the tower steps.

Gripping the large round metal handle, Hugo pushed open the heavily reinforced door. Heat and the aroma of food washed over the two weary travellers.Inside was warm and dry—a heavenly change— and quite big. Long wooden tables filled the expansive floor and were surrounded by basic wooden chairs. There was a large stone hearth blackened with use and age. In it, a fire crackled merrily.

A few soldiers raised their eyes, curious about the newcomers. Each soldier wore a coloured tunic with a dragon embroidered upon it. Two captains and a sergeant. Hugo ignored them as they blatantly assessed his bulk, his armour and his weapons. They kept a wary eye on him, noting his armour as that of a Queen's guard. If that wasn't enough to interest them, the way he moved was. It was enough to convince them he could use the weapons adorning his body.

An older, rotund man with grey hair hurried in through an archway, likely from the kitchen based on the smell of cooking meat and bread in the air. Saliva drenched her mouth. She was starving! Starving and near frozen.

"Commander Casimir? And Lady Gillon?" the man asked. His face was red, either from the heat of the kitchens or too much alcohol. Fleshy lips split into a polite smile, and he bowed as low as his stomach would let him. "We are expecting you. My name is Arthur. I am chief steward here."

Arthur nervously surveyed Hugo, but Diamond smiled at him, trying not to giggle at Arthur's greeting. Raising her eyebrows at Hugo, she mouthed, "Lady Gillon?"

His scar twitched, though he kept his face blank even as his eyes twinkled.

Arthur turned away, missing their exchange. "Take the commander and Lady Gillon to their room and ensure you see to their needs," he ordered the young servant boy lingering behind him.

Diamond almost burst out laughing as he addressed her as a 'Lady' again. Then she realised what he had said and blushed scarlet. They *were* sharing a room. That had to be Jack's doing. It was near impossible to hide the nerves that made her legs tremble. Hugo caught her expression, coughed and hid his smirk as Arthur turned back.

"Please, if you hand me your cloaks I will see they are cleaned and dried for the morning. I'm afraid many of the rooms here are already spoken for by the commanding officers. Although, on orders from his highness, we have managed to secure one of the larger rooms for you to share," he looked apologetically at Diamond.

She hoped her mortification wasn't too obvious.

"I have arranged an extra bunk to be brought in and some screens for my lady's convenience," he said a little uncomfortably.

Diamond smiled graciously and inclined her head, even though her heart nearly stopped.

"Thank you for your forethought and hospitality, Arthur. You are very kind. And I am sure the room will be most comfortable, for us both," she responded and gave him her best smile, though her voice trembled slightly.

Arthur puffed his chest out.

From the corner of her eye she saw Hugo wipe his hand over his mouth as if trying to hide a smile. *He knows how embarrassed I am*, she realised. Lifting her chin, she gave him a steady look. He raised his brows and affected an air of innocence.

"It is my absolute pleasure to be of service to you, my lady. William will show you up and be at your disposable for the evening. Would you like food brought to your room?"

"That would be lovely," replied Diamond, then she hesitated. "Is there any facility for bathing here?" she asked as sweetly as she could.

Arthur bristled a bit. "Of course, my lady. There is a small bathing room through that door there." He pointed to a wooden door in the opposite corner of the guardroom. "William will ready a bath for you after you have eaten, if that is your wish."

"That would be most welcome. Thank you so much for your kindness, Arthur," she smiled, fluttering her eyelashes at the older man and causing him to flush bright red.

Hugo snorted slightly but she ignored him.

"It's a pleasure for friends of his highness," Arthur stammered, bowing slightly to her before bustling off to the kitchen once again.

William walked off up the stone stairs.

Hugo cordially stood to one side, gesturing for her to ascend first. He gave her a low mocking bow as she passed.

Inclining her head haughtily, Diamond passed him by. His energy rippled around them, and she could tell he was still amused as they were shown into a large, plainly furnished room on the second floor. William quickly left them, vowing to return soon with their dinner.

A large double bed had been pushed up against one wall with screens placed around it. A smaller single bed rested against the other wall. They pushed the screens back out of the way, then Diamond moaned as she collapsed face down on the bigger bed.

"Hey, who says you get the big bed?" asked Hugo indignantly.

"Me. I'm a lady, don't you know?" she retorted, rolling over.

Hugo snorted loudly and stood grinning down at her.

Grabbing a pillow, Diamond chucked it at him. "I am, too. Arthur says so," she defended herself.

"Yeah? I wonder what he'd think to your ladyship if he saw you rip someone's throat out with your bare hands or turn them to dust with your magic," he commented drily, raising his eyebrows, hands on his hips and looking massive from this angle.

"Oh, do be quiet and help me off with my boots," she demanded. Waggling her feet, she tried not to succumb to the heat that flooded her body and face as she realised she was reclining on a bed with him towering over her.

Silence descended as he realised the same thing. Then a wolfish grin spread across his face. "Sure," he said and grabbed her legs, unceremoniously pulling her to the floor. Diamond landed with a bump, and he laughed, jumping in her place on the bed. "There. It's mine now," he declared, giving a satisfied moan as he flopped back with his hands behind his head and closed his eyes.

"Bully," she muttered in disgust, trying to ignore the mad rhythm of her heart as she raked her eyes over the full length of his body. It suddenly felt really warm. "That's no way to treat a lady," she grumbled from the floor.

He opened one eye and fixed her with a sapphire stare. "Oh, Diamond, I know precisely how to treat a lady," he drawled.

Her breath hitched in her throat and her stomach tightened almost painfully at his velvet tone.

276

"I'll even come and attend my lady in the bathing room to scrub her back if she wishes," he grinned lasciviously, laughing when she flushed bright red.

"No thanks. I'll manage," she huffed, not sure she could cope right now with this version of Hugo.

William knocked and entered, crockery rattling as he balanced the tray he carried. Diamond hastily pushed herself up off the floor. Poor William looked mildly confused as he saw her struggle up whilst Hugo kept his position, reclining on the bed with his eyes closed. The young servant placed the tray on a table near the small window and turned to leave, glancing nervously at Hugo, who still wore all his weapons and armour.

"Err, thank you, William," Diamond said gently, not wanting to startle the boy further.

"You're welcome, my lady. I will fill your bath now and make sure it's ready for after you have eaten," he said, still staring in awe at Hugo and his weapons.

"Thank you so much, William," Diamond soothed, looking pointedly at the door.

William looked away from the reclining Queen's guard and reluctantly left them alone.

Hugo deigned to get off the bed long enough to remove his leather armour. As he placed his weapons carefully within arm's reach of the bed, Diamond tried to ignore the way his damp shirt clung to the contours of his body. Instead, she busied herself with pulling the table up to the edge of the bed so they could sit and eat in relative comfort.

The roast pork, vegetables and potatoes tasted as wonderful as they smelled. They ate quickly and quietly; Diamond realised that if she was hungry, Hugo must be famished. He was almost twice her size and would have burned up fuel in a matter of moments when he used his magic. The wine Arthur had sent up was a bit sour, but it flooded

Diamond's body with warmth, making her cheeks flush and her limbs relax.

With her hunger sated, she sighed contentedly, then eyed the door. That hot bath beckoned. She ached to scrub herself clean; even she could smell the stink of stale sweat, horses and travel on her. It would be wonderful to feel her tight, magic-fatigued muscles relax, but she was so tired now, and that bathing room was such a long way off. She loosed a big breath, her spine slumping forward.

Hugo smiled, slid closer and nudged her gently with his shoulder.

"If you want that bath, you'd better go now, before you fall asleep. William will not think you much of a lady if you waste all that hot water he lugged into the bathing room."

Diamond groaned, "I know. Maybe you should go use it instead."

"Hmm, I might, but first," he prompted, putting his hand at her lower back and shoving her up off the bed. "It's yours. It will help you relax. Come on, I'll walk you down."

"Oh, I'll be all right, Hugo; you don't need to do that," she protested, not really seeing the need for an escort.

"Yes, I'm sure you'll be fine too, but I'll take you down and wait in the guardroom for you anyway," he declared, standing up.

"Why?" she frowned. "I'm only going downstairs. Why not stay here and rest?" she asked, almost pleadingly. The thought of Hugo *actually* coming to scrub her back made her hot and cold at the same time.

"Because *my* lady, in case it has escaped your notice, you are quite possibly the only female in this turret," he said, leaning forward and cocking his head. "And a damn gorgeous one at that."

Diamond willed herself not react to that comment and deliberately avoided his burning gaze, staring instead at the open neck of his shirt.

"And," he grinned at her, "I have not yet come across a bathing room in a soldiers' quarters that has a lock on it. It's sensible; we don't know who else is here, or what they are like, so it will be safer for you if I watch the door. Unless you'd like the company of another male in the bath with you? Maybe he could scrub your back instead?" he drawled, raising his eyebrows in amusement, but she didn't miss the hint of possessiveness in his tone.

"Of course I don't!" she snapped, using that as an excuse to move away from him. Hiding her gulp, she grabbed her sack with her clean clothes and toiletries. As an afterthought, she bent down and picked up a dagger.

Hugo smiled, turned and grabbed a couple of knives as well, thrusting them in his belt.

"Come on, then. Let's go, escort," she said, trying to glower at him as he opened the door for her.

He smiled and bowed mockingly. "I'm yours to command, *my* lady," he declared.

Flustered and not sure how to react to that statement, she flounced past him and smacked him hard in the belly for good measure.

"Oomph! Very lady-like," he laughed as she swept down the stairs. Keeping her back to him, she grinned.

CHAPTER FORTY

The bathing room was small and a bit damp, but it was also clean and warm. A small fire burned in the hearth, which had left the walls and roof covered in a build-up of black soot. A small Silverbore bath stood forlornly in the middle of the floor, full of steaming hot water. It dawned on her that iron could not be used for the fae officers; hence, the Silverbore.

Diamond dropped her sack at the edge of the room and undressed. She quickly slipped into the water. Hugo was right, there was no lock on the door. As she scrubbed her hair, she heard deep, male voices rumbling through from the guardroom. Stiffening, she leaned over the edge of the tub, her wet hand reaching automatically for her dagger. She cocked her head to listen, her heart banging hard. Then she relaxed; Hugo was watching over her. Lulled by the knowledge he would keep her safe, Diamond relaxed back in the water and had nearly fallen asleep when there was gentle knock at the door.

"Hey? Are you all right in there? You've been ages," complained Hugo from the other side of the door.

"Sorry!" she shouted, sitting bolt upright. "Nearly done!"

Quickly Diamond stepped out, dripping water in a puddle on the floor. Drying herself on the rough towels that William had provided, she kept a wary eye on the door. Her hair she left loose, running her fingers through its long silver tangles, grimacing at the knots. It would dry eventually, but brushing them out would take an age.

Diamond hastily threw on her shirt and leggings but didn't bother with her underwear or tucking her shirt in, or even doing all the buttons up. Her limbs were shaking with fatigue. A groan escaped her.

She just wanted to sleep. She'd have to ask if using magic would always ravage her body like this or perhaps she simply was not used to expending such energy from her soul. Aware that Hugo was waiting, she gathered up her belongings and, without giving her appearance another thought, rushed out like a sweet-smelling whirlwind.

"Sorry," she uttered breathlessly to Hugo, her attention solely on him. Hair tumbled over her shoulders, her face flushed from the heat of the water and her eyes glittered in the fire light.

The atmosphere in the room changed immediately, the background conversation stopping abruptly.

"Nearly dozed off," she explained in an apologetic rush as she closed the bathing room door.

Then Diamond noticed the four men sitting at Hugo's table. The two fae, who looked to be around Hugo's age, immediately lifted their chins and inhaled deeply. The two human soldiers, who were older, eyed the fae warily, their eyes darting to Hugo, who had become completely and utterly still. Silently the fae appraised her.

Diamond cursed herself. Young, male and fae were a bad combination for a half-dressed, half fae female. Extremely flustered and wishing she had dressed herself properly, she became very aware of her loose buttons, lack of underwear and bare feet. She had thought Hugo would be alone by now. It had seemed so quiet out here.

Hugo stood and glowered at her. She swallowed nervously when his eyes turned wholly black. He was ready to fight. Not really sure what to say to defuse such a volatile situation, Diamond gave all four males a polite smile.

The humans narrowed their eyes and, smirking at the fae, leaned back in their chairs, waiting to see what happened next. Both fae studied her intently, their eyes running over her, then lingering on the open neck of her shirt.

Hugo stalked around the table, his countenance curt, his face empty. Even so, she took a step toward him, glad of his intimidating air.

Stupid! Stupid! Stupid! she berated herself. This was an army of fae warriors, many of whom were going through their mating urge and with very little opportunity to assuage it.

"Gentlemen, I bid you a good night," Hugo said politely, even though his voice was laced with ice. He slipped a warm possessive hand around her waist and pulled her close.

Diamond tensed, then leaned against him, dropping her eyes demurely. Letting them think she belonged to Hugo, that she was his, was the safest action right now. The two fae eyed Hugo belligerently. Both backed down at the challenge in his coal-black eyes. Disappointed there would be no violence, the other two soldiers shrugged and struck up a conversation once again.

Hugo guided Diamond up the stairs, urging her forward with a hand at the small of her back. No sooner had he shut the door to their room than he hissed at her, "What in Chaos did you think you were doing coming out of the bathing room looking like that?!"

"Like what?" she asked indignantly. "I'm dressed!" Diamond looked down at herself. She *was* dressed and covered—mostly.

"Barely!" he spat, shoving his face up close to hers. His eyes glittered as he looked her up and down as thoroughly as the other fae had.

Her hand itched to slap him for looking at her like that. "What? I *am* dressed!" she retorted bitterly, turning away from him. Throwing her sack down in the corner, she fished out her comb and tackled her hair.

Hugo paced about like a caged animal, muttering about her lack of awareness and naivety. Most young fae had a remarkable degree of self-control around others, male or female, but sometimes things could get out of hand, and violent.

Embarrassment at her mistake turned into anger and indignation. Her magic sparked and, without conscious thought, she blasted him with a wave. His pacing stopped immediately, and he swung to face her.

"Oh, stop muttering, Hugo! I was trying to be quick so you didn't have to keep on waiting for me. I didn't think anyone else was in there with you. And you know it isn't my fault that they looked at me like that. They're fae, just like you. I can't poke their eyes out to stop them, can I?" she ranted, her eyes flashing as he stood and glowered, his arms folded tightly over his chest.

"Yes, you could. You could do a lot more than poke their eyes out. But before that, you could damned well dress yourself so the males around here don't want to break this damned door in to get at you," he growled. "Have you forgotten about their instincts, Diamond? Or mine? Because if you have, I would be happy to remind you exactly why you shouldn't tempt a fae who is of an age to be hunting for a mate," he finished, his eyes alight with silver fire.

Diamond swallowed, her hand shaking so much she nearly dropped her comb. Despite the sudden heat flooding her body, not to mention the way he was looking at her, Diamond stomped over to the big bed and flashed him a mutinous look over her shoulder. "Oh, I give up! You're being an unreasonable, arrogant pig! And I don't care if you are fighting some ancient biological need. It's nothing to do with you, or anyone else, how I dress. I don't belong to you, and I can do whatever the hell I like!" she yelled and flicked her wet hair down her back.

At that moment a hard gust of wind rattled the window and door.

Hugo immediately twisted his head towards the door as if expecting someone to barge in.

Ridiculous, Diamond thought. Fae were an extremely physical race and sometimes wild with their needs, but not stupid. Neither of those fae would risk the possibility of Hugo's wrath to bed a female they didn't even know.

Hugo grabbed a chair and wedged it under the door. Diamond almost laughed until she saw the look of rage on his face.

"I'm going to bed," she said petulantly. Then she pointed at the small single bed. "You get that one."

She knew the bed was far too short for him, but right now she didn't care. In fact, she took pleasure in the thought that she could punish him by making him uncomfortable — even if it *was* only a little bit. He deserved it. She then purposefully goaded him into losing his tight self-control by pulling off her leggings. Flashing him a dirty look, she bundled them into a ball and threw them at his feet. Only her loosely buttoned shirt covered her now, exposing her thighs. It was stupid and dangerous to push him, but she wanted to. Defiantly, she unbuttoned her shirt more.

Hugo glowered and snarled, his energy pushing angrily against her skin. Scowling, Diamond huffed once more for effect before slipping into bed, turning her back on his thunderous face.

Dangerous to turn her back on him when she was drowning in his rage as well as the burning, musky smell of his arousal. Her heart banged against her ribs even as his magic nipped at her skin. They needed to talk about what was happening between them, not fight. But Diamond balked at that idea.

Not now; we are both too angry, she decided, knowing she was being cowardly.

Metal rattled as Hugo threw his knives down on the wooden floorboards. Diamond flinched. The metallic clattering grated on her already tense nerves. Every move he made as he stomped around undressing made her tense even further. Eventually, he blew the lamps out. The room plunged into shadows, broken only by the glow from the dying embers of the fire. The little bed creaked as he reclined.

Diamond lost track of how long it took for his angry energy and the scent of desire to calm enough for her to relax slightly. As he turned or sighed, she felt a little spark of magic nip painfully at her exposed skin. She remained still, feigning sleep, though her mind and body buzzed with the awareness that he wanted her.

Diamond swallowed hard. Her father had always been candid about sex; being fae, such subjects needed to be discussed. He had told her to wait for someone she trusted. Despite everything, she knew she trusted Hugo. Sharing his past with her was his way of showing how much she meant to him too, that he wanted her to understand him. That *he* trusted *her*. A deep breath did not dispel the tightness in her belly. She and Hugo had so much to talk about: their bond, their feelings, his servitude. Gods, she didn't even know how their Nexus worked. Diamond squeezed her eyes shut and sighed.

Ignoring her nerves, she shuffled over onto her other side to ease an ache in her hip, only to find him staring right at her, his face wreathed in shadows. Unwaveringly, she held his gaze until the sheen of his midnight blue feathers caught her attention. Her breath caught in her throat; now all she could think about was the feel of those beautiful, silken wings wrapped around her naked skin. She bit back a groan of frustration and sighed. They had fought enough.

Diamond lifted herself up onto one elbow. "I'm sorry, Hugo," she said quietly. "I didn't even consider there may be other fae here who might be going through the urge. You're right. It was naive of me. Please. Can we forget this?"

The bed creaked as he sat up on the edge. He was wearing only under shorts. Diamond found her eyes glued to the ridges of muscle across his abdomen and bare chest, which flexed as he ran his hands through his hair, ruffling it into a mess. The sight of his naked body made her hot and unsettled. Swallowing hard, she was unable to tear her eyes off him as he stood and came to kneel next to her bed. Gently, almost reverently, he smoothed her hair back from her face, running his fingers through it until it cascaded down her back in a silken curtain.

Diamond closed her eyes enjoying the sensation of his touch in her hair. Gods, she had missed him this last week. After a while he cupped her face tenderly in his big hand.

"No," he whispered.

Her stomach lurched. *No?*

Hugo took a deep breath, shaking it loose before speaking. "Diamond, none of this is your fault. You don't need to apologise for being you. It's me who is sorry for being an *arrogant pig,* as you put it," his lips curled in a slight smile. "And you are right, it is none of my business how you choose to dress or who you choose to be with. But I want it to be, so much. And you know what happens to us foolish males when we want a beautiful female."

The knot in Diamond's stomach grew. It was impossible to tear her eyes from his face. His throat bobbed as he swallowed.

"It's just—those two fae were looking at you like they wanted to drag you to the nearest bedchamber. And I wanted to destroy them," he admitted, silver flames beginning to burn among the blue of his irises. "I am a warrior; I know how to control myself, but the longer I'm near you, the harder it becomes to remember that." He gave a small shaky laugh.

Suddenly Diamond couldn't inhale enough air. Her pupils were huge and dark as she stared up at him, her heart beating so fast she was sure he could hear it.

He loosed a ragged breath and caught her face in his hands. "You are driving me out of my mind. The thought of anyone else touching you, of even seeing other males look at you like they did makes me want to destroy something. I don't want *anyone* else to touch you. Not ever. I know that makes me possessive and selfish, but I can't stop myself."

Diamond watched his eyes fill with sorrow and guilt.

"I am so sorry for how I have hurt you, for what has happened to you since we met. What happened to Amy," his voice caught, "I couldn't let that happen to you."

Diamond dropped her eyes, her heart bleeding for him. His whole life had been built around violence and death, and now he was placing his heart at her feet, apologising for who he was.

"I'm sorry I could not save your friend. And I'm so, so sorry about Rose, I-I couldn't —"

Diamond interrupted him. "Hugo, *stop* apologising. What you said earlier, why you did what you did. *I* am sorry all that happened to you, that this happened to you," she said, reaching out and touching his scar. His hand was warm as he covered hers and pushed his cheek into her palm.

"No, you don't understand," he whispered. "There is something else that I need to confess."

Confess? Her teeth bit into her bottom lip. She pulled back, suddenly frightened. "What?"

Silence.

"Hugo?" Her stomach twisted with a surge of anxiety.

He dropped his head and heaved a sigh. When he brought his head back up she gasped in horror. Needle sharp blue teeth protruded from his gums.

"No," she whispered. The room spun as the blood rushed from her head. "No, you can't be like her." Images of Kitty and Rose swam through her mind and she scooted away from him, into the middle of the bed.

"I am nothing like her," Hugo uttered, those teeth disappearing immediately. His eyes turned pleading. "Diamond, please listen to me before you judge me. That day near Sentinel's Cave, when you fought so hard to save everyone, when your magic almost killed us, I couldn't let you die. I knew that you were my Nexus, but my need to save you was so much deeper than our magical bond. I wanted to protect you, to save you. I knew even then that my heart, my soul, was utterly lost to yours." His throat bobbed. "I couldn't let your magic take you from me, not when I had only just found you. You were dying, and I had no other way to save you." He gulped and met her eyes. "I bit you," he told her, his hands shaking as he reached out to cup her face again.

Diamond stared at him, trying to process his words. "You bit me? Like the Queen does to her warriors? You mean you can control my thoughts, my feelings?" She trembled from head to toe, feeling sick. "And have you?" she asked, already knowing the answer.

"Yes," he whispered, holding her gaze. "In the throne room. It wasn't you who killed General Edo, it was me. I didn't know if you could do it. I saw such confusion and grief in you. I simply wanted it to stop, to get you out of there. Gods, I did not want to use that whip on you—or the boy. You had both suffered enough. So I took control of your body. I have never done anything like it before and didn't even know if it would work, but it was so easy to find our connection. I am a killer, you are not. I *made* you kill him."

Diamond stared at him in horror. "It was you? Not the Queen?"

"Yes, I did it, so you wouldn't have to. So your conscience would be clear. I always planned on telling you it was me." He dropped her face and withdrew, sitting back on his haunches. "I know it was intrusive and that I should apologise, but I won't. General Edo betrayed you and killed your father. Gods, he wanted to *kill* you and Jack. He deserved death. I was not about to let the Queen torture you or that boy because of him."

Diamond pressed her lips into a tight line, unable to answer. Her mind whirled. Not only was their magic bonded, but he had injected her with venom and swallowed her blood. She hugged her knees, the implications of that last realisation hitting her hard.

"You could have used that venom bond anytime since. You could have made me do anything," she whispered. "Anything! Did you? At Gorian's inn, did you make me want you, did you make me touch you?" The moment those words left her lips she regretted them. Hugo would never do something so debase; besides, that feeling of fogginess in her mind had never returned after the throne room.

Hugo face fell into a mask of sadness, the sapphire of his eyes turning to endless shadow. "I have never coerced your thoughts or feelings regarding me. Every time I have felt your hate, your disappointment, your fear towards me seep into your magic, it has crushed me. There have been many times my self-control has nearly abandoned me, and all I want to do is hold you and kiss you. I could have taken advantage of you before, even now I can feel and scent your desire as much as you can mine, but please credit me with some honour. I know telling you this might cause me to lose you, but I want you to trust me, to think you can rely on me. I do not want any more secrets between us. None."

Diamond watched his muscles contract as he slowly shifted to kneel on the bed next to her, giving her time to stop him. The mattress dipped, tipping her towards him. Gently, his calloused fingers grasped her chin and turned her to face him. Diamond did not resist. Her mouth dried out at the tenderness swimming in his eyes. She needed to hear what he had to say, her whole being needed to know.

Hugo took a deep breath. "Diamond, I am drawn to you like no other person I have ever met. My soul craves yours as much as my magic does." With his other hand he took one of hers and placed it over his heart. His skin was so hot she gasped and closed her eyes. "There is something else. I know this sounds like madness but when you are in danger, I can feel something raging inside me—another entity. I have to fight to control it. It desires freedom, and it is only ever happy when I am near you, keeping you safe. Diamond, we are bound by venom and magic but my feelings for you run even deeper than that. It's as if my soul, everything that I am, is yours. I can give you up no more than I can stop breathing." His thumb brushed shakily over her lower lip. "I love you," he whispered.

His voice and words washed through her, warming her heart even as his magic tentatively caressed her face.

Her heart clenched so tightly it hurt. "You love me?" she whispered, her breath fanning his thumb.

"With everything that I am," he replied softly.

"But what about the Queen? You still serve her."

"No, I no longer serve her. When I first brought you to the palace, I was still confused about the depth of my feelings for you, and about our Nexus. I didn't understand how I could fall so hard or feel so drawn to a woman I'd just met. To start with, when we were in the forest, I tried to argue it was only my age, that my urge and instincts were affecting my senses, but I soon discovered it was far more than that. I am strong, I can fight with my body and magic, but as soon as those nightmarish wraiths tried to steal your soul, something changed inside me. I couldn't let you go, though I had no idea how to protect you from the danger I had forced upon you. I tried my best, but it wasn't until the Queen had us both in that throne room that I realised she knew how I felt and had been manipulating me for weeks." He shook his head. "I suspect she worked it out the night of the banquet when she saw me smile for the first time since Amy. I can only apologise for my weakness in not letting you go. Then it was too late. I didn't know how to get you out or how keep you safe. Jack had offered to help, but then he disappeared and I was alone. It wasn't until those rebels took you that I realised my soul would not survive without yours."

Diamond stared at his solemn face. Time. She needed time to process all this. *I love you.* Those words echoed around her shocked mind. And the bite. He had lied again. *No,* she reasoned, *he hasn't lied, but he should have told me before. And what would I have done then?* she asked herself. *Pushed him away like he thinks I'm going to now?*

"Diamond? Please, say something," he beseeched her.

"I don't know what to say, Hugo. You can have so much control over me now."

"That is not why I bit you!" he ground out.

"But you already have controlled me. In the throne room!" she cried out, still struggling to comprehend his confessions.

"I took control of you to save you. The guilt of ending someone you loved would have destroyed you. And no matter what he did, you still loved him. I have been there, Diamond, and that guilt *never, ever* leaves you. You did not kill General Edo. I did."

Diamond hugged her knees tighter and rocked.

Hugo's shoulders slumped at her continued silence.

The knowledge he could have controlled her, taken advantage of her, but that he hadn't, tightened her belly painfully. He wanted trust, and sharing his past with her, the horrific abuse he had witnessed and been subjected to, that was his way of reaching out to her, of starting to build far more than a magical bond. And so was telling her the truth about how she had survived her own magic's attack.

Diamond stared at Hugo's face. This warrior had saved her life so many times, in so many ways. Something inside her stirred, her heart fluttering. He had never truly let her down. He had only ever tried to save her from Amy's fate.

Hugo withdrew, wrapping his magic around himself protectively. Slowly, he backed away. When one of his feet hit the floor, Diamond knew she could not let him go.

"Where are you going?" she asked, her heart hammering in her chest, not from anger but nerves and anticipation. Hugo was being honest, now it was her turn.

"I understand your anger, Diamond," he sighed dejectedly. "I'll leave. Find somewhere else to stay."

"No!" The word burst from her. Reaching out she grabbed his hand. Slowly she looked up at her beautiful warrior. And that's what he was — beautiful, even with the twisted scar marking his face. "I'm not angry, and I do trust you. Please, don't leave." Her heart squeezed in her chest.

When he made no further move, Diamond spoke again. "When you bit me, did you swallow my blood?" she asked hoarsely.

"Yes," he replied, watching her intently.

Oh. Heat rushed her face. If he swallowed her blood a second time she would belong to him. A mating tie that could only be broken by death. Keeping her voice steady was impossible as she asked the words her father had taught her. She loved this complicated, scarred warrior, no matter how messed up their situation or lives were. Being without him did not bear thinking about. Raising her eyes and lifting her chin she began.

"You say you love me, Hugo Casimir. Does that mean you will forsake every other soul in this world — for me? That you will bind yourself to me, heart, soul and blood?" she whispered, holding his eyes with her own. Silver sparks ignited into flame as he heard those ancient words. This was the fae mating pledge. She was offering her heart to him and willing to trust he meant every word he had said to her. "Do you want me to be yours and ask I forsake every other soul — human or fae — for you? That you will…"

Hugo dropped onto his knees beside her and grasped her face in his hands. "Shh! Diamond, wait," he breathed.

Diamond fell into the heat of his gaze.

His eyes roamed her face, stopping briefly on her lips before he spoke again. "My love, I want you to be mine as much as I want to belong to you." His fingers brushed her cheek then moved lightly across her lips. "But when we take that vow and drink from each other's soul, I need to know you're certain."

Willing him to believe her, she held his gaze. "Hugo, I am not a child. I know exactly what I want. I have known it since the moment I looked in your eyes. I want to be yours. Only yours."

For a moment he seemed to stop breathing, the silver strands of his energy wrapping around her. Caressing her, they set her nerves on edge and her skin on fire.

"Then let me love you. Let me show you how much I adore you, and we will pledge ourselves to each other," he replied, in a low growling voice.

A sigh escaped her as the warmth of his magic flooded into her limbs and heat from his skin washed over her body. Closing her eyes, Diamond turned her face into his fingers, daring to kiss each one softly. His skin was hard and calloused but so very warm on her lips. Tiny silver sparks escaped the ribbons of his energy, nipping gently at her exposed skin and making it tingle madly.

She heard him catch his breath and groan as she took one of his fingers in her mouth, sucking gently. Her eyes flew open, and she moved closer to him. Her heart pounded chaotically. She desperately wanted to touch him, to touch his silky skin, to feel his warmth and strength under her fingers. He had just declared himself hers—if she wanted him. No one and nothing else mattered right now, not even the Queen.

Diamond reached out a hand, running it down the outline of his broad shoulder and muscled arm. His skin was hotter than she thought possible. He tensed as her fingers trailed to his naked chest, exploring the contours of his body. She gripped him, digging her nails into his waist; he wrapped one hand in her hair, bunched his fingers into a fist and held her head back. Slowly he tipped his head forward, keeping his eyes on hers, holding them unblinkingly. Her lips parted as he moved to kiss her but he held back, teasing her lips with his tongue until she moaned.

"You have to ask me," he whispered, pulling ever so slightly away. His hand tightened in her hair until she gasped, their hot breath mingling. "You have to ask me or I won't kiss you," he rasped, his voice shaking. "I need to know this is what you want."

She did not hesitate. "I do want you," she told him, not releasing his gaze. He needed to believe her. "I want you to kiss me and —"

Her words were lost as he groaned and pushed his lips against hers. His kiss was so very gentle, his mouth moving slowly and sensually against hers. A wave of desire exploded through Diamond, raging low in her belly and heating her blood. Nothing but Hugo existed; his touch, his smell, his taste. Grabbing at his head, her fingers got lost in his raven hair. She pulled him closer, not wanting to let him go. She splayed her fingers and slid her hands down, holding onto him as his weight slowly pushed her down onto the bed until he lay half on, half off her with one leg thrown over hers. Exulting in the feel of his rock-hard muscles, she ran her hands down his back, digging her nails into the scaly skin right under his wings as he gently and possessively bit her lower lip.

Growling her name, he arched his back, wrapping his fists in her hair and pulling her head down against the soft pillow so she could not move.

Experimentally, she raked her nails across that part of him again. His forehead dropped to the soft skin of her exposed shoulder, his breathing hard and ragged. Secretly she smiled, pleased her touch could affect him so.

After taking control of himself, he lifted his head. "Are you sure?" he asked, those fiery eyes staring straight into her soul.

Diamond's heart beat wildly, the scent of their desire and the touch of their magic filling her, but she wanted more. It was hard to stop her fingers from shaking as she reached for his face. "I've never been more sure of anything, but…I've never…" her voice disappeared.

Hugo traced his fingers down her hot cheek. "It's okay," he said softly, such tenderness in his voice that her bones turned to liquid. "You're going to be mine to love forever. There is no rush. We'll take this slow and gentle. If you want me to stop, just tell me. I will not hurt you—ever."

Diamond watched his throat bob as he swallowed hard. His eyes dropped to where her breasts strained against her shirt with every breath she took. Slowly he leaned in and kissed her, expertly moving his lips and teasing her with his tongue until she moaned, then he pulled back. She watched his strong fingers deftly unbutton her shirt. His face tightened as he pulled the folds of material apart. Breath left his lungs in a rush, his eyes raking over her naked skin.

"You're so beautiful," he whispered, his hand shaking as he gently traced the curve of her left breast with his fingers.

Diamond closed her eyes and gasped, arching her back. "Hugo," she breathed, a sound that became a yearning plea as he began to kiss every inch of her skin, from her mouth down her neck to the curve of her shoulder. His achingly beautiful eyes regarded her steadily before he smiled slightly. Moving his mouth across the bare skin of her chest, his teeth and tongue had her clutching at him desperately, her whole body on fire.

Slowly—so very slowly—his mouth trailed down her body until she arched towards him panting. Her fingers grasped again and again at the tensed muscles of his shoulders as he held his weight off her. With hooded eyes she watched him kiss more of her, unable to comprehend the sensations his touch awakened.

Tendrils of magic caressed her where his hands and mouth left off. Diamond lost the ability to think beyond those sensations. His mouth burned a trail across the soft skin of her left breast. The shoulders under her finger expanded as he looked her in the eye and inhaled — then snarled.

His whole body tensed, his energy recoiling from her with a suddenness that panicked her. Swearing viciously, Hugo literally launched himself off the bed, his wings tucked tightly into his back. Taking two quick leaps, he swept his weapons off the floor right as a fist hit the door and banged loudly.

"Cover yourself," Hugo snarled and kicked the chair from under the door.

The firelight glinted off his naked chest as he tensed, ready to strike down whoever approached outside that door. His hair shimmered as he nodded, the deep blue streaks glinting strangely in the dying firelight.

As soon as Diamond covered her bare breasts, she shifted off the bed too. The hilt of her sword felt cool in her hot hand when Hugo yanked open the door, wings armoured, ready to fight.

CHAPTER FORTY-ONE

Heat and the scent of their magic and lust poured over the two fae outside the door. Their eyes widened, realising too late that they had pulled this protective fae male away from his mate.

Hugo's eyes flickered with silver fire. He snarled viciously at the warriors. His future mate was half-dressed behind him, and the taste and smell of her still filled his senses. She was *his* and these males were not getting anywhere near her. She was his to protect, his to love…

Hugo knew he was being irrational. The sensible, calculating warrior part of his brain understood he needed to register the faces of these males, that he should discover their reason for wrenching him away from her. But the feral fae side of him did not care what they wanted.

The next few seconds passed in a blur. As his muscles contracted and he lifted his blade, the warriors each dropped to one knee, lowering their heads in a bow of subservience. But it was not enough to calm Hugo's wild wrath at them being near his half-naked mate.

"Commander, please forgive my intrusion," Elexon said, his voice steady and his eyes remaining downcast. "I mean no harm to you or Lady Gillon."

Hugo felt a warm hand on his arm, urging him to lower his sword. The burning inside his soul quieted at her touch.

"Hugo, Elexon is not a threat. You know he would not disturb us unless it was important," urged Diamond, her voice and magic washing over him in a soothing wave.

"What is it?" Hugo managed to growl down at the warrior. In a calculated move, Hugo lowered his blade.

"Sir, we have news of the giants. They are closer than we anticipated," Elexon answered, his voice unwavering and deferent. Slowly the warrior lifted his eyes from the ground. He did not look Hugo in the eye, nor did he look at Diamond. His golden eyes stayed fixed on a point over Hugo's shoulder.

Hugo appreciated the warrior's understanding; either action would have only fuelled Hugo's ire.

"Elexon? Your commander will meet you downstairs in a moment," said Diamond, her fingers curling around Hugo's forearm. There was a quiet authority in her voice that surprised and pleased Hugo.

"Yes, my lady," Elexon affirmed. Standing tall, the big warrior spun on his heel. "Havron," he ordered calmly. Without lifting his eyes from the floor, the other warrior stood, turned and headed downstairs behind Elexon.

As soon as the door closed, Hugo looked down at her, his whole body tense. Diamond deliberately stepped in front of him, those violet eyes huge as they travelled over the breadth of his chest then up to his face. Their magic had never stopped interacting the whole time those fae were on their knees. It was driving Hugo crazy. Dropping his swords with a clatter, he backed her up against the door. Her hands landed either side of his bare waist. All he wanted to do was kiss her and make her his, to pledge his soul to hers—but she had so many other things to overcome right now, and he had warriors to lead.

He cupped her face in his big hands, resting his forehead against hers. "Diamond, I want nothing more than to mark you as mine, to throw you on that bed and make love to you right now. I want to cover you in my scent so no other male tries to take you from me. But I can't, not until we have left this war behind," he told her. "We need to concentrate on winning, on surviving the giants and Ragor because I cannot stand the thought of being in this world without you. My soul will not survive losing you." Lowering his head, he kissed her, gently at first, until she responded and their magic ignited his blood. Her sweet flowery scent invaded his mind, fogging his thoughts.

Gods, I have a job to do, men to lead... Chest heaving Hugo pulled away. "I have — to go," he panted.

With great effort, he calmed more than just the rapid beat of his heart and pulled his magic gently from hers.

Diamond let it go.

"I know," she whispered, but those amazing eyes followed his movements as he dressed, making it almost impossible to concentrate. Metal buckles clicked as he fastened his swords around his chest and thrust his daggers into their sheaths.

"I'll find out what Elexon has to say and be back soon. Try and get some sleep," he said softly, caressing her face with the lightest magical touch before he strode from the room, not trusting himself to touch her again.

KAREN TOMLINSON

CHAPTER FORTY-TWO

Diamond rolled onto her back and stared at the ceiling. She must have been utterly exhausted because as soon as her head hit the pillow, she had fallen asleep. During the night Hugo had returned. Being pulled into the warmth of his arms had been bliss, but he had bid her return to her slumbers, stroking her hair with gentle fingers and wrapping his magic around her until she had done just that.

A happy smile stretched her lips, her stomach churning madly with butterflies at the thought of seeing her future mate this morning. Last night had turned her world on its axis. She rejoiced in the knowledge that Hugo wanted her, not only in his bed but as his mate. Dressing in her armour and donning her weapons, she made her way downstairs.

The guardroom was a hive of activity, full of soldiers and warriors. Some glanced up as she gracefully descended the stairs.

It did not escape her notice that some of the fae inhaled and tracked her progress down the stairs. It might have been flattering, if not for her circumstances; here in this warriors' camp, she needed to show she was not weak. A scowl instantly marred her features, and she laid a hand firmly on her throwing knives, sending them a clear message. She would stand no insolence or unwanted attention from any of them. Her eyes flashed, and she snarled a warning at the two fae from last night. They, along with the rest of the room, swiftly turned their attention back to their food.

Hugo was in the far corner surrounded by the fae warriors she had seen yesterday.

Her heart banged against her ribs, and she could not stop the heat that rose to her cheeks. He had tracked her progress down the stairs and was staring at her with a satisfied smile curling his lips. Her magic came alive as he sent his sweeping forward to touch her. Confidently, she held his gaze and pushed back, smothering his body in a wave of invisible energy.

The warrior at Hugo's side coughed loudly, as if he sensed their magical play. *Right, focus.*

Hugo smiled at her and, surprisingly, none of the warriors standing in their group showed any revulsion as his scar twisted.

"Diamond, you know Commander Elexon Riddeon. This is Havron, his second in command." Hugo told her, his voice matter-of-fact.

Diamond met Elexon's steady gaze. This close she could see flecks of russet in his irises. Riddeon. So that's where she recognised him from. He was related to the great and immortal Master Commander.

"Good morning, Elexon," she greeted the handsome fae warrior, then courteously greeted Havron and the others too.

"The giants are far closer than we anticipated. Our plans have been brought forward," Hugo said, completely immersed in his persona as commander of these men.

"When do we leave?" she asked, keeping her voice strong and steady.

His eyes studied her as he answered. "As soon as you are ready. Elexon, you have your orders. We will meet you outside in a few minutes," Hugo informed the warrior.

Elexon bowed to them both, fist to chest. The squadron of fae warriors parted respectfully to let him pass, then followed. Only Havron remained; he stood upright and vigilant near the door, watching them and the room.

Hugo frowned, clearly wondering why Havron was guarding them, then his attention rested on Diamond. She leaned against the edge of the table, using it to keep her upright as her legs wobbled—from nerves or his attention, she wasn't sure.

"I thought we had a few days to practise with my magic before we had to destroy the giants," she said, her voice wavering slightly despite her best efforts to appear in control.

"Diamond, we have no more time. I would not put you in harm's way if I did not think you could do this. Besides," a small smile curled his lips, turning her bones to water, "last night you managed to make your magic do whatever you wanted."

Her face heated and he grinned. "Fine. We leave now," she gulped, wishing her voice hadn't squeaked quite so much.

"Oh no, my heart, you are not going anywhere until you eat. It may be a long time until we get the opportunity again, and I don't want you passing out because you are weak from a lack of food. Remember, magic uses energy, no matter what you use it for," he drawled.

At that moment Arthur bustled over, pushing his way through the crowded tables. "Morning, my lady. I trust you slept well?" he enquired politely.

Diamond forced herself not to blush. "Very well. Thank you, Arthur," she replied, her stomach tightening painfully as she took the plate of scrambled eggs, bread and ham he offered out to her. Thanking the steward, she took a seat at the nearest table that was surrounded by other soldiers, a couple of whom gave her friendly smiles. Forcing herself to chew and swallow the plate of food, she did her best not to look at Hugo, who stood hovering at her back. Picking up her cup, she gulped icy water to wash the food down.

"Satisfied?" she smiled over her shoulder when her plate was empty.

"Not at all," he smirked down at her.

Diamond blushed scarlet. Hastily, she pushed her chair back and they left the noisy guardroom behind.

Outside, the tumultuous wind bit into her cheeks. Damp clung to her hair and clothes, raising a violent shiver from her. Ignoring it, she looked around with interest. Flags rippled upon the turreted walls of the tower, and in the grey dawn Diamond made out the watch soldiers staring down into the forest beyond the wall. Every bit of flat ground buzzed with soldiers, stable hands, delivery carts and people performing the essential tasks that kept Jack's army functioning. Makeshift shelters and cooking stations dotted the grounds. Their fires burned brightly, sending plumes of smoke and the aroma of food and burning wood into the air.

Hugo marched to the base of the wall where Elexon and the other fae warriors waited in neat formation. Their wings were armoured and extended, ready to fly. Save for one sword each, they were not heavily armed. Keeping their weight down would ensure better manoeuvrability in the air. In addition to a sword, each warrior carried a sack of explosives.

Elexon glanced at her, nodded in greeting then directed his next question at Hugo. "Sir? We are ready. Shall we go?"

"Yes, make for the village as planned. We will follow."

When the squad had risen, Hugo turned to Diamond. She had been dreading this moment. Nerves churned in her belly. *Will I be able to pull this off? Control my magic enough to fight?* Today she would become the immortal Queen's weapon. Hugo was right, though; the people in this valley needed a chance. She wanted to be the person to give it to them.

"Diamond? We need to go," Hugo repeated, holding his arm out as he studied her face. Support shone from his eyes, although he did not voice it. She was glad. It was up to her to find her confidence and bravery, not him to give it.

Warrior, weapon or both? There's only one way to find out, she thought. Raising her chin, the woodcutter's daughter stepped into the circle of the warrior's arms.

CHAPTER FORTY-THREE

By the time Elexon indicated they neared the village, Diamond's fingers and toes were numb with cold. Below Diamond's feet, the forest was wreathed in shadows. It was hard not to grimace. No matter how much she trusted Hugo, she still hated heights.

Elexon headed toward a small clearing. With practised efficiency the squadron of warriors landed one at a time. Hugo's wings thudded, slowing their descent, then his feet hit the ground in a smooth motion. He gave her one last squeeze before releasing her.

In the distance the sound of breaking waves rumbled. The tang of sea salt laced the air.

"Elexon. Let's go," Hugo said brusquely when they were all safely down. "Diamond, stay with the others. Do not follow us. Stay low and keep hidden until we return."

Diamond tried not to roll her eyes. He was back in the Queen's guard persona she knew so well. Knowing that did not stop her watching resentfully as he stalked away without waiting for a reply. Understanding he needed to become a detached warrior did not mean she had to like it. Before the scowl even left her face, the forest rang out with Hugo's roared warning. In one swift movement both he and Elexon had drawn their blades. Diamond's magic flared in response to a blast from Hugo's, causing her to cry out.

Dust Devils emerged from the trees, their rotting limbs giving them an unsteady gait. Not so the Wolfmen.

The fae warriors burst into movement, charging towards their enemy with blades glinting. Battle cries filled the air, amplified by the clash of metal on metal.

Diamond watched in horrified fascination as Hugo despatched two Dust Devils in the blink of an eye. An attack by two large Wolfmen followed. They came at him swiftly, their yellow eyes glowing with bloodlust and malice. Long, sharp teeth gnashed, and their razor-like claws swung at his chest. Surefooted and quick, Hugo drove them back, shadows curling around him and striking where he willed it. Diamond quickly realised the nightmarish beasts were working together. The large muscles of their back legs tensed before they pounced on him once again, one going for his throat, the other aiming a sweeping blow at his legs.

Fear punched through her gut. Without thinking, she drew both her swords and started running towards him. Before she could get anywhere close, two of the massive half-man, half-beast creatures ran at her. Seeing them from the corner of her eye, Diamond spun, greeting them with a snarl. Her senses shifted as she changed her vision. A whole new world appeared. Her eyes picked up the energy around her, but instead of the beautiful iridescent hues of the valley forest, this area was vapid and devoid of joy.

Dark yellow energy billowed and swirled about the Wolfmen like a noxious cloud of poison. She could easily see what their next move would be when that noxious cloud pulsed with intent. She gave a cold smile. The nearest one, a huge male beast, roared and showered saliva into the air.

"Come on, you ugly bastard," she whispered, pushing away her anxiety.

With startling speed and agility, the creature jumped high into the air. Diamond's heightened senses perceived his intentions in slow and predictable movements. Charging underneath him, she bent her spine backwards and slid along the ground on her knees. Her Silverbore blade glided smoothly along his belly, lancing him wide open. Slimy, purple entrails slithered to the ground before his carcass thudded down. Flinging her body upright, she spun swiftly behind her next attacker. Her blade sank into the Wolfman's hairy back before Diamond smoothly shifted her bodyweight onto her other foot, swiping her second sword across its neck. Blood gushed from the gaping wound. Diamond jumped away from the spray but did not save herself entirely. The smell of its body and blood was both familiar and disgusting.

Hugo dispatched another beast, slashing the tendon of its lower leg then cutting its throat with cold efficiency. A glance over at her and his eyes narrowed. Even with the clearing between them, Diamond didn't miss the flicker of worry that transmitted from his eyes and down through their magic.

That moment of distraction cost him.

A Battle Imp attacked from behind. Built of hard muscle, it towered above Hugo. There was no time to scream a warning. All Diamond could do was watch as the beast opened its maw to sink long blue fangs into Hugo's shoulder.

"Hugo!" Diamond screamed, instinctively throwing a bolt of magic at the creature.

Bellowing with fury, Hugo did not see her release that burst of power, and he spun directly into its path. Magic hit him squarely in the chest.

"No!" she yelled.

In that second, claws ripped through the air. Working on instinct and muscle memory alone, Diamond leaned back then spun on her heel. One set of claws narrowly missed her throat. Then white-hot pain lanced through her upper left arm. She screamed. Another other beast had caught her.

Control, Hugo had said. *Control your emotions and you control your magic. So be it.*

Diamond willed herself to push her fear and pain away. She locked it down so tight it almost suffocated her. Her heartrate slowed, and her eyes and senses focused. Less than five seconds later the beasts lay dead. There was no time for gloating, she needed to get closer to Hugo.

More Dust Devils attacked. Appearing from the gloom of the forest in droves, their movements were unpredictable and jerky. With no soul and no energy to warn her of their movements, her concentration and weaponry skills were sorely tested. Dust Devils did not move quickly in their rotting forms, but there were so many. Metal jarred against metal. Diamond glanced around, feeling her magic simmering under her skin. There were too many fae, too close to use her magic.

Diamond did her best to ignore her horror of the scene. These rotting creatures had once been men or fae with families and lives of their own. But her abhorrence faded as she cleaved head after head. The rotting bodies exploded into black dust, leaving it clinging to her blood-soaked clothes. These things were no longer people.

Snarls and roars of dying creatures resounded through the trees as the experienced fae warriors killed their adversaries.

Diamond grunted as she gutted another Wolfman. Her arms were tiring. More Dust Devils appeared from the trees to her left, their swords drawn. Relief made her legs wobble as Hugo bellowed a warning. *Thank the goddess, he lives and breathes enough to yell at me!* Her violet eyes aglow, she searched the small clearing for him. Quickly sheathing her blade, she lifted her right hand. With no fae in her way, Diamond sent a blast of magic from her palm, disintegrating the rotting, empty husks into dust.

Breathing hard, she stalked past gory corpses. Hugo had broken the Battle Imp's thick neck, and it lay dead at his feet.

The other warriors were breathing heavily, their swords dripping with blood and caked in dust, but all of them, including Elexon, eyed her with a mix of awe and wariness.

"Well, you don't think he brought me simply for my looks, do you?" Diamond inquired, hating that her voice sounded shaky. She stalked right up to Hugo, her eyes raking over his face and down his body, not stopping until she had covered every inch of him. Ignoring his warning glare, she looked around the back of his shoulder just to be sure. Though the Battle Imp's teeth had ripped into his thick leather armour, there was no blood. Satisfied, Diamond stepped away, looking anywhere but at Hugo's face as he returned the favour. His attention heated her insides, but it was the knowledge he was unharmed that had her legs shaking madly.

Ridiculous. Laughable. Hugo is an experienced warrior, not a novice like me. The forest settled around them, becoming calm and silent, yet the stench of death hung heavy and foul.

"Finn, Bram, double back through the trees until you are certain there are no more of our enemy nearby. Kalf, Reinn—cover them from the skies." Hugo clipped out orders efficiently, his voice strong and sure. "Diamond, let me bind your arm."

The warriors followed without question. Diamond found herself staring at him as he quickly and effectively staunched her bleeding wound. It was easy to see now what a good leader he was.

"Elexon, take point, and fan the rest of the squad out. We move in silence, hand signals only," Hugo ordered.

Elexon nodded. It was clear the golden-eyed warrior respected and trusted Hugo; he followed Hugo's orders without question.

"Stay close to me," Hugo rumbled quietly in her ear, his hot breath making her shiver. When he pulled away, his eyes burned into hers. "One injury is enough. No more."

Tempted to tell him she was capable of looking after herself, Diamond frowned at Hugo's back as he turned away. It was nice though, to know he cared for her enough to worry.

Leaving the gruesome scene behind, the group continued in silence through the dark forest.

CHAPTER FORTY-FOUR

The air became sweeter as they reached the forest near the coastal village. Hugo tilted his head. Seconds later the four warrior fae returned. The forest around them looked clear for now.

Hugo nodded. "Reinn, Kalf, Bram, guard the rear. The rest of you, stay vigilant and wait here."

But he wasn't looking at the warriors, he was looking at Diamond. Defiantly, she held his gaze and lifted her chin. His eyes narrowed as he seemed to read her thoughts. She would not wait here if he got into trouble.

"Elexon and I will scout the village. Be ready to move at a moment's notice. Giants might be ugly, but they are also cunning and vicious."

With a meaningful glance in her direction, Hugo stalked off with Elexon at his back. They disappeared into the gloom, melting into the shadows and leaving Diamond to impatiently wait for their return.

Plonking herself down on the carpet of dead leaves and pine needles, Diamond observed the attentive faces of the other warriors. It did not escape her notice that they formed a protective ring around her even though she had not heard Hugo issue such orders. She brushed it off.

Wrapped in her armour, her skin was hot and sticky, her heartrate still calming from that fight. She tipped back her head and closed her eyes, trusting the others to watch for more enemy attacks whilst she tried to ignore the stink of blood and gore that covered her. A briny breeze caressed her sweaty face and neck. It was heavenly.

Once she recovered, Diamond's patience wore thin. Shuffling forward into the trees, she tried to see if it was possible to spot Hugo near the village.

313

"Hey!" whispered Havron. "Where are you going?" He squatted a few feet from her, his short blond hair tousled but his hazel eyes clear and watching her with unease.

"I'm just taking a look," she replied in hushed tones.

Disapproval crossed Havron's face. "The commander said to stay here," he pointed out.

Diamond met his eyes. "I know." Crouching low, she moved away.

Sticks and undergrowth cracked as he followed her. Diamond smiled.

The trees gave way to rocky coast line and sand dunes. She dropped to her belly and, using her elbows and knees, inched toward the cliff edge. The ground dropped away, scree littering the base of the cliff and forming a slope that led gently down to the outskirts of a small village. *Goodison*, Diamond presumed. On her belly, she shuffled her knives so they didn't dig into her hips. The village appeared quiet, peaceful even; waves and wind the only sounds.

Diamond frowned, remembering what Jack had said about the giants destroying villages as they travelled to the wall. This village was in one piece, the buildings intact and seemingly untouched by anything other than the coastal weather.

A small river meandered its way out from the forest, tumbling over the small cliff edge before bubbling merrily through the village and onto the stony beach. A moment of sunshine broke through the grey clouds. Bright rays touched the beach, causing the wet pebbles to sparkle like jewels.

Diamond shifted her attention to the abandoned fishing boats pulled up on the shore. Strange, large rocks lined the sand dunes on either side of the river mouth. *Protection from the tides maybe?*

There was no sign of the two warriors. *Perhaps they have gone further along the coast to find the giants?* Maybe Elexon's information had been wrong. Not sure what to do now, Diamond sighed. Still on her belly, she turned to go back to the forest when, from of the corner of her eye, a movement snagged her attention.

Whipping her head back, she stared hard. It had been near one of the big rocks, the one nearest the village. No, not near it.

The rock itself had moved.

Blinking to clear her vision, Diamond swivelled back. Belatedly, she realised these were no rocks.

A giant unfolded its grotesque, grey-brown body and pushed itself up. Taller than the surrounding pine trees, it raised its bald, wart-covered head and inhaled—long and hard. Diamond realised that he had caught her scent. Milky eyes spotted her and narrowed as it loosed such a bellow that her ears rang.

With astounding speed for such a monstrous creature, the giant launched itself into a run toward the cliff. Raging footsteps vibrated the ground under her body, sending debris from the cliff face hurtling down below her.

"Damn!" she breathed, shocked that it could smell her from such a distance. Approaching the village from downwind had alerted the giants to her presence. It was too late to hide; the only option was to attempt to lead it away from the other warriors.

Diamond sprung to her feet and ran back for the treeline. Skidding to a halt, she spun on her heel, lowered her head and shoulders—then ran. Pumping her arms and legs as fast as she could she launched herself off the cliff edge. Havron bellowed at her to stop.

Ohhh! Why did I think this was a good idea?

Fresh, sweet air and weightlessness took her. It took everything she had to shove her panic away and yank on her magic. *Do as I say now or you will never feel your Nexus again,* she silently screamed at it. Magic surged, forming a cushion underneath her plummeting body. It didn't work as well as she hoped, but it was enough to stop her from slamming into the ground and breaking her legs. Her bones jarred and her breath seized. Her feet sank into the shale, down to her ankles. She thrashed around and dug with her hands. Soon Diamond was clattering across the loose shale, straight toward the bald and wart-covered giant.

Maybe if I get his attention, he'll miss the others. They'll come and help soon. They have to. Diamond knew without a doubt that she would be in for a roasting from Hugo if she lived through this.

The ground trembled under her feet. Horror widened her eyes as nine other boulders began to take shape. Tallo had the right of it. Swords were of no use here. Tougher, bigger weapons were needed against such creatures. Bringing down one giant between them would have been achievable, but all of these?

The sandy earth surged skyward, making Diamond lose her footing and showering her in fine grains of dirt. An overpowering stink of urine and faeces blasted her nostrils as the giant lumbered ever closer. She righted herself and blinked dirt from her eyes. Changing her vision, she was relieved to see an insipid brown-grey cloud of energy pulsing around the creature as it moved.

The giant's gnarled hand swooped, giving her only seconds to take a deep breath, summon magic and somersault high into the air. It was a move she had practised with Attion and Hugo over and over again lest she ever needed to clear a horse or another obstacle to escape. She had never expected that obstacle to be a giant!

Landing solidly, Diamond unleashed her magic in a violent burst at the massive head that passed above her. The giant, unable to stop his forward momentum, took the full force of her strike on the back of his rock-like head. Magic tore through its skull, erupting out through its forehead. Thick legs buckled and the huge creature toppled forward, smashing face-first into the cliff. Rock and sand exploded and the cliff collapsed, burying the giant's head. Diamond did not have time to stand and stare; she knew the other giants were attacking from behind.

The ground continued to shudder and dance, unsteadying her. Diamond spun around. Her mouth dropped open. Two of the monstrous creatures ran straight through the nearest stone cottages, decimating them instantly. Rubble and stone burst into the air, crashing down around their still-moving feet. Seven more giants pounded toward Diamond. Her heart lurched with sudden doubt and crippling fear. Steeling her nerves against a rising tide of terror, Diamond unleashed her magic in short blasts. Maybe she could slow them down long enough for the others to formulate a plan and dive in. *By the goddess, surely they would come soon?* Those damned explosives were the only things that could help her now.

Aiming damaging blasts of magic at the giants' thick legs worked for a time but then they began working together. Hugo had said they were cunning. The nearest one attacked, drawing her attention and blasts. Concentrating on controlling her magic, Diamond missed another large hand sweeping down to grasp her. Gritting her teeth and ignoring the stones that scraped away her skin, she rolled along the ground underneath it.

They will come soon, they will. Hugo won't let me die...

The acrid smell of burning flesh filled the air as she came upright and ran between the legs of the next charging mountain of flesh. She shot a long blast of white-hot energy up into its groin. A scream of pain rent the air, a horrible bellowing sound that echoed out across the ocean. Diamond did not stop; instead, she threw her energy at another giant that ran in on her left.

Focused on that attack, Diamond missed the ugly beast on her right who swiped his large foot in her direction. She was suddenly airborne. The foot's impact against her body drove the breath from her lungs. Pain wheeled through her. The world toppled and she spun through the air, then a sickening sensation took her stomach as she plummeted down toward the outstretched hand of another giant.

It roared with frustration when Hugo slammed his bulk into Diamond, catapulting her out of the giant's grasp. His speed and angle meant he could not stop their trajectory toward the beach. She screamed as his iron-hard arms and armoured wings wrapped around her, holding her fast as they slammed into the sand and rolled together into the waves.

Seawater filled her mouth and nose. Coughing and spluttering, Diamond fought to stand while big waves tried to knock her down again. Pain saturated her battered body. Ignoring it, she splashed to shore. Incredibly, Hugo was already there, his back toward her.

Shocked, her footsteps stilled, her mouth drooping open. He seemed to have grown two feet taller, not to mention wider. His armour was stretched and tearing apart at the seams. *And his wings? What in damnation was going on?*

"Hugo!" she shouted against the roar of the oncoming giant, who had recovered his balance and was heading their way. Hugo turned toward her, and she gasped. Silver flame swirled brightly, surrounding elongated pupils that flicked at her before he turned back to the giant. Rooted to the spot, Diamond stared as Hugo spread his wings, displaying scaly—not smooth—sapphire armour, tattooed in swirling patterns of silver flame. They too had grown in size, making him wider and more formidable than ever. Elexon bellowed a warning from above, and there was no more time to consider Hugo's altered appearance.

Hugo spun, shielding her with his body and wings just as a massive explosion covered them in sand and giant guts. Coughing and retching, Diamond immediately dived into the waves, washing the disgusting flesh and thick, dark blood away. No sooner had she ducked under the water than a massive hand grabbed the back of her armour, hoisting her upwards. Seawater cascaded down off her body and boots.

Hugo threw her upward as though she weighed no more than a child, then flew up to catch her to his chest. Hands gripping her waist, he lifted her until her face was directly in front of his. His bone structure had changed too. Small blue ridges protruded from above his eyes, along his cheekbones and down his jaw. Completely stunned, words failed her.

"Focus your energy at the one nearest us. The others will deal with the two nearest the village," he ordered, his voice deep and grating.

Diamond nodded calmly even though she was anything but. "Can you turn me around again?" she asked.

"In a moment," he told her, soaring upwards faster than anything she had experienced before, enough that the wind sucked her breath away.

Glancing down, she silently prayed he wouldn't drop her.

I won't, his voice growled in her head.

Scaled wings beat powerfully, raising them higher and higher. Preparing herself for the inevitable dive, Diamond changed her vision. Silver and sapphire flames engulfed them. That powerful energy made her skin blaze until heat seeped right into her bones. Diamond ignored it; instead, she spiralled down inside herself, pulling her magic up and curling it around her hands and arms where it crackled and fought for release.

"Ready?" Hugo growled, holding her tightly against him for a split second.

Diamond nodded.

Suddenly weightless, her scream hadn't left her lungs before he caught her to him once again. It took all her willpower to remain focused on her target below when she felt her back moulded to the contours of his body.

"Tuck your legs against mine. You will be more stable," Hugo ordered.

Diamond complied. Her silver hair streamed behind them like ribbons of starlight as Hugo dived from the sky so fast her eyes watered. Blinking furiously, she tried to clear them.

"*Now!*" Hugo bellowed in her ear.

Her magic exploded in a bolt of light from her outstretched hands. It hit the giant square on his chest, burning through flesh and bone all the way down to the organs in his chest. Diamond did not stop. Muddy, red-rimmed eyes widened until the whites were visible. Its whole body swelled, grotesquely pulsing with light until its warted skin ruptured, exploding in a cloud of bloody flesh and bone.

Breathing hard, she grasped Hugo's forearms where they were clamped tight over her belly. The corded muscle under her fingers turned to iron as he back-winged vigorously to slow their descent.

"Again!" roared Hugo, taking them back up in the air, then plunging to where Havron was trying to distract a foe from Elexon.

Hugo grunted, taking them in near to the giant's back. Magic swirled in a glorious pattern, dancing to the thrum of Hugo's wings. Diamond allowed hers freedom, directing it at the giant's monstrous tree trunk-like legs. Flesh burned and the giant toppled to its knees, leaving the back of its head exposed. Trying to ignore its hideous screams of pain, Diamond ended it.

Elexon and Havron somersaulted over the falling carcass, hurling their explosives toward the last two giants in amazing synchronisation.

"Pull back!" Elexon roared.

Hugo rolled in mid-air, clamping his teeth against the strain on his wings.

Diamond's legs slipped as he skilfully corrected his course, his muscles contracting like an iron cage around her. She gripped onto him for dear life as he rocketed upward, her legs swinging all over the place. Without warning, he threw her forward into the air again. Involuntarily, a scream wrenched out of her lungs.

Wings stretched wide, Hugo braced his back to the explosion, grabbed Diamond's waist and slammed her into his body for protection.

Explosive force dragged the breath from Diamond's lungs a moment before a rushing hot wave blasted over them. Even Hugo's bulk was shoved forward. The wide muscles of his back and shoulders contracted as his wings fought and worked against the turbulence. Seconds later, the world around them settled until only the waves and the wind murmured their song.

Hugo hovered, breathing hard under the grip of her fingers. Diamond kept her head down against his chest, clutching herself to the safety of his body, not wanting to face the condemnation she would surely see in his eyes. After a moment she felt a change in him. A shift.

Her mouth dry, she dared to peer up. Glittering black orbs looked right back at her, and his jaw flickered in spasms of anger. But at least he was back to the Hugo she knew. The ridges of blue bone were gone, and he had returned to his normal size. Not that it made any difference to his armour, which hung from him, ripped and stretched out of proportion.

His arms tensed until they were so tight she thought he might snap her in two.

"If you disobey my orders again and put yourself or anyone else at risk, I will take you out over the ocean, up into the highest clouds and drop you from a great height. And if you survive that fall, I will do it again," he warned, his voice ominously quiet.

Diamond flushed with shame. Her behaviour had endangered all of them, not only herself.

"Hugo — I — " she stammered, then looked at the uncompromising set of his jaw. An apology wouldn't help right now. This was a battlefield commander, not her friend or the male who had declared himself hers. This commander meant every icy word he had uttered.

"Understood," she nodded, knowing that a harsh reprimand was the least she deserved.

"Good. Do not test me again," he warned her.

He lowered them down to the devastated village. Sand squelched under her boots.

"I'm so sorry, Hugo. I just..." She tried again to apologise but her words dried up. An unwavering stare told her he was not interested in her excuses. So she nodded.

His eyes and his grip softened at that sign of her acquiescence. "I cannot lose you," he whispered, before he let her go.

Elexon strode over, looking at them both with concern. His golden eyes assessed Diamond's face and body before nodding respectfully at Hugo, inspecting him too.

"Is everyone still alive?" asked Hugo curtly, deliberately ignoring Elexon's scrutiny.

"Yes, sir. Although Havron sustained some broken bones in that last explosion. We need to get him back to the healers at the wall," Elexon answered, his voice steady, even as his eyes flickered back to Diamond.

"Agreed. Send one of your men with word to Prince Oden that the mission is a success," said Hugo.

Elexon looked at her thoughtfully, but she could not meet his searching gaze. Her mortification grew. She had let them all down.

"Of course, commander. Perhaps you should leave with the squad. Three others and I will stay behind. Havron will need a stretcher to get him back to the wall. His ribs and leg are broken."

"No..." Hugo said.

"No, we'll stay. I'll help you make it," interjected Diamond hastily.

Their voices clashed. Hugo raised his brows but remained silent.

Elexon shook his head, looking from one to the other. "That is not necessary, my lady," he answered.

"Please," she uttered, rushing forward and placing a hand on Elexon's arm. "He may not have been harmed if I had not been so headstrong and impatient. Please, let me help."

Elexon regarded her silently, and for a moment Diamond thought he might refuse. Shuffling her feet she waited, knowing she wouldn't blame him if he did.

"All right, my lady, but my men will construct it. It has to be strong enough to take his rather considerable weight back to the turret." Bowing slightly he gave her a small smile, and she relaxed a bit. "This way," he said.

Without another word, Hugo walked away to check the carcasses of the giants.

Diamond glanced at him surreptitiously, just to make sure he really was back to himself. She had no idea what had happened to him during that fight, and by the bleak thoughtful look on his face, she didn't think he did either.

CHAPTER FORTY-FIVE

Working with the warriors, Diamond helped gather the branches needed for Havron's stretcher. Whilst the warriors fixed the wood together with the ripped up explosives sacks, Diamond sank down on the soft sand next to Havron.

"Hey," she said, smiling grimly at the white-faced, sweating warrior.

"Hey," he rasped weakly.

"I'm really sorry, Havron. I should have listened to you," she sighed. "I'm far too wilful sometimes," she admitted, biting her bottom lip.

"So I've heard," he said wryly, panting in pain.

"Have you?" she asked, raising her brows in surprise.

"Yes. Powerful magic wielders are not usually allowed to survive in this kingdom. Word of your trials has travelled. You know? Through the ranks. And soldiers love a bit of gossip," he smiled wanly.

Embarrassed, she smiled back, "Really?"

"Really. A half-fae female holding her own against a group of elite Queen's guards is pretty impressive, even if our illustrious commander out-skilled you in the end."

"Yes, well, he cheated. I was already exhausted by that point," she pointed out dryly.

Havron gave a grin that was half a grimace. "I'll bet your magic can outshine his any day. In a fair fight, at least," he said.

"Thanks," she said, "but I have no intention of fighting him again. Ever," she added fervently.

Havron huffed a laugh then collapsed back in the sand. "After what I saw last night, I can believe that."

Diamond blushed, smiling at the brief twinkle in his eyes before he closed them. With nothing else to do, Diamond gazed around at the destruction. An idea formed in her mind.

"Can I look at your leg?" she asked Havron quietly.

"Sure, but don't touch it. It's damned painful," he rasped.

Pushing up on her knees, Diamond shuffled closer until she was next to Havron's misshapen lower leg.

Everything is made of energy, right? She had been able to see it from the moment Lunaria had unlocked her magic. And if she could see energy and summon magic to destroy things, maybe she could harness both gifts to fix things too. It was risky. She swallowed hard, dreading to think what Hugo would do to her if it went wrong—not to mention Elexon, who kept darting furtive glances in her direction.

One last glance around told her the others were busy with the stretcher, and Hugo was examining the giant that had met his end with his head buried in the rock face.

Gently, she placed her hands on Havron's leg.

He winced, watching her closely. "Hey, steady. What are you up to now?" he gasped, struggling to his elbows.

"Havron, I don't know if this will work, but I would like to try and heal you. If you will allow me?" she asked, not wanting to even try without his consent.

Havron studied her, his lips in a tight line as he nodded grimly. "Sure, why not? It's only pain," he murmured, eyes squeezed shut.

Diamond focused deep inside herself, blocking out the noise of the ocean and the quiet voices of the warriors nearby. She allowed a tendril of magic to escape her hands; keeping control of the glowing ribbon, she pushed it carefully through Havron's skin, feeling out the muscled layers beyond.

Warm blood thrummed against her magic until she found the smoothness of bone. Diamond concentrated, carefully feeling down the bone. The sensation of touching inside another living being was alarmingly intimate but also beautiful, like using sensitive fingertips that absorbed a picture of his soul. She gasped as the full impact of his pain hit her, but interwoven with that were feelings of trust, of love and of respect for his fellow warriors. It took every bit of self-control not to lose focus.

Havron panted, staring at her in awe.

Diamond gently pushed away his emotions.

The largest of Havron's lower leg bones felt jagged and out of line.

"Havron, grit your teeth," she advised as a shadow loomed over them. Hugo stared down at Diamond, eyebrows raised in question.

"I'm going to heal him," she explained calmly, in answer to his silent question, though her stomach boiled with nerves.

"Commander? Please let her try. I trust her," Havron croaked, beads of sweat covering his brow.

"Really?" Hugo huffed. He knelt down at Havron's side. "Rest then. Let's see if your trust is warranted." And he gave Diamond an unwavering look.

She swallowed hard. If she messed up, she was going to drop like a stone from the sky. Focusing entirely on Havron's broken bone with that sensitive ribbon of magic, she gripped the edges firmly, and slid them back into alignment.

Havron cried out.

Diamond jumped, nearly letting go. Hugo fixed her with a piercing look, his eyes flashing. The weight of his hand rested for a moment on her shoulder. Strength flowed from him into her. Diamond gasped. It wasn't a bad feeling; it simply took her breath away. Responding to his support, her magic calmed, allowing her to steady.

"Don't let go. His pain has to be worth it," Hugo declared. Moving now, he held down Havron's shoulders, his face remaining tight as the warrior grunted, sweat dripping from his forehead.

Diamond kept her resolve, determinedly holding the bone together. Her hands soon shook, but the bone reformed under her touch, becoming smooth and solid once again. Task complete, she withdrew her magic. Blood rushed through Diamond's ears and her vision fogged.

Mercifully, Havron fell unconscious.

Sweat trickled down Diamond's spine even as nausea washed over her. Swallowing over and over, Diamond ignored it. With trembling fingers, she felt her way down Havron's shinbone, reassured when she felt it straight and solid. He did not even murmur at her touch.

"It worked," she breathed softly, both shocked and pleased by the discovery she could heal as well as hurt with her gift.

"Of course," said Hugo, his voice full of pride. "If you set your mind to something, you're too damned stubborn to let it fail."

Diamond kept her eyes on Havron's leg to hide the flush on her cheeks.

Elexon and Kalf jogged over with the stretcher. An incredulous look fell over both males. They stared down at Havron's inert form.

"Did you just do what I think you did?" Elexon breathed, eyeing Havron's leg.

"I hope so," Diamond replied softly. On her knees, she shuffled up to the unconscious warrior's side. Havron had broken ribs too.

"What are you doing now?" asked Hugo, gripping her forearm. Worry flickered in his eyes as he took in her pale sweaty face.

"His ribs," she said by way of explanation.

Elexon opened his mouth to protest. Before either males could speak, she had summoned her magic and was focused entirely on finding the breaks in Havron's chest. Once again, she felt that intimacy with Havron's mind, but this time she was prepared. His altered state of consciousness seemed to make it less overwhelming.

Hugo studied her face and rumbled a protest. He could feel a connection to someone else too and was none too pleased by it. Despite that, her Nexus still entwined their magic and lent her some strength. After a few minutes, Diamond collapsed back on her haunches.

"There, it's done," she told them shakily.

Hugo flashed her a concerned look that she chose to ignore.

Elexon smiled and bowed low, fist over his chest in thanks. "That is one of the most amazing things I have ever witnessed," he said sincerely, his golden eyes studying her astutely. "Magic used to heal, not to harm. I have seen healers use spells in the past. But they are normally too weak to heal such injuries." He squatted down in front of her. "Don't worry, my lady. We'll get Havron on the stretcher now, whilst you rest. I'm sure he will be forever grateful. Healing from a few colourful bruises is much better than being out of action with broken bones. Although maybe we should splint his leg for the journey?"

Diamond nodded but stayed quiet, too nauseous to speak.

Elexon continued to reassure her whilst, between them, he and Hugo lifted Havron onto the stretcher.

The warriors were soon ready to go. The deference in their gazes was beginning to make Diamond uncomfortable. With Havron secured, she pushed herself up.

Hugo materialised by her side and offered her his arm. Not wanting to appear weak, she smiled gratefully but shook her head. Instead, she turned and walked toward the stretcher. In unison, all the warriors placed their fists to their chests and bowed. Diamond flushed scarlet. They all waited for her to reach the stretcher before straightening.

Hugo spoke, his voice deep and a little amused. "Elexon, you leave first and take Havron back. We will not be far behind."

"Yes, commander. Should we leave some warriors to escort you?"

"No, captain, I will ensure our safety," Hugo told him.

Elexon opened his mouth as if he wanted to argue, then snapped it shut. "Of course," he conceded.

Diamond didn't know what to make of all this. Salutes? An escort? Too uncomfortable to meet Elexon's gaze, she gave her attention to Havron.

"Havron?" She shook him a little.

Drowsily, he half opened his eyes. "Thank you," he croaked, but was awake only long enough for Diamond to squeeze his hand. The squadron of warriors saluted Hugo, then raised the stretcher skyward.

Elexon looked back once and gave her a farewell wave. Returning it, she watched them go until they became tiny dots in the twilight sky.

"Come on, let's get out of this gruesome place," Hugo suggested, his face registering his distaste.

He was right, the ground was covered in giants' remains, and the smell was atrocious. A large flock of sea birds and scavengers whirled overhead, waiting for the chance to feed. Diamond swallowed her disgust. She hastily nodded her agreement. Not waiting for him to ask, she walked up to him, slipping one weary arm around his waist and one over his shoulder. Strong arms squeezed her in close, and she gave herself up to the comfort and protection of his embrace. It was impossible not to, despite not wanting him to know how exhausted she was right now.

Hugo beat his wings, lifting them smoothly from the ground before gracefully heading out over the sea.

CHAPTER FORTY-SIX

Choosing the quickest route back, Diamond and Hugo flew over the raging sea. They were buffeted around cruelly by wind and rain.

Diamond's fingernails dug grooves in Hugo's ruined leather armour. There was no way she would fall into the black waves below. Soon her hands lost all feeling, and her eyelids drooped. Frightened she would lose her grip, Diamond wound her legs around his waist and pulled both arms up around his neck. She buried her cold face in the warmth of his neck and breathed him in. Concentrating on his warmth and scent calmed her fear. He would never let her fall.

"We're nearly there, my love," he murmured reassuringly in her ear. Vibrations from his voice shivered down her neck. She shuddered. Hugo responded by holding her tighter, cupping her head in one large hand and tucking her closer into the curve of his neck and shoulder. Diamond kissed his neck, not even raising her head as a slight zing of magic nipped her skin. They had passed through the shield, Diamond realised, feeling detached from everything other than Hugo.

Hugo bellowed the call sign to the watch soldiers, then he landed deftly outside the turret door. Panting hard and trying to recover from that flight, he merely held her, seemingly reluctant to let go.

Diamond breathed in his warmth, content to be held for as long as he wished.

They both felt it at the same time. Something was terribly wrong in the energy around them. Stiff with cold, her legs wobbled as Hugo lowered her to the ground, steadying her with a firm hand. Nearby, a small stairwell led directly up to the top battlements. Hugo shot up it as fast as his legs would take him. Diamond joined him, her heart beating hard as she ran forward and peered over the marble fortification and into the forest beyond.

Swift gusts of freezing wind and rain whipped through Diamond's clothes. Shivering and cursing at nothing in particular, she narrowed her eyes and concentrated on reaching out with her magic. The air in the forest was almost too thick for her to push her magic through. Even the storm couldn't reach into the trees and blow away the foul air.

Magic born of shadow touched her cheek, seeking to reassure. "What can you feel?" Hugo asked, his voice a controlled rumble.

Diamond allowed herself a second to glance at him. It was strange to accept—to feel—that magical bond between them. Allowing herself to be selfish, she wished they were anywhere but here. She wanted so badly to explore what this bond meant for them. For now though, all she could give Hugo was confirmation of their connection. She reached out and squeezed his hand. His fingers squeezed back. Steadiness and strength seeped into her magic.

Swallowing, she turned her attention back to the shadows. A frown creased her brow. There was nothing but inky darkness down there, no tell-tale auras or energy. "I can't see anything, no energy at all. But something doesn't feel right," she told him.

Hugo cursed under his breath. He leaned outward over the wall, gripping the stone.

A hissing breath escaped her. Darkness, black and threatening, had consumed the trees. Even the nearest branches were shrouded from sight. That was when the unmistakable dirty, yellow aura of wolf-like shapes charged into view. Among them swirled the grey-blue auras of Battle Imps. Diamond made out dark green patches of energy too. Her mouth dried. Seekers. Not many, but they were there. Suddenly the darkness lifted and revealed what awaited. The enemy plagued the forest below.

"They're here," she croaked. "They used that unnatural darkness to get closer. Oh gods, they're armed with bows, hundreds of them aimed at the wall—at us!" Panic laced her voice. Her legs buckled. She would have fallen but for Hugo's lightning-quick move to catch her.

"May the goddess help us. I can feel thousands of them out there. The darkness..." she gulped. "It's like nothing I've ever felt. It feels so *old*. So full of pain."

Hugo tensed. Malevolence rippled in a wave through their joined magic. It whispered of agony and death.

"Ragor," snarled Hugo.

"Oh gods, does Jack have any men out there? You have to warn him. And what about Elexon? Is he back?" she asked in a shaky voice. *They should have made it back by now. They should be safe,* she tried to reassure herself.

Hugo swore violently. "I'll send word to Jack and be back as soon as I can. Tallo will know where to find him. *Do not* leave this wall," he commanded. But his tone belied the fear in his eyes. "I'll come back to you," he promised.

Diamond could only nod as he launched himself into a run, making for the shelter that housed the nearest squad captains. Minutes later there was cursing and bellowed orders to his squadron. Those curses turned into urgent shouts when the soldiers realised this wasn't a drill. Running feet pounded against the marble as soldiers and warriors ran for their posts.

A welcome face appeared at her side.

Reese smiled grimly, still fastening his armour. "What are they doing?" he asked tersely, his normally jovial face hard.

"The Wolfmen are squatting like toads in the trees. They're waiting for something," she whispered, peering over the wall again.

There were shouts of surprise and disbelief when the watch soldiers saw the rest of their squadrons running toward them. Many denied having seen anything but blackness.

Reese looked at her questioningly. "Diamond, please tell me you and the commander have a good reason for waking me up and scaring the crap out of all these men."

"We do." She took a deep breath hoping he would believe her. "My magic gives me the ability to see the energy of living things—their aura, if you like. It flows around anything alive. You. Me. The forest. I am able to use that energy to feed my magic the same way Ragor uses energy from the souls he devours to give life to his Dust Devils," she explained, hoping Reese would believe her. "It's why the Queen wants me. I can turn my magic into a wild and destructive force using the energy around me. Please believe me, Reese; the Wraith Lord is here. Our enemy is waiting in those trees, about to rain a storm of arrows down on us all. Right now," she said urgently.

As if to give credence to her words, an arrow whizzed through the air, thunking solidly into the chest of a nearby warrior. He toppled over the battlements, his body dropping like a stone, dead before he hit the ground.

Diamond swore and ducked down under the protection of the wall. Anxious shouts and curt commands were bellowed into the night. Reese sprinted away to organise his men. A soft whine reached her ears, followed seconds later by a cloud of arrows that fell in a torrent of wood and metal. Sickened, Diamond watched men die around her, their screams filling her ears. Some made it to the shelters that had been built for this purpose, but many did not. Soldiers dropped mid-retreat, pierced by the vicious barbed weapons. Many fae warriors fared better by ducking under their armoured wings as they ran.

Thick, dark blood seeped across the marble. Horrified by the senseless deaths of so many, Diamond squeezed her eyes shut. Hugo's voice boomed in the distance, issuing orders and organising men.

That sound snapped her out of her trance. *Surely I can summon my magic this close to the wall?* She blinked, revealing the energy flowing around her. Instinctively, her magic reached out. With such a boost of power, shielding all those nearby should be easy.

A few feet away a fallen soldier stared with pain-filled eyes. Impaled by two arrows in his chest, he was unable to move. Blood ebbed onto the cold marble beneath him.

Hugo will not end up like that, vowed Diamond.

Setting her jaw, Diamond ripped a vast amount of energy from the air. Desperately, she tried not to steal it from the living. Instead, she pushed through her sorrow and took it from the souls of the dead. She could see them. Waiting. Echoes of the men and fae they had once been. Confused. Angry. Accepting. It did not matter, they had no choice but to pass on into Eternity. And there this energy would not be needed. With silent thanks, she harvested the energy lingering around their fallen bodies. Her magic fed on it, creating a storm in her soul.

Using all her training, Diamond gambled on her new-found control—and pushed. Magic shot from her body until a shield of white light formed a cloak over the heads of the closest men. Closing her eyes, she reached her senses towards Hugo's voice.

Diamond remained squatting under the protection of the wall. Her conscious mind soared, lifting free from the constraints of her mortal body. For a moment the feeling of weightlessness and vertigo nearly consumed her. Gritting her teeth, her body trembling, Diamond pushed out her mind. Shimmering over the heads of warriors and soldiers alike, Diamond's consciousness was just another streak of light in the shield she had created.

Her mind and energy located Hugo's with astonishing speed. Instantly, Hugo looked up.

"Diamond," he whispered, his eyes widening.

The warrior's body was immediately enveloped with magic, their bond singing as relief washed through them both. Arrows bounced harmlessly off the protective film as Hugo ran for the safety of the nearest shelter.

Exclaiming loudly and swearing at the magic that was saving them, men stopped dead in their tracks, gaping upwards. Those near her body ogled Diamond in disbelief. Use of such magic was unheard of in Avalonia, not when the Queen had outlawed it.

"*Move!*" she roared at the soldiers nearest. Controlling her physical body was such an immense effort. Her heart thudded against her ribs. "I can't keep this going!" she cried out. The soldiers close enough to hear dived under the shelter of the wall. Her shield faltered and exploded into a million tiny stars, sending her consciousness slamming back into flesh and bone.

Dizzy and retching violently, she collapsed in a heap against the cold marble. Heaving the bitter contents of her stomach, her body shook. It didn't matter, she took solace in the knowledge that at least these soldiers had managed to grab their bows and were firing back. Now it was their arrows raining down upon the enemy.

"Light the warning beacons!" bellowed Reese, catching her eye.

She understood his question. Nodding, she waved him away. He had bigger things to worry about than her.

Two of Jack's soldiers whipped the tarpaulin off the oil-drenched piles of dry wood. Horns were blown in sequence. With a whoosh, the warning beacons exploded into flame, one after the other around the whole expanse of the wall.

Recovered enough to function, Diamond grabbed a bow from the fallen soldier's clawed hand. His eyes were dull, his breath coming in slow heavy gasps. Death was no stranger to Diamond, but her heart hurt. Even if she healed his wounds, it was too late. Blood had pooled under and around his dying body. Shuffling forward on her knees, Diamond held his cold hand in hers. She didn't know if he was aware of her presence. It didn't matter. At least he wouldn't die alone. His eyes glazed over. Diamond held on tightly until his breathing stopped altogether. Swallowing her tears, she gently closed his eyes then wished his soul into the care of Lunaria, hoping the goddess or one of the mighty guardians would guide him to Eternity.

Composing her mind and willing ice into her veins, she stood and fired into the trees, her aim direct and true. Dust Devils moved towards the soldiers who had fallen from the wall to the ground below. For one terrible moment Diamond froze, unable to tear her eyes away from the dead as macabre shadows sucked their souls, kicking and screaming from their bodies until their light was devoured by the darkness. Enduring that horrifying spectacle caved Diamond's chest. This would happen to every single soul in the valley unless she could stop it. For now the empty husks of the fallen lay still. *How long would it take before their bodies became part of Ragor's army?* Clenching her jaw, she pushed those useless thoughts away.

When Diamond's quiver was emptied, she ducked down behind the wall. Sickening fear tore at her heart, and she scanned the melee of soldiers. Noise and death surrounded her. Hugo had not come back. She wanted to go and find him. *No, he promised to come back.* And he would. She did not allow herself to consider the alternative.

Her mouth dried, dread turning her insides into a mass of seething worms. If he didn't return soon, she would face this battle alone. There was no choice. The darkness that was the Wraith Lord had to be stopped. Desolately, her eyes scanned the mass of warriors who dashed around her. Hugo was not among them.

KAREN TOMLINSON

CHAPTER FORTY-SEVEN

Hugo grabbed a bow and a fistful of arrows from the nearest fallen soldier. He found Elexon and dispatched messengers to Jack, then he raced back towards Diamond. All he wanted was to get back to her side. That demonstration of her power had been staggering. Mastering her fear, using her magic like that, had saved countless lives — including his own.

Hugo heaved a sigh of relief as he beheld his Nexus right where he had left her. Only now she was loosing arrow after arrow into the enemy below. But Hugo's relief was short-lived as the shield sparked furiously above his head. Horrified, he could only watch the legion of shadowy vipers strike. A thunderous boom resounded across the valley as Valentia's ancient shield was breached.

Standing so close to the battlements, Diamond didn't stand a chance. A shadow whipped around her waist and throat. Cruel and unyielding, it yanked her from her feet, dragging her back at inconceivable speed.

"*No!*" Hugo yelled. He threw his body forward, arms outstretched trying to grab her.

He was too late.

Hugo roared his anger and despair, but these vile shadow servants were not done with him. They lashed around his middle and his neck, holding him fast as he bellowed his rage. Mercilessly, they squeezed, trying to wring the life from him. With desperate fingers, he fought to reach his swords, anger and despair lending him strength. Frantic now, he slashed out with his magic. Obeying him, his own silver-streaked shadow ripped the hold from his neck. Choking and gasping, Hugo pulled a blade from his back, but it was useless against the shadow snakes. No matter how many times he severed them, they regrew instantly and attacked again. A spear of darkness coiled around his sword arm as another thrust mercilessly into his shoulder, twisting cruelly. Icy coldness slammed into Hugo's blood. Cursing, he bellowed with agony. He would not succumb to this evil.

A frightened-looking soldier bravely ran to his aid. Hugo recognised Paige. She raised her sword and slashed at the shadow. It seemed to shudder with mirth. The last thing Paige saw was the dark lance piercing her belly. It disintegrated to leave a gaping hole. Disbelief flooded Paige's face as blood gushed from the wound. A moment later she toppled forward, dead.

Bucking and thrashing, Hugo roared with fury.

No! He had to take control of his fear or he would never get Diamond back. Forcing a deep breath, he shut his emotions down, concentrating instead on the burning entity that demanded its freedom. Right now. A sudden rush of strength blasted through him, fire burning through his veins and igniting with his magic. With that strength, Hugo could make use of his darker skills, his ability to absorb the magic of others — and use it he would.

Throwing back his head, Hugo arched his spine and sucked the serpents of Ragor's shadow inside himself. Screaming filled his head. It wanted to escape, to survive. Hugo gripped it, smothering it. No magic ever escaped him. It was how he had saved Diamond from the flames of her vision, how he had controlled her raging magic in the forest, how he had enslaved magic wielders for the Queen; he locked the magic of others inside himself. And there it stayed until the entity existing in his soul devoured it completely. Icy power barrelled into him.

A wild roar consumed the night. Hugo did not balk when he realised that sound was emitted from him. Gritting his teeth, he dropped to his knees — and roared again. Ragor was attacking Hugo from the inside out.

Followed closely by his men, Elexon charged into the throng of soldiers and warriors that crowded the battlements. All watched wide-eyed as the Queen's guard fought an unimaginable enemy. Elexon and his warriors threw men bodily out of their way to get to him.

Hugo emitted a wild roar as he felt pain rage through his body, his own magic fighting the dark, immortal force that attacked him.

"Commander!" Elexon bellowed.

At the sound of his captain's voice, Hugo whipped his head around. Even as he fought for his life, Hugo's eye narrowed upon the other warrior. Elexon's golden eyes now burned with red fire, crimson magic swirling around his hands.

The red warrior! It was Elexon who had kidnapped Diamond the day the guardian attacked the city.

There was no time to contemplate what that meant. Shards of icy pain ripped through Hugo's damaged shoulder. Ragor's shadow now attacked him inside and out. Hugo bellowed and fought with everything he had.

Elexon stilled, taking in the madness around them. The red warrior blasted out a wave of vermilion magic at the writhing snakes that stabbed over and over at Hugo's already bleeding body. Screeching, they headed toward Elexon.

That brief respite gave Hugo a chance. Trusting that Elexon was friend, not foe, Hugo shut his eyes and grasped Ragor's remaining shadow with all his might. Bellowing his wrath, Hugo hauled it inside himself smothering it with his own darkness. Scorching heat crackled defensively through his blood. The entity inside him consumed and devoured until nothing of Ragor's magic remained.

Hugo's eyes snapped open.

Elexon stood directly in front of him, head cocked, waiting.

Hugo met his red gaze with eyes of pure silver fire. Then roaring in agony, he shoved. His bones stretched and reformed, his palms slapping hard against the marble as he fell forward.

Elexon needed no instruction. With a small gesture of his hand, his red-winged warriors fanned out until they formed a barrier between Hugo and the other soldiers.

"What can I do, my lord?" Elexon asked, his voice steady and in control.

"Nothing," Hugo growled, the veins in his neck engorging. Under his already loose and torn armour, Hugo was healing. Muscle and skin throbbed as it knitted back together. "I'm going to get her back," he declared to the fae warrior. "Do not follow me. Protect yourselves."

Without warning, Hugo launched himself off the wall. He didn't let himself think about the danger Elexon and his men were now in. How, or even why, they had revealed their magic to aid him.

A resounding crack exploded through the night air when he snapped out his massive, armour scaled wings. The only thing that mattered now was getting Diamond back. Focused on that task, Hugo propelled himself after the sweet scent of summer flowers.

Elexon could only watch in consternation as Hugo disappeared into the thick, inky darkness. The red warrior would never disobey Hugo's order. Frustration etched his face. A moment later his fist slammed down on the marble wall, then he turned on his heel and ran, his warriors close behind.

CHAPTER FORTY-EIGHT

Flashes of light illuminated the sky, and something loosened in Hugo's chest. Diamond was fighting. Hard. He drove himself closer, the muscles of his back and shoulders burning with effort.

Diamond came into view, her silver hair streaming wildly in front of her face. She was fighting, working steadily at freeing herself.

Hugo's pride in her soared with each of her controlled blasts. *Come on, my love, you are far enough from the wall now. Use your magic and burn him to hell,* Hugo willed her with every part of his heart. As if she had heard him, a wave of white light exploded into the sky. The shadows screamed and recoiled, releasing her instantly. Diamond dropped from the sky like a stone.

Hugo's heart stumbled as he shot forward. In one smooth move he wrenched her into his arms. Flipping himself over, he beat his wings like never before, propelling them upwards away from the shadow. He only stopped when they burst through the storm clouds and the light of Tu Lanah bathed them in a soft silvery glow.

Diamond collapsed against his heaving chest.

"Diamond? Are you hurt?" he asked fearfully, holding her away from his body as if she weighed no more than a small child. He couldn't help but run his eyes over her.

She shook her head. "No." Her voice trembled.

"Thank the goddess," he uttered, pulling her back into him.

Diamond put the flat of her hands on his chest, stopping his embrace. "Wait," she gasped. Her attention focused on his blood-covered armour and the huge hole ripped clean through it. A storm of violent emotion hit him. "What did he do to you?" she breathed,

343

fingering the ripped remains. Gently, she brushed the healed skin beneath. Her touch burned him, their Nexus stirring.

"I'm fine," he rumbled. "Better than fine." Gesturing to his altered appearance, he held her so she could see. Her gaze raked over him, those glowing eyes flickering before she returned her attention to his face.

"How? Why?" she asked quietly.

Hugo frowned, knowing he couldn't explain it. "I don't know. It felt — right, to let my body change," he told her.

It was a relief to know his altered appearance did not scare Diamond, but he also acknowledged there would be more questions later, questions he could not answer.

"We should get back to the wall," he told her.

His voice lacked conviction, though. If anything, he was fighting the urge to soar away across the ocean, to take Diamond away from here. He would be hunted, of course; they both would, but he could keep her safe for a little while. Head cocked, she watched his face.

"We need to go back, Hugo." Her voice was quiet but steady.

Still, Hugo hesitated.

"We can't run from her yet, you know that. Jack is our friend, and he needs us; all these people do. They cannot beat an immortal lord and an army alone. I cannot let innocent people suffer at Ragor's hands and neither can you, not for me — and not for yourself."

Yes, I can, he almost growled. But she was right, he owed Jack a chance to regain his kingdom — to take his people home.

"Fine," he snarled, even though his heart screamed otherwise.

A moment later, warm legs and arms encircled him.

"Take me back, commander," she whispered, her body clamping around his.

Hugo nodded, not trusting himself to speak; instead, he turned his head and kissed her neck. At the touch of his lips, she shuddered. A tingle of pleasure rippled through their magic and, for a moment, he just held on. His whole being baulking at taking her back toward danger.

"Ragor came for my necklace. He thinks I still have it," she mumbled into his neck.

Hugo did not reply. Of course. This war had never been about lands or power, something he'd realised as soon as Gorian had told him about the gateway. From the moment the Queen had used Hugo to release Ragor from his prison, it had become a hunt for the keys that would unlock the door to Eternity and the gods.

"How do you think Ragor broke through the shield?" she asked shakily.

"I don't know. His immortality, maybe? But pushing through the shield, then fighting more than one magic wielder, weakened him. I could feel it when I absorbed his magic."

"Well, at least we know what he can do now." She tried to sound positive, to make light of the fact the enemy could breech what they had all thought a solid defence against his power.

Swallowing his growl, Hugo elegantly dropped from the sky. He scanned the darkness before arcing towards the turret.

"Elexon will be at the wall to greet us," he said as they approached the throng of soldiers atop the wall. He glanced sideways at her, trying to gauge her reaction. "We have much to discuss with him. You are not going to like this, but he is the red warrior. He took you prisoner the day of Sulphurious' attack. I don't know why he did it or why he put himself and his men in danger to help me just now, but I think we owe him a chance to explain."

Diamond had pulled back and stared open-mouthed at him.

"Perhaps you'll get chance to ask him about your mother." Hugo was trying his best to sound reassuring, even though his voice had a growling, animalistic quality to it.

345

Diamond blinked, her face a picture of confusion as she absorbed the information he had just imparted.

With his attention honed in on Diamond's face, Hugo missed the shadow hurtling in from his left. Something solid slammed into him, catapulting them sideways. Agony ripped through Hugo's side as his wing cleaved from his back. He screamed, losing all sense of direction. Over and over he tumbled, his vision darkening at the edges. Desperate not to lose her, Hugo grabbed tighter to his Nexus, pouring everything he had into the vise-like grip he had around her chest.

Sulphurious scooped them out of the air with curled talons. Roaring, the great beast hurled his prize sideways.

A petrified scream escaped Diamond. Hugo could feel her trying to grip onto him. Her fingernails gouged his skin through the holes in his torn armour. That scream froze his blood. And in that moment, Hugo knew true terror. Not for himself, but for his soulmate. He had failed. He could not save her.

The world spun past at horrific speed. Hitting a burning tree and sending embers flying, his body jerked viciously. The blazing wood sliced clean through his leather armour, shredding his skin and prying apart his grip on her. Then the most precious thing he had ever known was ripped from the safety of his arms.

"*Diamond!*" he roared in despair, just before his head slammed into something hard. His limbs turned to water and blackness swamped him.

Hugo jerked, consciousness returning. Heat seared his skin and throat, smoke stung his eyes.

A triumphant roar drowned out the noise of the raging flames, and his heart constricted painfully.

"No!" he cried, his voice breaking.

Hugo pushed himself up, crying out as his broken wing fell uselessly down his back. Ignoring the surge of white-hot pain, he pounded toward the dragon. Heat scorched every inch of his body. Totally focused on finding Diamond, his mind refused to register the pain. For Hugo, the flaming forest floor and falling branches did not exist. He had to reach her.

Breaking through the blazing trees, Hugo beheld Sulphurious. Smoke and fire distorted the dragon's huge body into a grotesque shadow. His red-horned head swung wildly; thousands of palm-sized scales across his back reflected the flames like dark mirrors.

And there, clenched tightly between the sharpest, blackest teeth was Diamond.

Grief exploded through Hugo's chest and, without thinking, he tugged wildly on their bond. Pain and fear swamped him.

"Hugo!" Diamond screamed, her wide eyes finding his.

Anguish rendered his limbs useless, and he collapsed to his knees, his heart breaking.

Sulphurious turned his big head and seemed to contemplate the warrior who knelt before him, then bared his teeth, malevolence pouring from him.

"No... don't..." Hugo pleaded, but the dragon only rolled his red eyes and shook his prey—hard enough to make her scream again.

Red-hot rage erupted through Hugo. Suddenly he couldn't breathe.

Mine! Mine to protect.

Heat from the burning forest fanned Hugo's body, and he did not fight the instincts that took over. Instead, he absorbed that heat, welcomed it and consumed it, like he hadn't feasted in years, sucking in more and more. The beast inside him roared as Hugo unleashed it.

Without warning, sharp agonising pain saturated his body; his every cell fragmented, his bones stretched, breaking and reforming.

Blackness swamped his vision, waves of dizziness coursed through his skull. With sheer will he stayed conscious, all his focus on Diamond as his wings snapped back into place, healing instantly.

Hugo's body expanded until he could feel himself pushing down the flaming trees, crushing those nearest to him with the great bulk of his changing body. Sapphire blue scales burst through his skin, clattering until he was covered entirely in rock-hard armour. Metal-scaled wings stretched wide, talons curving from the barbed tips. Whorls of molten silver tattooed his back and long neck, blazing brightly in the darkness. Sharp teeth thrust through his gums, the pain of his fae teeth a shadow in comparison.

In an instant, agony was replaced by ecstasy. Power more ancient than the earth and the heat from which it was forged tore through his blood. Hugo dug his talons into the burning earth and threw his head around, roaring loudly, needing to release his newfound strength and power.

There was no time to wonder about what was happening to him, only that it felt right. In harmony with the spirit of the guardian he had become, Hugo immediately launched himself upwards right as Sulphurious threw Diamond high in the air. Her arms and legs dangled haplessly as she fell towards the dragon's open maw.

Wind and smoke and flame rushed by. Hugo twisted, catching her limp body in one of his large back claws. Roaring his defiance at the bigger dragon, he snatched his Nexus away. Stronger and more powerful than ever, Hugo pulled Diamond close to his silver underbelly and snapped his wings open, thrashing through the air towards the wall.

CHAPTER FORTY-NINE

Air rushed by Diamond's lacerated body. She was thrown unceremoniously onto the silver ridges of an animal's neck. Pain lanced through her. Diamond didn't care; she was alive. Forcing her fingers to work, she grabbed onto the nearest bony spikes. Gusty wind tugged at her. Fighting it, she swung her leg over the beast's neck. Underneath her thighs, beautiful midnight blue scales gleamed.

A dragon! I'm sitting on a guardian.

Wide-eyed, she let her gaze travel over the dragon's entire body. A spiny ridge of solid silver merged from the base of three protruding silver horns, travelling down to the silver barb at the tip of its tail. Her grip tightened. Huge, majestic wings thrashed through the night sky, and she realised the stunning creature was taking her back toward the shield. The dragon's beautiful body gleamed with every ripple of his muscles. Shimmering whorls of silver flame, bright and blinding in the darkness. The patterns ran from the base of his neck, right down his back and shoulders and out across those glorious wings. But it was the dragon's sapphire energy shot through with silver serpents that made her gasp in disbelief.

"Hugo!" she breathed.

Silver orbs flickered back at the sound of her voice. Curling his scaly lips back, Hugo issued a familiar, challenging snarl.

Relief, awe and numbness vied for supremacy in her mind. Fighting the wind that threatened to pluck her off his back, Diamond had no choice but to lean onto Hugo's heat-soaked scales and tighten her hold on the ridges of his neck. She clung to him, trying to ignore the pain throbbing through her ravaged body.

The sapphire dragon soared upward into the clouds. Soon they left the sight of the army on the wall. He burst through the dark, smoke-laden clouds and into the never-ending plethora of stars above. Beautiful and serene, their light warmed Diamond's heart, but she did not have time to marvel at the sight. With a warning roar, Hugo flipped head-down. It was a move designed to unseat her.

Weightlessness had her stomach turning before he caught her to him and kept her in a vice-like grip as he dived.

Terror stole Diamond's voice. Hugo built up speed, then folded his wings flat into his back. Like an arrow, they travelled at phenomenal speed towards the shield.

The shield! He's going to kill us!

The dragon disappeared before they hit the dome of energy, and she was clasped in strong arms with Hugo's familiar scent surrounding her. Together they fell through the shield, the ground rushing up towards them.

Diamond released a petrified scream.

Bellowing loudly, Hugo tried to slow their descent, but the desperate thud of his wings and iron contraction of his muscles weren't enough. Squeezing her to his chest, he rolled seconds before they slammed into the shimmering dark lake together.

The impact knocked Diamond senseless. It was like slamming into a brick wall. The only thing that saved her bones from shattering was the cocoon of Hugo's body. Water swamped her mouth and nose. For one long moment her stunned brain froze, then panic set in. Thrashing wildly, she fought Hugo's grip. She needed to breathe! He did not let go but dragged her upwards at incredible speed until they exploded through the surface, coughing and spluttering. A shove in her back had her flailing toward the bank. Fighting her faintness, she kicked out, pawing across the surface and trying to swim. It was useless, her muscles wouldn't respond. Inky black water closed in over her head, and lower into the murky underwater world she sank. The desire to inhale nearly overwhelmed her. Diamond fought that instinct with all her might. She didn't want to die.

A sapphire and silver glow mesmerised her, commanding her attention. Rough hands grabbed her armour, yanking upwards until her head and shoulders broke the surface.

Hugo dragged her limp body through the water at incredible speed, then hoisted her into his arms. Cradled against the protection of his body, she floated through the air, feeling warm and cared for—until he placed her on the cold, hard ground.

"Diamond! Diamond! Come on! Wake up! *Now!*" Hugo yelled.

She felt herself dragged up off the ground. Frantically he whispered her name, pulling her into his arms and holding her tightly.

"Stay awake. Please. Come on. You have to stay awake," he told her, but his voice sounded broken, almost as though he were sobbing.

He was right. She should get up. They were needed back on the wall. But she was so tired. Wonderful, solid arms enveloped her. A cocoon of safety and protection as Hugo rocked back and forth. Her body felt fluid and light. Diamond smiled, all she wanted was to float away wrapped in Hugo's beautiful warmth. He would take care of her.

Cold, hard ground under her back jolted her awake. Swift and deft, Hugo unfastened the buckles and laces of her armour and ripped her shirt open. A sharp intake of breath and a steady stream of curses had her wondering what was so wrong. She was just tired. Smiling weakly she tried to lift her hand to his face, but it flopped uselessly by her side.

"Diamond, you have to heal yourself. Use your magic or you'll bleed to death!" he yelled, his eyes flashing with silver fury. He pulled her up and made her look at herself, supporting her head with one big hand.

351

Long ribbons of flesh hung from her body. Her belly, chest and hips were shredded and oozed a steady stream of blood that ran over her pale skin and onto the wet ground. Surprisingly, there was no pain.

Diamond blinked as he placed her hand over the torn skin of her abdomen.

"Don't you dare give up on me," he implored, staring into her eyes. "You've never given in before! Gods damn it! Heal yourself! Please, or you'll die."

"I. Can't," she whispered, her eyes rolling backwards in her skull. Her head was too heavy to keep upright and flopped backwards onto his hand, her wet hair tumbling to the ground.

Hugo's face turned rigid with fear. "No, this isn't happening," he choked out in an anguished voice. He cursed and cursed. Her. The Goddess. The Queen. Everyone. "You can't just give up! You can't leave me, not now. I won't let you."

She watched with fascinated detachment as he opened his mouth and she saw that second set of sharp, pointed teeth. Blood dripped from his wrist as he bit himself.

Diamond tried to move away, but Hugo entwined his fingers in her hair, holding her in place. He clenched and unclenched his fist above her mouth, making his blood flow faster. Warm and thick, it dripped steadily into her mouth. Unable to move, Diamond was forced to swallow it.

"It's all right, my love. No! Don't fight me. My blood will make you stronger. Just swallow. Please. Trust me," he crooned. Warm lips kissed her forehead, whispering soothingly against her skin.

"Stop," she uttered, gasping for air after he had forced her to swallow mouthful after mouthful.

Hugo freed his hand from her hair.

Diamond used her palms and heels to scramble away across the blood-soaked mud. Wiping the back of her hand over her mouth, she stared at him wide-eyed. The coppery taste of his blood filled her senses. Bewilderingly, she now had enough strength to talk and move. Her eyes fluttered closed as strength and magic invaded her limbs. An otherworldly heat rushed through her blood, burning from her toes right up to her scalp. It was as if he had ignited a storm of fire and magic in her blood, making it impossible to concentrate on anything else.

"You are my Nexus, and my blood is boiling with the magic of the guardian that lives inside me. It will make you stronger. You already are, aren't you? Now you can heal yourself. Please. Please do it," he pleaded, pulling himself on his knees towards her, his fingers digging anxiously into the soft mud. "Look. You're still bleeding. That evil bastard has ripped you to shreds. *Look! At! Yourself!*" he bellowed, gesturing violently toward her stomach when she just stared at him.

Diamond swallowed, unable to take her eyes off his face. All the while, heat continued pulsing around her blood stream.

Hugo shuffled even closer, grabbing her hands and kissing them over and over.

"Look," he urged again.

Diamond regarded her ripped flesh with disinterest, obsessed with the taste of him. It took her a moment to notice—to really see—the long open gashes that marred both sides of her body. Bright blood leaked a steady stream.

The heat from Hugo's magic-laced blood settled and awareness of her body returned. Every nerve, every piece of torn, ravaged flesh ignited. A torrent of agony erupted, and she cried out.

Hugo anxiously grabbed her hand. "Try. Please," he urged, pushing her hand over her stomach. "You can't leave me—not now. I love you too much to let you go," he choked.

Those broken words tore at Diamond's heart. For him she would try. Closing her eyes she strained to reach her magic. Nothing. Only emptiness.

"I can't, Hugo. I'm too tired," she whimpered.

Hugo thrust his still-bleeding wrist forward. "Drink." He gulped and his voice faded to a broken whisper. "We are meant to be together. We are Nexus. And I love you. Will you consent?"

The sun pushed its way over the horizon and the soft light of the new day reflected in the silver shards of his eyes. If she didn't heal herself, she would die, and that meant never seeing him again. She looked up, devouring every detail of his handsome face, a face now fraught with worry—worry for her. Hugo's desperation was clear to see, but she knew he would never force her. If she drank his blood a second time, he would be mated to her, bound to her until one of them died. Certainty settled in her soul.

"This is my choice, Hugo; don't ever think I am doing this only to save myself from Eternity," she panted, a wave of dizziness overcoming her. "I want to be with you—forever."

"Then drink. Now," he commanded, his voice harsh with torment.

It didn't matter what the Queen had done to them, or what her grand plan was, Diamond trusted Hugo with all her heart. Keeping her eyes on his, she gripped his arm. "I love you," she said and let that love shine through her eyes as she placed her lips around his wrist.

She drank deeply, barely aware of anything else but the feel of his skin under her lips and the tide of his energy flooding her body right through to the marrow of her bones.

The blood that bound them granted her entry to his mind. Gladly, he gave it. More intimate than even their Nexus, his emotions, his memories, his thoughts were now hers. A rapid hammering resounded inside her. Like a drum, it vibrated through her soul, followed by a deluge of feelings. Desperation, guilt, fury, pain—and something wondrous. It coiled through their entwined magic and settled around her heart, wrapping it in a protective shell. Love.

"Diamond," Hugo breathed with strangled emotion. "Now we belong to each other," she heard him whisper, though she knew that wasn't quite true; Hugo hadn't taken her blood a second time yet. Twice. He need to take her blood again. Then she would belong to him. Just as he belonged to her.

Hugo did not loosen his embrace as his blood bonded to hers.

Even when she knew she was strong enough to stop, she couldn't. In turn, it seemed Hugo was unwilling to pull away.

Understanding dawned. He would give all of himself if it meant she would live. Soon he winced at the drawing motion of her lips. Gently trying to pull his arm away did not work; Diamond instinctively clamped down on his skin with her teeth and gripped him to her. Her need to make sure he was hers was insatiable and wild. In her weakened state, Diamond could not control her fae instincts.

Hugo growled a warning and yanked his arm away, simultaneously clamping his other hand around the bleeding wound. He deliberately ignored her snarl of dissatisfaction, not to mention the angry flash of her eyes.

"Enough!" he grated, his eyes molten silver and blue. Blood dripped between his fingers. "Heal yourself! *Now!*" Hugo snapped.

Not thinking straight, Diamond growled her discontent.

"*Now!*" he hissed, pointing at her stomach.

Diamond looked down, pain forcing her to remember why she had been drinking his blood. This time when she reached for it, her magic flowered. Even the dampening effect of the shield could not contain it. Carefully, she forced tiny tendrils of magic from her hands. Her damaged flesh burned like hell as she split those tendrils into tiny threads and pierced her ragged flesh. Using those threads like a suture, Diamond drew her skin back together.

Hugo laid his hands over hers, steadying her, but he did not use any magic. She could sense his fear of the power that had enabled him to shift. He was unsure of what might happen so soon after shifting from dragon to fae.

A growling echo rumbled through their blood and magic, and a sense of reassurance seeped into them both. There was no time to wonder about that though, not when pain threatened to pull her into unconsciousness. Diamond's stomach was healing. Agony ripped through nerves and tissues as they knitted back together. Stars swamped her vision and sweat slid down her forehead, stinging her eyes.

Hugo tenderly brushed her hair back from her face. "Keep going. You can do this," he encouraged.

Steeling herself to control the threads of her magic, she panted, needing Hugo to steady her hands whilst she worked on her hips and legs, and then twisting to heal her back as best she could.

Time passed; neither took note of it until Diamond's wounds were nothing but angry purple welts along her skin. Utterly drained, she collapsed against Hugo's chest, gasping for breath. For a moment they clung to each other, and Diamond wondered if she really would make it. With grim determination Hugo thrust his wrist at her, not listening to her protests. Catching the back of her head, he held her still and made her drink again. For a moment Diamond fought her overwhelming desire to clamp down on his re-opened wound, but it was no use. Moaning in surrender, she fastened her lips to his skin. Savouring his essence, her body became fluid, her limbs heavy. His blood was like a drug, and she sensed a raw and animalistic presence simmering underneath, a presence that was overjoyed by their joining. A presence that was still Hugo but also an entity in itself too.

Diamond gripped Hugo's tense forearm, holding him to her mouth. She had no intention of stopping or letting him go. He was hers!

Through the haze of euphoria and magic, it occurred to her she hadn't used the mating words. Still, she had hardly been in any state to and Hugo *had* consented.

Gently, he wrapped a hand in her hair then pried his arm away.

"Enough," he whispered, using his thumbs to tenderly wipe a drop of dark red blood from her lips. Diamond couldn't drop her attention from his face as he carefully helped her dress. When the last buckle had been fastened, both of them sank down to the damp ground, eyeing each other with a mix of wariness and awe.

Diamond didn't know what to say to him. The gift he had given her, the absolute trust he must have in her to let her see inside him—to become her mate—gods above, it was overwhelming. She could still feel the potency of him, of his power, buzzing through her veins, making her stronger by the second.

Hugo went to rip the sleeve off his shirt. Blood still oozed from his wrist.

"Wait!" Diamond breathed, then moved to kneel in front of him. "Let me heal you," she said, swallowing hard. "Please."

Her heart bumped against her chest as she felt his eyes boring into her. With sudden butterflies in her stomach, she used a gentle touch of magic to pull his skin together. His throat bobbed, the air between them crackling with unspoken emotions and questions. She sensed his love, his exhaustion and his underlying fear. A vivid picture of his guardian-self flashed into her mind. She winced. All this—being party to his inner most feelings—was overwhelming, but she couldn't voice that or tell him how she felt. Their blood bond was as new and sudden for Hugo as it was for her.

His voice interrupted her thoughts. "We should try and get back to the wall," he said quietly, as if nothing held less appeal.

Diamond nodded tiredly. It was then she noticed the strange armour that seemed to have appeared on Hugo's body.

"It appeared on me when I shifted from my guardian to my fae form," he explained, noticing her scrutiny of him.

The armour was beautiful. It looked similar to the armour Diamond had worn in her dream, but in fluid silver and blue scales. It hugged the contours of his body, emphasising the muscles beneath. She nearly jumped out of her skin when a dragon's head appeared on it. The creature stared at her, then blinked before melting back and forming an outline on Hugo's chest.

"A gift from your guardian?" she asked.

Hugo grunted his affirmation before turning to the wall.

The shadow of the great structure was silhouetted against the glow of bright flames from the forest. Sulphurious had decided to burn more in his fury. It looked miles away to Diamond, and her shoulders caved a bit.

Warmth enfolded her fingers as Hugo pulled her up. Avoiding his eyes was hard, but she knew if she looked up at his face she might just throw herself at him and weep uncontrollably. She had nearly died, nearly let her will to live simply float away. If it hadn't been for this complicated warrior, she would not be alive right now. He had given himself to her. The greatest gift she could ever have. And it was unlikely she would ever stop reeling from it.

"We will have to talk about what just happened," he said softly. "And we will. But not yet. Not until this battle is done. I will try and keep my emotions to myself until then," he told her with a rueful smile.

Before Diamond could reply, before she could tell him how much he meant to her, Hugo turned away, letting his fingers slip from hers. Perhaps he too needed space to comprehend what had happened between them.

CHAPTER FIFTY

The armour on Hugo's wings retracted before he landed clumsily at the base of the wall. Knees buckling, they both collapsed. Hugo sweated and grunted with each breath he took, his skin so pale a bolt of fear shot through Diamond. She had taken too much blood from him.

Twangs of bows and bellowed orders echoed down from the battlements. All around them soldiers moved urgently about their tasks; none came to ask if they needed help or spared them more than a fleeting glance. Diamond was glad. It would be hard to explain Hugo's weakened state to anyone.

She pushed herself up off the muddy ground. She needed to find him food and water and somewhere to rest away from prying eyes.

"Diamond!" Jack's voice resounded from behind, making her jump.

Spinning on her heel, she pushed her exhaustion away and smiled at her friend. Jack hurried towards her, Zane and Gunnald at his back and Roin by his side. Jack's captain stared at her wide-eyed, and Zane swore as he saw Hugo collapsed on the ground. All the fae inhaled as they came closer. Their eyes flicking between her and Hugo. Diamond didn't notice. She was far too busy fighting a wave of nausea.

"What in the goddess happened to you both? There are stories flying around the wall about dark magic and red-winged fae and dragons. What the hell did you two do up there?" Jack exclaimed, catching her as her legs buckled. "Check Hugo!" he barked at Zane. But before Zane could even move, Elexon was in his face with a slight snarl to his lips.

Jack raised his brows. "Fine, stand back, Zane. Leave Hugo to his warriors."

359

Zane did not take kindly to Elexon's protective attitude. He gave the other warrior a long, hard stare before he grinned then stood back.

"I've been searching for you both all night. I wouldn't have found you at all if it weren't for Elexon." Jack motioned at the fae warrior. "It seems he sensed you, or maybe Hugo, the moment you were back on the wall. Where have you been? What happened?"

Diamond took a breath. Jack was her friend, but she could not answer all his questions. Not now. Not ever. She and Hugo needed to discuss what happened, what they should tell people. And Elexon. If rumours were already rife, it would not be long before the Queen found out about him and his warriors. She glanced at the warriors who had formed a circle around the group. Their wings were back to gold, but Diamond realised now it was a manipulation of magic that hid their red.

A frown furrowed Jack's brow as he realised he and his men were surrounded by a ring of heavily armed fae. Then his brown eyes flickered, and he seemed to shrug it off. He took in her dishevelled appearance, relief flooding his face when he registered the fact that Hugo's chest was actually moving.

Diamond open her mouth to answer his questions, but Jack held up his hand. "No, you know what? It's fine. Elexon has told me about the shadow attack, and Ragor has not managed to penetrate the shield again. You must have weakened him somehow. You can give me a full report later; just tell me what happened to you both. I've never seen Hugo in such a state."

Jack eyed her ripped and blood-covered armour, but Diamond did not notice; she was too busy figuring out what to do next. Elexon caught her gaze and nodded his head slightly before dropping his attention to Hugo. An agreement and encouragement. He knew she would need to tell Jack something. Diamond watched as Elexon dropped to his knees to check Hugo.

Right, of course. Jack already knew of Hugo's magic. They had lived and fought together at Stormguaard, and the mortal prince did not abhor magic as the fae Queen did. Besides, she had to tell him something.

"Ragor took me. Hugo followed me, he fought for me. We managed to escape and then…" She stumbled over her words, not sure what else to say.

"Sulphurious. It's okay. I've had reports of his attack. And the forest still burns. But there are stories of a second dragon. Did you see it?" Jack asked eagerly.

Elexon's shoulders stiffened, and Zane narrowed his eyes.

"Er, no, we didn't see anything like that. We had to run through the burning forest for the wall," Diamond lied without flinching. She knew it wasn't much of an explanation to the man who was running this war, but she couldn't betray Hugo—not even to Jack. It would be a huge mistake. Even if she whole-heartedly trusted Jack, someone else might overhear.

Diamond quaked at the thought of what the clever, manipulating Queen would do with Hugo if she found out he had the power of a guardian. "Please, Jack. Hugo's lost a lot of blood." She swallowed a sob as exhaustion tugged at her frayed nerves. "He's in such bad shape."

Elexon helped Hugo into a sitting position, but her mate still had his eyes closed and looked deathly pale. As Hugo slouched forward over his knees, the strange armour shifted, exposing a pattern of beautiful silver marks on the back of his neck that curved around his collar bone and down towards his chest. Understanding dawned in Elexon's eyes and, for a moment, they flashed red before he quickly readjusted the garments and covered the marks.

Diamond's heart flipped, her fingers instantly curling around her sword hilt. She shuffled her weight as though relieving her stiff body, until she stood between Hugo and everyone else.

Zane moved his eyes from Hugo to her. Diamond wondered why he did not challenge her to explain the marks he had seen glowing on Hugo's neck. Maintaining her composure was hard while she wondered if he would tell Jack. Hugo was hers now. She would protect him as fiercely as he would protect her. Drinking his blood had sealed his bond to her, even if she didn't belong to him yet.

Her knees wobbled as she held Zane's steady gaze. There was no arrogance or amusement there, only a gentle understanding as his eyes dropped to where she gripped her sword.

Shocked, Diamond realised she would do anything to protect Hugo, including kill for him.

Zane gave her a gentle smile and shook his head, telling her she did not need to.

Jack interrupted her dark thoughts, his brown eyes contemplative as he too eyed her grip on her sword. "It's alright, Diamond," he said. If he had seen the marks, he too was ignoring them. "I'm sure Hugo will be fine soon." And he lost no time ordering his men to fetch food and water. Jack gave her shoulders a reassuring squeeze before stepping back. He spoke to Roin in low tones, then strode forward and dropped to Hugo's side, his eyes scanning the Queen's guard. The rubies in Dragonsblood seemed to glint brightly as he moved closer to Hugo.

Hugo stirred and moaned as if in response.

"Hugo!" Diamond uttered, dropping to her knees.

Elexon quickly moved back to give her room.

Hugo's eyes opened and he smiled weakly. "I'm fine, my love. I just need to rest."

"Hello, my friend," Jack said, grim-faced. "You've looked better."

Hugo rasped a laugh.

"Relying on your mate to save you, are you now?" Jack joked, but Diamond could see the worry in his eyes.

Hugo's eyes flew open. "How d' you know?" he panted.

Jack grinned at Diamond's blush. "Don't worry, I haven't suddenly grown a fae nose. Although the reaction of these warriors would give me cause to wonder—if you hadn't just called her 'my love'," he pointed out.

Diamond didn't know what to say. Jack, however, leaned in and kissed her cheek before grabbing Hugo's hand. "It's about time! Took you both long enough," he chuckled.

Thankfully, Diamond was saved from explaining they weren't fully mated when Jack's soldiers returned with food. They helped Hugo into an upright position, then Diamond sternly encouraged him eat. She might have spooned the food into his mouth if Jack hadn't snorted a laugh when she grabbed the spoon. Even Hugo raised his eyebrows quizzically, but his eyes and that strange emotional connection told her he would have let her feed him if that's what she had wanted.

She gave him an embarrassed shrug. "Eat it all then," she commanded. "Or I *will* feed it to you, elite guard or not." Her heart flipped with relief as he smiled at her, his eyes glinting with amusement.

Sitting on the ground next to Hugo, Jack waited patiently for them to finish. Every now and then he would ask a question and listen carefully to Hugo's answer.

After a time Diamond wished Jack would simply leave. She needed to talk to Hugo, to sort out what was would happen between them now, even if it was only to figure out how to control the bonds they had.

Her stomach roiled. Ragor had plucked her like a flower from the top of the wall. It had taken her too long to react last night, too long to control her fear. She needed to be quicker or others might die because of her hesitation. Hugo might die.

"You know, the flames are still burning in the forest," Jack pointed out. "Ragor cannot send his main force against us until they fade. You should both rest for a while. You can have rooms in my turret. Or just *a* room if you prefer," he offered smoothly.

Diamond tore her attention from Hugo's face. She flushed, realising she had been staring non-stop at Hugo and not paying any attention to her friend or the warriors around them.

"Thank you, Jack," Hugo rumbled and reached for her hand.

Jack smiled at them and helped Diamond to her feet. She brushed herself down as he thrust his hand at Hugo, who grabbed it and let Jack pull him up. Diamond breathed a sigh of relief seeing him up on his feet again, even though he swayed a little at first.

Jack walked with them as far as the turret, Elexon and Havron following behind Zane and Roin. After embracing Hugo, Jack turned to Diamond and leaned in close so his words were only for her. "I'm glad you are finally together. When this battle is over, we will get you both out—before the Queen can find either of you. Remember I offered her my ships?"

Diamond nodded, her heart thumping madly.

"Well, I did not tell her about all of them. I have one more, in hiding..."

He grinned at her expression. "Every good monarch has an escape plan, Diamond. All you have to do is rid us of that Wraith Lord, then you can both run," he said, kissing her cheek before striding away.

Elexon was talking earnestly to Hugo, and Diamond decided their conversation was best not interrupted.

"We will join our warriors later," Hugo informed her as Elexon strode away, his wings folded tightly into his back. "Elexon will be

364

with Captain Reese on the wall. Havron is to be our guard. He too has red magic and can help defend us if necessary."

Diamond did not question him; she was far too tired to ask what he and Elexon had discussed.

Havron nodded and held the door open for them, bowing slightly as they passed. The blonde warrior remained at the base of the stairs whilst a servant showed Diamond and Hugo to separate rooms. They were both too exhausted to argue. Giving her a rueful smile, Hugo brushed his lips on her forehead before heading into his room.

CHAPTER FIFTY-ONE

Hours later, Hugo descended the stairs, his new armour moving fluidly with his body.

The guardroom was deserted except for Havron, who stood guard at the base of the stairs. Hugo exchanged a few words with the warrior before heading to the kitchen and talking the cook into handing over some cold chicken, bread and two tankards of wine. Balancing his cache, he ascended the stairs to where he knew Diamond slept.

He quietly let himself into her room. His breath caught in his throat at the sight of her. Placing the food down, Hugo sat on the edge of her bed, happy to watch her sleep and to listen to the precious sound of her soft breaths. He rubbed his tired eyes while his stomach clenched painfully. He had come so close to losing her. Offering her his blood, even knowing what that meant, had been the only way to save her. He would not feel guilty. She still had a choice. She was not bound to him fully yet. His chest caved at the thought of her rejection. *It does not matter*, he told himself. *If that is her choice I will respect it.* It would kill him to see her find another to love, but it would not change the fact that his heart and soul belonged to her forever.

Hugo scrubbed his face harder. That day, months ago, when he had first looked in Diamond's violet eyes, he had awoken from a trance of emptiness and horror. It had taken him so long to realise how precious she was to him. Now he had the chance of a future—with her. He would get her out of the city and away from those who sought to harm her—even if she ultimately rejected his feelings for her.

He flexed his wrist. Only a purple scar remained. Healing had never been a problem for Hugo, but his strength after such a short amount of rest was astonishing. For a brief moment he closed his eyes, trying to ignore the questions he had about the dragon that lived inside him. Never had he heard or read about a dragon shapeshifter. It was true Hugo didn't know his origins, but he doubted very much he came from the land of Eternity. Other kingdoms still worshipped the goddess and her guardians. He had heard rumours of fire breathing dragons being spotted in the Fire Mountains and the Sky Desert. He groaned. Gorian. His old friend had told them to head to the Fire Mountains when they managed to escape. *The old bastard always knew more than he let on,* Hugo huffed a quiet chuckle. *Maybe he knew what was inside me all along.*

Opening his eyes, Hugo stared at Diamond's lovely face, his gaze resting on her mouth. A curious feeling of warmth and love spread through him, which soon turned into something far more feral. His mind drifted back to their hot kisses and hungry touches. Face flushed, he shifted his body. He curled his fingers into the bed sheets to restrain his need to kiss her.

Expanding his lungs as much as possible, he exhaled a steadying breath. It would not take much for him to lose his self-control right now. Being half-mated was hellish when he wanted to take everything his mate was willing to offer. And she had been so willing under the touch of his fingers and his mouth.

A small groan escaped him. Stop. He had to stop.

Hugo gently shook Diamond. She would never forgive him if he kept her from the battle raging along the wall. Several giants and the first wave of Ragor's vile army were already rocking the earth and pounding the wall.

Diamond groaned and stretched languidly, causing her hair to tumble over her face and shoulders. Her eyelids flickered open, bathing him in violet light. "Hello," she smiled sleepily, reaching out her hand and touching his face to reassure herself he was there.

"Jack sent word." Hugo cocked his head and looked down at her. "The watchers have counted five clutches of giants." He paused and threw her a wicked grin to lessen the blow. "Shall we go and kill some more?"

"But that's fifty giants," she whispered, horrified.

"Yes," he confirmed, blinking in surprise as she shot out of bed and flung on her ripped armour. The sight of it turned his stomach, making it hard to keep his emotions locked away from her mind.

"Would you help me?" she asked after her fumbling efforts had her throwing her hands in the air in exasperation.

Taking a deep breath, he stepped closer, but remaining detached was hopeless; by the time he had secured the leather around her body, they were both flushed.

"We should go," she breathed.

Breaking his stare, she wrapped her hair in a knot at the back of her head. Ripped armour or not, she looked so beautiful and fierce and determined; his heart flipped in his chest.

"Wait," he uttered, as she made to walk past him. He couldn't let her go yet. Slowly, he turned her. It seemed she wasn't going to look at him, so he tilted her head back with a fingertip until he could stare right into her lovely eyes. "I nearly lost you twice last night. Please, stay close to me." He took a deep shaky breath. "I don't think I could survive losing you three times in one day. Besides," he added with a small smirk, "if you have to drink my blood again, I might have to take some of yours to keep us even, and then you'd be stuck with me forever."

Tears shone in her eyes, and Hugo could not stop himself lowering his face to hers. Warmth and sweetness invaded his mouth as he kissed her. Gently, almost reverently, he teased her lips open with his tongue. A small whimper and she melted against him. That sign of surrender almost snapped his self-control. Groaning, he pulled back and rested his forehead against hers whilst he mastered himself again.

"Don't you dare die," he uttered harshly. "I will fight for you and for this city until I no longer have breath in my body; but if Ragor comes for you again, you fight with everything you have. You turn him into dust. Do you hear me?" he ordered her harshly.

"Yes," she whispered, but determination shone in her eyes before he pushed her gently out of the door in front of him.

CHAPTER FIFTY-TWO

Thuds resounded from the wall. Diamond did not slow as she leaped up the steps two at a time. Hugo kept up with her easily, revealing his strength. Being physically weak had frightened him more than he wanted to admit. It had left him and Diamond vulnerable. He had relaxed only when Elexon had vowed that he and his men would protect her. Glancing over his shoulder, Hugo saw Havron was keeping pace with them.

The battlements were mayhem. Soldiers crowded around the edge of the wall, peering down at their enemy. Crossbows were cranked, but they were a hopeless gesture. Unless the archer could aim one through a giant's eye, the giant would not die—their skulls and hide were too thick.

Using his bulk, Hugo pushed a path through the throng of soldiers towards the wall. The stone was cold beneath his fingers as he carefully peered out. Diamond stood close, warmth radiating from the shoulder she pushed against his. Below them a giant pummelled its great fists against the ancient marble. The hulking beasts had spaced themselves out and worked in pairs. When one became tired, another stepped in.

Hugo turned, sensing someone's presence behind him.

Elexon looked at him steadily, his fist touching his shoulder. "Commander, it's good to see you both recovered. What are your orders?" Warriors stood in calm formation behind Elexon. It was an almost disconcerting sight among the mayhem on the wall, but not only were they highly trained, they were hiding magic—powerful magic— and had been doing so for years. Hugo wondered how many other citizens of Valentia had the skills to hide such power from their queen. Questions buzzed around his mind as he scrutinised Elexon.

"Hells teeth!" Diamond uttered, distracting Hugo from his thoughts. She cursed loudly as the wall vibrated beneath their feet.

Cocking his head, Hugo watched as his Nexus stilled. Steely determination crossed her features. He waited, swallowing his reaction to pull her away from danger. Instead, he reached for the calm and detachment that had protected his heart for so long, and hid the fear that twisted his stomach into knots. She was the best hope this valley had.

"I need your help," she declared.

Hugo simply nodded. He would fight for her until his last breath.

Indomitable heat pulsed against his blood cells right into his very soul, his bones aching to stretch and reform. The dragon's desire for release battled against Hugo's will to contain it.

He hoped he could do it again, that he could summon and control the guardian in order to help her. The shift had been extremely painful, but if he could master it, he could help Diamond travel the entirety of the wall. Together they could annihilate the giants. In his fae form he was too vulnerable, too easily killed by an arrow. But as an armoured beast he'd be Diamond's protector, her guardian — he could even try to summon fire.

A splintering sound and a roar cleaved the air. Around them, soldiers shoved Elexon's men in an attempt to get to the wall. Stronger, bigger and with magic to aid them, their wall of armoured-winged protectors did not budge. Hugo silently thanked them. He tracked Diamond's horrified gaze to the shield above. A tiny fracture had appeared, causing a wave of panicked shouts and yells.

"Look!" cried a soldier, his attention not on the fracture but the forest. He gestured frantically towards the smouldering trees.

Hugo leaned forward. Squads of Battle Imps, aided by grotesque Seekers, dragged huge rope ladders through the trees. The giant below huffed a deep chuckle. Not caring if he squashed the monsters under his feet, he grabbed the ladder and pitched it. Iron grappling hooks sailed towards the battlements. The first attempt failed, but the second didn't. It clattered into place among loud shouts from the panicked men.

The stench of fear was thick in Hugo's nostrils. As he looked around he realised that most of these soldiers were no more than farmers and lay men who had only received minimal training. They would fall apart if the enemy breeched the wall.

"Release it!" ordered a familiar voice.

Reese.

Diamond's old squad immediately complied, but their efforts were in vain; the iron hooks were too heavy for a man to lift and the fae could not touch them.

"*Burn it!*" bellowed Elexon, taking charge. "Burn the ropes! Now!"

Reese repeated the order, and men ran for the torches.

KAREN TOMLINSON

CHAPTER FIFTY-THREE

Diamond raced for the ladder, gathering her magic. She pushed men aside, aware her guard of warriors kept pace with her, holding the throng of soldiers back. With no time to explain her actions or consider theirs, she blasted the iron grappling hooks. They melted into nothing and the ladder plummeted to the ground.

Breathing hard, Diamond turned to find Hugo right behind her.

"We can do this," she said urgently, "or we can at least try. All these people, whether they are Avalonian or Rhodainian, they need a chance," she added, sweeping her hand across the dark valley towards the island city. "He'll take their souls. You know he will. We can't let that happen. Our magic." She deliberately tugged on their bond. Hugo's body jerked and he snarled slightly. "We can do this together," she told him, reaching for his hand. "But promise me you will not shift. The Queen cannot find out what you are."

The shield crackled. The ominous split spread a fingerbreadth down towards the wall. They both knew that if the shield fell, Ragor would sweep in, but worse: with no shield, the Queen could get out.

Hugo brushed loose strands of silver hair from Diamond's face, his eyes as dark as the night around them. The tightness of his face told her how unhappy he was. Straightening his shoulders, she felt the heat from his body when he stepped so close she had to tilt her head back to look at him. Both of them were fully aware that Sulphurious could be waiting in the shadows, ready to incinerate them or pluck them from the air.

"I promise. And we can do anything—together. The goddess has blessed you with her magic and me with a guardian," he rumbled, his arms snaking around her waist. For a moment he lifted her and held her close, as if needing to absorb the very feel of her. It was easy to let the softness of her body mould to his. He inhaled deeply, his lungs expanding, breathing her in.

Diamond closed her eyes and prayed to Lunaria to keep him safe. She returned his embrace, holding onto him just as tightly whilst burying her cold face against the warmth of his neck.

Elexon stood back, motioning for the others to do the same. Some warriors faced out, some in. A wall of armoured wings once again protected them from the eyes of the army around them.

Elexon's eyes and wings glowed red, rivulets of golden fire marking him. Diamond thought he looked truly magnificent, ablaze in the darkness. Even Hugo seemed stunned.

"We will fight from here. Our magic should be strong enough to weaken a giant."

"No!" ordered Diamond. "You cannot. We don't know who we can trust. The Queen..." her voice faltered.

"Diamond is right. We need to discuss your magic — and many more things. But do not reveal yourself to these men — not yet. The consequences are too steep." Elexon looked from one to the other. His eyes swam with discontent, then he gave in and faded into a warrior with golden eyes and wings. "Of course, my lord. My lady," he said in acquiescence, and dipped to one knee, fist over his chest.

Surprised, both Hugo and Diamond watched as the other warriors followed their captain.

Hugo did not wait for them to stand before he readied himself for flight. His wings stretched wide, silver whorls glowing brightly across them, then sparking down the exposed skin of his neck. He pivoted Diamond around and clasped her firmly around her waist. Gripping her tightly, he bent his knees and propelled them skyward.

Diamond stiffened as the shield zinged against their bodies. Her fingers clawed against his forearms, fighting the gravity that endeavoured to pull her from his grasp. His wings thudded against the air as they went higher and higher.

"I've got you," he whispered reassuringly in her ear.

Diamond turned her head as far as she could, a look of pure trust in her eyes.

"I know," she told him.

Up they went. Judging they were high enough, Hugo hovered right below the grey, rain-filled clouds. There was no sign of the black dragon.

"Are you ready?" Hugo asked, his jaw clenched.

Below them grotesque giants slammed their fists relentlessly into the wall.

Diamond answered by smiling wickedly, no trace of fear on her face.

Moving against hers, Hugo's body shifted, bones stretching and wings expanding until they were partially covered with scale.

Caught unawares, she uttered a stream of curses into the sky. Then she grinned widely, elated by the prospect of flying faster for longer.

"Well, you made me promise not to shift into a dragon, but said nothing about partially changing." He grinned.

Their magic intertwined. That bond—deep, strong and unbreakable. Before Diamond could do more than gasp, Hugo roared, "Now!" in her ear.

Her stomach was left behind as he threw them headfirst toward the giant nearest the cracked shield.

Cold air blasted her face, numbing her cheeks. Their speed was frightening, but Diamond trusted her mate to keep them safe. Hugo rolled sideways, and the first whoosh of arrows passed them by. He levelled out, and she quickly regained her bearings.

It seemed almost too easy to summon her magic, especially when weaved with her Nexus. Confidently, Diamond released a blast of white-hot power from her outstretched hands. The giant screamed as she burned its legs down to the bone.

Hugo banked, flipped them over and took her back in to finish the monstrous creature off.

More arrows glided towards them as they retreated. Diamond flinched as fletching almost touched her outstretched hands. Rapidly, but with breath-taking grace, Hugo soared skyward. More arrows fell uselessly back to the scorched earth.

"That one!" Diamond said, pointing towards a giant who was pummelling the wall near Jack.

Hugo gave her a squeeze to say he understood—and dived.

They worked together like this until the sun dropped from the sky, flying up and down the wall, despatching giant after giant. Soldiers and warriors gaped at the speed and destructive power of their attacks. Even the fae had not seen one of their own fly so impossibly fast and with such skill. Hugo and Diamond spoke only when necessary. Hugo's silver-veined shadow enveloped her, keeping her warm and focused, lending her strength. Hours passed as they flew to where they were most needed, killing giant after giant.

Without food and drink or rest, both became utterly depleted. Fatigue swamped their limbs but still they fought on; they fought until freezing rain fell and cruel winds buffeted their tired bodies, driving the cold deep into their bones.

CHAPTER FIFTY-FOUR

Together they surveyed the wall whilst hovering barely below the grey clouds. Hugo felt Diamond shiver, though she did not complain. Now was not the time to voice how proud he was of her; instead, he held her close. There was very little magic left in him, but what he did have, he would gladly give to boost her own.

They hung over Master Commander Riddeon's section of the wall, which gave them a reasonable view of the whole structure. Diamond made a satisfied noise in her chest when she realised there were only four giants left.

"This is getting too dangerous," Hugo muttered, his voice gravelly and harsh. "It's getting too dark to see properly, and I am too tired to sense their arrows now."

"All right, just one more pass. We can clear that one from near Commander Riddeon. That leaves one giant in their section."

"So be it," Hugo answered, trying not to show his reluctance. Narrowing his eyes, he peered down to where Erzion Riddeon's men were firing on a particularly big giant who pounded the wall with a fierce rage, roaring loudly with every beat of its fists. Gruesome remains were scattered about the base of the wall. The stink of burnt flesh and blood reached Hugo. Ragor's army of monsters swarmed over huge severed limbs and leaped easily up onto, then over, dismembered torsos.

Hugo ignored the realisation that the army on the wall was not making even a small dint in the numbers of the enemy. The Rift Valley might very well fall in the next few days, giants or no. Wolfmen and Seekers were using their fallen as a ladder, working with each other to pile up the remains of the dead. Soon they would breach the wall. Unless Jack risked bringing his army out, or—he swallowed his apprehension—he could summon his guardian—and try and burn them all.

"No," Diamond whispered, reading his mind, which had bloomed open in his anxiety. "Not until all is lost, and he breaches the wall. We are both too weak, even our Nexus is spent. We must get back and talk to Jack and Commander Riddeon. We need to plan."

She was right. Instinct told him he would not be strong enough to shift without replenishing his magic. His focus immediately turned to Diamond. A violent shudder racked her muscles as she tried to ready herself. Hugo kissed her hair, hiding his worry.

"One more time," he breathed, vowing he would then return her to the wall.

Sleet fell, stinging their faces and saturating their clothes. Even Hugo's fingers and toes were numb. Diamond's shudders turned into constant shivering.

Throwing his wings wide so they caught a gusting airstream, he pulled her in tight, then plummeted. As they got closer, Diamond summoned her magic. Hugo could feel it mingling weakly with his own. It became obvious he still had more left than her. He pushed his shadow into her white light, feeling the gratitude in her magic as he did so.

His eyes snagged on a large fissure in the marble wall. Their target was pounding his fists over and over into the same spot. Dismayed, Hugo realised how close Ragor was to destroying the wall. That distraction cost him. A sudden gust of wind caught his wings and threw him violently off course right when Diamond unleashed her energy. She swore as it missed the giant, blasting the ground at its feet instead.

"Again!" roared Hugo, flipping them over and making a second dangerously low pass.

With a yell of determination and exhaustion, Diamond burned a hole right through the giant's chest. The stink of burning flesh filled Hugo's nostrils as its carcass fell with a thunderous crash, squashing enemy soldiers beneath it. The army on the battlements cheered triumphantly, increasing their own efforts to thwart the droves of rotting corpses that pushed forward.

Within the circle of his arms, Diamond trembled. Hugo banked sharply toward the wall, his muscles screaming with fatigue.

Beyond them the forest was steeped in shadow. It was too dark to see arrows released by the creatures below, and he was too tired to fly high enough to miss them. Setting his jaw, Hugo beat his wings against the drag of the wind, aiming for the nearest part of the battlements. He had to bring her back inside the shield.

Frightened she may slip from his grasp, Hugo tightened his hold. Gods, he was so tired, his arms were shaking so much he didn't think he had the strength to turn her around. Even the guardian inside him seemed depleted and sluggish. Unable to prevent it, his body shifted back, his bones and wings reverting to their normal size, but with that shift he lost even more strength. The metal on his wings disappeared instantly, and the scaled armour that had protected his body became soft and vulnerable.

Gripping onto Diamond for dear life, Hugo pushed toward the approaching wall. Ghostly faces watched them. Dimly Hugo became aware of a familiar figure shouting and waving their hands in warning, Hugo raised his eyes from the ground. *Elexon.*

But he had no time to figure out what the red warrior was saying above the din of enemy soldiers and the sharp twang of bows.

Twisting his wing, he banked sharply, fighting the invisible force of the wind, focusing only on the battlements. Before he could straighten up, something thudded forcefully into his side, burying itself deep in his flesh. Hugo cried out as red-hot pain saturated his ribs and back.

They dropped towards the ground. Diamond's scream reverberated his eardrums. And no matter how hard he tried, Hugo could not move his wing properly.

A second arrow pierced his leg. Agony ripped through him. This time he dropped like a stone, his one wing unable to keep them airborne.

"*Jump!*" he thundered, gripping her wrists and dropping her down until her feet dangled down toward the earth. With a roar of anger and frustration Hugo let go.

Diamond tumbled over and over in a mess of hair and limbs.

Powerless to control his forward momentum, Hugo crashed with stunning force into the wall. Pain cleaved through his entire body as both of his wings snapped and his ribs shattered. He heard his own scream just as his skull smashed into the unyielding marble and everything went black.

CHAPTER FIFTY-FIVE

Breath whooshed from Diamond's lungs as the world stopped tumbling, and she slammed face-first into the dirt. Blood flooded her mouth and nose. She gagged, spat and jumped to her feet, drawing her swords in one swift move as Hugo crashed into the wall. Helpless, she could only watch as he fell heavily to the ground. Freezing darkness descended, shrouding the clearing and hampering her vision. She could make out the gruesome remains and bloodied carcasses of the giants and the monstrous forms of her enemy closing in.

Orders were bellowed from the wall. A second later, a red glow illuminated the night, giving her guidance. With no consideration for her own safety, Diamond sprinted over the burnt ground, ash exploding in plumes around her. Slashing sideways, her sword beheaded a lumbering Dust Devil, then eviscerated a Wolfman.

Blowing blood out of her nose and spitting globules from her mouth, Diamond ran faster and fought harder than she ever had in her life. Remorselessly, she slaughtered the endless stream of her enemy.

She scrambled over the dismembered arm of a giant, a sudden chill freezing her heart. Hugo was crumpled at the base of the wall. His wings sprawled at unnatural angles under him. Her stomach clenched with panic. His energy was grey. Grey and fading. He was dying.

An arrow released from the wall thudded into an enemy soldier behind her but Diamond did not look, unable to tear her horrified gaze from Hugo's face. The soldiers on the wall kept the monsters and dead things away from her, but she knew it was futile. Unless the warriors up there defied their orders not to leave the wall, both she and Hugo were going to die.

Diamond reached his body, crashing down on her knees. Her panicked mind barely registered the shouts of warning from above as she slid over the ground to his side.

Hugo's face was pale as death under the dark smattering of blood that covered his features. With a sinking heart, Diamond noticed a blue tinge to his lips. Thick blood streamed from the arrows protruding from his chest and thigh. And his wings! She swallowed her nausea.

They had been ripped apart by the force of his impact, their broken bones white and grotesque against his silky blue feathers. Blood dribbled from a wound on his head, down his neck, pooling along the exposed ridge of his collarbone where his strange clothing had been shredded.

"Hugo?" she croaked, grabbing and shaking his shoulders. Terror stole her breath when she looked at his chest. It wasn't moving!

No! No! No!

With shaking hands, she reached for his neck, her fingers slipping on the slick blood.

Nothing.

No matter where she placed her fingers, she couldn't find any flutter of life. Panic swamped her, and in that instant her whole world imploded. Her fingers dug into his soft armour, gripping until her knuckles turned white.

She shook him again and again. Fiercely. Desperately. It made no difference. He did not stir.

The ground tilted underneath her. He was dead. But he couldn't be. He was too powerful, too invulnerable and too *vital* to her life to be dead. He was her mate, her Nexus, he was her guardian.

Paralysed by disbelief, Diamond could not tear her horrified gaze from the mask of his pale face.

"Hugo? Please. Wake up," she sobbed, bringing her blood-soaked hands up to cup his head. Something inside her broke. The thread that had bound her spirit together, that had kept her going after losing her home and her father and after becoming the Queen's puppet, it snapped. Through that fracture in her soul, Diamond's remaining strength ebbed away. She collapsed against his inert, ravaged body. Unbelievable grief and pain built in her chest; it ripped at the shards of her heart and squeezed her lungs until she couldn't breathe. For a few seconds she just gasped; opening and closing her mouth, drowning in grief, not even registering the racking sobs that escaped her trembling lips. Her tears fell, hot and unchecked, onto his face. She dropped her head until she rested her forehead against his.

Oh gods, Hugo, I'm so sorry. I made you do this. This is my fault. I'm sorry. I'm sorry...

A broken sound escaped her lips, her voice a whispered plea.

"May Lunaria protect your soul and the guardians guide you on your final journey." She breathed the ancient blessing against his lips then kissed him, her tears cutting a path through the blood and dirt as they landed upon the pale mask of his face.

It sickened her—the realisation of how much she had taken him for granted. He was so strong, so formidable, she had never expected him to die. Pain twisted her gut, sending bile rushing to her throat. It burned viciously, and she tried not to vomit.

Just like that, these monstrous creatures had taken him away from her. She was lost. She had no future beyond this battle. She had no right to be here instead of him.

Grief erupted in a scream of rage and despair from her soul.

Soldiers stopped firing their weapons and stared at the distraught young woman, her sorrow reaching out through the night and across the wall, her screams gripping their hearts. They shouted urgent warnings as she was surrounded by a seething mass of rotting corpses.

An authoritative voice bellowed orders from above, and the red light glowed brighter. Diamond did not hear. When she ran out of breath and her screams stopped, her body slumped forward against Hugo's. For a few seconds that was how she stayed, oblivious to the danger she was in — or just not caring.

Then she pushed herself up and reverently ran her hand over Hugo's pale, blood-covered cheek. Gently, with all the love she had in her heart, she kissed his cold lips and, still on her knees, turned to face her enemy.

White-hot rage descended, invading her mind and burning her soul until she could think of nothing but revenge.

You trained me to become a weapon, so that is what I will be. I will kill as many as I can, until they lay dead at my feet or turned to ash. I will send them screaming for the hell of the afterworld. Back to Chaos where the dark god can devour what's left of their souls.

The torches and the red glow of Elexon's warriors revealed a seething mass of hellish creatures. But Diamond was not afraid. Her power grew, feeding off her hatred and grief.

She released that power, letting it take over her conscious mind. Her awareness expanded until she absorbed everything that was happening for miles around her. She felt no vertigo as she looked down from beyond the mortal world. Her mind whirled through the atoms, the fragments that made up this realm, seeing more than just the walking dead and soldiers of shadow.

Diamond perceived a shimmering, dark force that shrouded the forest, that held energy greater than the Wraith Lord. It was a darkness not of this world, overpowering and wicked. It wanted to smother life, to take the energy from all living things and all mortal souls. And it was hungry. That evil pulsed malevolently against her, like it had done before in her dreams. Needing to be free of it, she soared up into the moonlit sky until she could view the far-off glow of Valentia. So many people — so many vulnerable souls waiting to be harvested. Even now that darkness tried to drag her back towards its empty void. A cold, malicious laugh seeped through space and time.

"Soon they will all be mine; their souls, their life, their energy. And your blood will not stop me," it whispered threateningly.

Diamond recoiled, unable to think about what those words meant.

It did not matter. Hugo was dead.

Her consciousness hovered over her own body, searching among the blue energy of the living and the souls of the dead.

Where is Hugo's soul?

She would not let these creatures rip his essence into their darkness or use his body against his people.

Nor will Ragor take the lives of anyone in this valley tonight, not even the Queen's. Her wicked immortal life is mine, Diamond vowed, plunging back into her mortal body.

Then she felt him nearby, just a feather-light touch of his energy. She had only a moment to register his intent before he slammed the energy of his soul through her skin and it melded into her magic. Her cry was full of grief and rage as his power surged through her blood. *His last gift*, she realised, sobbing. The energy and magic to burn her enemy to dust. To live if the goddess willed it.

She would not waste it.

Diamond scrambled to her feet, unable to look at Hugo's ravaged body.

More arrows rained down from above onto the monsters that growled and snapped from so close by.

Warriors, glowing red and fearsome in the darkness, flew out of the protection of the shield, followed closely by golden-winged fae. Diamond could feel their anger. They had seen Hugo destroy their enemy hour upon hour, never stopping or giving in. They had come to protect his body. They had come to take him back inside the shield.

Diamond choked back more tears, honing them into anger. Elexon would bury Hugo properly in the temple of the goddess. The warriors who had knelt before him, who had wanted to protect him, would give his body a safe place of rest. Diamond stared upward.

Elexon looked down at her, his red eyes full of pity and grief. "Let us take him," he said quietly as he landed in front of her and bowed low.

A whole squad of heavily armed, red-winged, warrior fae descended until they formed a solid arc of defence. It was not arrows with which they killed their enemy, but short, controlled blasts of red-hot magic. Above them hovered more golden-winged fae, their arrows whistling as they were loosed with precision into the mass of monsters.

Unable to speak with the weight of her grief, she nodded at Elexon. Tears burned her eyes as he gently moved her to one side. Havron appeared and bowed his head sadly, touching his fist to his chest, a mark of respect for her and Hugo. Together they hoisted Hugo's broken body up between them.

Diamond watched them, seeking hope, but there was no hint that any of Hugo's beautiful sapphire and silver energy remained. He had given everything for her. Feeling utterly alone, tears ran down her cheeks and dripped off her chin.

"Stay there, my lady! I'll come back for you!" Elexon shouted at her.

"No. Don't!" she replied harshly, shaking her head. A move that sent her blood-matted hair free of its braid. Reflecting the light, it clouded around her head like a silver and red halo.

Elexon hesitated, sudden panic in his face, but before he could order his men to scoop her from the ground, a deafening roar went up from the hordes of Ragor's soldiers, a tidal wave of sound that shook the very ground she stood on.

Diamond's heart thumped against her ribs—from fear, yes, but also anticipation. Revenge was hers to claim. Hugo's last gift of energy and magic buzzed around her body, fuelling her ire. Dropping her gaze from Hugo's limp body, she focused on her enemy, on the monsters who had violently ripped away the one she loved. She would slaughter them—for him, for the people in the valley, for her friends and for Jack, so that he may reclaim his kingdom and once again have a home.

A vicious snarl escaped her lips as the seething mass of creatures surged forward.

The warrior fae could not stop them, even their magic was no use against such numbers. Horrified, the red warriors flew down to her aide. But Diamond raised her hand and sent an arc of energy upwards, forcing them all to retreat behind the safety of Valentia's shield.

Deliberately, the half-blood magic wielder turned to face her enemy. She drew more and more energy from the fabric of the world, from the magic that was her legacy. Mixing it with the gift of Hugo's energy, Diamond wrenched up a surge of power, unwinding the magic from her soul. Glancing up, she made sure Elexon was safe and had returned Hugo's body to the wall. Satisfied, she rolled her neck and grinned savagely.

It was time to kill!

Elexon looked down and roared her name, but it was too late; Diamond was lost in a world of revenge. Power surged through every cell of her body, turning the blood in her veins, and the marrow of her bones to pure energy.

Flinging her arms wide, she hurled a violent wave of power outwards. Exploding through the air in all directions, it surged toward the monsters. Faster than the eye could see, power raged up through the shimmering marble wall, healing the cracks the giants had rent, bursting through the shield and knocking the mortal soldiers and warriors off their feet.

CHAPTER FIFTY-SIX

Seconds earlier, Elexon and Havron placed Hugo down on cold marble. Both avoided looking at the warrior's broken body, but reluctantly Elexon's eyes returned to the male he had secretly sworn to serve. Bile stung his throat as he took in Hugo's injuries.

At that moment something strange caught his eye. Frowning, he yanked the arrow from Hugo's thigh. There was something wrong; it did not look like an enemy arrow. It was brightly feathered.

Hourian.

Quickly he threw it to Havron, who caught it in his fist. "Take that to the prince. Show him and no one else, then follow whoever he sends to find the assassin. Do it without being seen," he ordered curtly.

Havron nodded once and disappeared.

Elexon bowed his head to Hugo, silently begging forgiveness. His failure hit him like a solid blow to his guts. Elexon was a warrior of the First Legion, an army of fae sworn to protect Valentia and the descendants of the true heirs: the Arjuno line. It seemed the promises Elexon had made, the oath he had taken to protect the heir to the throne, meant nothing now.

Elexon looked to the wall. Diamond fought alone out there. Knowing she would refuse any help, that she may incinerate anyone who tried to stop her, only made his impotence worse. His father would know what to do, how to help. He had such vast experience. It often tightened something in Elexon's chest when he thought about how ancient his father actually was, how much life and death he had seen. How long would his father have to wait for an heir of the Arjuno line to return now?

Elexon knew his father had given up his life to fulfil the vow he'd made to the goddess. Erzion had hidden his wizard power from prying eyes, he had even hidden his red fae magic, not trusting any in the royal court other than his friend, Prince Lexon. One night had changed his father's life, the night King Noan Arjuno had left to face Erebos in battle—and was betrayed. The very same night his queen, the goddess, gave birth to a daughter.

The goddess had refused to leave her mate to fight alone and had extracted an oath from Prince Lexon—to become protector of her blood line. She entrusted the safety of her new-born daughter to him, bestowing a well of ancient magic to his soul. Then, before he could refuse, she had immortalised Erzion Riddeon. *"One day,"* she had told his father, *"my blood line will return. You must serve this city and protect it for when that day comes. You will become a traitor to your prince and serve the Queen. You must fight for her, lead her armies and ingratiate yourself with her; then, in the darkness of the catacombs under this valley, in the sacred place she knows nothing of, you will build an army of loyal fae."*

And that is what his father had done.

Elexon rubbed his eyes, trying to take control of his thoughts. His father had always believed the true heir to the throne of Valentia would return. But not even his father had been prepared for the boy the Queen had inducted into her guard, who would grow into the blue-winged warrior and who was prized above all others.

Erzion had felt the blood of the guardians in the boy and had brought Elexon up with the sole purpose of serving the heir when the time came.

Elexon knew his father had been there, watching when Prince Lexon had cast a powerful curse over the Queen, when the shield had fallen over the city. The vow he had taken to Lunaria had destroyed his father's heart. But his father, the half-wizard, half-fae general of the First Legion, had done everything the goddess had asked of him. From afar, he had watched his beloved friend grow old and die; he had loved and lost mates and children enough to break Elexon's heart. His father had told Elexon about his past family, for which Elexon was eternally grateful. He loved his father fiercely and was awed by his resilience to such heartbreak, by his ability to remain kind and keep his capacity to love. Erzion Riddeon had imparted his story only once to his son, on the day he had asked Elexon to swear an oath to serve a dark-haired prince, one who had no idea of his heritage or power.

Together, they had planned to tell Hugo of his claim to the throne, to show him the army that awaited his return. But when the prince had returned from the forest with the young, silver-haired woman from the north, his father had taken one look at her and known Lunaria's blood ran in her veins. There were now two heirs, two distant halves of the same family tree in the very city they were entitled to rule. Elexon had wanted to get them both out of the city, but his father, more versed in the intricacies of the Queen's actions, had made him stand down.

Elexon growled with frustration. His father had thought Hugo the safer of the two—and the more difficult to liberate. After all, the Queen held his blood phial.

When their bid for Diamond's freedom failed, the Queen had begun searching in earnest for the rebels. And Fedron, gods damn his big mouth, had led her to Rose. Now none of them were safe. Elexon's teeth ground together. He knew Rose would rather die than give up any of their secrets. But everyone had a breaking point. And Rose was a healer, not a warrior. He could not bear to think about what they were doing to her in the dungeons of that palace. His heart clenched, and he swallowed his nausea, looking down at the dead heir. Saving Rose from the hell she was in was all he had left to hold onto.

Before him, Hugo lay unmoving, his face a pale death mask. It had been such an impossible task to keep safe those he served and loved. Now his promises, his failures, dragged against his heart. Clenching his jaw, Elexon straightened up. He was not a novice. He had been trained from the moment he could walk to become a warrior, to deal with death. Resolutely, he strode to look down where Diamond stood in a glowing storm of radiance. If he couldn't save a descendant of the Arjuno family—if that dream was gone—then he would fight until he died for the people of Valentia.

A second later, the air around Diamond exploded into a sphere of raging white light. Elexon's ruby eyes widened in shock as that magical wave hit the wall, heating the air around him. It sucked the breath from his lungs and knocked the legs out from under him, throwing his considerable bulk violently to the ground.

The wave passed over the red warrior and struck the corpse at his side. Elexon gave a cry of disbelief at what he saw. Hugo's body jerked, his spine arching rigidly before falling limp once again at Elexon's side.

CHAPTER FIFTY-SEVEN

That first raging wave consumed hundreds of her enemy, disintegrating them into clouds of dust. Unleashing her wrath, Diamond allowed her magic to feed off her fury. Following the stink of rot and evil, her magic thrust through the forest into the darkness. No enemy soldier could hide. The shadow that had been their shelter was now their undoing as this fierce huntress became death and destruction.

Diamond's mind sent her mortal body onwards. She walked faster and faster, deeper and deeper into the darkness that shrouded the forest, shattering the bodies of rotting Dust Devils as they tried to use the burning embers and ash to change into columns of swirling dust. Laughing coldly at their pathetic efforts to thwart her, the huntress sent bright fingers of magic into the swirling clouds and ripped them apart. With swords of light, she cleaved Wolfmen and Battle Imps without a thought. Whips of crackling energy formed any weapon she desired: knives, spears, arrows. Vengeance consumed her. Stabbing and slicing, she shredded their flesh before she broke their bodies and turned them to dust.

Time became irrelevant. It passed by her until she felt the immortal darkness of Ragor watching from behind a wall of rotting soldiers. Diamond shrieked, wild with fury. Feeding on his fear and confusion, she launched herself toward him. The turmoil in his thoughts reached her. He had not expected this amount of raw power directed against him. A cold delight rippled through Diamond's heart.

The immortal lord was scared.

Diamond battled toward him, wanting to fight him, *wanting* to rip him apart for robbing her of Hugo.

He recoiled from her light, dissolving into fingers of dark mist that curled upwards into the night sky.

Diamond realised he was running toward the manifestation of wickedness that waited for a way into this world.

"Coward!" Diamond screamed, her voice echoing out into the ravaged forest. Enraged by his spineless retreat, she hurled her magic skyward.

"You cannot hurt me!" Ragor screamed, his voice tormenting her mortal mind. It was like hearing thousands of dying screams all at once. The Queen's voice had once felt like this.

Hurtling a dome of light to the stars, she caught the mist that was the Wraith Lord and slammed him down into the scorched earth. He bellowed with rage, unable to keep his ghostly form as her power enveloped him.

An emaciated body flickered between mist and solid matter as Diamond crashed back into her physical body. With little effort, she kept them both shrouded in a shield of crackling energy.

A mass of rotting soldiers pushed against the dome. Contemptuous of their weak efforts to rescue their master, Diamond ignored them. Her concentration stayed solely on the emaciated creature that had appeared in front of her. His face was skeletal. High cheekbones protruded from a layer of thin colourless skin. And his endless black eyes actually looked scared.

A wicked grin spread over Diamond's face. "Oh, I can hurt you, Wraith Lord, and I will. You have taken away the two people I love most. You threaten the lives of thousands more, and you have tried and failed to kill me. Now *you* are going to die. But there will be no afterlife for you. No Chaos realm. I will ensure your soul is obliterated from existence." Her voice was hard, shaped from ice and hatred.

"No! I can help you. If you kill me, she will set him free," Ragor argued, his face desperate as he pushed himself up.

"What do you mean?" Diamond asked stonily, only half listening as she studied the swirl of energy that enveloped her right hand, ready to be shaped to whatever weapon of death she chose. Maybe she would make him suffer for a while, carve away bits of his flesh, a bit at a time.

Ragor sensed an opportunity, a weakness in her knowledge.

"The Queen, Erebos' lover. She plans to set him free. Together they will destroy this world now that they have the keys to Eternity."

Diamond realised what that terrifying darkness and malevolence swathing the Rift Valley was. She recoiled in shock.

"She only has one key," she stated flatly, even as dread filled her.

The Wraith Lord chuckled. "So she does have your necklace."

Diamond kept her face blank, though his manipulation of her grated.

"I sent my Seekers to Berriesford for it. But you already know that. What you don't know is before I learned of the key you held, that lying bitch had already promised *me* part of the other."

Diamond almost stopped breathing. "Tell me," she demanded. "Tell me where the other one is and I will let you live, I will let you go back to the Barren Lands and rule there in peace."

Something between a snarl and a smirk curled Ragor's paper thin lips. It was then she felt this detestable creature probing her mind, stalking through her memories, violating her.

"Get out of my head!" she screamed, slamming a fist of energy into his face.

He grunted and fell to his knees. In a wheedling voice, he taunted, "She made you into a weapon to stop me. One of those dragon eyes is mine! She promised me! I want entry to Eternity, but all she wants is to give her lord physical form so they can destroy your world and take the land of the gods. Killing that warrior stopped her. If you kill me now, this world will be doomed. I can help you fight her—fight him—for one of the keys." His misty limbs shifted, becoming shadow as he inched closer.

Diamond could not think. Her thoughts were hampered and slow, like a veil of exhaustion was falling upon her.

"Please child, I speak the truth," his voice was simpering, creeping over her bones and making her shudder with disgust. Images of her father's face, of Hugo's face, flashed into her head. She didn't understand why killing Hugo stopped the Queen's plan to attack Eternity.

Ragor was tugging at her mind, confusing her. She could feel him stirring up thoughts and memories that were too painful. Grief slammed into her heart, causing her shield to wobble. Hugo had once told her not to let grief and sadness win on the battlefield. She had to fight it or those dark feelings would be the end of her, and Ragor would win the valley.

"*Get. Out. Of. My. Head!*" she screeched.

Heedless of her rising anger, the Wraith Lord grinned wickedly and continued. "Help me get the keys, and I will let you kill the Queen yourself. Give me what I want and I will give you your warrior back. She will never get him," he vowed, a small smile of triumph curling his pale lips when her energy flickered uncertainly. "His soul is mine. I can make him live again. All you have to do is pledge yourself to serve me. It's not too late. You can see him again," he insisted.

Diamond squashed the surge of hope that almost had her begging the Wraith Lord to make it happen. No, she would never join with an immortal who viewed the souls of others as his right, who could create such monsters as Ragor had done,

"No! Stop. Stop talking. You can't bring him back!" Diamond cried, not wanting to listen to his poisonous words. A bolt of energy flew from her hand to pierce his shoulder.

Surprised by the swiftness and force of her resistance, Ragor could not dodge the strike. Flesh burned. His scream rent the air.

"My Nexus, my blood-bound soulmate died fighting you. *You* killed him, just as you are trying to kill every living thing in this valley," she spat.

"*No!*" he raged. "Erebos would have taken the strength of your warrior and destroyed this world. With a guardian and a key, he would have turned his wrath on Eternity. I have saved you and the gods. All I ask in return are a few souls to feed me and a key. Then I will leave this world in peace. I simply wish to return home," he cajoled.

"*Stop!*" Diamond cried, her ears hurting from the sound of his voice.

Sensing her weakness, the Wraith Lord writhed to get free.

Diamond viciously twisted her lance of magic into his shoulder, so wrapped up in her anger and grief that she missed the coil of darkness sliding along the floor. It wrapped around her ankles and yanked her off her feet. The protective dome of light faltered as her head slammed into the ground.

Hundreds of Dust Devils surged forward.

Ragor screamed, "I told you I cannot die, you insolent child! You are too young and too stupid to kill someone as powerful as me!"

Diamond felt the icy cold touch of the Dust Devils as they reached out, trying to push through her remaining magic. Gritting her teeth, she coiled her energy down inside her body, twisted it into a ball of power and threw it outwards in a violent explosion of heat and light.

Ragor roared with disbelief as his soldiers disintegrated into dust.

Diamond created swords of light, slashing at his shadowy defences. In turn he formed writhing, snake-like creatures that screeched as she beheaded them, always repairing themselves until Diamond thought there would be no end to his darkness. A snake struck at her throat, latching dark fangs onto her neck. Icy-pain shot down her spine and across her shoulders, burning deep into her muscle fibres. She screamed. Simultaneously, a spear of darkness pierced the soft skin of her upper thigh. Diamond fought, not losing her focus even as her leg gave way.

This monster will die, she promised Hugo silently. *He will not take any more souls from this world.*

Full of determination and purpose, Diamond formed shards of magic under her skin, hurling them from her body in splinters. She drove them forward, impaling the immortal flesh of the Wraith Lord. He yelled in disbelief as the glowing shards embedded themselves in him. His darkness receded from her skin. With an inhuman growl, the huntress looked upon her prey, her eyes narrowed. For a moment nothing happened—then the screams of agony began.

Controlling the shards, Diamond drove them further inward, twisting them through to what remained of the Wraith Lord's dark soul. Struggling now, he roared with anger and desperation, knowing his end was near.

Another knife-like shadow slashed at Diamond's face, but she ducked out of the way. Bit by bit, his emaciated body began to disintegrate. Diamond looked into his swirling, soul-filled eyes, trying not to recoil in horror at the writhing tiny faces that screamed back at her, fighting each other to get out.

Set them free, Lunaria's weak voice implored her.

It had been too long since Diamond had heard that voice in her head. It gave her strength and purpose. With a screech, Diamond wrenched the shards from Ragor's body, leaving him oozing black, stinking shadow. Swiftly she coiled magic around her hands. It was hard not to savour this moment.

Revenge is sweet.

She snarled at the mess that had once been the fearsome Wraith Lord. Using the magic her Nexus had helped her tame, she blasted Ragor into oblivion.

Diamond held the dead soldiers at bay. Here, in the darkness, it gave her joy to see thousands of tiny spheres of light float skyward. The unbound souls rose towards the stars, free to seek out their ultimate fate. Breathtakingly beautiful, they flashed brightly before each one winked into Eternity.

"May the goddess protect you and the guardians guide you," she whispered, shedding a tear of happiness for them.

KAREN TOMLINSON

CHAPTER FIFTY-EIGHT

Shadows and rotten corpses writhed around Diamond. The Dust Devils were too mindless to run. Merciless in her vengeance, Diamond struck, killing them in droves.

Whilst her magic sought out her enemy, her mortal body walked swiftly through the forest, covering mile upon mile of ground. For hours she prowled through the devastation, wiping out any wickedness she sensed until the forest near Lord Stockbrook's territory loomed around her. Her mind registered the pain of her blistered and bleeding feet, but she ignored it. Her mortal body would endure this—or it wouldn't.

She didn't care, not at all.

Diamond knew she could not stop killing, because when she did, she would have to face up to the emptiness of her life, a future devoid of anything except agonising loss. Instead of confronting her fear and grief, Diamond twisted it, turning it into more anger and hatred. Only when a blood-red dawn burned across the sky did Diamond feel her power dim. Gentle warmth from the rising sun caressed her skin, forcing her mind to become aware of her body once again, of sensations she did not want to feel.

Weakness. Pain. Thirst. Raging loss.

Fighting her physical failings, Diamond fixed Hugo's eyes in her mind. Sobbing, she slaughtered more and more. She tried to stay in the shadows, but the sun caught her frail body in its growing rays. It gentled her rage, wrapping her in a soothing warmth, calming her until her exhausted mind tumbled into her body.

The well of vengeance and anger inside her soul was empty, depriving her magic of sustenance. Sensing her vulnerability, the remaining monsters came, crashing through the surrounding forest. Curiously detached from her fate, Diamond watched them step out from the remaining shadows. She no longer cared. Ragor was dead, and Jack's warriors would cut down any monsters that remained.

Lifting her face to embrace the kiss of the sun, Diamond became aware of a tremble through the ground and the thudding of wings in the air. Her remaining energy floated from her grasp, like a spirit on the wind. She realised then how utterly close to death her body was, that her bloodthirsty quest for revenge had used her up entirely. Her knees buckled.

At that moment, hundreds of horses thundered by, shaking the ground as she knelt.

Battle cries and screams cleaved the air as savage fighting began around her. The ground tilted, and she fell sideways onto earth strewn with the black dust and bloody remains of her enemy.

Only moments passed before strong arms pushed under her shoulders and behind her knees, scooping her off the ground. Then she was passed up to a hovering shadowy figure. A gentle hand brushed the hair back from her face and warm dry lips kissed her forehead.

"Get the healers to her as soon as possible. Ragor has wounded her badly. His poison will kill her if you don't hurry. My turret is closest." The hand drifted to her cheek. "Elexon? Don't let anyone stop you. Keep her safe. No one other than the healers is to be allowed near her until I have returned from this battle. Do you understand? And Elexon? Set your warriors to watch the valley. If the Queen sends her guards, you get her out. We all know you can," Jack ordered tersely.

Diamond felt Tallo's deep voice rumble through her and she looked up to see his tough jaw above her face.

"There is not a chance in hell of anyone stopping us, your highness. What she has just done...well, it's beyond belief. She has saved so many lives; they both did. It is our honour to guard her," he reassured Jack.

"I will get our best healers to treat her," reassured another voice. Elexon.

There was a slight tug of gravity as Tallo lifted them into the air. She wondered vaguely what they had done with Hugo's body, then her head rolled against Tallo's big chest and she passed out.

CHAPTER FIFTY-NINE

Diamond simultaneously became aware of the warm bed beneath her and a blinding headache. Her skull felt like it was about to split in two. A groan escaped her dry, cracked lips.

"Urgh!"

By the goddess, her mouth tasted foul. Like old blood and ash, her tongue felt so dry she could hardly swallow.

Diamond's mind felt fuzzy behind the throb of pain from her head, her thoughts fogged by the agony burning across her thigh and down her neck. Her body seemed in complete discord with her brain. For a moment she lay still, letting hazy memories float at the edge of her consciousness.

Images of Hugo dropping her, of him smashing into the wall, of his dead face swamped her. The devastating reality of his loss hit her, squeezing her lungs until she couldn't breathe. Screwing her eyes tightly shut, she heard a strange choking sound escape her lips. Grief ripped her heart asunder. Curling her knees up to her chest, she shoved her fist into her mouth, biting her skin to smother the sobs that racked her ravaged body. Shivering violently, her tears soaked the soft pillow. She wanted the image of his dead face to go, but it burned relentlessly behind her eyes. He would be cross with her for being so weak, for shedding tears for him. She pictured his rugged face snarling at her, ordering her to pull herself together, to get up and run from the city before the Queen could claim her.

She registered the sound of the door opening, then clicking shut.

Were they coming in or going out? she wondered vaguely. Not that it mattered, nothing mattered, nobody mattered, not anymore.

"My lady?" queried a warm voice. Gentle arms tried to lift her, but she fought and cried, albeit pathetically. She couldn't face anyone, not yet.

"Please, my lady," the voice said firmly. "You have to fight the Wraith Lord's shadow poison that's in your body. Get well, then I will take you to Commander Casimir. Please, don't let the darkness win. Fight it," the voice urged. A woman's voice. Diamond didn't care, she could only screech her rage at the mention of Hugo's name.

"Stop it! Stop it!" Diamond wailed, putting her hands over her ears. She didn't want to see his broken, lifeless body. Shaking her head, she tried to rid herself of this person's intrusion into her thoughts.

"My lady, Hugo is alive," another voice stated forcefully. "You must fight this poison. For him and your people."

Cool hands brushed her sweat-soaked hair from her face. "Be patient, son. She is trying." Then the female voice crooned, "He is right. Your mate is not dead. Your magic saved him."

Diamond's heart stilled as the shock of those words sank in.

The hands gently released her head and tentatively pulled the covers back from her tearstained cheeks. Covered in blood and dirt and armour, Elexon smiled grimly. So did the serene-looking lady to his right.

"Hugo is not dead," Elexon repeated slowly and concisely, his red eyes full of compassion. "You *will* see him again, my lady. But not until you are strong enough. You have to fight the poison in your body. You have to fight with everything you have left or Ragor will win. It's killing you."

Diamond collapsed against her pillows.

"You are safe here. The Queen does not know of this place, and Tallo is guarding your door. No harm will come to you, but only you can fight the corruption that is killing your body," Elexon said.

"Here, drink this," the lady ordered gently, holding a glass to Diamond's lips.

Numbly, Diamond drank. The liquid tasted strange, its bitterness washing over her tongue. Within seconds her head began to spin, blurring Elexon's tired face.

The lady smiled kindly, drying the tears that lingered on Diamond's cheeks. Diamond, in turn, had no choice but to fall into a drug induced sleep.

Diamond screamed as the god of Chaos came for her soul, his wraiths swirling around him. A dark, endless corridor stretched out before her. But there was hope. A light flickered in the distance, beckoning her.

'Run!' ordered an achingly familiar voice.

Her feet stumbled on the grey stone as she followed that order.

'Diamond! Don't look back. Don't look back, just run!' the beloved voice bellowed again. That voice had saved her so many times before, it had guided her and given her the strength to fight. It had saved her. So she ran—as fast as her shaking legs would take her.

The gentle healer did not back away as Diamond screamed with anxiety and frustration.

"Two whole days!"

Elexon threw open the door as she ranted her displeasure, the relief on his face almost stopping her tirade. He loomed in the doorway, his wings and eyes catching the light from the sconces that lined the strange cave room she was in.

Red, she noted.

"Elexon? Let me out of this room!" Diamond demanded, breathless with frustration. Gods, her body was so weak.

"My lady? It's good to see you awake, but please do as my mother asks. She has made you well again. Surely that deserves some compliance — and respect," he suggested with a warning glint in his eye, looking meaningfully at the kind-faced woman.

"It's all right, son. I'm sure my lady is simply anxious for her mate," she smiled compassionately.

Diamond had the grace to look ashamed. The past two days had been a blur of vomiting and sleeping, not to mention the agony of her wounds. She vaguely remembered gentle fingers applying strange poultices that burned, before they soothed.

Elexon nodded calmly at his mother, and Diamond caught the mutual love and respect between the two.

"I do respect her, Elexon, very much. I just want to see Hugo. Please, I need to know he really is alive," she said her voice breaking, feeling suddenly exhausted and near to tears. She collapsed back against her pillows, swallowing the ache in her throat.

For a moment poor Elexon looked at a loss, then his mother patted his arm. "Thanks, Elexon. You can go now. We'll be fine," she smiled, before sinking down onto the edge of Diamond's bed.

"Of course, mother." Elexon bowed to them both and returned to his post outside Diamond's door. With one last look at the two women, he clicked it softly closed.

CHAPTER SIXTY

"My name is Ophelia," said the kind-faced healer. Clear brown eyes regarded Diamond steadily.

Diamond gripped the covers, aware she was still too weak to force her way out of this room to find Hugo. She made herself uncurl her fists.

Ophelia noted the move. Her body relaxed and she smiled. "That's better, my lady. You need to eat and get cleaned up, then I will get my son to take you to your mate."

Diamond swallowed and nodded, impatiently she rubbed the dampness from her eyes.

Ophelia pushed her grey-streaked brown hair from her face and cocked her head. Green wings peaked out above slim, elegant shoulders. Diamond's eyes widened. *Green wings! Gods, what else—who else, was being hidden from the Queen in this strange place?*

Something told her this cave room was not an isolated phenomenon. Voices echoed outside her door; laughter and whispers came and went as though many people passed nearby. Power prickled her skin, irritating her enough that she absentmindedly rubbed her arms. For a moment Diamond closed her eyes. Whatever force rested here, it was feeding her exhausted magic.

"Don't worry. You get used to it," Ophelia commented. "It's the catacombs. They're as ancient and prickly as my husband." Amusement sparkled in her eyes as she pushed herself up.

Dumbfounded, Diamond couldn't bring herself to ask all the questions that ached to fall from her mouth.

"Bath first, then you need to eat or you'll collapse. I'll find you some clean clothes too," Ophelia said. "You will eat won't you?" Brows raised in question, she stared directly at Diamond.

Diamond could only nod in acquiescence. She had a distinct feeling this perfectly ordinary-looking woman was anything but. She had the air of someone entirely used to getting her own way.

"Good. I will go and arrange food. Now, you rest for a few more minutes. You are quite safe here." Her long slim fingers opened an old wooden door that was fixed into the rear wall of the cave room. "And just so you don't try and find your mate before you have taken care of yourself, be aware that my son and Tallo are guarding your room."

Elexon and Tallo stuck their heads in and smiled sympathetically. They knew this female was a force to be reckoned with.

A frown creased Diamond's brow but she was too tired to fight. A quiet curse fell from her lips. Tears threatening again.

"Don't fret, my lady. My mother only wishes to help," Elexon informed Diamond seriously. "We are all concerned about your wellbeing, and that of the commander."

"It's true, Diamond. So please, don't turn our bones to dust just yet," added Tallo jovially, but Diamond didn't miss the hard undertone of the warrior who had trained her, who demanded her respect and compliance. "You are safe from the Queen and so is Hugo; be patient and do as Lady Riddeon asks."

Diamond wanted to demand answers, to chuck something at them all, even to storm out, but her arms were far too tired; besides she had no idea where Hugo was being kept.

Sometime later Ophelia laughed at Diamond's shocked expression. The small door at the back of her room led into a small bathing room where a hot spring bubbled merrily. Not even considering her nakedness, Diamond let Ophelia help her out of her robe and stepped into the delightful, bubbling water.

412

The pain in Diamond's heart and the aching in her body eased a little as the searing hot water enveloped her body. For a moment she allowed herself to picture Hugo's eyes laughing at her back in Gorian's inn, to imagine his wings wrapped protectively around her. She quickly scrubbed away the dirt and blood that lingered on her skin. Ophelia assisted with washing her hair, and soon Diamond was out of the water and heading back to her room.

Feeling better in her soft cotton shirt and well-fitting leggings, Diamond let Ophelia dress her feet and see to her wounds. A young girl arrived with large soft boots that would fit over the dressings on Diamond's feet.

Diamond bit her lip. She wanted to ask about her friends on the wall, to know if the battle with the Wraith Lord was over, if they had won. She wanted to know if Jack was alive and well.

"All your worries and questions can be answered soon," Ophelia's soft voice reassured her.

Diamond gasped as the healer's eyes softened.

"Before you ask, no, I'm not empathic, not like the pearlescent wings of our kind can be. It's easy to guess your emotions when your feelings are written all over your face, my lady. Come, we will take you to the commander, then I will ask Elexon to gather news of the prince and the battle."

Ophelia's kind and patient demeanour had a fresh wave of grief squeezing Diamond's tender emotions. Rose and Kitty had been this kind to her once. Determined not to crumble under the weight of her guilt, she thrust away the pain of losing her friends. Instead, she tidied her damp hair, trying to ignore the sight of her pale face and red, puffy eyes ringed with dark smudges that was reflected back at her in the small wall mirror. She bit her lip nervously, studying her reflection.

Is Hugo awake? Will he be devastated if his wings are shattered? She also wondered if he knew what she had done. Was he proud of her? Was he in pain?

Whilst she was fretting, Ophelia spoke quietly, an uncompromising glint back in her eye. "We will go when you have eaten, my lady," she said, with a meaningful look at Diamond's full plate.

Stubbornness was a pointless exercise. And Ophelia was right, she needed to replenish her energy and feed her magic. She didn't know when she would need to call on her power again. Even here, enemies might hide in wait. Diamond remained silent but finished her food as quickly as possible, even though it sat like a brick in her belly.

No one knew how deeply her soul was entwined with Hugo's. Magic, venom, blood, and the fire of his guardian—they all bound her to him. Tears burned her eyes. They had been apart too long. The image of his blue lips haunted her every time she closed her eyes; it needed wiping from her brain—forever.

"Can we go now?" she asked, standing up and wringing her hands.

Ophelia's gaze flicked to them. Her hands were warm and comforting as she took Diamond's in her own. "Diamond," she said kindly, for once not using a formal term of address. "Hugo is recovering well. He is strong, he is fae. His magic—or maybe his guardian—is healing him."

Diamond nodded, swallowing the lump in her throat. So Ophelia knew about Hugo's ability to shift. Diamond decided not to dwell on or worry about that as Ophelia guided her to the door. The healer had not offered any information about Hugo's injuries, and Diamond had not dared ask. Part of her dreaded to know.

When she exited the room, Elexon and Tallo bowed, murmuring a greeting.

Diamond stepped in front of Elexon. Her attention snagged on his glorious red wings that glinted in the light of the sconces. This brave warrior had exposed his magic for all to see. He had declared himself against the might of the immortal Queen and unveiled there were others. Not only that, but he had put everyone associated with him at risk, including his father. She wondered if the Master Commander already knew what his son was. Questions raged in her mind. There was so much they needed to discuss. She ground her teeth, holding her tongue. Now was not the time. All that mattered was he knew how grateful she was for his help and loyalty.

Elexon studied her steadily, if somewhat warily.

Suddenly it was too hard to speak. Raw emotion made the words of gratitude stick in her throat. Tears stung her eyes as Elexon took her hand and touched his lips respectfully to her skin. The look on his face told her he understood her emotions. Releasing her fingers, he fell in beside Tallo.

Ophelia led Diamond down a surprisingly well-lit corridor, past numerous small doors. The smell of salve and magic tickled Diamond's nose. Neatly dressed, green-winged fae scuttled past, bowing in deference to her escorts. Diamond did not even notice. Her legs wobbled with each step she took nearer to the fae that meant so much to her. She gripped her arms tightly over her chest, feeling a little dazed by the enormity of her feelings. Elexon noticed her stumble and silently offered his arm. Determined to be strong, Diamond shook her head. Elexon merely nodded, though he walked close by, ready to offer assistance again should she need it.

A shiver raised goose bumps on Diamond's arms as Ophelia's footsteps slowed, then stilled outside an innocuous wooden door, much like all the other doors they had passed.

"Would you like me to come in with you?" Ophelia asked quietly.

Diamond shook her head. "No," she replied, trying to control her wavering voice. Her first moments with Hugo needed to be alone. It would be hard enough without an audience. "But thank you," she added, trying to impart how grateful she was to this female who had done so much for her.

Ophelia nodded, then leaned in and brushed a kiss on Diamond's cheek, her eyes grave. "Elexon will guard this door with his life. My son is sworn to you and Commander Casimir, as is every warrior in our secret city. You will be completely safe here." She glanced at her son, her eyes full of love and meaning.

Diamond's exhausted, emotionally burned mind could not comprehend that silent message, nor did she want to.

"Be strong, my lady. Your journey has only just begun," Ophelia whispered before she gave an elegant dip of her head and walked away. Tallo also uttered his goodbye, and followed the healer back down the corridor.

Diamond took a shaky breath. Her eyes briefly met Elexon's crimson stare as her fingers closed around the cold hard metal of the door handle. He pushed the warmth of red magic encouragingly against her hand when she hesitated. Straightening her spine, Diamond turned the handle and opened the door. Holding back her tide of emotions, she lifted her chin, swallowed and took a step towards her love, her mate and her future.

A BOND OF BLOOD AND FIRE

Find books by Karen Tomlinson

www.karentomlinson.com

Magic awakens. Darkness stirs. The Wraith Lord is hunting.

Sometimes magic can be a blessing and a curse…

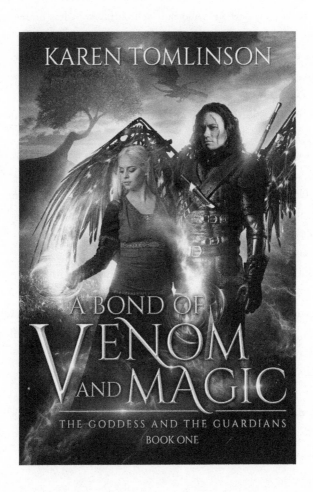

Acknowledgements

This novel started as an ending. Sounds strange but it did. I wrote a very long version of book 1 in this series: **A Bond of Venom and Magic**, and this was the second half of that book. It has undergone an enormous change but A Bond of Blood and Fire has kept all the elements of the original story that I planned and has loads more added adventure and romance. Hugo and Diamond have grown into characters that I love and I can't wait to see what scrapes they get in, and out of, on the long and dangerous journey they have ahead of them.

I have to thank my lovely husband, Aaron, and my twin girls, Annie and Abbie, first and foremost for helping me complete this instalment of The Goddess and the Guardians. Being a full time working mum and an author, takes up every spare minute in the day (and night sometimes) and you have all been beyond patient with me as I have dived back into my created world once again.

A Bond of Blood and Fire would not be the book it is now without the hard work and honesty of the fabulous readers who joined my beta team. I will not name you (you know who you are) but here is where I say a huge 'THANK YOU' to you all for giving me your time and honest thoughts. I appreciated every one of them.

To Zanny, thanks little sis for your continued support and interest in my writing. Mum and Dad, your copy will be with you soon!

To Jenny Baker, thank you for being such an awesome friend. Your cheerful, positive outlook, your company, and an ear to bend when I needed it most have meant a great deal to me.

I also want to say a huge thank you to the best mum-in-law ever. You were one of the kindest and most patient souls I will likely ever know. We will all miss you. I hope your Eternity is full of the colour and kindness and happiness you brought to us in this life.

Lastly I would like to say a huge 'thank you!' to you (awesome reader!) for buying this book. I hope you have enjoyed it and love the characters as much as I do. Please go here or to Goodreads to leave a review, even a star rating will be awesome! A review of any kind really helps with the visibility of a book in the ocean of other books out there in the world.

I love to connect with readers and you can find me here:

Twitter
https://twitter.com/kytomlinson

Facebook page
https://www.facebook.com/ktomlinson.author/

Facebook Street Team (Karen Tomlinson's Silver Guardians)
https://www.facebook.com/groups/1531458143821861/

Instagram
https://www.instagram.com/karentomlinsonauthor/

Goodreads
https://www.goodreads.com/author/show/15259538.Karen_Tomlinson

Join my mailing list for information on cover reveals, Advanced Reader Copies and news about new releases
http://karentomlinson.com

Made in United States
Orlando, FL
20 November 2021

10568319R00253